White Fur

This Large Print Book carries the
Seal of Approval of N.A.V.H.

White Fur

Jardine Libaire

THORNDIKE PRESS
A part of Gale, a Cengage Company

Farmington Hills, Mich • San Francisco • New York • Waterville, Maine
Meriden, Conn • Mason, Ohio • Chicago

Copyright © 2017 by Jardine Raven Libaire.
Thorndike Press, a part of Gale, a Cengage Company.

This is a work of fiction. Names, characters, places, and incidents either are the product of the author's imagination or are used fictitiously. Any resemblance to actual persons, living or dead, events, or locales is entirely coincidental.

Thorndike Press® Large Print Peer Picks.
The text of this Large Print edition is unabridged.
Other aspects of the book may vary from the original edition.
Set in 16 pt. Plantin.

**LIBRARY OF CONGRESS CIP DATA ON FILE.
CATALOGUING IN PUBLICATION FOR THIS BOOK
IS AVAILABLE FROM THE LIBRARY OF CONGRESS**

ISBN-13: 978-1-4328-4421-9 (hardcover)
ISBN-10: 1-4328-4421-0 (hardcover)

Published in 2017 by arrangement with Hogarth, an imprint of the Crown Publishing Group, a division of Penguin Random House LLC

Printed in the United States of America
1 2 3 4 5 6 7 21 20 19 18 17

For Neil Barrett Little

I take thee at thy word:
Call me but love, and I'll be new baptized;
Henceforth I never will be Romeo.
— WILLIAM SHAKESPEARE, *Romeo and Juliet*

I remember a little girl who had a white rabbit coat and hat and muff. Actually, I don't remember the little girl. I remember the coat and the hat and the muff.

— JOE BRAINARD, *I Remember*

June 1987

Outside their motel window, Wyoming is lurid with sunset. A billboard for Winstons simmers on the horizon of highway, as if the cigarettes might ignite in their box.

Standing rain has collected in the sagebrush close to the road, and heat makes a perfume from these puddles: herbal, medicinal, otherworldly.

Inside Room 186 of the Wagon Wheel Inn, Elise will be kneeling on the carpet, which is orange like a tangerine. Her hair is greasy and braided, and a name — tattooed in calligraphy on her neck — is visible. She keeps both hands on the shotgun — the muzzle pressed into Jamey's breast.

He'll be sitting on a chair in the middle of the room, hands on thighs.

"Don't you love me?" he'll ask, quiet and desperate. "Elise. Come on. Don't you love me?"

She bites her lip.

He's not wearing a shirt — just jeans — and his bare feet are splayed. The couple has been in this position for two hours and fourteen minutes.

Fifteen minutes now.

Her muscles are quaking. His should be.

In case the room seems small in this recounting, be sure it's not. It's gigantic, swollen, pounding on a molecular level like a billion hearts, the way a space does when the people in it realize their power. Elise will close her eyes, turn her head, and push the safety off.

January 1986

Connecticut is where it begins.

Elise sits on the couch and listens carefully to this evening's city song of church bells and police sirens. She tilts her long and fine skull in a minor way.

New Haven winter: sour, brittle, gray like ice that forms on milk.

Robbie's place — *and her place too,* Robbie insists — is bare as a squat, with a mattress and thin blankets in each bedroom. The curtains are smoke-soiled. The fridge door is scaled in decals from radio stations and hard-core bands, and stickers peeled off apples. One Lucky Charm lies bloated in the drain.

Taped to her wall, where someone else might hang a crucifix, is a page torn from *Rolling Stone:* Prince in a misty lavender paradise.

Elise moved in three months ago, after Robbie found her snoring in his boyfriend-of-the-night's unlocked Pontiac; she was shivering under a ragged white fur coat.

At first they thought she was a dog.

She squinted at Robbie and his friend, who both stood there with the door open.

"Whoops. This your car?" she'd asked, smiling lopsided, eyes clear, drug-free.

When she stood up out of the backseat, taller than them, a backpack hanging like a pendulum from her hand — then she looked scared. An elegantly sad runaway in generic white sneakers and gold bamboo earrings.

The men had to unclench their fists.

Robbie took her home, and the two became incongruous animals in a fable — a giraffe that helps a honeybee, or a rabbit who saves an elephant, having little adventures from page to page.

The new roommates bonded by cooking macaroni together, dancing in pajamas and socks to Michael Jackson, drinking soda, and watching late-night public access TV. Shit, neither of them has a clue what to do in life except live.

She's looking out her living-room window. Her and Robbie's building is rotted from its eaves down, the floors broken into discount apartment units. Their building has stoic — almost happy — bad health, the way a smile is gleeful if it's missing teeth.

Next door is a white townhouse where two Yale guys live. A chandelier glimmers inside, shining with leftover daylight when everything else is dark. Wealthy families lived there before the neighborhood slipped, and the house is forlorn like a society girl forced to get a job.

These boys happen to be smoking on the porch.

Now Elise is going to do it — before she thinks it over and backs down. It's been driving her crazy.

Now she zips up the knee-length rabbit coat with its vinyl belt, the name *Esther* stitched in violet into the taffeta lining that is threadbare and shimmering. (She traded her can of Pringles for the coat on a Greyhound bus one abnormally warm autumn night, while the factories of Elizabeth, New Jersey, ghosted by in the dark. The black girl was strung out and thought it was a good deal since she wasn't cold at that moment and seemed to revel in the dream she'd never be cold again. *But I already ate some of the chips,* Elise joked in protest, handing over the tube and taking the fur. *No, kid,* the girl murmured, *it's cool.*)

Elise leaves the apartment. Night air snakes into her seams within seconds as she walks down the sidewalk.

Everyone sizes each other up. She waves.

"Hey neighbor," says one guy for the first time since she moved in.

"Hey," she says.

"Where you going?" he asks, obviously intoxicated.

She sniffs and looks away. "Buy some beer."

Her accent is harder than they expected.

"We've got beer."

"What kind?" she says, eyes narrowed.

"The kind," he says, "you don't have to go walking in the cold for."

The three of them amble into the house as if this is an everyday meeting, as if no one is curious about anyone else. Inside, Matt goes to the fridge and pops the caps off three Heinekens.

Elise's heart is a broken machine, crashing and thumping.

"What's your name again?" he asks even though she hasn't said it.

"Elise."

Is she frightening? Is she pretty? The guys blink their eyes as if her body is rippling and morphing and they can't finalize an idea.

She's lanky with round and solid tits. Boys' hips. She's a greyhound, curved to run, aerodynamic, beaten, fast as fuck, born to lose. Her face is stark, outlined by dark cornrows. The features drawn down for velocity. The scalp — ghostly. Her skin and hair verge on oily, but the gray eyes are soft in black-liner confines. A divot in her cheekbone might have come from chicken pox.

"I'm Matt," says the one doing all the talking, his own face appraising, unkind. Nothing happens in his eyes except a vague fizz, like flat root beer.

"And I'm Jamey," says the one with the dimple. He looks like a matinee idol who got drugged — waxy, his eyes heavy with lust but also choirboy chaste.

Jamey.

Somehow he gives the impression of being a hustler, but also being the mark, his self twisted into a Möbius strip of innate glamour and his own exploitation.

"Nice place," she says.

Elise doesn't know what to make of it. A camel-hair coat on a chair. *Interview* magazines and *Wall Street Journal*s, cigarette packs and folded twenties and coins and Perrier bottles on the coffee table.

She moves around, in boots and that skanky fur, like an inspector.

"You at Yale?" asks Matt with a straight

face, even though they know she's not.

"Nah."

Jamey asks: "Are you from here?"

"From around. You guys from here?"

"We're from New York," Matt says, lighting a smoke, his tone polite considering the absurdity of the question.

"You brothers?" Elise prompts.

"No," says Matt, shaking out the match. "Just look like brothers."

"Grew up together," Jamey adds.

She's watched them since she moved onto the block a few months ago, and could barely tell them apart before tonight. Now it's obvious they're opposites. She's watched as they shaved on the other side of a steamed window, white towel around a waist. They buttoned long coats, getting into their cars where they talked on giant blocks of telephones.

Jamey gets up for another beer.

"Grab me one?" Matt says.

"Me too," Elise adds.

Matt shoots a look to Jamey, who just grins and shrugs, comes back with three bottles.

They sit there, drinking. Elise should go home, but she isn't standing up.

Late at night, Elise has watched them bring home girls in gowns (that drag the dead leaves on the ground) and big tuxedo jackets over their shoulders. Or a girl in a kilt will lean her bicycle against the porch railing and sidle inside on golden afternoons. The boys leave early for classes, hair damp and combed, the world moody with sleep. They wave to the elderly landlord shoveling snow from their walk.

"Well," Matt says in a disingenuous voice. "Bedtime for me."

She's also watched Matt shadow Robbie down the sidewalk to amuse his Ray-Bans-and-Shetland-sweater buddies, without Robbie realizing it (in fact after he'd waved hesitantly to them as he passed), Matt mincing his steps and hanging his wrist, making his face fey and pathetic.

"Guess we'll see you around," Matt says to her forcefully.

"Sure, yeah." Elise lights a Newport King. She stands to blow smoke in his face. "And if you ever get near my friend Robbie again, let alone make fun of him like I seen you do, I'll burn your motherfucking house down."

The blue smoke hangs, waiting, and she looks at him, her eyes half-lidded and suddenly red, deadened. The tiniest smirk touches her mouth.

"I'm sorry, what?" Matt says shrilly.

"You heard me," Elise says, mission accomplished but now having to control her voice from shaking.

"Are you coming into *my* house and telling *me* what to do?" Matt pushes her shoulder, testing the moment.

Elise looks at where he touched her then raises her head to stare at him.

"Okay, Matt. I don't think so," Jamey says, moving between them.

"She's out of here," Matt says to no one.

"You're fucking correct about that," Elise snarls.

Matt points Elise toward the door. "All right, let's move."

"I'll go as fast as I wanna," she says.

She glances back to lock eyes with Jamey, who — with a mystified half smile — is watching her leave.

Elise lies in her dark bedroom, ashing into a Dr Pepper can next to the mattress.

She's the uncommon baby left in a crib that consoles itself, that can stare for hours at the ceiling. Most people need to sleep once the lights are off, the sex over, and Carson's said good night; something's wrong if they stay awake.

Elise never separates things into day and night, rarely thinks about being a boy or girl, or alive or dead. Without divisions, there's less work to do. She floats, free in a cheap and magic way.

She happily replays what could have happened. She comes from fighters — her mom can drive a stick shift, smoke a cigarette, drink a soda, put on mascara, and deliver a smack to every member of the family without taking her eyes off the highway. Elise could knock that kid's teeth out with a single swing.

She grins into the dark, walks herself around the ring with one arm raised.

But it's the dimpled one, *Jamey* — she didn't know he could exist until tonight; it's like she was watching a jet cross the sky then realized it's a bird. She has to reorient herself.

She didn't leave home last summer with a plan. Twenty years old, she never finished high school, she was half-white and half–Puerto Rican, childless, employed at the time, not lost and not found, not incarcerated, not beautiful and not ugly and not ordinary. She doesn't check any box; her face has Boricua contours and her skin is alabaster.

She left her family and everything she knew the morning after a Sunday barbecue in June. They'd all taken over the grill and picnic tables in the Bridgeport park, the Sally S. Turnbull projects looming in the near distance but far enough away to forget for a few hours.

They sat hunched, swatting at black flies, laughing till they cried. Boom boxes, hot dogs, jean shorts and half shirts, Lay's potato chips, cherry soda, and sunshine that fried their brains and hearts. It was a rapturous last supper. She left the housing unit at dawn, when everyone was sticky with hangover. She walked out the way girls do in campfire stories, heeding a knock on the door that no one else heard, and vanishing.

And she hadn't known why till now. Oh, sweet mercy, now she knows.

New Haven is a skinny, sallow cousin to New York City; it's a town that pretends not to want anything or to need charity. This morning is like most others as the place tries to wake up and get presentable, spilling bums from the alleys, sending parolees to stab litter into a bag, sucking raccoons into drains.

Jamey glides through the cold cityscape, and there are ideas in him, fermenting, the heat of them purring from his mouth.

He walks down the sidewalk behind an old lady leaning into the winter sun. Her plum wool coat is open. Passing, he sees the York Peppermint Pattie of a mole on her jowl.

"Good morning, ma'am," he says, searching her eyes for consciousness.

She doesn't answer.

And he wonders if he meant what he said, if he cares what kind of morning she has. Or if it's just another empty thing he says out loud, a candy wrapper dropped into the street.

In the park, hardy men play speed chess.

The day is warm enough to melt icicles out of trees, making a rain that comes down when it wants, a rain more animal than mineral, a rain with a will, a sentience.

Jamey sees portals — the bubble window of that van, the unlit storefronts, the grate where the gutter ends — his subconscious hunting for patterns since it can't find meaning.

Sometime later, he finds himself drinking coffee from a paper cup, sitting on the steps of a random synagogue. He jumps to his feet, as if he just awoke, surprised to be there, amazed as usual at where he ends up when he hasn't intended to go anywhere.

Jamey knows what his advisor meeting will be like, and walks across a courtyard that's shellacked in ice. He tip-taps in suede bucks up the marble stairs, an Ivy League paper doll who holds the door for two rosy-cheeked white girls with books in their arms.

Professor Ford has reached the final stage with Jamey. They started the year amiable, but Ford feels played, disrespected. Jilted.

"Jamey," says Ford, opening his door.

"Hello, sir." Jamey smiles, doomed.

Ford's white hair is carved to the side. "Did you see what Professor Hilden gave you on the paper?"

"I did."

"The class is writing on *Othello* and you hand in a paper on the misunderstood altruism of honeybees."

"I was —"

"I *don't* want to know."

Jamey shuts his mouth.

Ford holds out his palms in an exaggeration of inquiry. "Do you not want to graduate next year then?"

"I do actually want to graduate."

"This has become, by the discrepancies between potential and execution, an insult."

Jamey looks down as he's meant to do while the sun creates a muddy heat from the shelves of clothbound books.

"And I do not care a whit who your father

is, nor do I care who your mother is," Ford lies.

Ford is like everyone is and has always been with Jamey: Ford had a crush, he wanted Jamey to like him, he expected the world, and now he hates him because Jamey won't respond.

"I'll do whatever you think is best, Professor Ford," Jamey demurs.

Jamey noticed it early in life. In a group of kids, a parent would speak to Jamey as the other adult in the room. Jamey would look at the floor, but whenever he glanced up, the camp counselor or parent or babysitter was still talking at him.

It even happened with people who had no idea who he was, who never saw his house in *Town & Country,* or read about his parents' divorce in the *National Enquirer,* or relied on his grandfather's predictions as quoted in *Barron's,* who didn't realize they were in the presence of a commodity, a publicly traded stock, a prototype of a child — like Huck Finn or the Little Prince.

If someone were fumbling with their wallet, the drugstore clerk would blush and summon Jamey, next in line: *Let me take care of you while this lady figures her stuff out.* Jamey wasn't impatient; he didn't even notice the line wasn't moving!

When he was little, playing at the Morrisons', Jamey cradled their new pet bunny, and Thomas whined and pulled for a turn — it was *his* bunny after all! Mrs. Morrison warned Thomas to stop, and warned him again, and then she violently grabbed Thomas's little hand off Jamey.

"Let Jamey hold the bunny, Thomas, *goddammit.*" Her mouth was bright red and open as she furtively stared at Jamey afterward, and he saw something in her face he would recognize for the rest of his life.

He always thought of these moments later as his "Let Jamey hold the bunny" moments.

People looked to him like one of those Tibetan children picked out as a reincarnated lama. They think he knows the secret to life. They get mad when he doesn't offer it up. What happens, anyway, when the village chooses the wrong kid as their prophet?

Every morning Matt waits for Elise to walk by so he can glare at her from the porch, ice hanging from the portico. Sometimes he even vaguely ashes his cigarette in her direction, shivering in his white Oxford.

"You're an asshole," Jamey says when Matt comes inside. "Why are you so threatened by her anyway?"

"I'm not threatened," he says.

"But you are," Jamey corrects him. "She's obviously nothing to you, so why don't you just leave it?"

"Because she *came* into our house."

"We invited her in," Jamey says, stirring hot oatmeal.

"That's because she 'axed' to come in. Doesn't mean she can tell me what to do."

"I don't know. I thought it was hilarious," Jamey says.

"Yeah, it'll be hilarious when our house is on fire," Matt says.

Jamey laughs lusciously, then sighs, and doesn't say anything more. He does this a lot lately.

Matt looks at him like: *What the fuck is going on with you?*

It's strange how much they resemble each other, these two men. But Matt — with his pale skin, dark hair, dark eyes, prominent pointed chin, fine clothes, practiced stances — should be handsome like Jamey. And he's not. There's a sense of moral failing here, the idea that Matt himself is to blame for not being handsome, which somehow makes him uglier.

Robbie is white and short, and studies airplane mechanics at South Central Community College, and waits tables at Red Lobster. His bowl cut and cornflower-blue eyes are gnome-ish.

With him tonight is a tubby black giant who stoops under the ceiling light.

"What's up, Leesey," Robbie says, chagrined at having yet another guy over.

Sitting cross-legged on the couch, Elise pulls back her sweatshirt hood. "Hey," she says, giving the new guy a once-over.

"Hello there," the guy says in a gracious, Darth Vader–deep voice.

The pair ambles, blushing, into the bedroom, like boys about to play G.I. Joes or Matchbox cars, and Robbie shuts the door softly.

They put on Depeche Mode. Each time a side ends, there's a rustle as someone reaches across the bed to turn the tape over and press Play.

She makes coffee, pages through the newspaper, biting her lip.

Elise grew up listening to her mom have sex in the next room — Denise growling and muttering naughty words — or her cousin giving head in the bed where Elise was sleeping. Hearing other people is arousing and aggravating, the way getting tickled is a mishmash of laughter and the possibility of throwing up.

She puts her hand in her jeans.

That evening, Robbie and Elise smoke on the roof, squinting at New Haven's squat and dumpy skyline dusted with stars.

The bedroom window next door lights up.

"Oh shit, that's him," she whispers, awestruck.

"The one with the dimple?"

"I'm getting sorta obsessed," Elise says. "His name is Jamey."

Robbie smiles uncomfortably. "They're rich kids. You know that, right?"

"Yeah, I know."

Robbie flicks ash into the abyss between houses, and the coal is fired up by its twirling descent for a second or two. "You like him though?"

Now Elise is shy. "He seems different."

They toss cigarettes over the ledge, pull coats tight, and take the steps down into the building.

"I guess you never know, honey," Robbie says over his shoulder. "Right?"

"Right?" she answers.

Elise trusts Robbie on a gut level. She gets being bisexual, and thinks everyone is attracted to anyone, but gay boys have it rough, they learn fast and cruel. This one kid who worked at a check-cashing place in her old neighborhood was famous for being queer. He was all buttoned up, saving money, determined to get out of that town, always wearing neckties and cardigans, polite in the Plexiglas booth, but he wouldn't hide his wrists or pursed mouth. She walked in there once with her Burger King check, and he was swollen, one eye bandaged, one ear burned. Necktie in place — green polyester with diagonal maroon stripes. She was fascinated by him — nearly destroyed for love, over and over, and refusing to lie.

She survived years of school fights herself, fights that came from real and imagined sexual and social conflicts. She knew what it was like to be forced to take the squatting posture against another girl in the parking lot, hair in her face and mouth, a tribe watching, a random extra girl coming into the fight once in a while to kick or punch, the creepy silence broken with huffing and a whimper. No matter how bad Elise got hurt, she never regretted standing up for herself. She was glad when that stage — fighting every week — was over. Although you have to be on guard forever.

Dove shit steams then freezes on the road. Icy light radiates into the house.

In the kitchen, Matt unpacks sushi lunch from takeout boxes.

"Let's see — what have we got here," he says.

"Yum, I'm starving," Abigail says self-consciously.

Abigail's Christmas-in-Bermuda tan is amplified by a white turtleneck. She's scared, in a titillating sense, which is how most girls feel near Jamey. He's not charming — it's something weirder, more potent, dangerous. He's so convincingly disconnected from his beauty that people look away, not wanting to be the one who tips him off with their gawking.

Jamey bends over the *Aeneid* in Latin, the only thing he studies anymore.

He's always taken classes off the beaten path: Japanese Swordsmanship, Thermodynamics, the Culture of Belief from Saints to Atheists, a course on Prison Ethics, one on Botanical Drawing, and one on Jainism. The barbs and thistles of these fields caught him. He had a double course load and immaculate grades — until now.

His classes . . . had committed mutiny. The simplest, most innocent concepts turned overnight into enemies, capable of triggering full-system shutdown. Light is not light but energy. A person will never see his own face, just its reflection, or a photograph of it. Brain waves are more active during dreams than waking life. Roses don't smell beautiful; they smell like ripe fruit, which is good for survival, and so they're defined as beautiful in our aesthetic beliefs. These are obvious riddles, in the league of conundrums that blow a thirteen-year-old's mind after his first bong hit.

Jamey wonders, vaguely ashamed, why they're getting to *him* now.

He carved ballpoint *x*'s into B. F. Skinner's eyes. He had to throw out his Kierkegaard.

And now, his last refuge — *amo, amas, amat* — disintegrates: the paragraphs don't hold, words fall apart. Letters degrade into tiny sticks and circles, and Jamey closes the book.

He dispiritedly gets up for water, and Abigail watches like a hawk.

Matt snaps his fingers. "Over here," he says, indicating himself, being funny. "Show's over here."

"Oh, shut up," Abigail plays it off.

"Jamey gets plenty of attention," Matt says.

"Do I?" Jamey asks drily.

"That one over there like spies on you," Matt says, looking to Elise's building.

"What?" Jamey's surprised he's angry.

Matt shrugs, psyched he got a reaction. "I've seen her, looking out the window."

"She's not looking at me," Jamey says, opening the fridge for something to do.

"And you defend her all the time. Fascinating," Matt says, tapping his chin with his finger.

"Oh, whatever," Jamey says.

Jamey ends up parking at the Chapel Square Mall, crossing the lot with hands in camel-hair pockets. He wanders the domed hall, following mauve diamonds on the rugs, passing potted plants that don't need sun. He likes the mall because he is *somewhere*, but he doesn't go into the stores so he's also nowhere.

He sits on a bench to observe the population. He's always relied on odd activities to soothe himself, like reading true-crime books in hot baths. As a kid, the encyclopedia was his security blanket. He sucked his thumb until he was eleven and a nanny started dipping his thumb in nail-polish remover.

Now watching strangers is his salvation.

Today it's backfiring, making Jamey feel particularly left out of the world's doings. He looks away from girls in tight jeans, from women in acrylic sweaters. He observes two losers by the food court throw out a nasty hello like a fish hook until they reel in a girl, play with her till she's not so disdainful, and then her friend joins them, and the guys clumsily sneak the girls a look at their freshly rolled joint. They all saunter off, the guys' arms over the girls' shoulders, newly minted couples, for a quick blow job on the loading dock then a grape soda at the arcade, or a car ride and a fuck at one of the girls' homes, with the second couple taking her little brother's room, his turquoise globe falling off the bed stand, cum on his Spider-Man sheets.

Jamey watches them leave the mall, his eyes golden with misery.

Elise rides a rusting Huffy BMX bike (whose handle grips are gone) to work, her body vibrating with energy. Passing the Harkness Tower and the translucent-marble library of the university, she then navigates a couple bad blocks where boys in black beanies and shearlings stand on corners.

The shop is downtown, past the movie theater and next to a hamburger spot. She unlocks the frozen door to a room humid with fish tanks.

Marianne, the shop owner, comes in later,

barely ever able to get there at all, dragging a cape of Mylanta and Epsom salts and cat litter vapors.

Marianne feeds the fish and watches soaps on a tiny TV.

"You seem awful happy," Marianne says.

"I'm in a good mood today!"

Elise wishes she could talk to Marianne about Jamey, but there's no point. Marianne has frizzy white hair and is obese, and is impartial to life, to living, without being bitter or blaming anyone. *I get along better with critters* is what she tells people.

Elise sings to Lionel Richie on the stockroom radio; hours pass.

At the pizzeria, she eats a slice while looking at a Jehovah's Witness pamphlet someone handed her. She sips Diet Coke from a wax cup, staring out the window at sun sliming the ice on the sidewalk.

At the Goodwill on Linden Street, she finds mirrored glasses for twenty-five cents.

Loopy Lex waves from the church steps. Homeless, his long hair matted and lip scabbed, he's still a raw-boned, handsome American.

"How's it going, Lex?"

"Going going going."

Back at the shop, she makes a paperclip chain.

Everything is about Jamey now. She'll wear the sunglasses for him. She could introduce him to Lex, tell him about the daughter in Vietnam that Lex never met, how Lex comes in the store to look at the fish. She wants to show Jamey the python Marianne keeps in the big tank, whose markings are like puzzle pieces.

She talks to Jamey out loud. As she bikes home in the dark, she's lost in a complicated conversation with him. Standing on the pedals to stall for a light, she suddenly worries she forgot to lock the door to the store, and has to go back.

It's locked.

In the evening, from her window, she'll watch him come onto the porch to see the moon, breathing minty air.

Yesterday, she had a clear line on him. He was reading in the chair in the kitchen, and she could see his chocolate corduroy pants and bare foot.

Elise looked at him gently then, the way a mother inspects a son for scratches or bruises when he comes back from a long day playing war in the woods.

His dad calls from Hong Kong as Jamey navigates twilit streets toward home.

Jamey can hear his father's smile — Hyde,

Moore & Kent closed on the Ho Lang acquisition. "I had to tell someone, Jamester. What would I do without you?"

Jamey imagines Alex at his hotel-room window, sipping iced tea, flushed from swimming laps, facing a blinking, chromatic, mind-bending cityscape, and seeing his reflection.

"I really want you to meet Randolph Sander's son — you know he's at Yale, right? First year? I've never met him, but his dad is a *good* senator, and they've got a place in Kennebunkport near Aunt Jeanette. Just a thought, Jamey-rooter."

Jamey makes a noise of acquiescence, stifles a yawn. He picks lint off his forest-green sweater.

Alex gossips about a car accident. "Unless you heard it from Sarah already. . . . no? Well, they're saying now Timmy was on drugs. . . . Yes, *terrible* for both families. . . . No, Catherine's a *Rye* Millford."

"How are Xavier and Sam?" Jamey asks at one point, as usual.

"Well, Cecily and the kids are in Vail, yes . . . ski lesson . . . the little one . . . Cecily and the kids . . . Cecily . . . Bats always said that about the Headleys, you know? . . . Cecily . . . This winter . . . to Italy to see his brother . . . Binkie won the winter orchid at the garden club . . . they fired Kathleen . . . well, the rehearsal dinner's at the Union Club. . . ."

Jamey's parked in front of his house, car running.

Elise taps on his window and he jumps, looks at her wide-eyed through the glass. She waves her pack of Newport Kings.

She waits.

He points at his phone and shrugs melodramatically, mouths the word *"father."*

She finally understands and keeps walking, into the night.

His stomach churns.

"Jamey, have you heard anything I've been saying?" his dad asks after what must have been a long silence.

At the Laundromat, a man in Carhartt khakis taps his cock, telegraphing with his eyes an invite to his truck. Elise doesn't even shake her head but still communicates *no.* They both go back to looking at magazines.

Aficionados of sex see her in a crowd. Some guys stumble upon her and crudely realize their luck halfway into it. Some have no idea, and turn her out of bed as if they did what they'd come to do, not understanding they hadn't even started. Those dudes smoked and hummed while they dressed and she felt sorrier for them than she felt for herself.

Redboy was one of the connoisseurs. He was something beyond this world himself — hungry, roaming, and furious. That boy would stay with her forever. It was something she couldn't regret, and she'd tried.

As early as seven she knew about sex, she felt it, she understood things. And she wasn't precocious from being abused, though she knew girls who were. Her mother was paranoid, for good reasons, and protected her — at shelters, Denise made her kids shower with her, and she tried to be meticulous and demanding about who watched them while she worked.

The first time Elise had an orgasm was at eleven years old, on a Bridgeport bus coming home from school — the seat was vibrating. Her cheeks got hot, and she felt a pressure, this sickness or desperation, the sense that something had to happen or she would die, and then it all broke open in her, hot syrup spreading in her blood, and she swiveled her head on her long neck like a bird, having missed her stop, trying to understand where on Earth she was.

His class watches the *Challenger* launch on the CNN school emission. Jamey slouches while a guy to his right jokes about gravity. Normally, Jamey would volley like a gentleman, but lately he doesn't have the energy, so he nods gently and doesn't answer.

Announcer: *It's the 51-L mission, ready to go.*

The rocket on the ground makes smoke and moves slowly out of the gate, like a sedated bull from a pen. Jamey is surprised when his stomach tightens up. Is he patriotic? That's mortifying — Jamey's always embarrassed when he catches himself being sentimental.

T minus fifteen seconds, we have main engine start, and four, three, two, one — we have lift-off! Lift-off!

The man's voice is so jubilant, Jamey pictures him as a kid in a Depression-era dirt backyard, squinting at the solar system and dreaming.

Challenger, *go with throttle up*!

The machine glides into the teal of the Florida sky.

And then: a disruption.

Flight navigators are looking carefully at what has happened.

Two bunny ears grow off a head of smoke. This chandelier of plumes comes slowly down the blue. The antlers, or jellyfish tendrils, drop: *Obviously there's been a major malfunction.*

Students whisper, transparent and shocked. The professor stands cross-armed near the television set, her back turned to the class.

Christa McAuliffe. The everywoman. Her face was as familiar and American as a gas-station logo or a rhubarb pie. She was someone you saw every day but only waved to, never knew. A woman of such bionically sober ambitions that the country agreed to take her into space. She was sent on a pyre into the big night.

Jamey walks out of the classroom — trying to hide his smile.

He crosses campus, passing under stone archways.

Jamey has a disconcerting flashback to his uncle's property on Long Island, many years ago. The parents talked and drank inside the main house, the kids set free for the day, moving through shadows and sunspots, woods and fields, running or loping, showing off, squinting into the sky at the roar of a plane, hanging in trees like leopards, making those connections cousins make that are almost lustful, the kids wanting to trade places, trade lives.

On this unchaperoned afternoon, the children ate at a picnic table while dogs swarmed around their legs, waiting for the crust of a ham sandwich. Topper, who was a perfectly likeable child, went into the potting shed. He screamed, hoarse and sincere, after the door closed behind him and he was trapped by a corn snake.

Jamey had a clear thought the second he heard his cousin's cry: *I hope he dies.*

Jamey's young eyes opened wide, ashamed, and he tried for weeks after to either delete the memory of what had flashed through his mind, or to forgive himself — and then he worked instead to be comfortable with the fact that he's just a wicked boy.

Now Jamey gets into his car under a dingy Connecticut sky pierced by gargoyles and turrets. He doesn't start the engine.

I'm failing, he realizes.

February 1986

Pigeons peck at frozen garbage. Sleet is punishing the city today, and everyone's despondent — although post offices are always despondent.

Elise stomps slush off her boots as she enters the room. A poncho is sealed like a plastic bag over her rabbit-fur jacket.

Standing in line, she feels her heartbeat triple when Jamey enters, and she waves him up as calmly as possible.

When he indicates the line will be mad, she comes back, eyes gleaming.

"I'll stand with you then."

"Okay," he says unsurely.

She unravels about twenty feet of toilet paper to show him a ceramic unicorn with a chipped gold horn. "I'm mailing this to my mom. She collects them."

"Gotcha."

"So?" she asks after a moment.

He smiles with embarrassment. "So?"

"Don't you want to go out sometime, make it up to me?"

"Do I want to take you out?" he asks stupidly.

"Like, for pizza. Whatever. Go see a movie."

He grins widely, wondering who in line is listening. "Um. Okay?"

"Tomorrow?"

"Sure," he says, drawing the word out so eavesdroppers know this is ridiculous.

They stand there.

The line isn't moving.

She looks at his creamy envelopes, an oxblood monogram — *JBH* — raised on the paper. "You want me to mail them?" she asks. "Then we don't both have to wait in this stupid fucking line."

"All right," he says, amused and horrified. "They just need stamps."

She winks, deadpan. "I sorta figured."

He walks out into a city that's smeared with filthy white, feeling like he just got smacked across the face, and is awake. She caught him in his schoolboy mode, polite and dutiful, mailing letters to his grandparents and stepsiblings, notes full of nothing, written in perfect script. Yet he feels like she caught him so unaware and alone that she saw the other side, the wolf crawling through wreckage, through broken walls, cracked Venetian mirrors, dust, blood, a turned-over rocking horse — the child who doesn't know its own name.

It's dark as midnight by evening. Robbie smokes while Elise tries on clothes.

She puts her braids in a ponytail, then takes them out.

"What. The. FUCK!" she shrieks in frustration.

"Leesey, sit," he says, pats the couch. "Time-out, honey."

She throws herself down, arms crossed, glaring at nothing. On her left foot, a white boot with scuff marks like a kid drew on it with black marker, and a white sneaker on her right. Gray acid jeans, a turtleneck.

He rubs her shoulders. "You don't need to go if you don't want to."

"But I do! You don't understand," she says, eyes welling.

Robbie takes her fingers in his hands. "Breathe."

Once she's calmer, he looks in the mirror with her, and he wipes a smear of eyeliner away.

He says to her reflection: "I just don't want you to get hurt, honey. Okay?"

She nods. "I know. I know that."

■ ■ ■ ■

Slouched like a lord in his car, Jamey waits.

She comes out the front door like a conclusion you don't expect after thinking about the same thing for too long.

Her hands in the pockets of the white fur, a thumb hanging over each rim. Eyes lined in turquoise.

"Hello there," he says, suave and distant, and drives in the direction of downtown.

"What's up," she says dourly.

Dour! he thinks. What happened to the bravado?

"So what'd you do today," he asks, making conversation.

She shrugs. "Worked."

"Where at?" he asks.

"The fish store on Main Street, like, the pet store, not the fish market."

"You're into fish?"

"Um, not really," she says.

"So, then, you work there because?"

"Let's see, I'm into paying my half of the rent. What, did you never have a job?"

He looks around elaborately at an intersection. "I've had a few jobs over the years."

"Like."

"Pumping gas at the Shelter Island Yacht

Club. I taught tennis another summer."

She smiles wryly out the window.

Inside La Forginni, white roses are reflected on the black marble bar. He picked this tacky and expensive place because he'll know no one.

He checks his camel-hair coat. Elise refuses to hand over her fur, giving the girl a death stare.

They sit at their table and unfold napkins.

"Let's see. Do you like Barolo?" he asks.

"Yeah." She has no idea what he's talking about.

"Should I order?"

"For me?" she says.

"A bottle, I mean?"

"Of?"

He pauses. "Barolo."

"Yeah."

She seems morose, charmless. No style in her delivery. No flick of the wrist, no tricks — just a dull, plain stare as he talks. Her voice is bare when she answers, the knobs and gristle of her accent out in the open. She talks the way she talks. Her voice isn't low or husky, yet it's somehow masculine. Her makeup is reminiscent of Cleopatra.

"So. I'm sorry about the other night," he says eventually.

She butters her bread. "Who cares. Let's talk about something else."

"I thought we were here to talk about what happened."

She grins. "But that's boring, is what I'm saying."

He's happy to be interrupted by the waiter. As he orders, Elise considers his heart-shaped face, those sleepy eyes — tired but electrified like he'd been up all night thinking.

He's got the surfeit of an only child: cream collecting on top, thick and rich, excessive. He's never been stirred. The loneliness shows up as latchkey keyholes for pupils.

"Why don't you tell me something about your life," she says eventually.

"What exactly are you wondering?"

"Tell me anything." She waits. "God, you suck at this."

"Jesus! Thanks a lot!"

"Sorry," she mumbles. "I get harsh when I'm nervous. You want me to start you off?" she asks. "Where were you born?"

He drinks wine. "New York City. Where were you born?"

"Hartford," she says, buttering more bread, hungry like a workman. "Where'd you grow up?

"New York City."

"Do you have brothers or sisters?" she asks.

He gives her a G-rated version of his family, the divorce, his stepfamily. He assumes she's heard of them because he never met anyone who hasn't — they've been in the papers since before he could read. It's like asking if she heard of the Eiffel Tower or Mickey Mouse and she shakes her head, befuddled.

"HMK. Hyde, Moore & Kent," he says.

"But what is that?"

"The family business. It's a private investment bank."

"Where's it at? This bank?"

"Well, I mean, HMK has offices all around the world." He blushes, feeling stupid for what sounds like bragging but is simply factual.

She fixes her eyes on his mouth when he's speaking, then she guilelessly explores his face. He sees her doing it. Then she looks away, bites her lower lip, eyes dull and damp.

Her style of self-possession is almost a matter of conservation, an efficiency, like she doesn't want to waste energy in affectations. There's no hair twirling or pouting.

"So . . . Are you, do you want to go to

college? Or were you planning —" he stutters.

"I didn't finish high school." Her *didn't* is *dint.* Her cheeks shine.

"Is that, you know, something you wish you could do?" he asks carefully.

"Obviously — it's easier to get a fucking job," she says.

"Sure," he says, and then worries that it sounds unkind.

"But at least I didn't have to keep *going* to school, thank God, because I hated it."

"You did? I like school," he says.

She smiles at him like: *Really? You're full of shit.*

The waiter asks if they'd like dessert.

"Definitely!" Elise says, finally relaxed.

Jamey's heart sinks. He's ready to leave.

They share chocolate torte, and Elise takes the lion's share, talking as she chews the black cake.

After dinner, he burps under his breath in the car, holds his fist to his lips for a moment before turning the key in the ignition.

A dead raccoon on the roadside. She looks away too late, which means some part of her wanted to see it.

There's a cul-de-sac near their block and she suddenly grabs his elbow —

"Turn here for a second," she insists.

It must be an emergency; her voice is desperate. He pulls to the side.

"Shut the car off," she says.

The air is balmy and cold, thick with smog and ocean and fir, like unmelted wax.

She gets out, comes around, and opens his door like a man does for his date. She flicks her gum out into the brush, leans down to kiss his mouth.

This shocks him; then she kneels. He puts his feet on the ground, sitting sideways. She unbuttons and unzips his pants, roughly tugs them down to mid-thigh.

When did I get hard? he wonders.

What she does makes him grimace. She looks up at him and keeps doing it. The air is freezing and her mouth is hot.

Headlights sweep by, far away, and he goes soft, waking up from a dream. But then she keeps going, and what scared him — being seen, doing this — makes blood rush down.

"Oh my God," he says, breathless afterward.

She looks up with no pretense. She holds one kneecap with each hand. He sort of wants to touch her face but is paralyzed.

She stands, gravel falling from her shins, and he zips himself, turns the key with a shaking hand. She jumps into the other side and slams the door like they just finished grocery shopping.

He tries to parallel park at home, but he can hardly get near the curb and gives up.

They sit in the dark.

"Thanks for dinner," she says.

"Yes, of course. Thank *you.*" As soon as he says it he regrets it.

She looks at him, then gets out of the car, and walks into her building without looking back. He should escort her to the door, but his manners have vanished.

Snow is clumped on the windows and the afternoon is greedy with winter gloom. It consumes the soul.

Jamey's brain is a kaleidoscope. He languorously wanders through halls, gets a hard-on in Latin class like he's fourteen. He watches the chem professor draw equations on the blackboard, but he sees Elise's chin, milky with cum. Her eyes are deliriously tilted up at him. Without speaking, she's communicating: *I will do this again. I will do this whenever you want.*

He gets home, exhausted and high from fantasy.

Jamey goes upstairs, looks out his window.

He hasn't talked to Elise since that night last week; he avoids her. He sometimes sees phosphorescent eyes staring from her living room, but it's probably his imagination. He's horrified by what happened, and fascinated.

He's been reminiscing about Millie, his high-school girlfriend, who went to Sacred Heart, and was blond, wealthy, sweet, skinny, bulimic, well-dressed in Carolina Herrera and alligator loafers and jodhpurs, polite, distant, with tiny teeth like baby teeth in a grown-up girl's mouth.

When they made out, and eventually had sex, they were two people. A boy and a girl in a bed. They never became one thing. They were just a sloppy, uncertain pair of adolescents pressing against each other. She liked Bombay Sapphire and tonic, and they usually did it after a party, so sex tasted like that to him: English and spiteful.

She used a sponge, and he had no idea what that was. He had sex with her as hard as he could, copying porn flicks he'd seen on friends' VCRs. She whimpered like a toy poodle, imitating women in romantic comedies. He tried to go down on her and she didn't let him.

Millie would talk for a half hour straight in a taxi headed south, and the minute they got out, Jamey couldn't remember a word. It was like owning a dream on waking, then watching the details get wiped from your brain.

Elise though. One minute she was a tomboy, provocative and defiant — then she was kneeling at his feet like a servant. Her skin and bones lit up as electricity ran from her through him, the switch flipped so the current could flow, and her masculinity morphed into heroic femininity. She was exquisite on her knees. She was aggressively submissive. One lick of her tongue meant more than hours of intoxicated sex with Millie. How could two girls be so different?

One clear and chilly night, Matt pulls the kitchen curtain like he's spying.

"She's feeding stray cats, man," Matt says.

"What?"

"The girl. She's in her backyard."

"Oh yeah?" Jamey says nonchalantly.

"Just what the neighborhood needs, more strays," he says sarcastically.

The second Matt heads upstairs, Jamey slips into his backyard. Through the chain-link fence covered in brown-leaf vines, he sees her squatting on the building's porch, under a bright bulb. His dad always gritted his teeth when they passed old men feeding pigeons in Central Park. *They're not doing anyone any favors, you know.*

In her yard, the lawn furniture is draped in snow, like a dead person's memories.

She wears the fur, belted, and her corn-rowed hair shines. She's holding a milk carton, which she poured into a bowl between her boots; two skinny cats work on it. Their markings are ordinary — gray and amber and charcoal.

He watches her watch the cats. A third cat lopes out of the dark to sip.

Jamey's body prickles, hot. It's like someone showed him a map of a strange country and said he'd grown up there, and he knew they were right. That long, narrow face — the smell of her breath.

He must have shifted his feet because a twig cracks. The cats don't look (because they already knew he was there and they don't care) but Elise does. She stares at where he's hiding.

Finally Elise says: "Are you going to say something?"

He grins, mortified, exhilarated.

They have a face-off.

"You got to say something," she declares finally.

"I'm not going to," is what comes out of his mouth. His voice is shaking slightly.

She frowns. Strokes a cat that nips her hand.

Eventually she goes inside, forgetting her milk carton, looking back as she stands in the threshold. Waits. Gives up.

Jamey lies in bed, and he can't sleep. *What the hell was that — am I fucking retarded?*

There's a baldness to Elise, a stripped-down sleekness like a car left for dead, its parts jacked and sold. The perfume she wore to dinner smelled like carpet cleaner. What she did to him was voodoo.

Was it even sex he had with Millie? Now it seems like he was just jacking off inside her.

But Millie used him too, when they had sex, but not for sex. She mashed herself against his body, like a toddler desperately snuggling a teddy bear.

To her, Jamey was a plaything, a present. Like a cupcake from her nanny, or an Elizabeth Arden gift certificate, or the blue ribbon at the Hampton Classic.

He'd been in love a few times — not with Millie — but always from a distance.

Nicole Andolino, who lived on the third floor of his building growing up, wore coats with gold buttons and bit her red-painted nails waiting for the elevator.

He loved a woman with a strawberry-blond braid who stood at the maître d' stand at a bistro on East Fifty-Sixth Street and stared with suicidal desperation out the glass as he walked by on his way home every day.

Matt's mother was his first real love; she ate a blood orange and wiped the juice off her lips, and he could play and rewind and replay that moment a million times in his dark bedroom.

Nobody he loved would have guessed it. Even as a kid, he was sealed, locked, cold. It's not that he was self-obsessed — he'd comb his hair or straighten his dinner jacket as if curating a stranger in the mirror. All his life, he could have convinced a lie detector he didn't need anything at all.

Jamey turns his face into the pillow, sees Elise's legs opening in his black heart.

Elise takes a bus through the dark morning, ice crackling down the sky, encasing buildings.

She doesn't carry her bag like a lady does, but like a hunter slings dead quarry over a shoulder. Her fingers are long and thin like a piano player's, with big knuckles. Her pigeon-toed feet meet on the bus floor. She has a mission today.

At the store, she cranks the heat.

She's going to call her mother, because

it's time. And she finally has herself staked in this new territory, and it's safe to reach back toward home.

Seven months have passed since she talked to her family, and since then, she's slept on more than a couple subways overnight, eaten chop suey dregs and pizza crusts from dumpsters, hung out with a fifteen-year-old from Memphis who was living with his leashed ferret in a church basement, and let a man take her into a loan office and jack off to the sight of her pussy — she pulled her jeans halfway down and he wasn't allowed to touch — for twenty dollars. And that's the tip of the iceberg.

"Hey, Ma," she says.

"Elise! How you doing." To Angel: "It's Elise. Jesus Mary, Elise."

"What's going on there, Ma?"

"We're watching television. You ain't missing *nothing.* Where you calling from? Someplace warm, I hope? Tell me you're in Florida, baby girl. Tell me everything's sunny and good."

"New Haven. I didn't get far. Can't really talk long either, Ma, just want to check in."

"Are you not gonna tell us where you're at?" Denise protests hoarsely.

"I'm in New Haven, Ma."

"Elise, come on." Snap and whoosh of a

Bic lighter.

"I'm getting settled. I'll tell you when I tell you. What's going on there?"

"Nothing. Everything." Big drag, exhale. "But I mean, at least it's the weekend now, so."

Elise fiddles with the desk drawer handle. "Yeah. It is the weekend."

"I got them unicorns you mailed me. I started looking forward to it each month, getting a little package from you."

"Yeah? I'm glad you like them."

"You not going to tell me why you left and didn't say nothing?"

"Ma. I'm twenty years old."

"Lise, if you was forty-two I'd expect you to say something."

"I guess I don't know. You guys didn't do nothing wrong," she lies.

"Well. At least you calling us now. Don't forget me."

"I won't."

Drag and exhale. "It's okay, baby girl."

"I love you," Elise says, trying to control her voice.

"I love you to pieces," her mother returns.

Denise asks her to come home for Cori's sixth birthday.

"I can't, Ma."

"Why not? Come back for two days. We're

having a party."

"I got something going on here," Elise says shyly.

"Oh, really," her mother says with a smile Elise can hear.

Fuck! Elise feels a panic of lovesickness. She misses her mama.

They say goodbye, and she sits in the stockroom, bent over on a stepladder, among metal shelves of fish food and empty tanks, and tries to breathe.

Elise thinks of Denise's laugh cracking like thunder over the Turnbull houses, the paprika in her chili, the way her bra cuts into her back, the powdery heat of her body when they'd lie on the bed in the summertime, the afternoon too hot for anything but gossip and game shows. Her mother played with Elise's hair like it was her own, absentmindedly twirling it as they smoked.

Denise looks like a white-trash Swiss Miss: blond with a jolly face corrupted by cigarettes and methadone.

She had Elise at sixteen, and gave a teenager's violent tenderness to her baby. Their bond is ironclad. She named her Elise so their names would rhyme. They wore matching pink tracksuits when Elise was a kid.

Of course, her mother also misses Elise

doing dishes, buying diapers and Kool-Aid with her own paycheck, watching whatever orphaned children ended up at the apartment, cleaning when case workers were due, sewing torn clothes.

And most important — going down the street for daily lotto tickets.

Elise thinks of the apartment: roach shit, a defunct fridge in the window to block stray bullets, and leftover Christmas decorations shedding glitter on the floor. Someone's black-eyed toddler sick and sleeping on the couch.

I pulled the short straw, so what, Denise likes to say, about anything in her life: men, money, health.

And she *is* beat up. She lashes out in inefficient ways. Like she doesn't dump the garbage if she's overworked, living with the smell just to get the family miserable. Elise remembers more than once the can moving with maggots. Her mom believes in love. Angel broke her ribs, and sold her TV, but they have that thing, the fire that goes out and comes back from the smallest cinder, the flame of god. Denise will not give him up because her world would turn completely cold. *You got to let it go,* Elise thinks now. *It's not your life. Let her go.*

■ ■ ■ ■

Early morning — the sky is lustrous like a pearl, and cruel with dampness. Matt and Jamey get into the BMW and wait for it to warm up.

"So you *did* drop that girl off the other night," Matt says. "Abigail saw."

"*Abigail saw?* Are we in junior high?" Jamey flicks cold eyes at his friend.

"But I mean — you did."

"Yeah. Took her to dinner to make up for, you know, the incident."

"Huh."

The heat roars.

Matt wants to say something else. "She freaks me out, dude."

"Why?"

"Well. She's a hustler, don't you think?"

"I don't know." Jamey blows into his Purdey gloves of copper-brown leather.

"You're nice to her because you feel guilty. Correct?"

Jamey shrugs.

"Don't you think she knows that?" Matt presses, looking at Jamey who just looks at the ice-crusted windshield. "Don't you think she's counting on that?"

"So *she's* to blame for you pushing her?"

"I barely touched her! How else could someone in my place react?"

"There's lots of ways someone could react."

"She's a *townie,*" Matt observes.

"She's not even from here."

"Wherever she's from, she's a townie there."

"Why do you care?"

"Um, she looks like she didn't finish high school and is casing our house as we speak."

Without answering, Jamey steps out and rakes ice off the windshield.

Matt watches, the light in the car a frozen blue.

Jamey gets back in, takes off his gloves, and puts his hands to the heat vent. Then he turns to Matt.

"Anyway, you went out with that girl Beth."

"Brenda? From Port Jefferson? What does that have to do with anything?"

"She wasn't from your social circle."

"You sound like my mother!"

"You know what I'm saying."

"We went out for two weeks," Matt says, unrelenting. "She gave the greatest hand job in Suffolk County."

Jamey stares out the window.

Matt sighs. "I'm just looking out for you, man."

"Please don't." Jamey smiles.

This makes Matt angry. "What, am I supposed to feel guilty because I have a great family, and we have money, and I got a really good education? Should I be miserable all my life because I got lucky? Sorry. I don't feel guilty at all."

Jamey says nothing.

"Dude," Matt says, flustered and giving up. "I'm sick of your shit."

They drive to school over roads pitted with salt, mute.

She watches from her window as the car drives away.

Him and Matt — that's no good. She has the urge to pry them apart, like photographs on album pages that got stuck together, the faces sealed.

The cold is mean. Cheeks are red and raw, and hands hurt when they take up pens in the classrooms, knuckles thawing. Snow melts off a boot to watery mud on the marble floor.

Jamey sits in a classroom, and his is the only desk to get an angle of sun. He resists closing his eyes. He can't warm up. He pretends to stare at the professor. Dust moves around his head but barely; Jamey could be a photograph he's so still. When the class is over, he leaves as if he just got there, as if he didn't hear a thing.

A mitten is half-sealed into a dirty snowbank outside the science building. When a bird shrieks, everything that already felt fragile suddenly feels broken.

In the dining hall, he sits with Matt and friends, pretending to listen to their Gorbachev debate.

Amber pendant lights, blue curtains, mashed potato on blue-rimmed plates, wood walls, ginger ale — Jamey holds on to the table like someone on a stormy sailboat.

Because he's watching Matt (collar popped, jaw set, leaning back in his chair with his arms crossed).

I don't like my best friend anymore, Jamey understands, and actually tears up.

Matt watches the debate. He always gauges how an argument will lean before choosing a side. His French-blue cashmere sweater is new; Jamey's never seen it. That's how well they know each other.

Growing up, Matt gave Jamey the birthday gift Matt wanted for himself, dragging his nanny to FAO Schwarz; Jamey did the same. A toy Ferrari to pedal in circles around your bedroom! A Japanese robot whose chest shoots real sparks! The most extravagant water gun the world has ever known!

Matt recently decided to be an investment banker. He wants to ski triple black diamonds at Vail. He wants a loft in SoHo. He wants to marry a supermodel. He wants a Rhodesian ridgeback, like the one some cowboy bond trader brought to a party in Montauk last summer. He wants a sixty-foot sailboat like his dad, and he wants to win races in Jamaica, Newport, Antigua, and then he wants to do a victory sail with the boat full of supermodels and his Rhodesian ridgeback.

Matt always had Jamey over because Jamey's home was a ghost land, with the nanny-of-the-month drifting through rooms, and his father in Gstaad or London or Lyford Cay. The families lived on the same block — East Seventieth between Park and Madison — and were of the same social status: both dads were East Coast royalty but chose wives who knocked them down a peg, or skewed them sideways at least.

Matt's mother, Yasmin, is a megawatt beauty from an Iranian oil family. Matt acted out if she gave Jamey too much attention: Matt would spit food, fake-cry, slit his eyes in drastic boredom. She questioned the boys in an opulent accent about their day, the new Latin teacher at Buckley, the books they were reading. Her gold bracelet's one charm clanged on the marble counter or the phone receiver.

Matt's sister was named Asha, and her room spun with mobiles and Madame Alexander dolls. A cave of glitter and porcelain and grosgrain. Her hamster, Rod Stewart, nibble-sucked the silver water pipe in his cage with blank eyes.

Asha once stared at Jamey through dinner, then asked: *Why are you always here anyway?* Her parents shushed her. Matt hissed: "He's like my brother that's why, you stupid," which is something he never said out loud before or since.

The Danning apartment had things the Hydes' did: a junk drawer of twine and batteries and menus; a linen closet that smelled of lavender sachets; a foyer table where mail collected; and a master bedroom the kids couldn't enter. That wing was often empty at Jamey's house but full of light at Matt's. Jamey once got up to pee, and saw Matt's mom and dad in the hall — she was in a robe, he was in boxers. The couple faced each other, and he tucked a wisp of black hair behind her ear before kissing her. Jamey felt like someone lit a Roman candle in his mouth and aimed it down into his soul.

A blizzard is predicted, snowflakes cartwheeling across the TV screen all day as New England gets hysterical, waiting to see if it will come true.

Robbie's new boyfriend, Craig, wears a Metallica T-shirt tucked into jeans. He eats pistachios on the couch, delicately putting shells in the ashtray.

Robbie and Elise grind to Grace Jones, "Slave to the Rhythm."

"Shake your boo-tays!" Craig yells out.

Each time the song ends, they rewind the tape and play it again.

"Wow," Robbie says, and looks out the cold glass.

Elise and Craig smile with him as the white crush of sky lands on the earth. Snowstorms are mortally gentle, a silence dropped from heaven to stifle houses and highways, factories, dumpsters, and statues and fences and motorcycles and bushes and sheds. Birds and squirrels and stray cats vanish into hiding places that seem preordained, since the disappearance is seamless and immediate.

Next door, the guys watch CNN until the

lights flicker and die.

"Blackout!" Matt says, lighting a candle and grabbing a box of Triscuits. "Want some?"

"Sure," Jamey says.

They sit in the dark and eat crackers but can't think of much to talk about.

Luckily, Jonas and Thalia knock on the door with a bottle of scotch.

"Party time!" Thalia says throatily, unwrapping her plaid scarf, a veteran of Bermuda storms and Swiss Alps blizzards and heavy rains on private islands in Maine. "I told everyone to meet here. I *love* blackouts. So fun."

Later, Jamey sees silhouettes in the next-door yard.

He gets up.

"Got to piss," he says in a ridiculously casual voice to the people gathered in his lightless living room.

He sneaks out the door, toward Elise and two guys making snow angels.

The trio freezes, then Elise, finishing the wings, clumsily sits up and smacks her hands together.

The small guy takes charge. "Crazy storm, right?"

"Totally," Jamey says.

The guy holds a plastic cup. "Making

snow and syrup, man. You want to come upstairs?"

"Sure, I guess."

Jamey walks over. Elise's face is blotchy, and steam comes from her mouth. She wears white sweatpants and a rainbow sweater, tufted with snow.

Jamey nods at Elise. "Hey," he says.

She grins and ducks, like someone with braces. "Hey."

"What's going on," he says, offering his hand to Robbie and Craig. "Jamey Hyde."

What am I, running for president? he thinks.

They feel their way up the stairs, their footfalls especially loud in the darkness. In the apartment, Robbie pours Aunt Jemima into a cup of snow and hands it to Jamey.

"Thanks," he says.

Jamey bristles with discomfort and desire, standing like an exclamation point — ramrod straight and perched on a dot.

"You doing good?" Elise asks him.

"Yeah, you?" he says.

She nods, licks ice from her cup.

Candlelight makes her eyes black.

They all sit on pillows on the floor, telling blizzard and blackout and hurricane stories. Jamey hears himself guffaw and ask simple questions, and he's reminded of his dad or some other middle-aged man talking to teenagers.

But he won't leave. Everyone can feel it, and it's thrilling and freaky.

"Why don't we go for a little midnight walk!" Robbie says theatrically to Craig.

Elise and Jamey sit there on the pillows, stranded. When she finally looks up, he's staring. He's dumb, gauche with lust. This makes her flush. She puts her mouth as close to his as she can while letting him be the one to start the kiss.

And he kisses her.

She takes him to the bedroom eventually, pulling up sweatpants unglamorously pushed halfway down her thighs, sweater around her neck.

She's taken his shirt off and unbuckled him, and he holds his pants closed as they walk hand in hand into the dark room.

"Ouch," he whispers, after stubbing his toe, and she nervously laughs with him.

They sit on the bed, and she tosses her boots into the corner, where they land heavily. She pulls her sweater off and stands to step out of her pants. Sitting, he circles his arms around her hips and puts his cheek against her stomach, where blood beats like a drum.

She moves his mouth down. He licks her, and she makes him stop, trembling, because she's about to come.

He looks up, bewildered, in the dark, for directions. She shakily leads him to take off his pants, and lie down. Straddling him, she's so swollen, he thinks he must be injuring her. But she eases down, then moves, slowly frantic and unstoppable, and they both come so hard it hurts.

She lies next to him, on cold blankets that haven't had time to warm up. She kisses his damp neck where the artery throbs.

"I'll do anything in the world for you," she says quietly.

Her hand spreads flat on his belly.

And he hates her.

He stays awake and sneaks out when dawn washes the room with a bisque-cream light. He tiptoes by Robbie's open bedroom, sees dirty socks hanging out of the quilt.

Later in the morning at his own house, Jamey yawns, makes tea on the gas stove, acting like nothing happened. Matt looks at his friend with dull hostility.

"I almost called 911," Matt says. "Why didn't you just tell us you were going over there?"

"I heard something outside," he sputters,

"and they invited me upstairs for a drink."
"Who's they?" Matt says.
"Elise, and her roommate, and his, you know, friend."
Jamey bounds up the stairs like a kid home from a first date.
The blizzard takes days to plow, and classes start slowly.
Jamey doesn't go to her place that night, or the next night, and can barely sleep. He jacks off quickly and without ceremony because he has to.

She's eating Kentucky Fried Chicken in the living room, and she finds herself motionless, paralyzed, holding up a drumstick, unsure how long she's been like this — lost in the dream. The room is dim; it's become evening without her noticing. Elise can barely eat because her stomach is shrunk in obsession.

Since their biorhythms are yoked, Jamey's distraction, even though he's not doing anything about it, is driving Matt insane.
"You seem a little unfocused," Matt says acidly.
"What do you mean?" Jamey asks.
Jamey's *extremely* focused on those thighs, and hard tits, the way her kiss summons his

blood and sends it gushing through his veins like a fucking river!

That weekend, Jamey gets tipsy at the Eggnog Social, where high-society kids do cocaine and listen to the Rolling Stones. He isn't drunk, just buzzed enough to slide out of the wood-paneled clubhouse when friends aren't paying attention, turn his coat collar against the crackling Connecticut night, pop into his BMW, driving and grinning, to park at his house, even though he goes into *her* building, whose door is unlocked, taking two steps at a time, and knocks on her apartment door.

"Whatsup," she says.

She's in sweatpants and a tight leopard shirt, her cornrows slick.

He's got a holly sprig in his lapel; she looks at it, looks at his face.

They have hours of sex. He's not very good at it.

"Easy," she says, more than once.

They fuck four times, till daybreak, birds piercing the giant pale winter morning. Elise and Jamey are both sober but strung out as if they've been partying for hours, and she throws on a T-shirt to make them coffee, which she brings to the bed. They sit with backs against the bare wall, and sip the

black coffee, listening to the city wake up.
"I have to go," he says.

Jamey won't look Matt in the eye when he throws on his coat to see her, which he does almost every night now, like a junkie.

"Later," Jamey says, humming uncomfortably.

Matt shakes his head one night, without looking up from his newspaper. "You better be pulling out or wearing a condom, that's all I'm saying."

"Did you just tell me to 'pull out or wear a condom'?" Jamey repeats, because he can't think of what to say.

"So you don't get her pregnant —"

"I know what you're implying, that's not the point," Jamey says, his voice oddly high.

Matt sounds like a politician: "I'm on your side."

"There aren't sides!" Jamey says.

Silence.

"This conversation really upsets you," Matt says.

Then Jamey laughs that devilish way. He slips Doublemint into his mouth, and sneaks a look in the hall mirror at his freshly combed hair. In the darkness between houses, for the brief time it takes him to cross yards, he feels as inevitable as an animal.

Elise moves from tank to tank, cleaning the water with her tiny net. Fish dart down to the gravel, afraid of her hand.

Her pussy hurts, and her thigh muscles are sore, and she's buzzing with love. She smiles as she works. The tight seam of her jeans runs between her legs and amplifies the pain, and she cherishes it.

Jamey gets to know Robbie's men.

Craig loves pistachios.

Steven has orange hair and a pig nose but is somehow charming.

Gilbert is too young for his double chin.

Barney's white turtleneck clings to his breasts.

The characteristic linking them all: harmlessness.

They sit around the living room together, watching *All in the Family* or *The Jeffersons,* ordering Chinese, groping for small talk.

Jamey sounds condescending if he asks about their jobs or lives, arrogant if he doesn't.

And he can't read them either.

"That BMW out there yours?" asks Barney with a straight face. "Great car."

"So do you like Yale then?" asks Robbie

with a straight face. "Great school."

Tonight, after sex, Jamey showers the stickiness off.

Suddenly Elise steps in, douses her face, then hands him the soap. He's never showered with a girl.

He's not sure what to do, and gingerly washes her arms.

"You can kiss my cunt but you can't wash it?" she asks.

Jamey crookedly grins and holds the bar uselessly.

She pulls his hand between her legs.

Their skin is rubbery and slick, stained by the amethyst curtain. She kneels in the basin and gives him head.

Afterward, while she blow-dries her hair, he pretends to look for aspirin but wants to find the birth-control pills she says she's taking. He doesn't see them, although he's not sure what they look like, and he feels sick.

He leaves, his hair wet and face blank, and she can tell something's wrong. She can often tell something's wrong, since after sex he usually hates her and wants to disappear or die, but then he comes back the next night, or the night after, and that's all that matters.

■ ■ ■ ■

Some mornings, he studies while she sleeps. Or she watches him read, trailing nails along his arm, their bodies crisscrossed with sunlight coming through tattered blinds. She can do this for an hour. It always leads to the same thing. She's wet when he touches her.

To her he was a virgin and she took his virginity. He was an unpicked fruit turned to sugar. His lack of skills in the beginning, his brutality, his wide-eyed need for her to spell things out, to guide his hand or his mouth — all this made her want him more.

And his cock is thick, long but not so long that it's silly, with a pink sheen like marble on a humid day. When she sees the spot of pre-cum on his boxers, she shudders — and then she's a queen of sex, a Maria Callas in bed, an Olympic track star in the sheets, a sensual and deliberate teacher.

But they never do anything outside this room. They don't go to dinner again. They don't do breakfast or lunch either. Sometimes she asks if he wants eggs when they wake up, asks what time his first class starts. She gets upset when he has to leave. She crosses her arms at the door as he goes down the stairs but she watches him to the last step, till he's gone.

She starts calling his house every evening to see when he'll come over.

"Hello?" says Matt.

"Is Jamey there?"

"He's not back yet."

"All right," she says glumly like she doesn't believe him.

She calls every half hour.

"Is Jamey there?" she asks.

"I will *tell* him you called," Matt says in an aggravated, measured voice.

"Yeah, tell him I called."

"I will —"

Click — she hangs up.

When Jamey walks in, Matt looks at him.

"What?" he asks.

"That psycho is stalking you."

At work, Elise takes a smoke break in the bleak lot, staring at a shopping cart capsized in dead grass. She taps ashes and keeps her shoulders high against the cold.

She believes he might love her at some point. She never kidded herself that this would be easy; she just knows it will be worth it. They hail from different planets but that doesn't mean it's impossible. He's coming around. The cold wind makes her eyes wet.

Matt's taking Thalia to the Winter Ball, and Thalia has a friend visiting who needs a date, and that's how Jamey ends up taking Cornelia Founder to the dance. A Southern girl in a powder-blue gown, she laughs all night, like archaic flute music, holding Jamey's arm.

There are shenanigans in the ballroom, where tinsel hangs from chandeliers. An a cappella rendition of "I Just Called to Say I Love You," boys in the girls' bathroom sharing pristine cocaine, Timothy Gerrigan vomiting into a Champagne bucket.

"I've heard about you," Cornelia breathes into Jamey's ear as they sit at the silver-cloth-draped table late night.

Jamey and Matt, Cornelia and Thalia, and the rest of their *Social Register* crew, either grew up on the same block or went to boarding school or summered or skied together. They were raised in a pod, incubated in the thick and slippery gel of legacy. They arrived at Yale intact as a clan.

The group looks fine in tuxedos and dresses. Harry Smythe III, there, laughing with Beth Von Trotta and Alexandra Essex — they glitter with importance.

Why shouldn't they? They've been doused in lessons, experiences, attention, books, toys, films, saltwater and sunshine, space and quiet, vitamins, music, discipline, orthodontia, reward, vaccinations, role models of gentility and success, cake and lemonade, support, guidance.

Harry wears his granddad's cufflinks: tiny gold fox faces that look at the world sideways, unblinking, in the blur of his gestures.

Jamey does one bump of coke, and finishes his scotch. Cornelia is warm, and giggles into his neck when someone cracks a joke. She smokes like she never had a cigarette, coughing, pearl earrings winking.

He drives her home, concentrating on the yellow line but thinking about unfolding the blue silk. He wants to put his hand down there. At the house, he parks and turns to her, touches her mouth with his thumb, then leans in to kiss her.

Soon she's spreading her legs a little as he reaches down, the car dark and scattered with light. Her mouth is too wet on his mouth. She doesn't do much else.

Eventually they break apart. He smooths his hair and smiles at her, in his way — apologizing, happy, nihilistic.

She furtively snaps open her clutch and hunches over to swipe on Clinique lipstick.

"Shall we go inside?" he asks.

"Sure," she says too loud, drunk.

They walk without touching each other at an awkward fake-stroll pace to his house.

It's late when they wake. The sun is indistinguishable from clouds, all of it bright gray.

Cornelia puts on her grandmother's black mink and stands up straight.

They walk out quietly, since Matt is probably asleep and hungover and might have a hungover guest. They move toward the car, followed by their stately shadows on the frozen ground. It's only when they get to the BMW that Jamey sees key scratches and a shattered windshield.

"Oh my God!" Cornelia says. "Was that — did that happen last night?"

"Must have. It's been happening on this block lately," Jamey says evenly, and ushers her into the car, desperately collecting the dress's hem like dropped sails onto a boat.

He feels eyes watching from Elise's window.

"We can't drive like this!" Cornelia says shrilly.

"Sure we can," Jamey says, getting in the front seat.

Cornelia looks at him — and she suddenly loathes him, knowing something, without knowing what.

On his way back, he checks himself in the rearview mirror. The day comes through the cracked glass to make a map of lines on his face, a diagram, a collage like the magazine cut-ups girls create for mix-tape covers. Dull light is harder to handle than bright sun — he squints, barely able to keep his eyes open. It makes him look like he's grinning.

March 1986

For the next couple days, Elise paces the apartment.

Girl, you fucked up that car!

She's violently jealous, a plastic toy thrown into a fire, her white body turning liquid in the heat. She keeps playing a film from what she assembled — a blue dress, the idea of that rich, perfumed cunt, his drunk tongue, his bed (where Elise has never been), tuxedo slippers under a chair, and the couple sleeping, rank and sweet, while the sun rises like a peach.

Pull it together, Elise, she thinks one morning, and shakily puts on mascara.

At the kitchen table, she smokes and calls his house.

He comes over that evening, hands in coat pockets, looks at her overfilled ashtray.

"Sit down," she suggests coldly.

He does.

"I'm fucking really sorry about your car," she says, and she does sound sorry.

"Okay."

Silence.

"Your turn," she says, snapping her gum.

"For?" he asks.

"An apology."

He doesn't respond.

"Right in my *face,*" she says. "You think I deserve that?"

"In your face? What, were you spying on me?"

"Spying?" she sputters. "You live right fucking next door. I have to see you."

Ugh. He couldn't even get hard in his room that night. Cornelia resorted to a hand job, but she looked like a kid tying a ribbon on a kitten or putting the head back on a doll, earnest and flustered. He pretended to pass out.

"I didn't know we couldn't see other people," he says without conviction.

"So you can just use me and all that."

"Why is this a one-way thing? Are you not getting anything out of it?" he flails.

"I'm not getting enough."

"What else do you want?"

"I want to do things with you," she says softly.

"But. I don't know what you want to do,"

he says nonsensically.

She thinks. And then, guardedly, she states: “I want to go to Paddy’s Arcade.”

Nervous and uncomfortable, they walk down the stairs.

He unlocks the car as she winces at the sight of the windshield.

“Whoops,” she mumbles.

“It’s okay,” he says.

“Can I smoke if I roll down the window?” she asks, desperate.

“I guess,” he says, doing a U-turn.

She lights her cigarette and looks at the dull city lights. She turns to him. “So what have you been up to?”

When he looks at her, she’s trying not to smile.

He can’t help but smile too. “You’re something else,” he says.

At the arcade, she’s immediately giddy, grudgeless, unrepentant. He notices it right away. She becomes royal here, strutting with her endless legs and high chin. He changes dollars to quarters and they cruise around the mad, loud space. The spirit infects them, and they stare with big eyes at everything.

“Whatcha gonna play? Pick something, Jamey. You got to pick.”

She puts a Red Hot in his mouth as if to

give him strength.

The glare and *ring-bop-ding* of the games, the black lights illuminating the neon shapes on the carpet, make a dreamscape of wins and losses.

The soldiers and aliens die bloodless deaths, careening through space in pixelated pain.

Jamey's face is dappled in these lights, a palette of lemon-yellow and pink and lavender stars, and he ignores the other boys, who smell like popcorn and fabric softener, and his eyes focus like lasers on the tilting screen after he drops in his coins.

"Play again. I just want *you* to play," she says when each game is done.

He puts in more quarters. He leans, his shoulders narrowed, he jerks back. He fires and fires, decimating the machines, and his thumb is almost bleeding. Numbers float! Monsters help!

When the game is done, his cheeks are hot and his eyes are radiant. He's broken out of the shackles of himself.

She sucks on his lip after kissing him, jumping at him like a kid too big to catch and hold. While they walk, she pulls his arm around her, then matches her gait to his.

She finally plays one round of Donkey Kong against him.

He looks at her, jaw dropped, after she destroys him.

"What can I say." She grins, shrugging with one shoulder.

She rips cotton candy with her long magenta nails and stuffs it in his mouth. She holds out her Diet Coke in a big waxy cup for him to sip through the straw.

He's unexpectedly excited by what they must look like. He's enjoying being self-conscious tonight. No one he knows is going to show up.

He's seen other couples look like he and Elise must look, and he knew they knew things he didn't know. Those couples were always at movie theaters, or in Central Park, in New Haven pizzerias, at Montauk carnivals. Kids who chew gum with mouths open. Kids who yell and scream, with pleasure, with juvenile madness, fucking around, wrestling and flirting, making a scene, making fools of themselves, the girls in the guys' laps, all singing one line in a radio song's chorus together, and then falling apart and laughing at their outburst. Kids who pile later into one car whose side mirror is duct-taped on and whose ratty seats are covered in tiger-print towels, and they have nowhere to go.

■ ■ ■ ■

He's on his way to swim laps when Thalia comes out of the pool room with Darcy, goggles pushed up on their sleek heads.

"Jamey!" says Thalia, as if running into him in a hotel lobby in Rome.

"Hey there," he says, trying to move past them.

The aquamarine mist rises.

"Cornelia said to say hello," she says with a twisted smile.

"Please say hello from me," Jamey says.

The women watch his back as they dry their faces with towels, not moving to the locker room until he disappears.

He swims with great energy. He could have repaired things just now, charmed these girls back, righted the ship. It reminds him of a story that a drunk man at a beach club party once told him whose significance he didn't understand then but might understand today. The guy dropped his suit at the dry cleaners on Eightieth and Lexington, and decided not to get it, for no reason, and to never go to that dry cleaners again. The man laughed when he told Jamey this tale, sipped his Dewar's and ginger ale, and wandered off in a cheerfully unbound way.

■ ■ ■ ■

When he gets to Elise's bedroom tonight, she's wearing a cheap red negligee, and while he built himself up before coming over, he now feels sorry for her and her trashy nightgown.

Dammit, he thinks.

"What?" she says.

"Nothing," he says, deflated.

They make love, and lie in bed.

"How come you never ask me anything?" she says, turning the light back on after he turned it off.

"What's your favorite color?" he tries, and he's not sure if he's being kind.

She takes it seriously. "I've got a few. Black cars. Pink roses. You know? I like the blue what's in Club Med commercials. That kind of beach, I never even been near."

"You want to go to a beach like that?" he says because he has to say something.

"I mean, who wouldn't? What else you want to know?"

"Umm. What do you want to be when you grow up?"

Elise shrivels her nose. "I know what I *don't* want to be."

"What's that?"

"That's a whole other conversation," she says.

"What's the saddest you've ever been?"

"When my sister died. She wasn't my blood sister, but I loved her." Elise holds her hair so he can see the name on her neck: *Donna Sierra* in azure-blue italics. "She died a asthma."

"I'm sorry, Elise," he says, turning on his side to look at her. He suddenly wonders why he never asked about the tattoo.

"Ask me something that's not upsetting." She's lying back, one arm across her eyes.

"What would you be if you were an animal?"

"Shit, I don't know. A jaguar." She smiles.

"What would you be if you were a flower?"

"I got no idea," she says defensively, because she doesn't know flowers.

"A black iris," he tells her grandly, feeling different now.

"What's it look like?"

"It's . . . unusual. It shines in this really dark, strange way."

"Well, fuck you too."

"That was a compliment!"

"Yeah, yeah."

"Let's see," he says, and he runs his hand up her thigh, distracted.

"What's my favorite ice cream," she says.

"What's your favorite ice cream?"
"Peppermint at Friendly's."
He kisses her neck.
Elise puts her hand between her legs to close it off. "I'm sore."
He takes the straps off her shoulders and bites her nipples.
"It's my turn," she says. "Even though I already know all about you. Since *I* pay attention."
"Ha," he says dully but playfully.
"What's your favorite color?"
"I don't discriminate."
"Gee, aren't you fucking correct. What's the saddest you ever been?"
"I'm always sad."
"That's not true."
"I was born sad."
"What kind of animal are you?"
"I'm a human animal."

He tastes her neck, kissing, soft as a cream puff. He moves so slowly that she's the one who arches her back, starting over, finding his mouth with hers.

And here they are again, and it hurts but that makes it pungent, evil, and good. "Wait — wait for me," she tells him sternly at the end, teeth gritted, and he does.

They're spent. Bodies light as ash.

"Dayum," she says a few moments later.

And for a while, the room isn't grim, the paint isn't cracked, the sounds of toilets flushing and dogs barking and people fighting don't make it through the disintegrating walls. Their golden chamber is oily with incense, studded with jewels and stars and thorns, hidden from the city, the floor covered in fur rugs.

Her red negligee is divine.

They discover a diner, with a quilted-metal exterior, always busy with senior citizens and kids from the nearby Hebrew school and housewives in jogging suits. Each table has a miniature jukebox, and the grilled cheese is butter-crusty on the outside, creamy on the inside, the milkshake too thick for a straw. It's their station, their headquarters outside the bedroom.

She mashes an onion ring into her mouth. "This kid just keeps tapping on the glass tanks. I said if I *ever* fucking see him again, I'll crush his junior-high ass."

Jamey stares at her.

"What?" she asks, eating.

"Do you listen to yourself?"

"I'm not deaf."

"Are you unable to express things without curse words?" he asks, sounding like an old-lady teacher. "You're going to alienate people."

"People who? What the fuck do you care?"

What does he care?

She plays with the fake-gold necklace hanging over her turtleneck and grins, watching him be flustered. Later, she'll think this conversation revealed that — at least subconsciously — he thinks about a future.

When they drive somewhere, she scratches his neck like he's a cat, distracting him so he forgets to turn or signal or stop. His face is masculine, in a bountiful way, and she stares at his dimple, his teeth, his sly mouth. He has a way of sluggishly shrugging, or winking — or slowly fingering a shirt button — that works against the way his mind darts in strange directions, and the chasm this creates draws Elise down into him.

"When I'm not with you, I just sit around and think about fucking you," she says at the diner one day, and he winces.

"Why would you say that in a public place?" he hoarsely whispers. "Everyone can hear you!"

Now that he's told her to stop cursing, she does it more. Is she playing? She's poker-faced, like an Indian, like Pocahontas, eating onion rings.

■ ■ ■ ■

One night he's tired after writing a paper in ten straight hours on coffee and Vivarin.

She lights candles in her room, turns up the R&B station, and breaks out the baby oil.

He's terrified. "You're not serious."

"Oh, I'm gonna take care of you, boy."

She straddles his back on the bed and hums to Luther Vandross as she works. He grins into the covers with humiliation. He doesn't do this. He's not here. His body battles being relaxed. It's like he landed in some MTV nightmare, some late-night boots-knockin' remix. But it feels good, and he ultimately can't pretend that it doesn't, not even to himself.

Spring break's coming up. The guys are hitching a ride out of Teterboro, meeting Matt's family in Aspen — for a week of skiing, Armagnac, and braised elk!

Jamey's got a better idea.

The Newport house is empty: a briny wind whipping the trees, surf pounding the ice-laced beach, a fireplace, a bed. And no one watching.

"Not going to make it to Aspen," Jamey

says one day, clapping his hands like a corporate breaker of bad news.

"Why not?" Matt says.

"The Newport house'll be empty, so I was thinking about that."

"Of course it's empty, it's freezing and it's a beach and there's nothing to do," Matt says.

"It'll be cozy," Jamey says, and actually blushes.

"So you can't leave her for one whole week?"

"I could easily leave her."

"You know, the fact that you never bring her over says ever-y-thing there is to say," Matt singsongs.

Jamey rolls his eyes. "She'd feel so welcome."

"Why not?"

"You said she was 'casing' the place."

"Forget about that," Matt says, because he can't bring himself to apologize.

Jamey snorts. "It's not like she *wants* to come over, trust me."

They stare at each other.

"Who *is* she? Do you know who her parents are? Do you know *anything* about her?"

But Jamey doesn't want to know her for the same reason that — (his brain starts fuzzing up here, trying to save him from the thought he's about to think) — for the same reason a farmer isn't close to his animals — it's not supposed to last. Jamey burns with shame at this unbidden idea, and Matt sees his face redden.

"Are you in love with her or something?"

"Are you fucking out of your mind?"

Watching her eat toast, or tie her sneakers, or sleep — Jamey is repulsed.

The slant of her eyes is lower-class. She chews gum like a whore. She leaves skid marks in the toilet. The fact that she irons her jeans is pathetic. Her face is wide and empty when he uses words like *disingenuous* and *amorphous.*

He doesn't even know where he gets these notions. How does a whore chew gum? Who says *whore* anymore?

And the disgust breaks like a fever. He sees the light in her eyes when she laughs, braids falling over her face. The way she looks at him when he walks in the door. The smell of her neck when they come together, something feral and otherworldly, salt and roses, life and death.

And his head goes back and forth. What's he doing hanging out with this girl? And then he thinks *he's* just really fucked up.

And then he wants to fall asleep and leave consciousness behind before it ruins him.

But he invites her to Newport anyway.

Packing, she feels excited. And stupid. She knows the trip will be humiliating in vague, as-of-now-unknown ways, and she stands outside in the brisk morning with her backpack, smoking, waiting for him to leave his house. So much of life is about standing on the curb, willing to see what rolls up.

She squints at birds on the telephone wire, the line of small bodies never static — as one lands on the cable, one from the other end of the group takes off into flight. A masterpiece of balance.

Driving, Jamey tries to fill the silence, saying inane things like: *Ever been to Newport? No, well it's a pretty town. You like lobster? Maybe we'll have a big seafood dinner one night.* A "seafood dinner"? He sounds like a TV commercial. *Did you pack your bathing suit? Just kidding.*

They get cheeseburgers at McDonald's, and she holds out a greasy paper of ketchup so he can dip his fries and drive. She finally asks if he minds listening to the radio; the Knicks game is on. He can tell she just wants him to shut up too.

■ ■ ■ ■

Late afternoon, they turn into the gate. Her eyes take in the long driveway and the elms arching over it, and then the size of the white house, the dozens of windows reflecting sky.

"Wow," she says. "It's huge."

But she doesn't give much away, holds her cards tight as they walk up massive slate steps to the door, flanked by pots where camellias flourish in the summer.

He and Elise bumble around, reviving the foyer, the kitchen, the library, stirring the sunshine-thick rot of a still environment.

She opens a closet to put away her jacket and finds it stuffed.

"Whose are these?" she asks.

He looks at slickers and sandals and umbrellas. "Everyone's. No one's in particular."

"Did people forget them?"

Jamey tries to understand her confusion.

"I mean," she begins again. "Who lives here?"

"It's a summer house. A second home. No one lives here."

Elise shuts the door, unconvinced. She imagines people walking around somewhere without jackets.

Mouse droppings have collected in an antique bowl on the piano like rice grains in a monk's cup. She plays one note and looks at the painting on the wall.

"Who's that?" she asks, intuitively intimidated by the portrait.

"My grandmother. They call her Binkie."

The house is rejecting Elise like a body refuses a transplanted organ. Cells conspire. The rugs, the roll-top desk, the sun-faded *Economist* stacks — they want her out.

They drink coffee on the couch. The chintz looks to Elise like outerspace flowers: unnatural, unearthly, a pattern of symmetrical asymmetry. A garden written in code. Sinister.

Elise wants him to be glad he brought her, and she knows part of the reason they're here is sexual fantasy, so she does what she believes will make him happy. She starts to kiss him on the sofa, pushes up his teal sweater to lick a line down his stomach, then she unzips his pants. Of course she got her period yesterday, which couldn't be worse timing, but she can put off his knowing if she gives him a blow job now. Her eyes flick up to his eyes as she works.

Dusk hits the windows and turns to inky

night. The silk lampshades are brighter. Finished, she moves back to the couch and leans against him. He sits with knees spread, eyes bright, and then sighs and pulls it together. A couple drops of milk on the Persian rug.

They eat roast-beef sandwiches for dinner. He listens to her talk without hearing what she's saying. If he closes his eyes, the hard way she ends words, the youngness in the middle stretch of a syllable, the innocence caught in one long lilt, followed by jadedness in a staccato phrase, like gunshots — he could be listening to a sixteen-year-old boy.

She hunkers down while she eats, a quarterback on the bench.

When she's quiet, she sometimes looks cross or like she's trying to remember something. She seems so lean in moments like this, and ungiving. A lot of bone and fury, and nothing else. She's dry metal, the glint of mica ringing in your ear.

She takes Jamey's hand, kisses his knuckles.

He's suddenly aware of how plush she is, how luscious, within, or somewhere. What's so exciting about her is there's no room, in theory, for what's inside. Her heart is voluptuous, it has a tongue and a pout, dense fur, a huge lake of blood, a dazzle of lash and white fire, where he floats and dreams, borne on lust.

In the morning Jamey jogs. He runs like an athlete — light and unerring. The road cuts into the rocky coast over the ocean. The sea throws up plumes of water — viciously cold.

No one's here this time of year except caretakers: often alcoholic friends of the family who can't handle society, who hide and take care of mansions and animals.

He knows every family on this route. The Galloways over there have albino peacocks. The birds usually strut by the old eggplant-purple Mercedes, maybe because they're narcissists and they like their dull reflection in the paint.

Here's the pale-gray castle where the widow Rutherford, last of her line, throws bridge parties and grand dinners at the age of eighty-six. She remembers Jamey whenever he takes his turn greeting her, small as a girl in a wicker throne shaded by lilacs and robins.

The Tennyson house, blocked by tall privet hedges, was the site of a sad birthday party. Jane Tennyson was turning twelve, and her best friend, Eileen Choward, dove into the shallow end and broke her neck, paralyzed for life. Jamey still thinks about these two girls, almost every day, and he doesn't know why.

He runs by Sarah Stanhope's house, his best friend in their early summers. They traded books at the beach club. Now she wears gold bracelets and a topknot, and he thought for a while she'd be the person to love. At a wedding on St. John's, they tried it, while jasmine-spiked moonlight leaked through the window, and drunk guests squealed on the beach, but he felt like he was kissing his sister.

His hair is damp and cold as he runs on the cliff.

He runs past the pier where he's launched and docked many a sailboat. This is where family and friends have evening drinks, sitting in captains chairs on the wharf, smoking, having wandered down in loafers from their homes with their own drinks in their own glasses.

Jamey often sailed alone, and they all got quiet when he approached to dock the boat. Jamey was the promised child and the cursed child. The sun would set through his sail as he got close, and he would loose the mainsail to luffing by turning the bow into the wind, and make a perfect landing.

They always helped tie her up.

His young body was intended for sailing — he moved like a cat on a hot roof — he looked to his relatives as they exchanged rope, and his uncle or second cousin bent to cleat the line with one hand while holding a scotch in the other, and no one looked back at him.

It wasn't a cruel silence. They were all just waiting. Jamey continued growing, changing, his mother's otherness maybe showing in his skin, in his full mouth, his elegance. He should be the family legacy, and they want him to properly and exclusively claim his Hyde blood. They don't shun him. They just don't know what to do with him yet. Someone offers him a hand off the boat. He takes it, steps to the dock, letting the boat gently rock behind him. *Atta boy,* someone says.

He starts to become aware now as he runs, conscious of his moving parts, of the unlikelihood they'll continue to interact. Synchronicity ends.

In a class last month, the professor conducted an experiment by telling students not to think of a white bear for five minutes. To suppress that image. And then to record how often they thought of the white bear.

Not only did Jamey think of the white bear

a hundred times in five minutes, he thought of it for the rest of class. Then the rest of the day. Then that night. The white bear sits in his head now, like Jamey's skull is a circus ring and there's no ringmaster. The bear cracks a whip and grins with yellow teeth.

When Jamey gets back to the house, he pulls off his sneakers, wet with sand, walks quietly through the rooms.

He finds Elise in a bedroom, bending over a vanity table where many girls have cut bangs and tried on their aunts' earrings and whispered and squabbled.

She's looking in a jewelry box.

He wonders what's in her pockets. The second he suspects her, a phantom hand — his own — slaps his face.

"Hey." She smiles.

"Hey."

"How was your run?"

"Fine." He looks at her.

"What?" she asks.

"Nothing. What are you doing?"

"Looking for a safety pin to hold my stupid bra together," she says.

"Oh. Yeah, there might be one in there."

He wonders, as he showers, if she heard the real question: *What do you think you're going to find?*

He doesn't really know her; it's his right to speculate. *Isn't it? She's a stranger.*

As he towels dry, looking at a Dior perfume bottle next to a conch shell on the glass shelf, he thinks of a scene at his dad's place in the city, years ago. Alex was yelling at a housekeeper, who'd brought her daughter along that day. The girl was ten or eleven. She'd taken a perfume bottle off a dresser and the cook had caught her hiding in the pantry and trying it on.

"I don't care that she gave it back — she gave it back because she got caught," Alex was saying to her mother.

The girl looked up and Jamey didn't want to see the poor thing's eyes; he expected humiliation. He was surprised to see pinwheels of pure hatred spinning in her face.

Photographs line the walls of a hallway. Jamey stands behind Elise as she looks, and he wonders — Do I really want her to understand all this?

"That's you!" she says, pointing to a kid in a Brooks Brothers blazer by a Christmas tree.

"Yeah, in Palm Beach."

"And this one! Look at you, so skinny," she says of Jamey — he's alone in a bathing suit, his body painted with the cobalt shadow of blooming rhododendrons. Braces and a pale chest — even at his most awkward, he was awkward with grace. It's funny that, grown-up now, groomed and charming enough, he still identifies most with that boy, with that photo, with that moment of gloom and radiance, possibility — and solitude.

He watches her scan pictures, sees her realize the woman in the snapshot there is Nancy Reagan, and that it was taken in the dining room of this house. Elise doesn't say anything.

His dad as a prep-schooler in a rowing shell, his grandmother on a Technicolor golf course. Many weddings, but not Jamey's parents'.

"Where's your mom?"

"Nowhere," he says. "According to them, she never existed."

Adults on a sailboat, laughing, off a blindingly white beach. Square-jawed women in gowns with baby-faced men in tuxedos at balls in Manhattan, Boston, London. Children on a ski slope, black trees in the background. Newborns, eyes looking glassily from a bassinet.

How can he explain the Hydes? Their pockmarked DNA, aged like blue cheese, traditions browning like the edges of a sliced pear? They're more than a family — they're an institution, a culture, a regime. And he, technically, is a high-ranking member.

The women are smart and lanky — a few exist on Ritz crackers and gin — no one sees them consume much else. The men range from chieftains, eminent rulers — like Bats and Uncle J. P. — to their henchmen, like Alex. The family has legendary parties — whiskey juleps at the Kentucky Derby, summer croquet in East Hampton, and holiday caroling from house to house in Newport. They have backgammon tournaments, and the guests wear herringbone slacks, sipping Glenlivet outside in the cool autumn twilight.

The old cat, Ducky, is pictured here in a grove of peonies, and he represents another facet of the Hydes. He fought a one-cat war with raccoons all his life, his face rearranged after bloody, moonlit altercations, and one yellow eye blinked on top of his head, and his tongue hung out the side of his mouth. He died on a Thanksgiving night, heaved and gurgled at the top of the stairs as the family ate turkey and potatoes dauphin. The Hydes didn't move — they admired his self-sufficient courage, and they admired themselves for being unsentimental. The children helped dig his grave under a holly tree the next morning.

After looking at the photos, they eat cookies in the kitchen, play "Chopsticks" on the piano, and see the view from the third floor — a long dark gleaming glitter of ocean. There are more staircases and hallways and closets and rooms than seems scientifically possible from outside.

This isn't new to her, being new in a house that isn't hers. Elise checked off many addresses on her journey. She saw herself in medicine-cabinet mirrors, she slept on couches covered in dog hair and took the dimes and pennies from under the cushions, she nipped a slug of orange juice before she left, she stepped out of buildings and looked left then right and simply moved in a direction so it looked like she had a destination. The lightning fork on the city rooftop gleamed with dirty light as she set out, again and again, newly put forth after getting through a night, rising like a bird into the world.

"I want to see the beach!" she says around midnight.

"Now?" he asks. "You're insane."

They grab a blanket and walk, blanket over shoulders, down a path that in summer is hedged by hydrangea blooms. Tonight the plants are sticks.

On the beach she pulls away and tears to the ocean, runs to the surf's edge, wets her boots at their tips.

Jamey drops the blanket and they race in circles. The moon clarifies the sand's ripples and the half-buried driftwood and the frilly edge of the Atlantic.

When they stop, she coughs, bending over.

"God is telling you to quit smoking," he says.

"Yeah, that's gonna happen," she scoffs, but she collects his statement of concern like a seashell in her pocket, another souvenir of their future together.

They lie on the blanket and roll into it. He puts his hand under her shirt, she yelps — her torso is blazing. So slim, and so much heat! She slips her icy hands in his sweater, and finds it's hot there too.

They barely move and yet the sand stirs audibly, minerals turning, squeaking.

Her face painted by the stars. The light sanctifying each curve and lash. He thinks about how human bodies are made from time and space: meteors and blood, lava and brain, plankton and bones.

"Let's sleep here," she says.

"It's way too cold," he says.

And she *could* almost sleep in the dunes. It's about being hardy as well as disobeying conventions like homes and buildings, rooms and beds, addresses, belongings. She left them; she unbraided those things from her identity. She signed off.

"*I'm* too cold," he admits.

"You're a baby," she teases, and they lie there for a while before standing up, brushing off sand, folding the blanket, and walking back.

He wakes up in the dark, confused — the rooms divide memories into compartments. His father and Cecily in this bed, hungover after their engagement party ten years ago, reading the paper all morning and drinking bloody marys Jamey delivered. In the sitting room, an argument between his uncles over a card game. An afternoon of buttery light in the kitchen, cigarette smoke, a couple visiting from Saudi Arabia — who were they? Someone's dog cowering in the hedge, in shock after being hit by a car.

He wants to get rid of most of what he remembers, comb through it, toss it, but he feels guilty. His head is packed with tie pins, soda caps, pressed violets. Girls' things, or things collected like a girl collects things. There's a feminine side to him, an almost indolent, timid part of his soul. He's affected so easily. Once in a while, he can feel everything shift one way, and he lurches to the left, seasick on recollection and devotion. An object like a metal spatula — he sees his dad in madras shorts and no shirt at the grill — shimmers now in the far distance like a friendly warning.

The next day, he has to shit but he can't do it with her around. When they're in New Haven, he goes to his own house because he can't at her apartment.

Now he sneaks to the cold, unheated servants' wing. He yips as he sits on the freezing seat.

And suddenly she's calling his name through the house. *Why? Why now?* He's mortified, and holds his breath. He wipes his ass, quietly stands — *She's near!*

He lights a match from a Le Cirque matchbook in the French ceramic dish on the back of the toilet. But he doesn't want her to hear him flush.

Her voice recedes. He waits and waits, flushes, tiptoes up a back staircase so he can come down the front stairs like he was just out of earshot. His heart is pounding.

They're reading *Smithsonian* magazine and

drinking beer when Elise hears a noise upstairs.

"This place is haunted!" she says.

This house *is* haunted, he explains — by a charismatic, manic red-head named Henrietta, who loved gardenia perfume, mystery novels, caramel candies, and her employer: Aaron Balthazar Hyde, Jamey's great-grandfather. Loved him too much, loved him the wrong way, loved him over and over. Everyone thought her bloated nose and pink eyes were because she missed Ireland, but the worldlier girls saw the slight weight gain, almost imperceptible, just a shifting of the body's priorities. And one day the girl was found hanging in the bedroom she shared with two maids, her tongue ice-blue.

"To be honest, I've heard so many versions over the years, it's probably not true."

"But she was real?"

"As far as I know. And he was certainly real."

"And they had an affair?"

"That's hard to confirm. She could have said he was the father but it was actually the driver, you know?"

"Or your great-granddad could've raped her."

"Yes," Jamey says slowly, not sure if he

should be defensive.

"Or maybe she was like delusional. Was she definitely having a baby?"

"That could be rumor."

Elise now pictures this girl arranging daisies in a vase, polishing silver.

Jamey keeps putting her beer on the magazine so it doesn't water-stain the table. Elise sees old scuffed furniture, but this is an eighteenth-century English sideboard. She twirls her hair with black-tipped magenta nails, a Turner seascape as her backdrop, and luckily she doesn't catch his expression. It's the face he makes when *their* story sounds like a rumor. What on Earth are they doing?

"You have to open the flue first," he says, reaching up into the charred space. "Like so."

He crouches, wedging newspaper cones under an *X* of kindling and logs. He touches a match to the paper. Fire consumes Jamey's construction, popping and hissing, and twigs turn molten orange and sizzle into smoke and ash, while the alligator bark starts to glow.

Jamey's face and neck and hands are yellow as he watches.

They gaze at the fire, throwing on another

log whenever the time is right, looking through art books like James Whistler paintings, Edward Weston's mountains, an Audubon tome whose plates Jamey turns from egret to pelican to raven.

When they go to bed, she drinks a glass of water because she's parched. She's deeply dreamy and sleepy. That fire changed the whole house, like it finally got a heart, but the sheets feel extra cold, and they hold each other.

He sips orange juice in the kitchen, and he smells on the glass his own breath — his mouth — in that way that's usually impossible, even if you blow into the cup of your hand. Nothing has ever made him so aware of mortality. *He gets it.*

Then, bang! It's gone again.

He hands her a tartan cape to stay warm, and she looks like a Scottish warrior as they go walking through the lanes. Massive houses are almost visible behind hedges and ivy-covered brick walls, looming, moving as they pass. Once in a while, a bronze square indicates that someone's home, or smoke chuffs slowly from a chimney into the dark sky.

"I was out in a place like this, upstate New

York, for like a week," she says.

"Oh yeah?" he says. "Was it nice?"

"It *was* nice, we went swimming, played softball in the town. It was just weird, you know, 'cause I was staying with this family. It was like a program."

"A Fresh Air Fund sort of thing?" he asks after a moment.

"Yeah."

They look at each other like: *I wonder if we can talk about these things.*

"That's cool you got to go, but yeah, I imagine it was strange," he says, his tone gently closing this part of the conversation.

He's thinking of a summer, he was fourteen or fifteen. The Kellogg family down the road hosted a brother and sister from Harlem, Josiah and Kelly (or Kerry? or Cary?), and Jamey ended up bringing Josiah over for a barbecue. Everyone treated the kid well, including Bats and Binkie, asking about his school and his summer. Josiah was tall and spindly, wearing someone's Izod shirt. But Jamey overheard Bats the next day laughing with his friend Greg Lamar about the Kelloggs. *What, they're Mother Teresa now? Better than the rest? Feeling especially guilty about that IPO, are we, Jeff?* Jamey thought about how the maid Lysoled the downstairs bathroom right after the barbecue was done and the guests gone, and he knew someone in his family asked the maid to do that, and he knew why.

"Are you listening to me?" Elise says now, halfway through a story about strawberries and a sunburn.

Walking with Elise is like walking with a hyperactive child, because she turns around and strides backward to talk to him, or runs a few steps forward to dunk an imaginary basketball, or does a Crip Walk with a straight face while he bends to tie his shoe.

But when she holds him around the waist as they stroll, he doesn't respond with his own arm around her waist, and she eventually lets go. Even though there's no one looking, he still feels seen.

The morning they're going to leave, Elise stands at the kitchen window, the T-shirt she slept in falling off one shoulder. A deer has come to the yard to see if there's anything green to nibble. She's watching the animal.

The doe steps through the grass, muted by dew, as if moving through a mine field of light and dark. Jamey steps behind Elise, wraps his arms around her waist.

What if, he's thinking, for the first time. She leans back, easing weight against him.

And he feels it as her saying, *Yes, exactly.*

The deer stops, bites, chews while listening — her big brown eyes not frightened but intensely alert.

Elise is taking one last hot soak when he comes in to brush his teeth — she's fallen in love with the claw-foot tub and is sad to leave it. She lies back, braids hanging over the ivory edge. Her eyes are closed, goose-bumped knees high.

Then he sees it: threads of blood from between her legs, unspooling in the slow motion of ethereal things.

He knew she had her period; they'd been putting down towels in the bed. But there's something about this — so delicate and terrifying. . . .

In the car, she bites her nail while he drives.

"So, you wanna drop stuff at your house and come over?" she asks.

"I sort of need to collect myself."

"Collect what?"

"Get it together for this upcoming week."

She looks at the highway, the neon signs for Arby's, for Jiffy Lube. A white van next to them has cheap black letters glued to its side: ST. LUKE'S HOUSE FOR MEN. Beyond, a landscape of suburbs and industry is dark rubble covered with a thousand rhinestones. The stars in the sky are browned out. She uses a fake smile to hold her place in the world.

A couple times, Jamey has the almost comical urge to swerve into the oncoming stream of headlights. He hasn't felt that in at least a month, and he's disappointed to feel it again, his hands sore when they get home from gripping the wheel.

When Jamey makes it into his house, he's weirdly pleased by the *clack-clack* of a jeans button spinning in the dryer, and the lamps blazing, the furnace on high. He closes his bedroom door, and only then realizes how tired he is after he and Elise had to generate enough humanity between them to battle the cold and empty mansion in Newport. He's exhausted. Finished.

He thinks about the things they maybe left there — a satin thong in the sheets, Diet Pepsi in the fridge, a *People* magazine. Drops of bacteria that can grow and change the environment, evolving the empty house.

"So, what time you gonna be here tonight?" she calls to ask the next day.

"Not sure." He squirms. "I have a lot of work."

"What work?"
"Schoolwork, Elise. I'm in school."
"Just come after."
"I don't know when I'll be done."
"It doesn't matter. The door's unlocked."
"It matters to me."
"Why? Just wake me up."
"Goddamn. You don't give up."
"I'm sorry, am I hearing that you *want* me to give up?"
"Elise, for God's sake . . ." he says in exasperation but without answering yes or no.

He and Matt get pizza in town, and Matt tells him about hotel-room partying in Aspen and this guy who puked all over the parquet floors, the curtains, the bed, and how they put him in the hall, naked and unconscious, on a room-service tray for the staff to handle.

Matt asks him carefully about Newport, and Jamey answers that it was "relaxing," the house was "peaceful," the beach was "beautiful with no one there."

Jamey didn't think he was going to do this — there were even moments in Newport when he imagined a murky, quivering future of sorts — but he doesn't want to see her anymore. He's playing with a human heart. He needs to stop this experiment. It *was* an experiment after all.

She calls the next afternoon.

Matt says: "Um, hold on a sec."

He raises his eyebrows at Jamey, who shakes his head and mouths: *I'm not here.*

"He's out right now, but I'll tell him you called."

Between his BMW being there on the street and Matt's politeness, Elise knows.

Actually, she knew before they left the house in Rhode Island, as she locked eyes with Binkie's portrait one last time. His people have a kind of power she thought only existed in myths. The way the fireplace lit him up, the way he stretched out in the four-poster bed, sheets to his hips — that house doesn't want to let him go.

She tries to reach him, sporadically, over the next week. Even Jamey is surprised at how infrequently she calls. Then she stops.

Robbie and Elise are cooking Hamburger Helper and dancing to Madonna, using the greasy spoon as a mike. *Get into the groove, boy, you've got to prove your love to ME!*

They eat, watching *Dallas.* Elise is holding a cotton ball soaked in hydrogen peroxide to his ear, which he got pierced yesterday.

"So, you throwin' in the towel?" Robbie asks during a commercial, blue eyes wide.

She shrugs, very uncomfortable. "He doesn't know *how* to love anybody. He just has no idea."

"I mean, he should love you, Leesey."

Elise smirks at Robbie, grateful, and dabs at his ear. "We got too close on this trip. He has to step back."

"Yeah?" Robbie says, trying to be supportive.

"This is gonna be" — she can't look at Robbie when she says it — "a test. He'll come back. He'll miss me. I just gotta wait."

"Why don't you break out those ninja skills?"

She laughs, drums up some bravado. "I'll wait like a ninja."

Robbie smokes schwag, offers the one-hitter to Elise, who says no thanks. He coughs, and they keep watching TV, but Elise is remembering the beach that night, the glittering sky and the glittering ocean divided by one dark line, and how she let Jamey put his cold hands under her sweater, and his hands warmed up.

April 1986

New Haven blooms; dogwoods open their petals of tea-streaked porcelain, and birds tune up like a symphony; rain falls on stone one day, simple white puffs fill an azure sky the next.

Students are euphoric, high on thin sunshine. Tender skin is revealed to the air in golf shirts and knee-length skirts. Kids shiver at the sidewalk café, determined to drink their coffee outside, hunching over notebooks.

Elise sometimes goes to the basketball court on Montague Street that's annexed to the church. A program for troubled teens uses it when school lets out, but it's deserted in the mornings. She squints into the frail light as she shoots. Her face is expressionless whether she misses or scores.

One day, a nun offers her banana bread in a napkin and a can of cream soda.

"Oh, wow," Elise says. "That's really nice of you."

"I see you playing here," the nun says. "You're a *strong* girl."

"Seriously, thanks," Elise says, the ball between her pigeon-toed feet as she eats — she needed this kindness.

The woman's face is turtle-like in the short tuck of her nose and the bleary, innocent eyes. She wears gray orthopedic shoes, and when she waddles back to the church, her beads sway.

Elise bikes through neighborhoods she doesn't know, skirting the campus, taking in its massive mismatched buildings, the castles, the hospitals. Mainly she cruises residential areas, watching a mom zip her girl's jacket on a stoop, smelling garlic in butter through a window, riding over empty dime bags.

At night, she dances with Robbie at the Anvil, where the music is thunderous and morbid, and they can each afford one drink, which they nurse over the hours.

One day she goes to their diner. She doesn't really expect to see him, but her stomach is still twisted as she waits to be seated, eating a mint filled with yellow goo. At the table she picks at her cheeseburger and fries and lemonade.

She's always been an outsider. She isn't clearly black or white or Puerto Rican, and the world where she grew up was easier if you were one thing or the other, or if you claimed one thing or the other, which she could have done but never did.

Elise didn't bond with other kids; parents watched her on a playground — throwing rocks into a bucket or talking to herself on a swing — and said: *Elise got to do it on her own, always.* And when she started running away at thirteen, Denise would hiss when they got her back: *Why you think you can just fucking do this? Makes me crazy, Elise. You're not on your own yet, girl. You belong to me. You stay put. Hear me?*

Jamey is trying to be alone. But his mind is flooded with a psychedelica of sexual positions, fantasies invading like an army of Elises who blow kisses, snap the waistbands of their panties, strut, suck the straw of a million milkshakes, curse, and grin. A regular pinup parade of this girl in her red negligee and white fur and black sneakers, smoking, staring with irresistible boredom in her dead eyes like a killer.

He has trouble sleeping, but hates admitting it so he petulantly lies in bed, arms crossed in the dark. When he was a kid, his mom's assistant gave him sleeping pills, and taking them sends him back to groggy and frightened nights in half-lit hotel rooms or a producer's pool cottage in California or Portugal, so he leaves them alone.

Maybe I just need to define terms better, he tells himself one morning. Yeah, that's it!

On the phone, he feels twelve, but a twelve he never was. He should be chewing gum, baseball in mitt, cartoons squeaking and honking in the background.

"Hey," he says slowly.

"What's up?" she asks matter-of-factly.

He's thrown off by her tone. "Um, wondering if you want to have lunch." Silence. "I miss that grilled cheese!"

"You miss the grilled cheese, huh?" she asks.

"Yeah."

When they get there, they try to hug but make a mess of it. She pulls away before he can tell she's trembling.

Seated, he says: "I'm thinking that — we can hang out. But this time it's clear —"

"We're not girlfriend-boyfriend."

"We're obviously *something* to each other."

"We're just gonna fuck," she says.

He gets wide-eyed. "You're in an eloquent

frame of mind."

"Sounds great," she says, and taps the menu. "Turkey club."

"Okay then."

"And I gotta have onion rings." She looks around the diner like she's bored.

Sunlight illuminates dust in her bedroom, garishly exposes every stipple in the carpet.

She strips like she's getting in the shower. Tells him to strip too. She runs nails over his naked, daylit arms, his chest, his groin, looking him over while ignoring his eyes.

She licks her palm, then kisses him while reaching down and stroking him with an economical rhythm. She puts her hands on the bed, and looks over her shoulder. "You fuck me," she says. "Come on."

He's harder than he's been in his life, swollen, and thick at the base. She's so wet her inner thighs get slimy. She rubs her clit and comes in a series of bucks, before he does. She pulls away and sits on the bed.

"Jack off on my tits," she directs.

And he does. She watches, unflinching.

She wipes translucent cream off her nipple to lick.

He stretches out on the bed but she puts on her clothes.

"I'm not in a mood to lie around today,

Jamey," she tells him gruffly.

"Oh. Okay." He dresses in a daze, dark hair falling to his nose as he looks to button his shirt.

Kissing him and folding her hand in a goodbye at the top of the stairs, she goes back into the apartment. Only then does she let herself sink onto the bed, exhausted, grinning at the ceiling. She rolls over and takes a deep breath of him from the sheets, closes her eyes.

Aaaannnndd they're back! Together almost every night, under cheap blankets. He sleeps with his back to her but doesn't mean anything by it.

They're making bacon and eggs when he says his mother is coming to town.

"You have things in common," he says.

"Like what?"

"You're both . . . feisty."

"I'm feisty?" Elise asks, grinning. "What's she look like?"

"You've seen her."

"Where?"

"In movies!"

"She's famous?" Elise asks, nibbling bacon grit off the spatula.

"I thought you knew that. Tory Boyd Mankoff."

No reaction.

"She was in *The Canyon*?" Jamey prompts. "And Polanski's *The Father's House.*"

"What's Polanski?"

"Or . . . you must have seen *Star City.* She's the card dealer. She finds the body. She has sex with Peter Fonda in the elevator."

"That's your *mother*?" Elise sits on the counter and looks at Jamey with giant eyes.

"Yup. Yale is showing a retrospective of Abernath films, and she was one of his muses," Jamey says.

Elise stares at the ceiling. "I can't believe you had to watch your mom fuck that guy."

"It wasn't real."

"Sure looked real, let me tell you."

Tory is supposed to meet Jamey for breakfast, but changes it to lunch, then calls to say she's an hour late. Par for the course.

When she pulls up, he can see through the car window her long straight hair, and he knows she's as tough and skinny and glamorous as she ever was.

He gets into the ivory Jaguar, entering its force field, sinking into leather.

Tory looks at her son, the way she does.

Suddenly his shirt is too tucked in. His hands can't find rightful places on his knees so he crosses his arms. His mouth, eyelids, teeth palpitate with wrongness.

"Hey, babe," she says with a casualness that makes him feel his self-consciousness is self-created.

The light changes. They're off.

"How you doing?" he asks.

He made a lightning decision between *How are you* (formal) and *How you doing* (mistake).

"How'm I doin'?" she asks, in a godfather-of-the-mafia impersonation.

Her face is straight, but then she grins at him. "How's life?" she says, without answering.

"School's great," he says. "Yeah. Been a great semester."

As he rambles, Tory takes a Merit Light from the soft pack between her skinny white-denim thighs. She lights it, cracks the window with the cigarette in her mouth and eyes half-closed against the smoke.

"This is such an ugly city," she interrupts.

"It is," he agrees.

"I've missed you," she says without looking at him, which is how he knows she means it.

"Missed you too," he says.

"You're coming to the screenings?" she asks girlishly.

"Tory, of course."

She tosses the cigarette and rolls up the window.

Red light at Haney Square, where the vacant department store stands. A dead tree comes out of the sidewalk, a deflated balloon caught in its branches.

At lunch, she tries, as usual, to find out what Alex is doing — since they haven't spoken in about eight years. "So! I hear HMK has a massive lawsuit from some Japanese company."

Jamey fills her in with what sound like top-secret details but are not. He knows how to do this to both parents, head tilted forward, shoulders slumped back, tapping the table with his fingers — generously indiscreet. Whoever he's talking to always stares like his mouth is smeared with honey.

Then they chat about Jack Nicholson coming tomorrow, about the documentary she's funding on Moroccan schools for girls — *Wait, no, girls in Istanbul, is that it? They changed it on me — shoot, I can't remember* — and various parts she's been offered in films that are in various stages of possible production. Jamey stifles a yawn.

"I'm just in one of those periods, James, when there's so much being thrown my way.

I can't commit to anything and everything someone begs me to do."

Even as a kid, Jamey knew that his mother's thinking so hard about acting, studying lines, being absentminded, *was* acting. Her trailer was a curated mess, with fan letters and cigarette packs and banana peels everywhere.

But she couldn't act all the time. Her dark moods were renowned, and genuine.

In her hotel room now, skin creams and homeopathic pills and clothes exploded everywhere, she presses the phone's red light as Jamey talks; a woman says *Jack is unable to make the screening and wants Tory to know he's sorry.*

Jack is sorry. . . .

Oh, there had been benevolence till now. A playfulness in the air.

Now Tory evades Jamey's eyes, touches her hair in the mirror.

"What am I even wearing?" She laughs rabidly.

Jamey's stomach twists.

Instantly Tory turns sulky and wants to go shopping.

"Um, sure," her son says, racking his brain for stores. New Haven is not exactly Paris.

He should call Elise to put off dinner

tonight, since his mother will now be especially dangerous. But he's never alone with the phone.

Tory and Jamey are drinking wine when Elise knocks on the door. She's wearing acid-washed jeans and the white fur. She got her nails done for tonight: burgundy with gold lightning streaks. *Great!*

He sees shock on his mom's face.

Reflected in each of his mom's eyes is a tiny ghetto demon who waves her hand and bites her bottom lip.

"What's up!" Elise says.

His mom is speechless.

"Tory, this is Elise. Elise, my mother, Tory."

"Hi," Elise tries again.

Tory seems to decide this is not a joke and she should proceed. "So nice to meet you," she says haltingly.

"I didn't know who you were!" Elise says. "I mean, Jamey had to tell me you were who you are. You know what I'm trying to say?"

"Um," Tory says. "I think I do."

"Well, it's cool to meet you."

"Yes. Thanks. Cool to meet you too."

Tory doesn't speak in the front seat of the BMW. Jamey knows why.

Jamey tries to ask Elise harmless questions.

"So you had a good day?" he says, looking at her in the rearview.

"We got a shipment of dead angel fish, but that happens."

Tory's eyes widen.

"And Lex had pneumonia, we found out, which is why nobody's seen him recently. But he's doing good now."

Jamey doesn't follow this up either.

"Lex is a friend?" Tory asks Elise and Jamey.

"Not really," Jamey says.

"He's not *not* a friend," Elise corrects.

"He's a homeless guy," Jamey explains, which doesn't help anything.

"Ah, I see," Tory says.

At La Maison, the host warmly greets Tory and Jamey, then looks too long at Elise. While the others check coats, she pulls her fur tight.

"So where do you hail from, Elise?" Tory asks as they look at menus by candlelight.

"Do you mean where do I come from? Connecticut."

"*Where* in Connecticut."

"I kind of grew up all over the state."

"So you're not from anywhere."

"Well, Hartford, New London, Bridgeport."

"What do your parents do?"

Jamey shoots his mother a look, but she won't make eye contact.

"I was never, like, in touch with my dad. But. My mom's done every sort of job there is, practically." Elise tries to laugh.

Tory smiles in a small, controlled way. "I love how you grew up everywhere, and your mother has done everything."

Elise tries to laugh again, her face damp. "Well, not *everything,*" she says.

"I guess that's good," Tory answers as if they were conspirators. "I'll have another Stoli," she says to the waitress with warmth so theatrical it's actually designed to be understood as insincere.

Jamey orders escargot, and Elise looks at the round plate bubbling with butter.

"Want one? It's a snail," he can't help but add.

"What?!" Elise says, the slug poised on its tiny fork in her hand.

Jamey tries not to smile. "Protein. It's good for you."

Elise pops it in her mouth, grimaces as she chews. "Oh my *God.* Disgusting."

Tory baby-sips her potage aux pommes, watching.

This is going so badly, Jamey almost wonders if Elise is playing it up.

Tory turns to her son. "Well, James. Perhaps I should have been checking in with you more frequently this semester."

Tory was never supposed to be a mother.

Her own parents joked that she came out of thin air — two alley cats mated and had a Siamese kitten: Victoria.

She was fourth out of ten kids. From the age of five she said lines along with TV actors.

Tory even wondered if anyone famous had come through their Indiana town around her conception. But she had her dad's skinny legs, his thin mouth, and the eyes that misled people into thinking she was tender and emotional.

The baby brother, Benji, had a harelip, which the small-town doctor took a crack at fixing. Tory dragged him around like a toy, a stuffed rabbit whose ears were dark from getting teethed on. She played mommy, bossing him with ludicrous affection. It was her first good role.

Having a real baby was different.

The labor lasted thirty-three hours. Alex came from his cousin's engagement party at Tavern on the Green with scotch on his breath, held her hand as she cried in the hospital bed.

And she *cried.* (This girl he met at a Beverly Hills party, a seemingly feral seventeen-year-old in flared jeans and gold wedges. The torchlit garden burned around her that first night as she blew cigarette smoke out like opium, daring him.) She roared like a dying tiger till the body slipped from her bloody thighs.

When Jamey was three months old, Bats made Alex go to London for a few weeks to oversee a merger.

Tory, left on her own, stood in the doorway to Jamey's nursery one night. The hall light lit the infant's eyelashes. She was supposed to think he was beautiful. He made her hurt, on a cellular level. Tory didn't realize her cigarette had burned to the filter, or that her cheeks were wet.

Into a Gucci duffel she tossed a nightgown, a pack of smokes, a curling iron, a couple scripts. She never used that curling iron, but felt the bag would be too light without it — this was her logic in the moment.

She didn't decide on a hotel until she was in the cab.

"The Carlyle," she said.

A couple hours later, Teddy the doorman

got a call from Mrs. Hallock. *The Hyde baby's crying, and* — pause — *it doesn't sound like anybody's at home there.* Teddy let himself into the apartment, called Binkie, and rocked the baby in his arms. She was at the Goodyears' dinner party on Seventy-Seventh Street, and her silver gown crinkled as she made necessary phone calls in their kitchen. *Surprise, surprise,* her eyes said to Balthazar as she exhaled cigarette smoke.

Weston Briarcliff, a trusted family friend, was dispatched to the Carlyle once it was determined Tory checked in there. A night nurse was hired on the spot. Binkie braced herself for calls from tabloid hacks, but nothing.

And so it went, almost every night. Tory left, checked in to the Carlyle, Weston went to give her a martini and bring her back eventually, but now round-the-clock nurses watched Jamey.

Binkie could handle anything. An Astor, a debutante, a Daughter of the American Revolution, a Southerner, a Northerner, Binkie had bet horses with gangsters and shot doves with diplomats and flirted with presidents. Binkie ruled Palm Beach, a gravelly voiced hostess who remembers you like your Manhattan stirred, and knows you'll be fired after Christmas bonuses —

she probably advised Bats to do it.

She had no sympathy for Tory, who had more trouble *having* a son than Binkie had losing hers — the first James Balthazar Hyde drowned in a sailing accident in the Bahamas at the age of nineteen.

Binkie took to her bedroom then, corpse-like herself in French handmade-lace coverlets, a gin and soda on her bedside table, its ice melted and the lime pulp hanging in the liquid like tadpoles. Pink light through drawn curtains stained Binkie's friends, who talked to the help since Binkie was silent. She looked at the wallpaper for one week, as if counting fleurs-de-lys, mute. Then she got up and never spoke of that Jamey again.

This afternoon's sun is high-pitched, the sky as cold as glass. Lex opens the store door partway, sticks in his big, damaged head.

"Elise, can you help me for a second?" he says in his giant booming voice that has the formality of a radio announcer but is warped.

When she comes out to the sidewalk, she finds Lex standing with a dog.

The hound strains the rope; a kerchief tied around his neck signals that someone loved him, even if his ribs show. He flinches as

Elise tries to pet him, and bares shiny onyx gums.

"O'Harris got picked up a couple nights ago, and he ain't getting out, but I can't take care of this fella of his. I wannu but I can't."

The dog pulls, and Lex restrains him. Elise crouches in the winter light, holds pizza crust to his mouth.

Marianne watches, wisps of white hair standing up on her head from the excitement.

Eyes dark and wet, he snatches the food, attacks it on the pavement. His patchy fur is tawny, with black outlining his ears and snout and paws.

"He's a hungwy widdle one," Marianne says.

"What's his name?" Elise asks.

"Jessie, but he'll take whatever name you got."

Jamey's banking on Annie, who always makes things better.

And the next morning, Annie prances into the hotel lounge, with luggage and chauffeur, to meet Tory and Jamey. Apple cheeks and donkey teeth. A washtub torso and rooster legs. Nice round breasts that have lasted, without work. Dallas Annie, get your gun!

"Look at my Jamey." Annie smiles, and rocks him with a hug full of perfume and Hermès scarf and gold necklace. "I'm so happy."

Annie met Tory when they were young at a big party thrown by Warren Beatty. Somehow Tory and Annie ended up in a room with a glass ceiling, banana plants, a hot tub, and a couple bikers. Annie swallowed the Quaalude, but Tory shook her head. *Oh, not tonight,* she said, fumbling with a cigarette, and Annie realized she was scared. *Leave her alone,* she said. The biker unbuttoned Tory's dress, and Annie threw her drink — BAM! — blood and vodka–orange juice ran down his forehead — *Oops!* she peeped, hand over mouth, like a silent-era blonde. Later the two girls lounged in Annie's penthouse suite and giggled.

Annie, heir to Hanesworth Oil, with a face carbon-copied from her CEO dad and a bank account the size of a small country's GDP, fit snugly with this creature who was impeccable on screen and disastrous in life. They never left each other's side.

At the hotel bar, the ladies drink martinis, eat peanuts, talk about PETA, the Italian Alps, *Miami Vice,* artichokes, their friend

Jerry, their enemy Helen, Armani's spring line, and cats.

Then Annie turns to Jamey: "Your mama tells me you're in a very interesting relationship. Now, do I get to *meet* her?"

"Yes, tonight — she's coming to the screening," he answers.

"Stupendous!" she cries in her bright-as-Texas-sunshine voice. "What's her *name,* darling?"

"Elise."

"Elise what?"

"Elise Perez."

"She's not at Yale, is that correct? You met her outside of school then?" Annie pops a peanut into her glossy mouth.

"I met her outside of school, yes."

"Well, I couldn't be more excited. And you know, I'm truly of the mind that everyone needs to *stretch* their parameters, see what's out there." Annie's looking at Jamey but addressing Tory. "And if you end up right back where you started, with someone a little bit more like yourself, you at least know *why.*"

The theater is full, people are turned away. The curtain parts, and Jamey looks around at the light and dark shapes playing on faces. The story seeps through everyone's forehead and into the subconscious, creating a dream inside. There's a rustle of a slacks leg being crossed, a cough drop unwrapped. Rows of people breathe in these moving pictures like they're smoke.

The dinner after is a VIP group of Yale film scholars, another NYC director, and Annie and Tory's friend Tristan, who drove in from Litchfield. Jamey is introduced to everyone he doesn't know, embraced by everyone he does know, and he's left to introduce Elise since his mother simply isn't doing it.

Annie greets Elise with a debutante smile and a church hug.

"Sorry," Tory says to Elise when they have to ask the waiter for another chair. "I forgot you were coming."

That's when Jamey notices Elise's posture change, her chin tilting, face hardened one tiny degree.

"I loved being reminded how solid that film is," says one of the scholars, dripping a forkful of risotto.

"Right?" says Annie, the MC, stirring up praise.

The group murmurs complex statements.

Elise doesn't wait long. "Jamey said Jack Nicholson was supposed to come," she says to the table.

Silence, and Tristan tinkles the cubes in the glass.

Annie says, "Oh, Jack, he's probably tied up in some hotel room in Bangkok with a hangover," and the table laughs.

Except Tory, who looks at Elise as if seeing her for the first time.

Elise eats her pork chop, wide-eyed.

"Tory, can I ask you what your next project is going to be?" a professor inquires.

"I'm choosing," Tory says. "There's not a lot of great material out there."

"Can I ask a question?" Elise says. "What was it like when you were famous? Did everyone want your autograph?"

Tory now looks like she's about to come across the table, WWF-style. "I was just asked for my autograph at the screening."

"Oh, really!" Elise says.

"Really," Tory answers.

"That's cool," Elise says with a straight face. "That they still ask."

Jamey looks down, watches his hand play with his napkin, hiding his amusement, his amazement.

"I mean, thank God they don't stalk you like that guy did — remember, in Cannes?" says Tristan. "In '78? That was like unreal."

"Oh my dear lord, I do remember that!" Annie says, her hand on her forehead. "That was a great year at Cannes, though, wasn't it?" she says.

Normally, a person exits backward, like a geisha, for Tory. But Elise throws her napkin on her plate, zips her jacket.

"Nice to meet you all," Elise says. "I got to get up early!"

She allows herself to look at Tory with clown-crazy eyes, flashing raspberry-red lights. "Good night, Tory. It was a pleasure." Then leaves.

Jamey and Elise walk the dog in eager but ineffective sunshine. The sores on the dog's back are scabbing already, and his ribs aren't as brutally visible. Now he smells of White Rain shampoo.

"I can't think of a name!" Elise says.

They walk by a school playground shrieking with kids.

"I loved this one book, *Call of the Wild,* about a dog named Buck," Jamey says finally.

"Buck!" Elise kneels to look the dog in the eye. "Do you wanna be Buck?"

They wander into the park, neon green with new buds and leaves.

Sitting on the bench, Elise zips her fur, puts on mirrored glasses. Jamey rubs Buck under his chin.

He needs to apologize, and explain his mom.

Elise waits, her face gentle, like a bell open for ringing.

He tries. "Tory is — she's funny. She's always been such a — performer," Jamey says, biting his lip, reaching for something truer.

But he fails.

Elise waits, and waits, then nods almost imperceptibly. She looks away.

They sit there a long time, freezing, ankles and knees locking, but they don't want to leave. It's cold, the day giving up without a fight.

"It would take more than that, Jamey, to scare me off," she says, without looking at him. Her face and neck turn scarlet. "I'm in love with you."

Then she stares right at him.

"Well, I like you a whole lot too," he says in his funny voice.

He focuses on throwing the stick for Buck, who doesn't chase it, because he chooses this moment to shit behind the leafless bush.

Jamey watches with a bizarrely bland smile, like an old man observing ships drifting into a harbor. He's stricken with terror and prays for the afternoon to end.

■ ■ ■ ■

One more night, he thinks.

Annie rented the penthouse suite at the hotel, and gathers his mother's admirers there.

"Hi, babe!" Tory calls out to Jamey as he walks in.

"Hey, Tory," he says.

Then Tory shows how when she's good, she's the greatest, and she and the crew go on a run of fun.

The hotel room is full of folks, talking, drinking Mumm out of paper cups. Tory smokes, sitting on the floor with her impeccable posture, the gang of disciples around her. A few are straight, two gay, a couple in between, none more beautiful than her, most of them broken, half parasitic and half delightful.

She asks them questions so rude she must be kidding, and they pretend to be offended, and try to figure out if she's joking at all.

She'll throw a grenade of gossip into a silence, or hand out candy in the form of praise and affection — when it's least expected. She riles them all up, churning a pile of puppies, tickling and pushing them away, pulling them gently back by the ear.

"Oh my god, I'm so demanding!" she says. "Why do you people put up with me? I'm like — *I need this, I need that!*"

"We love you!" they say.

"Look at you guys. You're all goddamn beautiful."

There's a group sheepishness.

The room groans like a cruise ship forever changing direction, seeking the sun.

"I mean," Tory says, "Look how beautiful Annie is. Look."

Everyone coos at beautiful Annie.

"Annie, let's go skiing! Can we?" Tory asks like a girl to a boy.

"Anything you want, sweetie pie," Annie says, lying on the rug, getting drunk.

"Come to Vail," says Tristan, " 'cause me and Toby are there all month."

They're all talking about how fabulous Vail is.

And Jamey knows by bringing up this story, he'll ruin the night.

"Remember when you left me there, Mom?" he asks, smiling.

When Jamey was five, she and Alex — divorced but sharing custody then — muddled a handoff in Vail. When she arrived at her friend's house in Santa Fe and found out, she almost threw up with cold fever.

She thought Alex had the kid, Alex thought she had the kid.

She called the hotel. *Where is he? Okay, give him some ice cream. You have a pool; take him swimming, for God's sake! I'll be there soon. Just tell him that.*

Her friend Marie asked what was the matter; her husband walked up behind her with a tray of drinks. *Nothing, I'll be right back,* Tory said, even though Vail was a six-hour drive. She couldn't bear to tell them. She squeezed her keys so hard walking to the car her hand bled on the white leather steering wheel.

She drove through aspens and snow, and they were one piece — the trees and the land — a single whiteness.

Alex told the story whenever he toasted Jamey on his birthday and reminisced about his son's "madcap" childhood. Tory never joked about it. That drive to Vail took a couple years off her life, although the way she talked to the hotel staff and even to Jamey when she got there would have convinced anyone it was nothing but a god-*damn* inconvenience.

Now she looks at him, and waves him away. "Jesus, I shouldn't have gone back for you," she jokes, and the group whistles shrilly, *oh là là!*

"You're so cruel, darling," says Evan, purring in his leather pants next to her.

"I can't help it," she says throatily, provocatively.

Jamey sneaks out when the group is hitting their peak of tipsy, catty hysteria, the boys trying on Annie's scarves in the mirror, Terry and Sylvia having a serious talk in the corner, and Tory floating in the center of the ring, cigarette poised near her lush naked mouth.

Jamey is supposed to meet Tory the next day but he's in Elise's bed, happily stoned on fucking, eating graham crackers, and getting crumbs in the sheets.

Next door, Tory rings the doorbell, and waits on the sunny porch in her white jeans and trench coat. When Matt answers, she pushes her chin up and her tiny breasts out.

"Matty! So good to see you."

She hugs him briskly and strides into the house.

"He should be home by now. But please make yourself comfortable — or take a look around," he adds, since she's already on her way up the stairs.

As she comes downstairs, she asks if he has any vodka.

"I don't mind going out and getting

some," Matt says in a panic of etiquette, pulling at his Polo shirt like he's hot.

"You're sweet. Get Stoli if they have it."

She lounges in their living room, looking through magazines, smoking. When Matt comes back and pours her a drink, she scans his face and sighs. "You dear boys. You have it so easy, you'll never know what it feels like to make it on your own."

Matt rushes to agree: "That is a problem."

"*I* got to see what I had in me, you know? I had to prove myself."

"Totally, I agree."

She asks about Elise.

"It can't last," Matt says.

"He's just acting out, right?"

"Definitely. They have nothing in common. And it's good timing that the school year is over, almost, and he'll be gone for a while, you know?"

"If that's what it takes, sure!" Tory says, recrossing her long legs.

Matt awkwardly checks his watch. "I don't know why he's not here yet."

Now Jamey watches from Elise's window as his mother's shoe kicks the air. He's an hour late. No shirt, just corduroy pants. Deodorant wax smeared through underarm hair. His mouth parted as he stares. He's enthralled.

Elise joins him at the window.

They watch Tory leave finally, and she waves to Matt, who sees her off. The Jaguar toots out lavender exhaust and slides into the city.

Elise plants kisses on Jamey's back, and she runs her hand up his neck to his jaw, rubs his lip with her finger, until he sucks her finger, and then they're on the mattress again, and she says *Oh God* with each thrust as if she can't take any more when all she wants is more.

He spent time on movie sets as a kid, before his mother's manager decided he was too distracting — Tory blamed the manager entirely when she gave up custody.

He did throw a rock at his mom during shooting when he was four or five, an out-of-character act of defiance. A seamstress with a dirty tan and bleached hair was assigned to take him to a burger joint. He cried, and she gave him two ice-cream sundaes, and he stared at them, dumbfounded, while she smoked. *Two!* she kept saying. *You can have two. Look at you. You've got two sundaes, sugar.* Her voice throaty and gruff. He could see the dark oyster pearls of her molar fillings when she yawned. He ate both and threw up.

His favorite people on those sets were the animal handler, Dominic, and his collie, Starlight, good memories in a sea of strange ones. Dominic told stories about wild hogs in Texas and a church burning in Vermont.

Jamey was an extra too. He had a speaking part in *Bad Hand.* He's the kid at the gas station when Lorraine and Jessup are on the run. Jamey's character says: *Hey mister, where'd you get such a fast car?* and his mom's character, Lorraine, says to Jessup: *Jess, let's go. We can't be wasting time.* But when the Shelby Cobra peels out in a storm of dirt, Lorraine forlornly watches the boy from the car window, as if she already knows how the story ends.

May 1986

May's unrelenting rain paints a sheen on houses, daffodils, cars in the slick streets, umbrellas. Everyone at Yale is finishing exams, barely sleeping, coming apart, wearing shirts inside out, and staring into space.

Jamey decides to finish the year as right as possible. He runs across campus in the monsoon, handing in papers, his hair wet — a messenger delivering well-intentioned and pointless letters.

The sun shines onto graduation, making a rainbow over the lawn. Mosquitoes arise from fountains and birdbaths and rooftop lakes. He and other underclassmen slouch on the sidelines, with button-downs rolled up at the sleeves, to watch the ceremony. Students in black gowns sweat, standing in the bright yard as the speaker tells them they *are* the future, they are the great minds of their generation, *they* will steward grace and dignity and knowledge into modern society.

Which may be true of many graduates, but Jamey looks at some of the people he knows best in this crowd: Andrew Chesterton, who tried to fuck a drunk, unconscious girl last weekend in a Volvo parked behind his house; Molly Easley, who has a two-hundred-dollar-a-day cocaine habit; and Brady Fitzgerald, who shoved half a frozen bagel up Jacob Murotzky's ass in a hazing ritual.

He tries to fish the word *greatness* out of his brain like a fly from milk but it sticks to the glass.

Restless, Elise takes Buck out. He walks without a leash, already loyal, and glares at anyone who gets close — his black snout seems sinister, but he wouldn't bite unless someone strikes first.

She throws him a tennis ball on empty basketball courts, sometimes until dusk, stopping because suddenly they can't see each other.

She likes the mystery of that changeover, those fifteen minutes of sundown when the streets and trees and people and parked cars are delicate and immediate, every sound and smell and movement amplified by the lowest light or the lightest darkness. Even a city that's broken and dirty can, in that time, be divine and intimate.

Elise and Jamey eat breakfast at the diner, rain pinging on the metal roof. Her sweatshirt tag stands up, and her hoops dangle as she reads the menu.

"Yeah, I'm leaving in a week and a half," Jamey finally says.

"That soon?" Elise asks, as if she's been thinking of anything else.

They're both weirdly formal.

"So, what *is* your plan?" he asks, using the side of his fork on his pancakes.

"Well, the lease is up end of May. Robbie's headed to Miami, Caspar hooked him up with a hotel job."

"Are you renewing the lease?"

"Nah. Can't afford it. I might not stay in New Haven," she says. "I dunno."

"Where would you go?"

She shrugs. "Anywhere but home."

"You have money saved?"

"You're fucking hilarious."

"What if you end up without a place to live?" Jamey asks.

She laughs, but not meanly, swipes egg bits with a long-nailed finger to lick. "What would *you* do if you had no roof, and you had no money?" she asks. "You'd figure shit out."

"Me?"

"Where would you sleep?"

"I wouldn't."

"Everybody has to sleep."

"I'd find a park," he says, amused. "Sleep on a bench."

"Where everyone can see? Cops see you? Sleep under the bushes. Until you make friends."

Silence.

"Have you slept under bushes?" he asks.

"Oh my God," she says, annoyed, and drains her orange juice.

He puts money on the table and gets up, does a fake yawn-and-stretch to seem casual, his shirt rising to show hip.

Of course he thinks about inviting her to New York City this summer. He dreads being alone in the downtown loft a family friend is letting him use, but he can't combine her world with his, for her sake. Gasoline and fire.

When he thinks about asking, he gets woozy, like a kid who can't see the road over a dashboard.

He should use this natural juncture for farewell. But if she lived with him (tucked away — a secret playmate), the summer could be different.

When did I get so creepy? he wonders.

"Why don't you come with me for a few weeks?" he says one night, turning off the light and getting under the sheets.

Did I just say that? He's instantly high like he sucked helium.

"To New York?" her voice asks in the dark.

"Yeah. I'm staying downtown. Working at an auction house."

"What's that?"

"They sell people's belongings."

"We call that a pawn shop, brother."

"What options do you have?" his voice asks, and he feels too aggressive.

Elise grins but he can't see. Her voice is quiet: "Of course I'll fucking come with you."

When Jamey was little, he was driven alone in a limo from the Hamptons to the city, or vice versa, and he'd look up, and there was always some kid on the overpass above the LIE, face pressed into the fence, crude blue sun streaming around her silhouette.

He was afraid of those kids — or threatened — not for what they could do to him. They couldn't touch him, let alone see behind his smoked windows. It's that he thought they knew things and he knew nothing. He was star-struck by how sad they were, how little they had, what they went through, what they saw.

And now he's opening the limousine door wide, patting the leather seat.

Elise and Robbie go dancing at the Anvil one last night.

They spend hours getting dressed, drinking rum-and-Cokes, jumping and jiving around the house. Robbie's wearing a silver tank top and Elise has on overalls, a black leotard, and gold chains. They leave the house without jackets because the jackets will get stolen, and they both shiver, ecstatic, as they walk.

The club is empty when they arrive, and the dance floor is calling their names. They get down, hold nothing back, lost in the shudder of strobe lights and beats. Robbie's lovers show up, and they sweat as a tribal group, never taking a break.

"I love you, honey!" he shouts to Elise.

"I love you! Yo, I want good things to happen for you, Robbie — hear me?" she yells.

"I *know* good things gonna happen for you, Leese!" he screams among laser beams while the DJ nods to the record.

The guys pack. The radio plays classic rock

and commercials for New Haven car dealers and sports bars as Jamey and Matt put books and desk chairs on the curb, and dump food into garbage bags.

Jamey remembers moving in — the rooms had been quiet with autumn light and shadows, mattresses bare and closets empty. The house was a question, and it got an answer.

Matt and Jamey sit on the porch when they're done. Matt sips a large Pellegrino and smokes a cigar, and the spring sunset is vivid. Matt's off to Zurich in a week, to assist on a trading desk.

"You should be coming with me," Matt says as if he's joking. "With my bedside manner and your brain, we could destroy Wall Street, smash it to smithereens."

"You'll do just fine," Jamey says, knowing Matt's fantasies are real. "And I'm locked into Sotheby's."

"Which is a great job. If you have a *vagina.*"

"Ha."

"Well," Matt says after a moment, without looking at Jamey. "It was a good year."

"It was," Jamey says, appreciative of Matt's attempt to connect. "A weird year."

"I mean . . ." Matt says, shrugging, but leaves it at that.

Jamey has the opportunity, like with Thalia at the pool, to stay friends, to make the other person comfortable, to apologize.

They sit in silence instead.

In the past, Jamey did ridiculous things to keep Matt company — like standing in the empty VIP section where Matt wanted to be even though the fun was outside, or approaching a pair of girls Matt wanted to meet, who looked vacuous and sadistic. Jamey owed Matt, who discreetly — all their lives — got Jamey invited on Matt's family trips, took him to concerts (front row and chauffeured), made Jamey sit with the Dannings at school functions.

Matt told Jamey's stories as if they happened to Matt. When Jamey got a surfboard, Matt got the same one. When Jamey wore a tomato-red Polo shirt, he looked louche, edgy, and accidental. When Matt wore that exact shirt, he looked like someone who desperately wanted to look louche, edgy, and accidental. None of that bothers Jamey. But Jamey has reluctantly and bitterly accepted that his friend isn't going to be a good person when he grows up.

Jamey's hitting the city first, and Elise will meet him in a few days. They say goodbye at dawn. Elise insists on coming down to the street — the sky is still dark, no birds.

She holds him, and he smiles as they pull apart.

"I'll see you really soon," he says. "Right?"

She nods, and stays there till brake lights flare at the end of the block.

Climbing the stairs, Elise tells herself to stop worrying. It's a done deal. She'll see him soon.

But what if he just never calls? She lullabies herself to sleep for a couple disoriented hours: *It's a done deal, it's a done deal.* Closing her eyes — he presses her mind from the inside out. Opening her eyes — the silent apartment makes her sick.

The sun comes up, thick like cheap butter, as his car rolls down the Merritt Parkway, passing a linden tree in bloom, then a horse chestnut tree on the brink.

The loft on Crosby Street is care of Martine, whom his father dated after he divorced Tory and before marrying Cecily. A beauty editor for French *Vogue,* Martine lives in Hong Kong, Paris, and NYC, and she was too young when she dated Alex years ago, and is now too old for Jamey but has always looked at him in a certain way.

He's never seen the place, but SoHo is good and far from the Manhattan where he grew up.

He parks on the wide, empty cobblestone street.

The building's super is Giacomanni, who has a twisted head like he'd been wrenched from his mother's loins by a barbarian — and an old Little Italy accent. He wears a dusty jumpsuit and lets Jamey into the loft.

"This used to be a lightbulb factory," Giacomanni tells Jamey while unlocking the door.

They enter a white hangar whose floor is scarred with sunlight. The king bed is in one corner, and a dinner table that seats twenty stretches down the middle of the room. A Julian Schnabel painting takes up a wall. A birdcage dangles from the ceiling (which is a confusion of pipes), and Jamey realizes it's a piece of art from the signature scrawled on its base. But he still makes sure there is no bird.

"Here's the key," says the man, and nods as Jamey thanks him.

Jamey sees his dad the next day for lunch on a South Street Seaport pier.

"Jamey-roo!" his dad says, pulling his son's earlobe, sitting down.

Alex barely has time to eat, late like the boarding-school boy he'll always be — making chapel by a second, his coat misbuttoned, eyeglasses askew.

"Hey, Dad, good to see you," Jamey says, nervous Alex will detect something.

They're sitting in wind laced with brine and oil, drinking beers among suits. Alex's car is waiting downstairs and he has to "make it quick," which is one of his phrases.

"*So,* how's the loft?" Alex asks.

"Amazing. Thanks for your help with that."

"And the job?"

"Starts tomorrow."

"Still not sure why you took a girl's job, Jamey —"

"Come on, it's not —"

"Well, if you're the only fella there, I guess you get your pick of the lot."

"Not my agenda."

"You're putting off your career, which I don't understand."

"At HMK? Well, it will come soon enough. How are *you*?"

Alex rants about the Stockholm office, and Cousin Hallie in East Hampton and the boat issue, and then he tells a story involving Xavier and a bicycle and a frog.

Alex asks for the check before they're half done, crams cheeseburger into his mouth, and rubs Jamey's head.

"Glad you're here, Jamester," he says, and disappears.

Jamey wonders what he feared, since Alex has never noticed *anything* about Jamey's life.

He gets another beer. He's been coming to the Seaport since he was little, eating pickles from the Fulton Market barrels, watching waves swirl up the docks. He used to visit Bats at the HMK headquarters on Rector Street, where Jamey was walked through executive offices like a child king in line for the throne.

On his way back to the loft, Jamey watches three sparrows fly through a chain-link fence without pause. *How the fuck do they do that?* He smiles, and keeps walking.

Jamey wakes to sunrise covering him like a hot blanket.

He shaves in the sink, thrilled by the gigantic and unfamiliar space. He knots his tie and clasps his watch. Steps into the morning a new man.

Takes the 6 train to Fifty-Seventh and Lex, and then walks east, then up York Avenue, as he's early, and it feels good to see the million faces, the grubby sidewalks, the river shimmering to his right.

His job is assisting Clark Woodford, an

asexual buyer from Virginia who wears Ben Silver periwinkle suits and tortoiseshell glasses, and who loves Jamey at first sight.

"Well, well, well, nice to meet you," Clark says. He *seems* young but certain signs — stained teeth, loose skin on his tanned hands — put him older.

"You too, sir."

"Oh, God, not *sir,* anything but *sir.*"

Everyone seems affected by New York's fresh May flowering, the petals cracked open in the middle of the night so you wake up to hope and possibility.

This office is titillatingly new to Jamey, ripe with Hermès cologne, duck rillettes at lunch, magazines from Italy and Japan on desks. He hopes to lose himself this summer, to hide among the etchings and furniture and jewels. At HMK, he'd be out there in the clearing, out on the bald plains of finance, where he'd be called to fight, to choose sides. All that.

Stella walks him from floor to floor of the Sotheby's empire, introducing him to everyone, and he shakes many hands. He's a racehorse paraded through barns, and they make a fuss — *This is Jamey Hyyyddde* — so belittling! By the end of the day, he's skanky with fatigue, his mouth in a state of rigor from smiling. Two girls watch him, giggling, scheming pornographic social-ladder dreams.

Jamey hangs suits in the closet, and folds T-shirts and jeans into empty drawers.

Onyx earrings, with gold backings, gleam in the soap dish. Martine must have taken them out in the bath — they look like black soap bubbles.

Jamey is intrigued and repulsed by bathing where other people have bathed. The ceramic basin has a perfume to it, of water and skin and lavender. A non-American smell.

He reluctantly imagines Martine there, her dark hair coiled into a chignon, in a Cubist fan of images. She's there and not there. He's fantasizing and also repelled. She pisses in that toilet. She plucks her eyebrows in that mirror.

The closet is foreign and adult too. Shoeboxes line the floor: Balmain, Mugler. The clothes have been worn; there is fragrance, pedestrian life, days and nights aromatically accordioned into the slacks and dresses.

The cookbooks are in French, with transparent ovals where oil seeped through the paper. The refrigerator door is crammed with fish sauce, Worcestershire, grapefruit marmalade from Spain.

Jamey arranges for D&E Car Service to get Elise and Buck on Saturday.

When that morning comes, he paces the floor, moving through the exotic hour of anticipation.

He sees the black car pull up below the window, and feels sick with anxiety.

"You made it!" he says, greeting her on the sidewalk.

Everything she owns is crammed into a cheap suitcase she bought at the Salvation Army. Buck pours out of the backseat, nails clicking unfamiliar cement.

"Hi," she says.

"Welcome."

They're both shy and ecstatic.

He's never lived with a girl! Notions of domestic life always grew on his horizon like lichen, furry bumps of children, money, furniture, cars, second homes, trips, dogs.

But Elise eclipses the woman from Jamey's future, the lady in tennis whites flashing her diamond as she drinks orange juice fresh-squeezed by a maid. A woman Jamey never quite believed in anyway.

Elise doesn't say anything fake and grand when he shows her around the minimalist loft; she just asks: "Where's all the stuff?"

They sit on the gold-plugged magenta sofa and Buck laps from a china bowl.

"What do we do now?" she asks.

"Whatever we want."

"Should I get a job?"

"I mean, if you don't know where you want to be after this, then maybe not?"

She nods, understanding. He doesn't want anything permanent.

"But I'll miss you every day," she says, trying not to seem weak.

"We can meet for lunch sometimes?"

She can't help seeming sad, and fidgets with her necklace. He's worried, like a new dad with a crying baby that seems hungry but won't take food. What should he do?

That night they just lie together before having sex. Her thighs around his hip — rough fur against his skin.

The whites of his eyes — electric milk — his tongue is hot, her mouth is hot, she feels his jaw, strokes his neck, and this is when doubt reverses and charges along the golden train tracks, hooting and hollering, like a machine once stalled but conquering this territory again.

It makes *him* sure she should be here.

But she's uncomfortable. They sleep fitfully, wake up in pale light. They make coffee, and he gives her grocery money — if she *wants* to shop, he adds, terrified it sounds like giving orders.

"What should I get?" she asks, trying to read clues for what he wants from her.

"I don't know. The basics, I guess."

She knows enough to know their basics aren't the same. When she arrived, there was stinky cheese and black bread and Pellegrino in the kitchen.

She goes to Key Food, whose windows are plastered with white pages of purple or red block letters: *Chicken, $3.99,* or *Milk .99.* She buys cold cuts, spaghetti sauce, an iceberg lettuce head, soda.

She balances the bags on her hip as she unlocks the building. She hasn't seen other people, only intuits a cat across the hall, an electronic keyboard somewhere.

"Yeah, Buck," she says when he greets her. "That's my boy."

She puts things away, a trespasser in a stranger's cupboards — stealing inverted.

The clouds part for a demure sun.

She stacks Jamey's change on the table and thinks of her mom counting change to Angel like a cashier. When Angel was doing well, he'd throw extra dollars to her. She bought the girls used roller skates, laid out feasts from Kentucky Fried Chicken, paid off debts to neighbors for formula and diapers.

When Angel was locked up, she'd use the money his friend delivered for whatever she wanted, like a kid's birthday party, because he wasn't there to yell about it. Denise bought the mega-cake at Carvel, and ordered a dozen metallic balloons.

Now Elise is so anxious for Jamey to come home, she paces, and Buck whimpers. When she finally sees Jamey down there on the sidewalk (*the way he walks, he's not like anyone else*), her knees almost fail, and her face turns white with passion.

In the morning, he says goodbye, and she stands at the threshold in a T-shirt. She seems to have the power of a great bird — like a heron or a swan — to lift into the sky with just one swift and glorious flap of the wings.

Her lunch is an egg-salad sandwich and ginger ale, but while washing up, she drops the glass. She keeps Buck away as she picks up pieces.

"Why're you so clumsy," she moans.

It's this stupid loft. She feels shitty here, so she takes Buck for a walk, but every time he lifts his leg, she waits for a shopkeeper to yell. Women walk by, stupendous with tall shoulders, stilettos, briefcases. Elise dodges them and gawks.

And when she comes back, she realizes her keys are in the jean jacket in the bedroom.

And it starts to pour.

She and Buck huddle under an awning next door. Rain seeps into her high-tops.

A guy unlocks the building, avoids looking at her, and pulls the door shut.

Elise fumes at herself.

A woman with freckles, grocery bags twisting off her fingers, rambles up like a mailman in Denmark who's delivered letters in the snow for decades.

"Aren't you staying here?" asks the woman.

"Yeah," Elise says, mortified.

The woman unlocks the front door. "Go ahead."

Elise mumbles a thank-you. "Can I take a bag?"

"Sure." The woman is panting a little. "You're on three too, right? You can get into your place?"

"I'll just wait in the hall," Elise nods, awkward.

"I'm Gretchen," the woman says.

"Hi."

"And what's your name?" Gretchen finally asks.

"Oh, Elise."

In five minutes, Gretchen gives Elise a mug of tea. Winks. Closes her door.

Elise hopes Gretchen isn't looking out her peephole, and she stares at her own feet. *What's wrong with you?* she thinks scornfully. *You're out of practice.* She knows very well how to accept love from strangers.

Once he gets home every night, she stops freaking out and trying to guess what he wants, and just savors every minute they get to spend together. A Chinese food menu is slipped under their door so they order from there. They watch a show about gorillas on PBS. They eat powdered cookies she bought at one of the Jewish bakeries. She puts her wet finger in his asshole as she sucks his cock, and he comes in a great epiphany.

Elise looks through the house one day when she's bored. In the bedside-table drawer, under the almond hand creams and white Cartier fountain pens and notepads from hotels in Japan, she finds a tiny vial of cocaine. In the bookcase is an album of photos, people looking serious in dark, tailored clothes — they seem grown-up in a terrifying way. Martine's dildo is in an underwear drawer, but Elise doesn't know what it is at first. Even the sex toy is couture. Pale glass with gold beads — it looks like an angel's penis, or like something that fell out of a museum and landed here, among the palest pink slips and bottles with French prescription labels. Elise cradles it like an egg, then places it back in its nest.

Clark holds the idea of sex away from himself like it's a baby who just pissed its diaper. He often drinks martinis at lunch, and after that his mouth is sort of askew, his grin hanging like a door off one hinge. He sometimes speaks terrible German or even worse Italian on the telephone, and is really fun — to everyone but Edna the intern.

Clark sends Edna on coffee runs. She's an art-history wunderkind from Vassar. When she leaves, he mutters under his breath for everyone to hear: *Little exercise can't hurt anyone.*

Summer employees aren't supposed to lunch with senior staff, but Clark always brings Jamey along. Normally favoritism would make someone unpopular, but in this office, where Clark is king and the code is beauty and cynicism, it makes Jamey popular. They eat Dover sole and drink Chablis at La Grenouille, suck down chilled oysters at the Plaza, sip milkshakes at Rumpelmayer's in the Hotel St. Moritz.

The offices are domestic with Oriental rugs, mahogany desks, maritime art, and Arabian textiles on the walls. The staff are dealers who get high on their own supply. A silk curtain hangs between office and showroom floor, between artifice and reality, the buyer and the bought, the pitch and the truth. The auction operation seems to Jamey an upending of civilization, all the articles that normally convene to create homes are spilled, removed, undone from their worlds, separated from one another.

Ever since Lady Esperanza Von Laighton Phillips was rumored to have a *cough,* Clark has been daydreaming about her estate, and once her obituary ran, it was Christmas and his birthday rolled into one. The trucks are arriving today, and he's even managed to excite Jamey about the incoming crates of sterling silver and ceramics and oil paintings.

Clark is over the moon; he loves objects as if they were alive. He loves the chain of people who loved the objects, the story of ownership and inheritance. He's good, too, with grieving families, like a morgue keeper who can slide the rings off a corpse's fingers in one chic swipe.

▪ ▪ ▪ ▪

Saturday morning: cinnamon rolls and black coffee with the windows open. Elise is putting on her shoes to walk Buck when Jamey sees the holes.

"You need new shoes!"

"They're fine," she says.

"Stop lying," he says, half-kidding.

At Henri Bendel, a guard welcomes them into the chocolate-brown-and-white canopy.

They see their twins in the mirrored walls: a man in lime-green shorts and espadrilles, hair tousled like he just walked out of a Paris disco all-nighter, and the girl, tapping a long nail on the escalator railing, rhinestone jeans creased, braids pulled back in a rubber band so her eyes are catty.

"What else do you need?" he says casually.

Jamey's in a funny mood. This thing he always had — money — was never anything besides an abstract truth, but today it's a silk trick pulled from his wrist. He has accounts and credit cards (which are massive but tiny compared to the trusts) that no one watches; he could buy a house, and the family's manager wouldn't blink.

"Try something on at least," he chides.

"Humor me."

She awkwardly collects jeans, looking at him over the racks with a twisted smile of discomfort and glee.

Jamey sits on a loveseat while she's in the changing room.

"Is thut Jamey Hyde?" trills a voice.

Alastair Waddingford's mom appears in a trench coat and massive sunglasses.

"Hi there, Mrs. Waddingford."

"You know you must cull me Joan," she says. "How ah you, darling?"

"Never better," he answers while his mind bursts in a constellation of social connections, the friends and friends of friends Joan will tell about the girl she saw with Jamey Hyde at Bendel's — if Elise comes out right now.

"Are you in New York awl summer, darling?" she asks.

"Pretty much. How about you? What's the family got planned?"

She turns coy, mewing to him about this and that.

"Is that right?" he says occasionally.

His voice has a soothing, loving, everything-will-be-okay growl to it, like the favorite uncle who spends half the cocktail party in the kids' bedroom telling stories, lulling the children into dreams, capable of this magnanimous and lazy lavishing of his adult time in a nursery seeing as he has no hope for his own life, and can give it all away.

She bats her lashes.

But what would normally be for Jamey a sugary cotton-puff of nothingness has an allure of fear to it — not unpleasantly. He doesn't want Joan to meet Elise.

And he *does* want them to meet.

But Elise doesn't come out in time.

"Toodle-oo!" Joan says, swaggering off in Ferragamo flats.

A rare Japanese print collection hangs in one of Sotheby's galleries. Jamey's working late, with no one around, so he calls Elise.

He turns on the lights, and they walk around the exhibition, and he points to favorites. The room feels like a garden at night, ripe with mountains and birds and chrysanthemums, and they're alone in it.

"You like them?" he asks.

She half smiles at Jamey, her upper lip shadowed with peach fuzz, eyes limpid, and shrugs. "Yeah, I love them."

He's so awkward, she thinks, trying to figure out how to include me when no one's looking. Another woman would be insulted, but Elise is touched, and thinks it's tender.

Neither of them wants to leave, and they keep moving around the room, looking at paintings they already looked at. It feels pretty silly.

They amble through Washington Square Park on a bright afternoon, the trees reflecting green onto their skin.

A man in a denim hat hisses: "Little smoke, little horse, got some white."

They walk past him, faces down, holding hands.

Sitting at a sidewalk café, she can tell he's going to ask her finally.

"You don't do drugs at all?" he asks, as if asking what she'll order for lunch.

She thinks for a second how to answer. "Yeah. I've done some. Have you?"

"Not much. What does 'some' mean?"

She can't help smiling uneasily. "Do you want to be hearing all this?"

"Hear what?" he asks, spinning a fork in his fingers.

"We never talk about our past."

"We don't?"

"I always want to but you never do."

He's quiet, accepting the accusation while maintaining eye contact.

"I've done drugs," she tells him, moving things forward bluntly. "And seen every drug *being* done. That's probably not something we have in common, right?"

"Depends on what you mean."

"Do you understand where I come from?"

"Bridgeport."

"Subsidized housing in Bridgeport," she clarifies. "No offense, but it's a different galaxy. And you know, my mother had me real young —"

"How old was she?"

"Sixteen! And *her* mother, well, that woman was evil. Messed up in the head. She drank. She was sick. So my mother was in the streets as a kid. My dad was some homeboy from San Juan, didn't speak English, he was sent upstate and got killed."

"You didn't know him?"

Elise shakes her head. "Never met him."

Skinheads play soccer down the middle of the street, but Elise and Jamey pay attention to each other.

"So we grew up with not much, that's for sure. We lived crammed into these housing units. My mother had kids with two other men, men who never stuck around. Everybody I knew, everybody I looked up to, they all did drugs to some extent. Not counting one or two people. Cocaine, heroin, smoking herb. With their children, all day, all night sometimes. You understand?"

Elise lights a cigarette.

"I took care of the younger kids 'cause of being the oldest," she continues. "My mother had two jobs and I did the housework. But when I was ten, she got in a car accident, which put her on this medicine, which she had a problem with once the medicine was done, and then one day — she's a junkie, shooting dope. Angel starts coming around then, 'cause he's a junkie too. And I'm the one getting kids to school, cooking beans for dinner, begging money off neighbors for baby formula."

Jamey ignores a dog who sniffs his shoes, and the owner pulls it away.

"Angel beat the shit out of my mother, and she beat him too, for real. He beat us kids — you know, and I'd try to get him to focus on me. Then one day him and me, we had it out, and he put a knife on my throat. I went fucking crazy, and I did everything I never did before."

"Good lord."

She raises her eyebrow: "I don't want any pity from you. I'm just saying."

"No pity," he agrees.

She breathes smoke through her nostrils, and continues. "So, yeah. I was *trouble* from twelve to fifteen, barely living at home, I neglected those children, I left my mother on her own, I was selfish, and no one could stop me."

She flicks her cigarette onto the street, flicks her braids over her shoulder.

"Then?" Jamey asks.

"I was fifteen. Living with this man, Redboy, he was sort of redhead black — his family's Caribbean. He was older, you know, he introduced me to things. We did all kinds of shit. He was a mad soul — furious, you know? He taught me about love."

"That sounds . . . I'm not sure how that sounds," Jamey says, coming off paternal and regretting it.

"Naw, trust me, it was . . . He —"

Here she tears up, quickly —

She wipes a tear with her long nail and tries to collect herself.

"I really cared about him," she tells Jamey, her voice yolky.

"Was he — what happened?"

Elise looks down the street, eyes big and glassy. "Poured gasoline, lit hisself on fire."

"Why?" Jamey asks, incredulous.

"He was doing PCP for days. I couldn't find him, nobody could. Turns out he locked hisself into a Holiday Inn in Hartford, and the police try and get him out, 'cause he was making a ruckus. TV news got it on tape, so we had to see it later even though I didn't want to. He finally come out the door at dawn."

"He burned to death?"

"Truthfully? He hated the world he got born into, and he was gonna get out no matter what."

Tears are smeared on her jaw, and he touches her hand on the table, and she pulls her hand away to light a cigarette.

"Then Angel got locked up, he got four years, and Donna Sierra died. My mother was gonna fall apart. So I went home. And me and Redboy, we *had* been doing drugs together, but I stopped. My mother went on methadone, and Angel was out of the picture, so we got back into order as a family."

Jamey feels useless.

She stares at nothing with red eyes, smoking.

But then she gives him a quarter smile.

Dusk. Blue shadows in the loft. They've been having sex for hours. He went down on her as soon as they got home, on the floor, making her come twice before they found the bed.

They're standing. Lily-white, he gleams in the mirror, and she holds his waist from behind, staring at their reflection over his shoulder.

He used to glance at his body like catching someone's eye and looking away fast to discourage conversation.

His cock twitches up as she rubs his stomach. He watches, hypnotized by the cardinal sin of staring. He's here: *dimple, arm, eye, foot.* This is James Balthazar Hyde, and a woman's warm body is pressed against his back so he can't run.

In bed, they smoke and talk.

He asks about her first sexual experience. It's like he suddenly needs to know everything.

"Guess it's storytime today," she teases. "I seriously was wondering when you'd want to know me."

"Come on," he says defensively.

She shakes her head, meaning *never mind.*

He pulls her braids off her face, arranges them on the pillow.

"Well, I heard people fucking my whole life," she finally answers, "which is an education all by itself, *trust* me."

"I'm sure."

She pulls the sheet off her lower legs because she's hot. "When I was eleven, me and my friend played hooky and met these guys at 7-Eleven. No one talked about what was gonna happen, and to be truthful, how did we know what we were about to do? It's just what you did.

"So we go to this empty house. It was burnt up and all graffitied, but it was like a hangout for kids in the neighborhood. We smoked a joint, probably. And then my friend and the guy she was with go over to one area, and me and this guy hang out on the couch.

"And the guy I was with couldn't get hard. But he told the whole school I couldn't give head. So I of course had to set him straight. I ended up having an abortion when I was thirteen, another one at fourteen. I had let my friend Monique convince me I couldn't get pregnant if I douched with *soda* right after."

"Who was your first love?" he asks.

"Redboy. What about you?"

This is the moment he's dreaded, when he says out loud: *I'm an alien, I can't love anyone.* He grits his teeth.

"Nobody."

"Tell me who!" she says.

"No one."

She pulls herself up so she can look into his eyes. And then she rests her head on his chest, and they listen to night traffic and street voices and dogs howling. He waits to be ashamed.

"No one yet," she whispers instead.

The next day, she gets out of the shower and listens to the echoes that fill the apartment — different notes and chords in the morning. She wants to go out, play a part in the story of the city. She'll walk Buck into a radiant turquoise world.

No amount of roaming around town will satisfy her today, and she'll be wanting more hotel taxi lines, more hot-dog-cart fumes, more car horns, more newspaper stands, more dog piss, more, even more!

Something's changed; she feels different.

She buys a coffee with a couple quarters and sits in the park. She fools everyone, and always has, letting her mouth fall open (untended, obviously dumb), and never blinking her eyes, which are mean, simple marbles, one-dimensional and lightless. Her shoulders hunch, the long masculine hands uncertain where to rest or hang. But she's tracking, computing, and either discarding or accepting factors other people barely notice. Her costume — the gray jeans, the fake-gold *E* on a chain — doesn't blend in and doesn't stand out. Her awkwardness is strategic, turning people away in boredom or discomfort before they register the vague, haughty, delicious joy she takes in being alive.

He didn't want to leave the loft Sunday for this Bedford horse-farm wedding but his absence would have triggered questions. The bride walks between hundreds of white chairs in a field while the groom awaits, the sky touching everyone with quicksilver light.

Jamey says the same things over and over: *Sotheby's, fantastic, Clark Woodford, SoHo, Martine Boulton-Locque, amazing, sure, yes, let's, fantastic, I'll tell them you say hello, that would be fantastic, amazing, sure, yes.*

He drinks Champagne. Horses in a corral look on suspiciously, manes and tails braided for the occasion. The bride, with puffed-up sleeves and elbow gloves, glows from attention.

A bouquet soars through the air. Men in suits and sunglasses, ankles bare and vulnerable like women, stand in groups, ruined from coke at the party last night. A buttermilk-white 1936 Cord Phaeton rumbles up the dirt road to fetch the couple, and Jamey is amused to see the exquisite machine trundle through shit.

He brings home tuberoses from his table for Elise, who fell asleep on the couch waiting. Even though he closes the door quietly, she wakes herself up. She's devout about making love every night, no matter if she's barely awake, or if he has a Champagne headache — which seems to go away within minutes anyhow.

When he gets up to piss around four a.m., he sees Elise smoking by the kitchen window. She hugs one arm across her ribs, and sometimes looks at the cigarette between drags like she has a complex relationship with it. He doesn't realize she's scheming, and she's so intent she doesn't notice him.

Another night he goes to Dorrian's for early gin-and-tonics with Webster and Vanessa, who then beg to see his loft so persistently he says he doesn't feel well and must go home immediately. *How much longer can he do this?* Vanessa watches him go, standing in Dorrian's doorway in her pink gingham shirt, the uniform of certain spies.

At Sotheby's, a netsuke collection comes in from a British doctor who lived in Japan, and Jamey organizes the tiny wood and bone sculptures for appraisal.

Clark assigns Edna to assist: "Ed, help out Jamey, however he sees fit. He'll tell you what to do, 'kay?"

They spread the fawns and dragonflies and rats on the conference table.

Edna holds one in her plump, butterscotch-freckled hand: "Tagua nut?"

"If you say so," Jamey says earnestly. "Screw what Clark says — you're in charge."

She considers him, and her lips turn up at the corners. "You know what, Jamey Hyde? You're full of shit. You could have said that when Clark was in the room."

She walks out, her green plaid culottes stuck in her ass crack.

Jamey's bloodless for a few minutes, until Clark arrives.

"Holy Mary, you're pale," Clark says. "Did you make little Edna vewwy angwy? She just marched off!"

"Did she leave the floor?"

Clark shrugs happily.

Sometimes when Jamey's falling asleep at night, Clark stomps into his mind, and stands there with hands on hips, spectator shoes splayed in a demented ballet pose, and he grabs Jamey's jaw and says: *Honey, you can sleep when you're dead.* Or he shakes him by the shoulders in a pantomime of child abuse and says: *Pour Daddy more Champagne, chop-chop, don't be shy and don't be stingy.*

"Shoot, I'm going to see if I can find her."

Jamey runs out, to Clark's uncomfortable

amusement.

Why does Jamey work to please Clark? All his life, Jamey's hustled to make people feel good, so they don't feel stupid or guilty for whatever stupid or guilty thing they just said or did. No one asked Jamey to be the policeman and pastor of egos. Why does he think this is his obligation? Clark is fabulous in many ways — he can make a rainy Tuesday at the office into a circus, complete with gossip and candy and afternoon Pimm's Cups. But he's also a prick. Why shouldn't Jamey tell him so?

Jamey can't find Edna, and he stands with hands on his hips at York Avenue and Seventy-Second Street, under ever-changing and fast-moving white clouds.

Elise and Jamey agree on a ravioli craving and walk toward Paolucci's, a red-sauce joint on Mulberry Street.

They pass the junk shop, and Jamey points to the tattered harlequin puppet, the torn Bible, the bleached and vanishing maps in the window.

"My brain is full of things like that," he says.

"What do you mean?"

"From work."

"Your job is weird."

"My job is ridiculous."

They eat lavishly, slowly, and drink red wine at a table outside. They have cappuccino afterward, which Elise never had before they started eating in Little Italy, and she loves it, pours sugar on the foam and licks it off like a cat. She watches Jamey sip his espresso and look around — he's lost and determined at the same time, eyes always roving.

She suddenly feels so good, she gets flushed.

"I'll love you till the day you die, Jamey," she says, cupping her hands to light a cigarette, hiding her face.

"Who says I'll die first?" he jokes.

"I'm tougher, I'll last longer," she says back, smiling. Then she gets serious. "To be honest, I'd rather die before you."

She takes a deep drag, and they both watch the smoke as she exhales, quiet. Nobody has said anything about her continuing to stay at the loft — Jamey said *a few weeks* when he invited her — but she doesn't feel like he's about to kick her out or anything. Still, as they sit here in the bright spangled Manhattan night, she wonders how to make him love her.

Goddammit, what's it going to take?

June 1986

One morning she watches him eat Corn Flakes, and says:

"I'll make dinner tonight."

She might as well try this ancient route to the heart.

He knots his tie. "Great." He smiles.

Leaning against the couch, legs bare, she's drinking coffee. Even though she washed her face last night, traces of makeup darken her eye sockets.

He suddenly wants her, and he shouldn't be late for work but they do it quickly, against the couch, standing, grunting, and he leaves with face flushed, a figgy musk reeking from his armpits.

She stands naked at the door, kisses him goodbye, and he thinks about it all day — how the door was cracked, how anyone could have seen her.

She looks through Martine's cookbooks:

crème fraîche, veal stock, herbes de Provence.

"What the fuck?" she murmurs.

At Grand Union, she wings it from memory.

And she can be seen through the lazy and sullen crowd of shoppers, a girl with cornrows and a basketball jersey, head turned down with some kind of dignified everyday precision, looking through grapefruits under a fluorescent light. She's examining the bumpy hides, the rash, the strange color that isn't pink or orange, myopic but also aware of the world like a cat is when it focuses on one thing but is really focused on everything. She'll choose a fruit and move on to peppers, and she smiles as she pushes the cart — at no one, briefly, at this hour, this task, at herself.

Back at the loft, she empties bags and turns on Howard Stern.

"Buck. You wanna help?"

Martine's copper pans just seem old and battered to Elise, but she sets them on the stove. Outside, taxis honk at cars, buses grind, people shout across the street while the sun ricochets off mirrored buildings.

She cooks a Puerto Rican feast, like her aunt used to do sometimes. Bright-yellow rice, a roasted pork shoulder, the green sofrito, plantains caramelized to a crisp at their edges.

The air comes in the window, its sweetness cooling, like a cake just taken from the oven. It's a perfect summer night. She waits.

The phone rings.

"I got to meet these friends tonight," he says unhappily. "I can't get out of it."

"Really?" she asks.

"I've said no too many times, I don't have any excuses left," he says, then feels funny about what he just said. "You know?"

"Yeah," she says, her voice hollow.

"I'll see you around ten or eleven," he says, and she realizes he forgot about dinner, or didn't understand what she meant when she said she was cooking, and she could tell him now, but her voice catches, and she barely says *okay.*

At Dorrian's, Jamey drinks greyhounds with Brent and Walter while girls with charm bracelets and madras blazers lean in to talk to him, their alcohol-and-Dentyne breath tickling his ear. It's fun to be here but only because he has a secret. Otherwise it would be boring.

A dull ache throbs in her rib cage. She should have spoken up — he'll feel bad when he realizes the one night he spontaneously chose to do something was the night she made a real dinner. A proud woman would throw a tantrum, toss the food, and leave the candles to burn down like in the movies. A vengeful woman would get drunk, call someone else. But Elise lovingly and carefully packs the rice and plantains into dishes, covers everything with aluminum foil, to be brought out and reheated when he comes home.

In the morning, realizing what he's done, he insists on eating it all for breakfast, with a scrambled egg. He grins, telling her it's so good, as she sits in her T-shirt and watches him devour the food, her face spiked nicely with amusement, and she smokes her cigarette on the other side of the table.

When they can't sleep, they lie on the sheets, trading tales in the dark.

These are tiny stories that they never told anyone else — smudges of incidents, not worth repeating before but now important.

He watched a woman on a horse, and the horse stepped into a wasp nest. The bodega owner on her block always gave the kids a Swedish Fish; Elise heard shots — then saw blood run into the sidewalk seams. . . .

On a NOLS trip in Wyoming, a girl went

over a cliff, and her body was helicoptered out. Elise helped Monisha lock her cheating boyfriend into a motel room by nail-gunning the door closed.

Andy Warhol came to his tenth birthday party.

The drunk hibachi chef on her seventh birthday fell onto the grill, burning his hands.

His mom gave him a puppy for his eighth birthday, and his father gave it to another family three months later.

Her mom taught her to swim in the metallic-cold lake where *her* mom swam as a kid. During drowning drills at the yacht club, he and Matt saved each other. She sometimes went to a public pool whose surface rippled with a rainbow of Afro-sheen. His friend grew up in a penthouse apartment with its own tiny movie theater.

She draws figure eights on his belly with her finger.

Each time one finishes, they say: *You still awake?*

Yeah, I'm awake.

What can she do besides cultivate a daily schedule? Make coffee for him and say goodbye in the early light, watch *Good Morning America* (red skirt suits with black buttons, concealer on the man's face, potted flowers in the window), take a shower and pick out clothes, put on eyeliner — which takes a mighty long time, the way she does it.

She smokes her menthols on benches, squinting at people passing. She finds a hair salon that braids hair the way she likes it. Sometimes she shoots hoops if she finds an empty court, and if someone's there, they alternate shooting, moving in sundial curves and not speaking, and throwing the ball back if it bounces to the wrong owner.

She wonders if she *should* get a job, if Jamey wants her to now that she's staying longer than a month. She peeks into shops. She asks if they're hiring, but she acts odd, nervous, and they think she's shoplifting. In a thrift store, she touches a row of slips the colors of wine coolers, puts her hand into one to see the silhouette of fingers through fabric. She rubs the zipper of a motorcycle jacket, silently composing words about working here to the Japanese man behind the counter. Her body produces an attar of insecurity, and he looks at her with suspicion. He even sighs loudly, meaning: *Fish or cut bait.*

Fuck, this lack of confidence is bad for business, she knows that. She's been here before. What girl in love doesn't know this territory? *Don't get weird. Chin up.*

She eats McDonald's in Washington Square Park, and leaves the cup and crumpled yellow wrapper on the sidewalk when she's done, stretches, yawns, and lopes home.

Elise was so shy as a kid, but at ten, she found a friend, Phara, from Haiti. The girl got dumped with some relative after her parents faded into trouble. Phara's smile was curved and cherry-red, and she talked to everybody. Even at eleven, she worked the sidewalk or the playground or the bodega. Tagging along, Elise saw the world open like a flower.

Phara talked to strangers.

After Phara left a year later, deposited into another random home, Elise forced herself to do it. To talk. Other girls watched and sneered: *You're not Phara, and you never will BE her, so give it the fuck up.* But Elise practiced, somehow knowing curiosity would be the key to her life.

Walking Buck today on the piers, she surveys the hustlers ambling, or sunbathing in coconut oil. One dude in army boots and tiny denim shorts hands out flyers. This is a frontier.

She moves through the invisible net of power dynamics and mating signals.

No one meets her eyes but they aim their own eyes as close as possible without making contact — *I don't want you — but I'm not looking at the ground or the sky like I'm ashamed.*

Tugboats groan on the river.

She walks close enough to one guy — in parachute pants as thin as rice paper — that he has to see her.

"Got a light?" she asks.

He looks confused.

"I mean, an actual light," she explains, taking out her cigarettes.

"Sure," he says gruffly, his voice heavy with interrupted conquest.

He flicks a Kelly-green Bic.

"What's her name?" he asks.

"It's a he. Buck. Like from the Jack London book."

The guy smiles, cracks his gum. "I loved Jack London. When I was a kid, in school," he adds cheerfully.

"I never read any of his books," she says, taking a drag. "But my boyfriend talks about them."

"Read *John Barleycorn.* Fucking outstanding."

"I will. Thanks, man.

"Anytime."

She waves, giddy now. "Have a good day."

"You too," he says, resuming position like a mime going back to work.

She hangs out the loft window, the way everyone did where she grew up. She's inquisitive, runs her fingers over the street like reading Braille. Who's shouting down an alley between apartment buildings? Whose pit bull sits in the auto-body shop window there, pale eyes wise in the caramel face?

This is how Elise prays, how she gets keener, how she bows.

The music from that man's car, as he wheels down the street, is it opera, some Italian immigrant stuff? Blue smoke comes out his window, and she sees his fat hand as the huge Cadillac passes, he's older, belting out the lyrics, cigar held high.

What makes him so happy?

She likes to imagine his house in Queens, his wife, a parakeet in a cage, a gold-framed mirror, fake roses in a vase, veal parmigiana for dinner. . . .

They go to Balducci's and buy French goat cheese, fresh-squeezed juice, English muffins, lemon curd, rib-eyes, Champagne grapes, fresh pasta from Italy, a case of Perrier bottles, a bouquet of orange roses, romaine salad, cooked shrimp with cocktail sauce, bagels, and capers.

Elise thinks she heard wrong when the cashier says the total, but Jamey doesn't seem surprised. Elise stares at him bug-eyed as he hands over the cash.

On the way to work in the morning, Jamey gives a dollar to a homeless man; he never used to do that. Not because he thought he shouldn't, but he couldn't figure out his motivation for charity, and that drove him nuts. *Did he want to be seen as good? Did he want to be admired and thanked? Did he want to control the man by giving him money?*

Now he doesn't care about the reason and hands out coins all the time.

This man, he's seen him before: he resembles a bodybuilder in rags, with muscles veined like worm-eaten rock.

"I fear not," the homeless man says to no one, as if practicing for the stage. "I know not."

The old Jamey would have walked away, but now he lets himself watch.

The man traipses from one persona to another, changing shape and color, shining under the morning sun. The man is President Reagan, now he's Ulysses, he's a baby, he's a corpse, he's a drug addict, he's a preacher — he's a piece of meat through which pass the divinities and rascals of human imagination.

Tonight it's dinner at his old home. Jamey thought about bringing Elise to meet Alex and Cecily and the kids, but decided he'd just *tell* them about her first. One step at a time.

Jamey arrives at his childhood block: there's the gold lobby table in the corner building, arthritic Mrs. Grant walking her Yorkie, Town Cars idling along the curb.

Marvin opens the door and Teddy sits behind the desk.

"What's up, Teddy!" Jamey says.

"How you doing, James."

"Long time."

"Too long, young man." Teddy smiles broadly — meaning: *Do not hug me while I'm on the clock.*

Upstairs, Cecily is arranging giant, falling-over peonies. White petals razor-cut with red.

"How good it is to see you," she tells him.

Xavier and Samantha play with wooden trains on the parquet floor, their sibling-talk unintelligible and calming.

"We've missed you," she says, kissing his cheek.

Cecily's a very good wife. After Tory, Alex found someone benign. His friends warned him about Tory, then rode her fame with him, then rejoiced when things went sour, pranking Alex by taping articles to his desk on the "divorce of the decade."

"I ran into Caroline Stallworth at a party, and she said she hadn't seen you around this summer. Where have you been hiding?"

Cecily's face is round as a plum, and she waits guilelessly for an answer.

"Oh, I've been, you know, laying low. Just getting the hang of this job, and, yeah."

She nods. She's from powerful Seattle shipbuilders, but the Pacific Northwest humility plus Scandinavian disaffection cuts through prestige, and she's not like East Coast empire daughters, even if she is as wealthy.

She takes a man at his word.

"Well," she says, looking at a stack of envelopes. "You have a number of invitations that have come to the house."

"Ah, thanks."

The kids stand on chairs to peel potatoes or snap the ends off beans. *You monkeys,* she calls them when they squabble, or she tells them, with a measure of sweet and stern in her voice, to *go play nicely in another room.*

At Palm Beach last winter, Jamey walked into a bedroom where the three of them were napping, tangled on a king-sized bed with a banana-yellow coverlet. They were in dried bathing suits, Solarcaine in the air, books on the floor, and visions cast on walls: Peter Rabbit played with a hungry caterpillar, girls stood in straight lines with umbrellas while a bird flew around looking for his mother.

Alex runs in, newspapers shoved under his arm.

"Want a beer, Jamey-roo?" he says, hugging his other children.

"Sure," Jamey says.

"I've got to make a call, Cece," he says. "Back in a flash, don't wait on me."

While his dad talks to London, Jamey looks through the *Encyclopaedia Britannica,* the same volumes (now somewhat outdated) he loved as a kid. The dog-eared "Butterfly" section reminds him of the hatchery he created in the guest room when he was nine. Glass jars lined up on the Louis XV bureau and on the bookshelves — with caterpillars inside and enough leaf to make a cocoon.

Jamey now reads a line he'd highlighted in awe back then: *In the chrysalis, the cater-*

pillar must disintegrate into pure liquid, with no form at all, and no parts, before its cells start to realign themselves, as per the imaginal discs, and develop into a new creature: the butterfly.

His science report got a gold star, and the teacher wrote a note home that most children don't have the "exemplary patience" to complete an experiment like this.

Every time a chrysalis broke, Jamey took that glass jar to Central Park, and let the butterfly go. Sometimes the Painted Lady Monarch walked the shoulders of his little blazer before dusting its oily wings enough to fly.

The nanny was bored to *death.* But Jamey didn't let that stop him from infatuation, seeing butterflies in his sleep, doodling spots and legs and thorax, talking about butterflies to anyone who would listen.

"Dinnertime!" Cecily sings.

Jamey joins Cecily and the kids at the table for coq au vin, but Alex never makes it. Jamey leaves after pantomiming a goodbye to his dad in the office, and his dad pantomimes his regret about the length of the call.

On the street, he tosses the envelopes — to weddings, summer balls, twenty-first birthdays on yachts, engagement parties at

Point O' Woods — into the nearest trash can.

Walking home from work that week, Jamey impulsively buys a Polaroid camera at a RadioShack on Broadway. The sales guy has a silver cap on his canine tooth, and breath to kill an elephant. He calls Jamey "my man" over and over.

Jamey photographs a dog pissing in the street, and a red mannequin in an out-of-business shop. The flash burns the night like an X-ray, and everyone looks.

He knocks on the apartment door, and when Elise opens it, he presses the button. She's startled, then captivated as they watch the square develop into her face.

He looks at it longer than she does, at something in her eyes and mouth, something willing yet resolute.

They go eat dumplings on Bayard Street, walk back hand in hand. Asian gangsters smoke foreign cigarettes and barely register this American couple; there's a gridlock of energy, conversations, arrangements, and tension on this block, as on every block. Elise and Jamey don't figure in, and they glide by like extras in a movie.

At home she picks up the camera and walks backward to the bedroom, snapping a picture of Jamey.

"Come here," she says.

She's kneeling on the bed.

"Take down your pants," she says.

He undoes his belt, and she reaches with one hand to do the rest. She manages to take a picture, and they laugh at the awkwardness.

He grabs the camera, and she lies, naked, on the bed, and smiles calmly.

In moments that would make other people shy or awkward, she becomes supernaturally natural.

He shoots her lying there.

They pick a gladiola from the vase, pose it between her legs. He takes a close-up.

Elise sets a brooch from Martine's jewelry box on his breast and shoots that — it looks like the gold pin goes through his skin.

Jamey manages a shot while they have sex. He seems half robot, half man — a bedroom centaur.

The film gets pushed out with a succinct noise.

Afterward, they spread the pictures on the floor: cloudy, shady poems of bodies, a lyrical record of love. That's us, they think silently.

"But I don't want anyone else to see them," she says.

"We could burn them," he suggests after a hesitation.

They go to the roof in their pajamas with a matchbook. Under the constellations and a thin scythe of moon, they set fire to each Polaroid, starting with a corner. The images get distorted first, as if the bodies are returning to some primordial shape closer to the soul.

They save one: her legs spread with the flower between them. It's impossible to tell what it is. The pale globular shapes are part animal, part blossom.

The photo is like the dream that someone had in a dream: doubly inaccessible.

Jamey wakes up in a nest of sunshine this Sunday morning. He feels like a fire is burning in him, and all of a sudden, the wood will shudder and shift, send up lazy sparks. Something in him is getting rearranged, or destroyed.

At the Ground Zero Gallery, she tells him she never went to an art opening before. This exhibition is graffiti paintings, and everyone's high, rambunctious. Jamey and Elise are bumped around the mad crowd, and their eyes get shot up with Technicolor stuff.

It's nice and late, the sky a damaged purple, when they squeeze out.

She walks beside him, hooded sweatshirt off and hanging from her head, T-shirt tucked into jeans. She's holding his hand, swinging it, then slowing down, dragging him to a stop as if he were rushing the night away.

Sometimes she stalls to light a smoke, grimacing over the Bic, its flame reflected in her gold necklace, then she resumes her streetwise lope — pigeon-toed — a gait he's become addicted to watching. *Addicted?*

They have nowhere to go tonight. Nothing to do.

And that's heaven. *Heaven?* he thinks.

But it *is*, to wander and explore, to play, to talk with this girl. . . .

Tonight — seeing her laugh, head tipped back with abandon, with sarcasm, with pleasure — he's struck by bizarre lightning. Diamonds of heat prickle his face: *You idiot. This is all you need. This is all you ever wanted. You just didn't know it. You prideful dickhead. You blind piece of shit. You retard.*

"What?" she suddenly asks.

He must be grinning like a lunatic.

He shrugs and keeps smiling, refuses to tell her.

She smirks awkwardly, intuiting he's

happy for some reason that has to do with her, and she walks with an extra-clumsy strut.

It's like a daydream he forgot to have. It's like he forgot to daydream at all. It's like he never wanted anything, but only thought and fretted about what he *should* want, what other people wanted him to want. He's a brat all of a sudden now, turned back into a child, and he wants four, no five no six no seven lollipops from the deli. He's going to waddle away with them, through traffic, hearing no one call his name. He'll go lie in a field of toys and video games. The babysitter can go to hell. His teacher can get fired and cry. He'll suck on candy and watch airplanes make their silent way across the sky.

That night, in bed, he says: "I want you to stay all summer. I don't want you to leave."

She laughs, with old-fashioned joy. "For real!" she squeals. "For real for real?"

"For real for real," he says.

Right before she falls asleep later, she murmurs it one more time: "For fucking real for real . . ." She sleeps like the devil, basking in victory, smiling while she dreams. Her exhaustion is the best kind. *I did it.* The words hover over the bed — a crown of golden hearts, spinning in infinity.

July 1986

Elise walks Buck in the early-morning light. He sniffs overflowing metal cans before lifting his leg. She smells trails of nightlife, of narcotic musk tracks left by party people roaming from one after-hours club to the next. The darkness, just a couple hours ago, seemed so invincible to the night crawlers, but the sun turned out to be stronger, and the poor insects were flushed into the street, black sunglasses on, shoulders hunched in a grenadine-red suit against light.

The *New York Times* is on doorsteps, a sack of ideas and facts, the city's brains and tongues gutted by masterful hands, arranged into sausage.

The cobblestones shine; horse phantoms clop over them still. And how do you know this turd is human shit? The deli bag that wiped someone's ass is crumpled next to it, and a cloud of wounded pride hangs dense as flies.

She shoots the breeze with the bagel man, and the guys who loiter on Broadway and Prince don't whistle anymore but wave instead. This is her neighborhood now.

She brings home a cheese Danish and coffee, and puts them on the kitchen table in a graph of sunshine. She's draining her coffee when she senses a disturbance, and she flinches.

"Hello?" says a woman who just let herself into the loft.

She has long, dark, lustrous hair in a blue leather headband, and a dress with asymmetrical shoulders. Her eyes are incredulous and her mouth is resigned; the two features creating one meaning, the way Chinese characters are built.

Elise is dumbstruck, swallows in a hurry. "Hi."

"And you are?" says the woman.

Elise clears her throat. "Elise."

"Am I supposed to know you?"

Elise can hardly think. "I'm with Jamey, I'm his girlfriend."

The woman hesitates and then holds out a thin hand to shake. "Martine. This is my home." She gives a stoic and un-warm smile. "I never heard about a girlfriend so forgive me for not calling first — I assumed Jamey would be at work."

"Oh, yeah," Elise says nonsensically.

Martine is holding a bottle of Champagne that she can't hide, with a navy grosgrain ribbon. "Well, this was meant for Jamey," she says tightly, and puts it on the counter.

Elise nods, not sure what she's supposed to do. Apologize? Leave? Is the Champagne not meant for Jamey anymore?

"Don't mind me," Martine says acidly, "I'm just going to pick some things up and I'll get out of your way."

Buck wanders toward them, a soiled panda bear in his mouth.

Martine looks at Buck. She glares at Elise.

"I'm going to walk the dog," Elise says.

Martine is silent for a moment. "Fine."

Elise gets a leash on him and vanishes, walking a full block with her hand over her mouth, barely breathing.

"Oh fuck," she whispers when she finally sits on a West Fourth Street bench, in front of a basketball game.

She thinks of the ice in this woman's voice.

After a while, Elise realizes she locked herself out again.

"Goddammit!"

At five, she stands with Buck outside the building. The street burns under the July sun, which acts like it will last forever and not vanish one day in September, with no warning, the way it does every year.

Who else but Gretchen should come home?

"Let me guess," she says gleefully to Elise.

Elise makes a wistful smile and follows Gretchen up the stairs. Elise is grateful, but she has a feeling Gretchen likes girls, and Elise worries about getting into debt. Everybody wants something, don't they?

"Come in," Gretchen says, and this time she means it.

They enter the huge loft, a spatial variation on Martine's, drawings and photographs taped to the walls, the furniture arranged as if people, late at night, huddled to discuss Marxism or Rothko or volcanoes here — who knows. Nothing ordinary could be debated in these formations.

"Keep me company while I cook."

She asks Elise about her life as she takes things out of the fridge.

"What's his name?"

"Jamey."

"Where'd you meet?" she says, cutting shallots.

"New Haven. We were neighbors. It's funny cause we're *definitely* from different worlds."

"Where's he from?"

Elise shrugs. Buck is lying at her feet, and

she rubs his tummy with her toes. "Money. High-class family."

"*You* got class, girl."

"You know what I mean."

"Class isn't money."

"Well, the woman who owns the apartment came in today, and —"

"Martine?"

"Yeah."

Gretchen laughs shortly. "Oh, she's a cunt."

Elise can't help but grin. "Whaaatttt?" she asks with pleasure, drawing it out.

Gretchen wipes her hands on a rag. "You think she even likes this building? Someone told her it was cool to live here. That woman has no soul. What, did she make you feel unwelcome?"

"Well, she's letting Jamey stay there, but she didn't know about me. Think she was surprised. Surprised some ghetto bitch is sleeping in her bed."

"You're not a ghetto bitch."

Elise shrugs.

The women look at each other. Elise is uncomfortable, stares at the floor. Gretchen takes mercy and changes the subject. When Elise hears Jamey coming up the stairs, she thanks Gretchen and flees.

"Hey!" she says. "I forgot my keys *again.*"

They kiss, and enter the dark loft.

Jamey usually comes home and immediately turns on every lamp, but Elise can sit all evening without light. To Jamey, this darkness is sinister.

She throws herself onto the couch now, the city roiling beyond the open window, and she rakes under Buck's chin. Jamey curls next to her in the grayness. He fears this half-light, when artifice's power blinks off and the natural world — in its capriciousness — reigns, but it feels right tonight.

"Martine came by," she informs him.

His heart double-beats. "Really."

"She didn't seem too *happy* finding me here."

"What'd she say?"

"Not much. That was the problem. I just let her look at me like I'm nothing."

Elise has a thousand talks with Martine from this day on, in her mind. The two women face off like gladiators. They bang foreheads. *I don't know who you think you are,* it often starts.

And this French succubus hangs over Elise's bed, waiting for her to fall asleep.

Or Elise is standing in the bathroom, putting on mascara, and suddenly Martine will be in the mirror too, in her stupid blue headband, like a scene from a horror movie.

Fighting is an inevitable necessity. Like God or rain or illness, it will happen; it's not a matter of *if* but *when.* It's beautiful, the ugliness of it, and girl fights are especially awkward and unredeemable aesthetically. There's no boxer's punch, no fast feet. There's strength and intention, hatred communicated with nails, with teeth, box cutters. Hair in the eyes, or caught in the mouth, girls move and heave like fat animals even if they're skinny. They grunt and squeal inside, not audibly. It's oddly silent, a mute disaster.

Elise wishes she could have done battle and moved on.

Alex's secretary calls to schedule lunch on Saturday for Jamey and his father. What a surprise!

When Jamey gets to the New York Yacht Club's gilded lobby, Alex is jangling coins in his pocket.

"Hey there, Charlie," Alex says to a man passing.

To the people Alex reveres he gives an operatic hello and stretched-arm handshake. The people he despises get a happy punch on the shoulder. His oldest, closest friends get something melancholy, distracted.

"Jamey," he says sternly, hands on hips.

Alex studies the menu even though he knows it by heart. He has to order carefully because his stomach is tricky. He goes to doctors in Switzerland, Japan, California who prescribe seaweed and other regimens, but Jamey can always tell ten minutes into a meal when Alex is preoccupied.

"Look, Martine told me there was a girl in her loft when she stopped by the other day."

"There was. There is. That's Elise, she's staying with me."

"She's staying with you."

"She's my girlfriend." Jamey aims his heart-shaped face at his father and doesn't let himself look away.

"Your girlfriend who you've not mentioned nor introduced to anyone."

"If you want to meet her, maybe we could all go out to dinner."

"James. I'm not sure how to say this, so I think I'll just say it directly. Martine told me about Elise, and to be honest, this whole thing has me concerned."

At the next table, the sommelier uses a pince-nez to look at a decayed label before uncorking it.

"Martine and Elise barely spoke. What could concern you?"

"Listen." Alex painfully folds his napkin

and begins his speech. "Certain people see the world as small. They're directed by fear, Jamey. They get what they can, when they can, because in their experience, not much is coming their way. Their life is hard, and that breeds a certain attitude. Do I think these people should be helped? Absolutely. They deserve all the help they can get, and I think it's *most* helpful to teach them how to do for themselves. Do I think someone like that makes a good companion to my son? I don't, Jamey. It doesn't add up. They've been beaten down. They have certain instincts, trust me. Guy goes into prison. He comes out, he knows exactly what to say to get by, to get over. It's survival; he's living in hostile environments. He learned to cry at his parole hearing. And he's learned even better skills to rob you blind when he's freed. It's a cycle. They're caught in a cycle. You can try to get them resources and programs, give some of these kids from certain neighborhoods some scholarship money. But usually? Known behavior is hard to get rid of, Jamey. Instinct wins. It's not their fault."

Jamey stares at Alex with mouth agape. "*What* are you talking about?"

"I think you understand." Alex takes a big sip of wine and surveys the room, the maritime paintings and boat models lit by golden lamps.

"No one gave Elise any scholarship money, I can tell you that."

"Well, let's also talk about how challenging it is, even in this modern world, which isn't really racist anymore, thank *God,* for you to be in a mixed affair."

"Dad. Elise is white. Her skin is white, that is, which is what I think you're talking about."

Alex looks flustered. "Is she? Forgive me, then. Martine gave me the impression that Elise is —"

"She didn't go to Yale. Is that what you mean?"

"Look, I don't know what's going on. I do know that I love my Jamey-roo. I've got meetings in Stamford and the car's waiting. But this was a good talk — we nailed it, I think. Right?"

"You've really enlightened me," Jamey says sarcastically.

Alex is so used to his son being nonconfrontational that he either doesn't register or can't acknowledge Jamey's bitterness. "But um, you do need to fix the situation."

Alex gets up and clumsily rubs Jamey on the head.

Jamey sits at the empty table and stares at

red tulips. All around him, men tell stories over oysters, laugh, order another gin. Jamey washes his hands in the Old World bathroom, and then leaves, dazed with rage.

Walking down the street, he questions everything — why he's doing this, why she's doing it. He sees her in Newport, opening the jewelry box. He almost loses the will to keep walking. *Is* he naïve?

But it's . . . the way they lie in each other's arms, the way they sweat, the way they laugh and whisper, the way they sleep and dream together. *Right?*

He walks with hands in pockets, face collapsed into a disappointment. He's disoriented, capsizing like a tiny sailboat in a big wind.

When he gets home, she's sprawled on the couch, and WKCR is playing Ornette Coleman. The sun is a brutal glowing heat in the window. Buck is curled into Elise's stomach, and loves her too much to greet Jamey. The dog wags his tail instead.

"Yo," she says. "What's up?"

She's just listening to strange notes and chords ricochet around the space, putting Cheez Whiz on crackers and feeding one to the dog and then eating one herself —

And he believes in her.

"Nothing," he says, smiling, throwing his

keys on the counter.

Hungry for dinner, they leave the loft, listening to how their footfalls sound together down the stairs. As the building door closes behind them, they get that New York City exhilaration of launching into the unknown.

It's immediate; they've arrived into the night, into the intimacy of strangers, the second they step outside.

They walk up Broadway; Jamey wants to go to a sushi place he heard about. They pass a spectrum of human beings: pierced, shorn, manic, grounded, painted, torn, distended, shriveled, innocent, guilty as sin, foreign, local, young, old, dying, regressing, growing. Jamey in his seersucker slacks and Elise in her gold hoops and overalls are citizens too.

He stops next to a record store, under a tree, to kiss her.

She smiles when he's done.

They see a cat on a stoop, and the cat sees them. The cat moves his head to watch certain people pass, showing his inner ears — iridescent with membrane.

A group of club kids pops out of a door. They're birthday cakes of sex. Ludicrous fairy-tale animals on the run. Clowns made of drugs. The cat won't look at them, won't feed their egos; he licks his paw instead.

At the restaurant, Elise takes a Polaroid of a tiger fish in the tank.

"Is it just raw fish?" Elise asks, looking at the menu.

"No, we should get edamame, some miso soup."

"You order. I trust you."

Elise puts tuna in her mouth like taking communion of some religion she doesn't follow. It tastes like a girl at a juvenile program in Massachusetts, and Elise flashes back to bunk beds, drills, the girl, that time — and then it's gone.

Jamey convinces her to try eel.

She spits it out, and they laugh, and cry, and toast again.

"Let's get another one," she says of the empty sake pot.

They remember paying the bill, scribbling a tip, finding the door, then careening down the street.

Make out against a building, sneakers in poisoned grass, a rat, *Whoa, whoa,* one moans, they stagger on, making out in the street, twisting together like a couple in the rain but it's not raining.

They fall, lie there, as if to sleep, laughing so their rib cages stutter up from the asphalt, holding hands, and someone gruffly says *Get off the street,* and there's streetlamps for moons, glass in the tar.

Jamey's been drunk, of course, but mainly he avoided it when everyone around him was bingeing and crashing cars. Yet tonight is a good roughening up. *Jamey, I'd like you to meet indignity.*

They manage a photo of the ceiling when they get home.

Masser-piece, Jamey will say after looking at it blearily for a long time.

This is how it feels to sleep in your shoes. You're supposed to take them off. You should have brushed your teeth, said your prayers, kept your hands out of your pajamas. If you die before you wake, I pray the lord your soul to take. I pray the lord your toys to break.

Jamey's not even cognizant when he makes it to his knees and lifts the toilet lid, just in time. His stomach muscles work of their own volition. He breathes and spits in between.

He crawls into bed. Elise shakily sits and pees, and then understands they had sex without taking out the tampon. The cotton plug is jammed, and her trembling fingers work a while to remove it. Her eyes are hot and wet when she gets back in bed.

Jamey smiles miserably, roughly throwing one arm onto her shoulder.

"It's not funny," she says.

He grunts. After a moment, he asks into the pillow: "Why don't we just decide it's funny."

"What'd you say?"

He moves his mouth. "Why don't we choose to make it funny?"

She considers, nauseated and curious. "All right." She presses against him, so they can feel as bad as each other, or make each other feel better.

They start to have sex, with no foreplay — just rancid kissing and rough fucking — but he has to stop, cross-eyed, to keep from vomiting.

"But it's funny," Elise says slyly, eyes winking in a blur of makeup.

He holds up his finger. "Please don't talk," he pleads, knowing if he laughs, it's over. His body has gone wild, sick and aroused, and he can't figure out what to commit to. The madness of the situation is awesome.

He watches, smiling, with nothing better to do.

In Martine's kimono, she's pretending to be a sex slave, pressing her palms together at her chest and making up gong-ringing fake words, stuttering across the floor as if her feet are tiny, not gigantic.

When the game gets old, her real posture takes over, and she sits with legs spread on a kitchen chair dragged to the window so she can smoke into the night sky.

"So in line at the bodega this morning, this girl was ahead of me," Elise says. "She had crazy long blond hair, and white lace-up stiletto boots? But she turned around, right, and there's black stitches from her mouth up her cheek."

"Did you ask what happened?" Jamey says, because Elise usually feels no shyness in these situations.

"No, I just thought: *Little sister, I feel for you.* Who knows. Sometimes we have to see what life is doing to us, it has to be physical to be real."

Jamey adores the shooting stars of her mind, the powdery galaxy of her thoughts. Her intelligence isn't organized the same way his is. She never finishes more than a few pages of a book, but loves to talk about what she read. She thinks in wild gardens, and his thoughts are espaliered into an introduction with a thesis, then supporting paragraphs, and a conclusion.

She waits now for the Empire State Building to flicker on, and then makes a childish yelp and points it out.

He's aware Elise is moving around the city every day, roaming, with no professional design for her future. She apparently put in a job application at a hair salon, and they're going to call if something opens up, but she doesn't want to go to beauty school. And she spends afternoons at the record store on Broadway, where guys scratch on turntables, and she nods to the beats and asks them questions about DJing. But that's it — she listens and keeps her hands in her pockets, talks shit, laughs. This kind of aimlessness, according to how Jamey was raised, is a sin. She's supposed to have elaborate ambitions.

But why? The girls he knew who were on their way to conquer Wall Street, or run art galleries, or start PR firms — were they really going to improve the world so much? He grew up thinking you're supposed to work till your eyes bleed, be exhausted all the time, get money, get houses, get prestige, do good, be important, be busy, get on the board, run out of time, cancel lunch with friends, run out of gas. Why? Why did he believe them when they said that? Why did he believe anything they said?

■ ■ ■ ■

Four in the afternoon. Gretchen hollers to Elise from the stairwell, unable to knock because she's got bags in her arms. There's a dinner party tonight and Elise is helping cook.

Gretchen's potbelly swells her corduroy shorts. She cooks with rabid and decadent accuracy.

She asks Elise to mince the garlic.

Elise coarsely chops cloves on the board.

Gretchen grabs Elise's forearm. "What the fuck are you doing?" she laughs. "Mince means tiny pieces. There you go."

Gretchen wipes her cheek with her shoulder when her flour-covered hands aren't free, chewing her lip as she reads the cookbook.

She teaches Elise to pick the membrane and veins from the sweetbreads.

"You've got the perfect tools for the job there," Gretchen says, indicating Elise's neon-pink curved rhinestone nails.

"This is so-o-o-o nasty," Elise finally says, smiling.

Gretchen laughs, stomping her feet. "Oh man. I like you."

When Jacek arrives home, he gives Gretchen a hug, and she gets gooey eyes. She acts like a teenager, her body somehow becoming girlish and slight.

"Jacek, this is Elise," she says.

"Very pleased to make your acquaintance." He smiles, chewing a black licorice rope.

Elise is flabbergasted at her wrong ideas. It takes her ten minutes to process the truth: *Gretchen loves Jacek.*

Gretchen doesn't need anything from Elise.

Jacek opens a dark Mexican beer and talks about Britton, who got a teaching post in Umbria but has been lying in bed with depression for the last month.

"Delilah's going over to be with him," Jacek tells Gretchen.

"Well, that's good at least," Gretchen answers, forehead furrowed.

"You guys are from here?" Elise blurts out, overwhelmed by how natural and secure they are.

"Michigan," Jacek says. "I came to school here when I was a kid."

"I moved from Nebraska to be with this guy."

Elise thinks about Gretchen's journey. How she was raised up, by a hot-air balloon of a heart, and she floated over fields and hills, chubby ankles hanging in the sky, across the many miles.

Jamey appears with a chilled bottle of Sancerre.

"Finally we meet the mystery man!" Gretchen says happily.

Guests arrive — Jemma, a woman in a bronze lamé jumpsuit who is otherwise casual, looks unbathed, unconsidered; Timor, a small man with a bow tie and an air of extreme compassion; Estella, an older lady with a modern architectural haircut and Italian accent and gnarled hands heavy with gloriously unusual jewels; Sam, a man in white overalls who brings Gretchen and Jacek library books on Nova Scotia.

"Jamey and Elise are staying at Martine's place while she's gone," Gretchen explains.

"Dear God, thanks be that she *is* gone," says Timor, and then looks apologetically at the couple.

"No need to censor yourselves!" Jamey's throaty, wayward laugh gets everyone's attention, as always. "We already battled with her."

Elise does a razor-sharp imitation of Martine's heart attack when she caught Elise in her loft, *Ohmygod, who on Earth are you,* and they all cackle. The group makes fun of Martine relentlessly — buying whatever art a dealer tells her to buy, chatting them up in the hallway when she's high on coke and then ignoring them the next day, pulling her chinchilla tight at the neck and putting on massive glasses.

"She used to hang out with Carolyn Von Terrire," says Jemma.

"The girl slumming with Jean-Michel, the girl who ODed?" asks Sam. "That was sort of heartbreaking."

A dinner party is the oldest experiment. Trap a bunch of souls in a room. Faces move like painted moons, rising and setting, as talk blows in from the east. The *thunk* and freckles of a hand slammed down on the table in laughter, the noise of a long night unscrolled like a map. Madeira and Roquefort. Paper towels for napkins. The maroon wall telephone rings: next round of folks on their way!

At dinner, Jemma grills Elise on her thoughts about life.

Elise finally and clumsily sums it up as: *See what comes your way.*

Jemma says, "You're a cool kid, baby."

"You grew up where?" Sam asks, listening in.

"Bridgeport. The Turnbull houses."

"And you're still alive," he says bitterly. "No thanks to Ronald. Half the population might as well be crossed off these days."

Elise is a little flush with wine. "We don't exist out there, it's like — war. Families with babies living up against a bunch of sociopaths who don't give a fuck."

The room is silent.

"Sociopaths?" Jemma asks finally.

"Half the people in the houses aren't human," Elise says antagonistically.

"Everyone is human," Jemma says soothingly.

"What the fuck do you know about it?" Elise asks. "They're addicted, they're zombies, humiliated to death. Or they're making money off it."

"Sorry, I understand now," Jemma says quickly.

"You do?" Elise says, heating up for a fight. "Spend a lot of time out in Bridgeport?"

Alert! Alert!

"Elise, I think she means she understands that she doesn't understand," Sam says smoothly.

The group survives that sinkhole, and deftly finds new subjects.

Later, Elise says to Jemma: "I didn't mean to be like that. I just don't like people talking about something they don't know, and being all correct about it."

"I totally get it," Jemma says, properly terrified of the discussion starting up again.

"Okay, good," Elise mumbles, apologetic and also still wanting to argue, but letting it go.

By the end of the night, Gretchen's teeth are stained gray with wine. She guffaws and stamps her feet as she tells a story to Jacek while he washes dishes, a cigarette hanging from the corner of his mouth.

Over dessert — port wine and braised peaches — Estella squints at Jamey.

"You're the kid in *Bad Hand,* aren't you," she asks.

"Yup."

"Tory Mankoff's son," Estella says. "I knew her, back in the day. Must be wild being her kid."

"I would hardly know," he jokes. "I see her once a year. Which is fine."

Jill and Crane show up, in the middle of an argument, moving to a corner to hash it out. The table is dirty with foreign cigarette packs, sticky glasses, abandoned threads of talk about de Kooning and Kathy Acker and spaghetti westerns.

Elise licks her stinking fingers — she never had cheese like that. More plates are piled in the sink for a wash, and Sam takes over, cigarette hanging from his teeth too as he talks and scrubs. Someone's neon-pink stilettos are jumbled in the corner.

Two blond children are putting a paper crown on the cat in a beautiful nighttime project the cat patiently tolerates. Jamey keeps looking at the pits toothpicked in jelly jars on the kitchen windowsill, sprouting roots and leaves. He's having a lovely time, he really is, but he's separated from the group, including himself; he's a ghost hanging in the corner of the ceiling.

Then he looks at Elise, who is uncertain but fascinated by everyone, she's learning them, understanding them, and she joins in, laughing, unafraid now. He loves when she forgets to hide the anarchy of her bottom teeth. These people are above his people, certainly in their minds. They're anti-snob snobs.

Elise is thinking she and Jamey were invited as curiosities, but everyone in the room is a curiosity — that's the currency of this crew. It doesn't offend her. Everybody wants something after all — why shouldn't they?

His dad calls him at work.

"I'm calling to touch base," Alex says perfunctorily. "Make sure you took care of things."

Jamey doesn't answer, rolls his eyes, plays with the straw in his Schweppes ginger ale can on the desk. "What does that mean?"

Alex stalls. "Did the girl move out?"

Jamey's face heats up. "No. Why?"

"Why? Because that's what we agreed on."

"We never even mentioned it."

"Martine wants her gone," Alex says after a moment.

"Well, then, I'll move out too," Jamey says, testing him.

After a moment, Alex clears his throat: "I guess you should."

Head reeling. "Wow. Okay. Just because this woman decides to judge someone she met for thirty seconds —"

"The deal was for *you* to live there, not some stranger," Alex rushes to explain.

"That's not it," Jamey says quietly, touching the rim of his desk.

"Look. If Bats hears about all this, Jamester — he'll be unhappy. Do you understand?"

Like Bats has anything to do with anything. Ever since Jamey could remember, Alex told him he was the favorite grandson — Bats asked how Jamey was doing at lacrosse camp, at Race Week, on his SATs. Alex reported it like Jamey should be proud — because Bats didn't look out for other grandchildren this way.

"Dad, Elise is a harmless —"

"Just be a big boy, okay?" Alex sounds weary, like this girl he's never met has exhausted him simply by existing. "That's all I'm saying."

In the middle of that night, Jamey wakes from a vision and recognizes it as a memory.

It starts as a blister of honeysuckle — he's a kid, running though a garden, playing hide-and-seek, it's a summer party in the Hamptons. The dogs don't know what's happening but they love it anyway. There's a luxury, a July paradise, the kind of time kids get lost in, when an hour lasts a year. But now Jamey remembers seeing his dad's silhouette by the pool, drinking with other men, as Jamey went inside to get a lemonade. He remembers noticing his dad's shadow was shorter than the others, and he had a visceral sense his father was weaker than the rest, and that he was more dangerous as a weak person with a lot of power than a powerful person with a lot of power. Jamey knows he didn't know that truth in words back then, but he knew it in a deciphering of silhouettes on a lawn whose green is turned turquoise by eastern light, the salt and chlorine, some mingling of blood and dusk and threat. . . .

August 1986

The streets are hot, the sky is hot. The loft is hot no matter how many fans oscillate. Jamey's also on fire, livid — he's never been this pissed. Elise sees it in his eyes.

It feels really, really good.

Thus begins their spree, Jamey using his Platinum Amex to playfully stick needles in his father's heart.

Elise and Jamey go to the Odeon one sweaty, sticky evening, lured by its orange-red neon sign. They walk into a star grid of tables — is that Harvey Keitel? Paulina Porizkova? They're guided through downtown algorithms to a booth under a hanging globe of light.

Elise chews gently on her thumbnail, hunched over the menu, self-protecting as she does in a new place. Then she stares glumly out the window while peripherally gathering information on her surroundings — methodical while seeming indifferent.

She looks at the Bakelite skyline on the wall.
Satisfied, she sits up and smiles at Jamey.

"What are you getting?" she asks.

"Steak tartare," he answers happily.

"What's that?"

"Raw meat."

Elise gets a New York strip. Jamey orders his own steak tartare and one to go for Buck. Gets a martini and doesn't drink more than a few sips. Takes a cheeseburger to the homeless guy on the corner.

"Um. What's going on here, Jamey?" Elise asks as they climb the stairs in their building.

"Just feel like spending money," he says with mordant delight.

He's looking like the gothic version of a preppy boy, blood smeared on his Izod persona, his smile wrongly polite. This perversity is what makes Elise kiss him as he unlocks the door, and they close the door and lock it behind them.

They become regulars at Fanelli's, Odeon, Chanterelle. Jamey buys everyone sitting at the bar a round. He and Elise eat prime rib, lobster, salmon, truffle fries, crème brûlée. They always get the prize on the menu, the show-off item dangled in front of the rising Hollywood child star, the Russian mobster, the insider trader; they order caviar from Finland, the Lafite, the 24-karat gold-leaf chocolate dessert — *Bring it on! We're hungry for treasure.*

Jamey doesn't even consider finding a new apartment. Elise notices he's just less respectful of the loft. He leaves dishes in the sink, towels on the floor. Sprays Martine's perfume in the air for fun. Opens bottles of wine from her rack, pours Elise a glass.

"What if she comes again?" she asks one day, watching fruit flies vibrate over the peaches on the counter.

"I hope she does," he says, sitting at the table like a king in his boxers and nothing else.

The truth is also that he doesn't know how to rent an apartment. He's always been given places to live, and Elise would laugh at the limit of his life skills. So — *tra-la-la, everything is fine!*

One night, they fight outside Indochine after he buys drinks for a couple sullen models, teenagers wearing lime-green Lycra dresses and cherry-red pumps.

"Why do you feel the need to fucking treat everybody in a place?" she asks, ashing on the dusk-silver sidewalk.

"It's not about them," he says.

"What's it fucking about then, Jamey?"

"I don't know!"

"You don't? Me neither."

They glare at each other. Then they start laughing.

"You're a piece of work," she tells him.

They're standing next to a Volvo, and they realize there's an androgynous toddler in the backseat, in a diaper. The kid looks out the window with shy blue eyes.

"Hey, baby," Elise says, clicking her long nails on the glass.

The child stares at her.

"Let's get some ice cream," Jamey says.

They buy a Popsicle on the corner and pass it through a cracked window to the hand. When the parents return, this stained wooden stick and gooey smile will be a whodunit — *What self-important Good Samaritan fed our child?* There's pleasure in changing a static environment, but Jamey doesn't know if it's a decent and moral pleasure, and he doesn't care if it's not. Elise realizes he just wants to give things away, to a sixteen-year-old from Slovenia wearing Gaultier and high on heroin, or to a nameless baby. She tries to be okay with it, she really tries.

■ ■ ■ ■

Jamey hands the bouncer three crisp hundred-dollar bills to slip into the Ninth Avenue club. He and Elise hold hands when they enter the stenciled door like kids about to jump in a pool.

Inside, the bass churns the crowd, rumbling through bodies. It almost seems that a stage disintegrated and the performers fell into the crowd. A woman in white slacks with duct-taped nipples smokes a Cuban cigar. A banker wears a Savile Row suit, his tiara tilted, his eyes ruined. A fuchsia crocodile hangs on the wall, life-sized and dead, descending to eat everyone. The girl in the dime-store satin dress scrounged train fare from Massapequa to get here tonight. Anyone can tell by looking that she bought a one-way ticket, and this is the underpinning of her glamour.

They go from club to club. Egos crow like roosters, all these inner childs coked to the gills, and the coat-room boy and society man fall in love for one hour. The ladies in diamonds won't come out of the stall, having too much fun, watery liquor spills from plastic glasses, a gown is violently slit to the thigh, computerized music pings and twangs. *What time is it?* A blond girl checks — *Where?* she asks, because each of the eight transparent watches on her arm represents a zone.

Jamey gets home after a meaningless day at Sotheby's, inventorying porcelain Bavarian plates. The evening sky is dry with hot clouds. Jamey is supposed to meet Alex at Harry's for another "talk," but he suggests to Elise they go dancing instead, and glibly leaves a message with Alex's secretary.

"Won't your dad be mad?" Elise asks.

"Very," Jamey says.

Jamey suggests starting the night with oysters at the Plaza. Their taxi driver is an old man, with white sideburns under a fedora, who speeds up at red lights.

They meet a couple as they finish their second dozen at the bar.

"I'm Tom, this is my wife, Sheryl. Mind if we take a seat?" the man asks, pointing to the wooden stools.

"Go ahead," says Jamey.

"Oddly enough, we've been here before but never on a Wednesday," Tom says, surveying the place.

Later he says, "My wife and I, weirdly enough, were born on the same day, just two years apart."

"Isn't that bananas?" Sheryl asks, touching a cocktail stirrer to her bottom lip.

Tom buys the next round. Jamey reaches for his wallet, and Sheryl puts her hand on his arm; her burgundy nails flex. "Oh, let him. He's had a good month. He gets sort of spendy, and I don't see why not."

The four of them are giddy, Elise and Jamey not sure why, until eventually they realize, and then realize they've known all along.

Sheryl is telling the couple they should join her and Tom on a cruise in December.

Jamey and Elise look at each other, and almost lose it. Elise cuts eye contact with Jamey in a desperate attempt not to laugh. "Where to?"

"Meh-hee-co," Tom says.

"God, I wish I could get off work long enough. Sounds fun!" Jamey says.

"Next time," Sheryl says.

The bar's closing. Tom invites them up for a nightcap, one last drink before they go home. "Our room's got a stupendous view. Why not. No reason why not."

Elise and Jamey grin hesitantly at each other. Try to read each other's face.

"Why not is right," Elise says, making the decision, and looking at Jamey as she says this.

As they all walk the opulent carpet on the tenth floor of the hotel, Jamey takes her hand, and voltage jumps from his body to hers.

Jamey hangs the Do Not Disturb sign on the door.

It's strange and beautiful for Elise to taste Sheryl's perfumed lipstick; it's like hearing her own voice on the radio or something.

Jamey and Elise sit on either side of Sheryl. They all have their thighs squeezed shut, like nervous and polite schoolkids on a bus seat, and Jamey and Elise each have a hand inside Sheryl's unbuttoned shirt.

Jamey ends up on a king-sized bed, positioned between four legs. Elise is lying on top of Sheryl; he moves from Elise, to Sheryl, back to Elise. It shouldn't be that different, but one has nothing to do with the other.

This can't be happening. It's like finding out that the Easter Bunny or the Tooth Fairy, after years of nonexistence, are alive and well. It takes effort.

Tom is doing something in the peach jacquard chair, and encouraging them all sincerely, in a low voice.

Jamey is starting to operate in a trance, biting his lip. He's a mystical version of an orangutan in a nature show. He actually has the thought: *I'm a monkey, and that's okay.* He's got a dumb look on his face and that's okay. For a minute, an hour later, right before he comes again, with two tongues licking him like kittens, he understands everything.

At daybreak, Tom is knotting his tie when he thinks of something.

"You two want our tickets for tonight? We got third row for *Chorus Line.* Can't use them. You'd be doing us a favor because otherwise the tickets will go to waste."

"Why aren't you going?" asks Elise, lacing her high-tops, braids hanging to the floor.

Sheryl's brother just got engaged and they're flying down for the party.

"Overnight Bobby decided," Sheryl says. "That's how he does things."

"Yeah, so, he got in a boat accident a couple months ago. Two catamarans, actually — in Florida. And he fell in love with a girl on the other boat."

"Nice girl," Sheryl adds, clipping her earring on. "I think. We haven't met her."

Sheryl moves to the window, one hand in her Gloria Vanderbilt jeans pocket, the other holding a croissant smeared with apricot jam. She starts tearing up.

"What's wrong?" asks Jamey when he notices.

"It's okay," Tom assures him.

"What happened?" Elise asks.

"It's so beautiful," Sheryl finally murmurs, looking at the pale-blue buildings, the massive world they can't hear through the glass.

"She loves the cityscape in the morning," Tom says, almost proudly.

They're tired when they get home from the Broadway show. Fucked out, eyelids full of spotlights, starry-brained. They fall asleep holding hands.

The phone rings at dawn. Elise picks up.

"Who's this?" Alex asks roughly.

"Who's *this*?" she says.

"Give me my son."

"He's sleeping," she says crisply, and hangs up with finality.

Jamey groans, but doesn't wake, while Elise listens to her heart pound.

Something in that man's voice sounded like doom, and she decides right in this moment not to tell Jamey the truth about their future. Not now. She'll carry it alone, as long as she can. She kneels in the sheets, still and silent in this game of hide-and-seek, feeling invisible just because she closes her own eyes.

■ ■ ■ ■

Walking to work the next morning, Jamey's gait has an extra beat.

He thinks of himself as a telephone that was off the hook till now.

Any couple in any oyster bar could have been Tom and Sheryl, but Jamey never listened to their catamaran stories, never said yes to nightcaps from strangers. The world looks so different today; he catches the eyes of other pedestrians, shopkeepers smoking on the sidewalk, riders of a bus stopped at the light. He sees every window in every building as exceptional, a possibility. He thinks of the way Tom held Sheryl's limp, manicured, gold-braceleted hand as she stepped into her heels before leaving, and she said *Thank you, darling,* and Jamey was just bowled over by their bourgeois manners and futuristic ethics. He stops and buys a Twix at a newsstand. Candy for breakfast, and why the hell not.

Jamey and Clark are having petite tender roasts with béarnaise for lunch, the steakhouse lively and loud.

"Clark," Jamey says. "Don't you think Edna could use a break? She's been getting the short straw all summer."

Clark squints. Jamey's acting suspiciously earnest.

Then Clark laughs, merry-eyed.

"I'm serious," Jamey says, freeing the bee in his bonnet.

Taken aback, Clark turns tomato-red. "Oh, you're . . . being genuine. Of course. Poor Edna. I'm not sure I know what you mean, but we can always be a little sweeter, I suppose."

"Fantastic!" Jamey says, which is something Clark always says, and Jamey doesn't ask permission but orders a second martini for himself with a Hollywood smile.

Cross-legged on the magenta couch, Elise sweats in the afternoon heat. Buck is waiting for drips from Elise's Klondike Bar, at a polite distance but attentive, when the phone rings.

"Hello?" she says, licking her finger.

"Hope you're sitting down!"

She cocks her head. "Who's this?"

"Trent Black from Venture Prizes, and today, miss, is your lucky day."

Elise puts her ice cream in the sink.

"Is this, let's see here, Elise?"

Elise furrows her brow. "Yes."

"And you're staying with Mr. Jamey

Hyde, correct?"

"I never heard of Venture Prizes."

"We're a subsidiary of American Express. Surely you've heard of American Express."

"Yeah, of course."

"Well, you and Mr. Hyde have cause to celebrate, because you have won a trip to the Bahamas, and that's not all!"

"How did we win?"

"Mr. Hyde's a loyal Amex customer, and his name was in the sweepstakes pool. Truly exciting, don't you think? We sure think so!"

"What else did we win?" she asks, getting a thrill.

"Two tennis racquets, and, wait, there's more."

"What?"

"A magnum of Moët Champagne!"

"What's a magnum?"

"A very large bottle. All I need now is your social security number."

"Why do you need mine?"

"If you have Mr. Hyde's handy, that'll work."

"I don't."

"Why don't you give me yours, I'll put these prizes in your name, and you can celebrate the good news this evening, how's that?"

Elise looks at Buck, who looks at her.

"Okay." She smiles nervously.

When Jamey gets home, Elise is grinning, arms crossed.

"Guess what," she says.

"What?" he asks, pulling his necktie loose.

As she gushes out the news, he looks mildly confused but happy.

"Bahamas?" he asks, eating Brie and Ritz crackers standing at the counter.

"Yeah."

"Nice work," he tells her.

Alex calls him the very next day. "I've got something for you."

They meet at a Murray Hill bistro where Alex rarely goes, a place with greasy menus and red candles. Alex hands his son stapled pages with Elise's name and social security number at the top, and his face is self-righteous but also apologetic.

"You're doing this out of guilt," Alex suggests as Jamey reads.

"I'm not doing anything out of guilt."

"The way you immediately deny it — speaks volumes! Look. You've always been a sensitive kid."

Jamey stares at him in his pink Brooks Brothers shirt — his father's eyes are kinder and softer and sadder than usual. This "problem" has brought Alex closer to his son than anything yet.

"I'm not a kid."

Alex sighs. "What I'm saying is — no one would hold it against you, what you've done so far. But you're getting damn near making a mistake."

"What mistake?"

"Just get her out of that apartment."

Jamey won't answer, looks away.

Alex pats his mouth with his napkin. "You belong to this family. This family loves you. Why would you create problems?"

On the curb, father and son awkwardly scan for cabs, the night fragrant with the incense of New York — taxi fumes, perfume, cinders, bread baking somewhere.

"There's nothing wrong with this relationship," Jamey tries one more time.

Alex rocks heel to toe, hands in slacks, looking at the avenue. "Then why do you keep her hidden away like you're ashamed?"

Jamey walks the long way home, broad shoulders squared and hands in pockets. People, streetlights, headlights, they blur, foggy and dreamlike. One stranger's eyes trail a milky brightness as he passes Jamey. A dog pisses black onto the stone building, its hind leg raised in a terrible way. Nothing is right. Jamey looks down on his own body from the night sky, and sees a lost boy.

When he opens the door finally, Elise is sitting at the window in her basketball shorts and a bra. She's eating Lucky Charms from the box, handling a palm full of cereal the way a bored man jingles coins.

"Yo," she says.

Jamey sits heavily on a couch, his big thighs spread. Stares at her.

Elise widens her eyes. "What?"

"I can't believe you've been arrested and never told me."

"Arrested for what?"

"Shoplifting, public intoxication, assault."

She eats the last Lucky Charm, and smirks. "Jamey. Nobody who grew up where I grew up doesn't have a record. Mine is *short.*"

"But — assault?"

"I probably pushed some girl at the bus stop."

"That's not what it sounded like."

"Cops have a quota, they hand out tickets for nothing, haul you in if you give them trouble. Of course I'm gonna talk back if I feel like it." Now she's mad — her skin almost tinged with green.

Jamey sighs.

She smacks the back of one hand into her palm: "I've seen your friends from Yale, high and drunk as *shit,* falling in the streets, driving into brick walls like retards. No one is *ever* gonna cuff them."

"I don't need a lecture."

"Who told you anyhow?" Elise asks.

"My dad."

"How should he know?"

"He had your info printed out. For your whole family, actually. Your mom's record is like three pages."

"I don't understand."

Jamey sighs. "There is no Venture Prizes."

They don't have sex that night.

At one point, he kisses her forehead in the dark bed. "What else don't I know?" he asks quietly.

She turns on the light, furious.

"Fucking plenty! You don't know shit!"

"Okay, okay."

"I can't believe your *father* would do that. Was that him on the phone?"

"He paid someone to do it, I'm sure."

"I would of told you *anything* if you had asked. Fuck all-a you."

"I'm sorry."

"You better be. You know what? Go sleep on the couch — I can't even be near you."

He gazes at her — she lies down and won't return his look. He slinks onto the couch but can't sleep.

She eventually turns off the light again.

The August morning blazes like petroleum through SoHo streets.

Elise and Jamey sit in silence on the magenta loveseat and drink grapefruit juice.

Suddenly Jamey gets up, rubs his neck, deciding. “Let’s go celebrate your record.”

She tries to interpret his expression; he looks like one of those smug, bored baby-faced Cali boys who drive Mercedes sedans with big trunks for shopping bags — that’s their virility.

“I have a stupid idea,” he tries again. “Just come with me, okay?”

They take the subway, hanging onto the pole as the car heaves and bucks. The door doesn’t quite close, and the girl in the Salems ad has a black Magic Marker gap in her teeth.

Uptown, they walk in off the steamy street, and Elise and Jamey swivel their heads to take stock of the store, expensive air shining them.

Crude transactions are done in muted, eloquent tones.

An old woman gets her shoe heel stuck in the escalator pleat. Her spun hair tall as a fruit basket, she almost topples, but a gang of sport coats saves her.

"What are we doing here?" Elise asks.

His cousins always played the Tiffany's game, where they'd crowd around the baby-blue catalog, and every girl picked one thing on each page.

"Playing a game," Jamey says.

He puts his hands over her eyes, and they walk awkwardly toward a bank of glass cases. She grins, blindly holding her hands over his.

"All right, point your finger, and whatever you point to is yours," Jamey tells her.

"What?" she says in a childish voice.

The counter man has dyed hair and a snarl like an aristocrat, although he probably still lives with Mother in Lindenhurst. He glances to the door to make sure security is watching — and they are.

"Should I assume you two are having fun?" the salesman asks in a careful voice.

"Sure," Jamey says.

Elise puts her finger to the glass and Jamey releases her eyes. It's a floral moonstone-and-ruby pin.

"It's a grandmother pin," Jamey says.

"I love it," Elise says, because it's psychedelic.

The salesman uncomfortably asks: "Would you care to see it?"

Jamey shakes his head. "Just put it in a

box, please."

The man clears his throat. "Will this be cash or credit, sir?"

"Credit."

The man's eyes flick to security again, but he slowly wraps the pin in a baby-blue felt bag.

Elise scowls at the man. "What's your problem?"

"Elise," Jamey says, smiling.

"That will be four-thousand five-hundred ninety-nine dollars, please, sir."

Jamey hands him a platinum Amex. The man looks at the name on the card, clears his throat.

Returning the card, he smiles, sensual with apology. "Thank you, Mister Hyde," he purrs.

She sticks the pin on her leather baseball cap, and turns the hat sideways, blows a bubble and cracks her gum, busting through the door into the world of sunshine and true, stinking, boiling air.

He's going to do it. Just as other ideas lately have shed onion skins to reveal a wet heart, this one is impossible to parse any further. He's taking her to Theodore's christening — a monumental Hyde family convention.

Morning simmers in the loft like golden

milk on the stove.

"Is that what you're wearing?" he asks.

"What's wrong with it?" She looks at her denim miniskirt, red tank, gold necklace.

"We're going to a church."

She shrugs and shakes her head, meaning: *So?*

"Don't you want to maybe do long sleeves, or a longer skirt?"

"I don't *have* the outfit you're thinking of, Jamey," she says harshly.

"Elise — it's a bunch of conservative, gossipy ladies."

She slumps on the bed. "I could borrow something of Martine's?"

Jamey shrugs. "Why not?"

They hijack her closet, handling clothes delicately at first, but then Elise spins and models, throwing castoffs on the chair.

Jamey watches her. She pouts in tight white Azzedine Alaïa, twirls in the Sonia Rykiel sundress, grabs her tits in a Chanel jacket.

"Fuck, I dunno," she says, surveying the mess.

"You look good in everything," he says honestly.

She smirks, like: *Shut up.* But she's infected with his hopefulness.

■ ■ ■ ■

They're almost late, but dressed to the nines. They enter the massive bronze doors, and walk into the church. Pink granite pillars hold up the arches on each side, and a Tiffany glass dome sends jeweled light onto the altar.

Everyone else is pleated into grass-green blazers and whale-print skirts. They all move like bees in a hive, buzzing for Bats and Binkie.

"James, darling!" says Aunt Jeanette.

Jeanette's popular in the family. Powder-blue suit worn like a field-hockey uniform. Freckles on her tan, athletic hands. All the family traits of sociability and charm are there but unpollinated by entitlement. She's a perfectly benign ambassador from the family, and he introduces her to Elise.

"Well, hello, Elise." Jeanette beams, her face convulsed with extreme delight. In another culture, she might look insane, but here — this is grace.

At the center of the crowd, the baby — Theodore Stanhope Hyde — is five months old, born at New York–Presbyterian.

His mother wears a canary-yellow shift. Black hair in a chignon. Her bum is still a little wide, and she grins at her husband, Jeb, who has the baby over his shoulder. He bobs slightly to the left and to the right as he talks about the US Open to Cousin Marshall.

And the king and queen arrive, make their way up the African-marbled floor between pews.

Binkie leads in a rose-pink Oscar de la Renta suit, her raspy whisper doled out in endearments and greetings. Occasionally her voice catches fire in a cackle. *Well, hello thuh-r, sweetheart!* Binkie's fun, even in God's house.

Tall Bats has a way of looking into the eyes of whoever he's talking with, then gazing out, to make sure everyone is safe — from train bandits, bad weather. Bats is not actually handsome. His face is wide, mouth and eyes like a stretched rubber doll, skin turning watermelon-pink when he drinks or plays golf or goes shooting, and his nose is almost porcine. He combs his yellow-white hair, once dark like Jamey's, in the side-part he's had since he was sixteen and taking Mary Blixworth out for a milkshake. A shard or two falls over his forehead.

Women follow him like cats after a fishmonger — tails raised, chins elevated. Intelligent women giggle and sip Champagne with head tilted down and eyes girlishly tilted up. Even now, in his late sixties, hands covered with sunspots, he's the object of longing looks from Sacred Heart girls on the subway. He can get away with halitosis, and drunken finales to formal dinners, and the odd nasty comment. Even the maid who has to bleach his hemorrhoid-bloody sheets has a crush.

People hardly talk about his bad behavior, as if they live in a dictatorship and everyone's a spy. He swims at the club every morning in Manhattan, and in East Hampton, he swims the ocean — his eyes cold and impenetrable as the Atlantic in March.

Everyone keeps talking in stained-glass-lit groups but they're waiting to see if Bats singles them out for a hug, or a wink and a wave. They have to be ready — but can't look like they're waiting. So Bats moves through the distracted crowd.

When he finally makes it to the baby, a pulse of love beats in the room.

Bats is shown his grandson — the parents beam, their mouths vulnerably open. Bats *tsk-tsks,* shakes his head: *Fine specimen,* his expression says.

Jamey watches, rolling the engraved program tight and sweaty.

And now Bats heads toward Jamey —

slowly — talking to people on the way.

Elise should be a Dartmouth lacrosse star whose granddad went to Groton with Bats, and she should be bronzed from the Vineyard, lips opaquely shiny from Chapstick. *So happy to meet you, Mr. Hyde!*

But no! Jamey is pushing forward the real Elise, in a couture dress, shins bruised from basketball, cornrows latticing her lean head, feet wedged into slingbacks.

Elise who never graduated high school, never got her teeth fixed, never heard of a country club, never flew on a plane, never attended a christening like this, never met a man like Bats.

"Elise, is it," Bats says, eyes twinkling.

"Yeah," she says, face drawn into unprettiness by a determination to do this thing right.

"Well, it is a *pleasure,*" Bats says, and Jamey knows the verdict.

Elise thinks it's going well.

That turns Jamey's stomach.

They slowly move into rows, sit on the carmine cushions. Elise wants to hold Jamey's hand, but doesn't. The priest speaks, but the baby's bleating makes a spectral fan of sorrow in the dome.

The two girls in front of her, hair Pantene-shiny and French-braided identically, are up to something. Jamey's actually watched these cousins braid each other's hair in the sun-rooms of mammoth apartments, like monkeys picking bugs with love.

They giggle now.

The girl next to Elise is leaning away — almost imperceptibly, her face stoic, a caricature of politeness. She smoothly moves her purse from next to Elise to her other side.

One of the girls in front sneaks another look back, and then glances at her pew mate, and they go into a paroxysm of stifled mirth. The girl next to her tightens her face, almost grinning but not, and then Elise realizes that she, Elise, is the joke.

Elise, burning like white stone, made of nothing that isn't pure and right. Gold earrings and man's feet, and the ill-fitting Valentino sheath, blue eyeliner. Truer than the Holy Spirit.

Her blood freezes.

She stands up.

Jamey tries to meet her eyes as she brushes down her dress.

She murmurs at the girl next to her: "Fuck you."

The girl blanches.

He watches Elise walk down the aisle, chin up, shoulders back.

No one turns, but everyone is attuned to her departure.

Jamey's face is hot. He picks at his nails. He doesn't go after her, thinking he should stay and repair what he can, protect the idea of her, see what he might save.

Elise was six, her mom was working a double shift, and Jeri-Lynn was watching the kids and smoking dope with two guys from the Bronx — Danny and Rat had come out to the "countryside" because they'd done something. Danny's acne made his face looked mauled. The radio was loud and no one could hear the baby wailing except Elise, who whined around Jeri-Lynn's knees, worried: *Dawn's crying in her crib. She need her bottle, Jeri-Lynn.*

Help me get this thing out of my fucking face, joked Danny, and the two guys dragged Elise into the closet in the bedroom, laughing. Rat, a scrawny guy with a ponytail, blew smoke in her face. *Stay put.*

None of this was out of the ordinary. *No!* she yelled. *I don't want to!*

What makes this day sting in her cellular memory is what happened next.

She got quiet seeing Danny's expression.

He pulled down his sweatpants and pissed on her, and then he closed the door. The wetness felt hotter than her skin, and she sat in the dark as it cooled, and she stayed quiet this time, and a new dimension to her was born, a space carved inside her to be filled with emotions all through her life.

Tanning Junior High. When twelve-year-old Elise came out of the bathroom stall, Mary Gonzalez was dabbing on lipstick. Elise heard Mary's brother got shot a few nights ago, paralyzed from the neck down, and she smiled uncertainly at the girl in the mirror.

"I like that color," Elise said.

Mary grinned. "Wanna try it?"

Elise took the tube, and glided it on. She made a smile.

Mary laughed in a practiced way. She even clucked as she put the lipstick into her fringed purse. "Shit, girl. Nothing gonna help you. You. Are. A. Dog. You know that, right?" Mary was still smiling, talking to Elise in the mirror. "You're the ugliest girl in the whole fucking school."

Elise watched Mary toddle out the door on spike-heeled boots. Normally Elise would have punched someone who said that.

Instead, Elise's blood froze and her skin got mottled. She tried to look okay as other girls came in, smoking and shrieking, and

Elise kept washing her hands with her head down. She somehow slipped out of the fluorescent-lit room, and walked down the hall, not looking into anyone's eyes, breaking out the door into the autumn day and moving briskly with no direction, just getting away, just getting off the school property. Was she crying?

She realized she was, and then she was sobbing, hurrying past the Laundromat, the deli, a junkyard, and she needed to go somewhere to be alone and she finally found her way, walking toward the dam, where she could be above the rushing dirty water.

She sat on the matted grass and let her jeans get damp from the soil, and cried like a mixed-up and stranded runaway, the descent of water just out of reach behind the chain-link fence, but the water was there, crushing and sizzling, icy and sad. She was telling me the truth, is the only thing that Elise was thinking. Someone finally said it out loud.

She peered into her Maybelline compact. The hard-lined eyes, the long jaw, studs in her ear, greasy hair. *You're an ugly fucking cunt,* she told herself, face screwed up in a monstrous way.

The sky was an incandescent backdrop, and she felt a physical phenomenon she would never forget. It was a cracking, a separation. She was finally and irreparably removed from the pack, the gang she never understood or belonged to, that she ran with to look right, that she tried to join. *You are on your own, kid,* she thought, and she could barely catch her breath because there was so much heartbreak to this, such devastation.

But then, after an hour of sitting there and letting this news run through her, she also started to feel — up there on this crest of earth, its tall dead wildflowers tangled with Kleenex and gum wrappers and plastic straws and bird shit — she felt free.

When he gets home, after making milky, distracted small talk with family, and telling everyone Elise had a stomachache, and they pursed their mouths with compassion — *Poor thing, I hope she feels better* — he finds her on the couch with Buck.

"Well," he says, uncomfortably. "That sucked."

Elise is glaring at *Geraldo.*

"I understand your leaving," he tries. "I wish we could have handled it differently."

Elise turns red eyes at him. "You know what sucks? You do."

She gets up and throws herself on the bed,

the headrest vibrating.

After a moment, he approaches, biting his lip, cufflinks winking as he puts hands on hips.

"I'm sorry," he whispers.

He lies on the bed, spoons her, kisses her sweaty neck.

Apparently that's not the right thing to do.

"What are you *doing*?" she moans, pushing his hand away. "Get offa me."

She cries, sobbing.

"What?" Jamey asks stupidly.

"*What?* How come you let me walk out by myself?"

"I didn't even know what you were mad about!" he tries, his voice shrill.

They're sitting up now, disheveled and mad.

"You couldn't feel what those people thought of me?"

"I mean —"

"You didn't see the way they looked at me? Are you fucking blind?"

"No one said anything but nice things to you, Elise," he says weakly, without conviction.

Her jaw drops.

Suddenly she's hitting him — he grabs her wrist and she bites his forearm as hard as she can, tearing his shirt, breaking skin —

He manages to contain her, holds her down on the bed, and breathes *I'm sorry* into her hair, over and over.

"You're saying I'm crazy," she weeps.

"You're not crazy," he admits. "You're not."

"Why would you say that?" she sobs.

"I'm not saying that now, I won't say it ever again," he tells her, over and over.

They don't even eat dinner that night; they just eventually fall asleep. Jamey dreams in a jittery, jagged way, a bandage taped onto his arm. Elise snores, nose stuffed from crying, her eyeliner smeared.

When they wake, they seem hungover though neither drank. He makes breakfast, takes care of her like she has the flu. He watches her eat toast and drink juice, her face swollen, and he asks her what else she needs.

He thinks about an exchange between Bats and a friend once on the salty porch of the Newport house, a conversation he always tried to forget. Jamey was on the other side of the screen door when he overheard Bats say: *I didn't blame Alex at first, she's a looker.* His friend said: *Yeah, no offense, Bats, but every good family can use a showgirl or stewardess in the bloodline once a decade, spruce things up.* They laughed together. Bats sighed: *Truth in that, Harold, truth. Doesn't mean he had to go marry a Jew.*

It's a dark Saturday, and Elise and Jamey go to the Museum of Natural History.

They gawk at the whale model hanging from the ceiling. A Japanese family tilt their heads back too, exclaiming in their own language, pointing.

A stuffed monkey family stands in a fixed jungle environment, the parents holding their kids' hands. Elise slings her arm over Jamey's shoulders and points her lollipop at the world inside the glass.

"Happily ever after."

In another room, she runs her hand down a bear's arm. "So soft," she murmurs.

"Hey you," snaps a guard. "No touching the animals."

"Sorry," she says with aggressively fake contrition, and the guard makes a surly mouth.

Watching her act like that to security guards (and bossy cashiers and cops), Jamey realizes he's always been nice to these people. But not because he's nice. Because they're beneath him, and above him for being beneath him. But Elise is just a dick back if they're dicks to her.

The gemstones room! Like standing in a jewelry box with black velvet walls, surrounded by rocks chiseled into luxuries. They gape at all the dazzle.

When they come out, it's raining so hard the drops bounce back up from the sidewalk.

They stand under the awning and watch the city get pummeled, green leaves falling off stems onto the sidewalk, coffee cups floating in the gutter.

"I'm not going back to school," he says, hands in pockets. He looks at her with derelict glee.

"What?" Elise asks, incredulous.

"Not going back."

Elise is elated — and crushed. They'll blame her, and she knows it.

"How long you been thinking about this?" she asks, hands cupped to light a cigarette.

Jamey looks at the sky. "It's possible I knew before we left New Haven."

"Well, Christ," she says gruffly, exhaling, trying not to smile.

When the rain lightens, they jog to a café and drink cappuccinos, and share a slice of coconut cake. They take turns sketching people sitting at nearby tables on napkins, making cartoons of them, furtively studying bunny teeth and heart necklaces and stoned eyes. Outside, a rainbow appears over the Bronx.

On Sotheby's stationery, Jamey jots a letter to his dad about not going to school. After he mails it, he grins at the Rolodex, the Limoges teacup, the pale blue telephone on his desk, absorbing his decision. I have to do this in stages, he thinks, and even he doesn't quite know what he means.

He tells Clark he has to run an errand, and ducks into the first bar he sees on leaving, an Irish pub. It's three in the afternoon, and a construction crew rolls in. Jamey lets their conversations boom around him.

His dimple deepens as he smiles at his beer.

He told Alex he was taking off the semester to restrategize, so his last year's course load will be calibrated for his HMK "career."

Jamey had lied with joy. A ruthlessness burns the tallow around his heart. Maybe it's one way to become honest.

The men collect under a neon-light bowtie Budweiser sign, and the biggest guy orders a round of Bushmills.

"Give one to this dude over here," the guy said, pointing a bruised-black fingernail at

Jamey. Then to Jamey: "You gotta drink with us, buddy."

They all tip their heavy shot glasses, wipe mouths in staggered unison.

The next day, he and Clark are eating takeout Waldorf salads at Clark's desk, where trinkets are spread on the ink blotter: a crystal swan, a Purple Heart (Clark doesn't know whose), and an ivory comb, monogrammed, that belonged to Carole Lombard.

"Clark, I wonder if I could work here for September, maybe October. I'm taking a semester off, so I can focus on my future, and I just love working here." And it's an easy paycheck.

"How nice to hear this enthusiasm! I suppose so."

"Great, thanks!"

At the end of the day, Clark and Jamey wait for the elevator.

Clark fluffs the lavender hankie in his pocket. "But you will be going to Yale for spring semester, won't you, James? You wouldn't throw away that opportunity, right?"

"I'm sure I will."

"Great, great," Clark says, but with suspicion. "You're not, like, doing drugs, are you? Should I be concerned?"

"No! All's well," Jamey says, giving his best smile.

Perhaps he can tell Jamey knows he'll never go back to school.

Not next semester, not next year. Not ever.

But for once, Jamey doesn't feel like he has to explain himself to some nanny or proctor or anyone else acting in loco parentis.

Clark smells a rat.

For Elise's birthday, Jamey conjures up a four-course dinner on a rented yacht, circling Manhattan. She has trouble walking down the pier in high heels and he holds her elbow, and she looks nervously around the sparkling dusky marina.

"Here we are," he says, and salutes the captain at the boat.

Elise takes off her shoes, and is helped onboard.

"Happy birthday, mademoiselle!" says the first mate.

The table in the cockpit is set with white linens, antique silver, and roses. The water rises in triangles of liquid black licorice. New Jersey blazes away across the river, and a black-tie waiter pours Elise a vodka sour with a cherry — her favorite.

"Can I smoke on this thing?" she asks

under her breath.

"You can do whatever you want," he says. "Tonight's your night."

They eat filet mignon, with profiteroles for dessert.

Passing under the bridge, its darkness and echo is an otherworld.

All week she's been stressing about how his family will look at him playing hooky — she'll be the culprit.

It's so beautiful out here — the stink of the river, the baubles of light. She suddenly knows she won't fight his decision. The family will decide it's her, *that she led him astray,* no matter what he says or does now.

And hasn't she?

SEPTEMBER 1986

On September first, they take up residence in a railroad crib at Second Avenue and Seventh Street.

They read their names on the lease.

"Wow," Elise says, looking to him for assurance. "We're doing this, huh?"

"We're doing it."

Elise and Jamey walked around for a couple weeks, looking for apartments. Elise taught him it's as simple as hunting for cardboard signs posted in delivery entrances or first-floor windows, or asking the guy sweeping the stoop if he knew of vacancies.

They were drawn to the East Village. Kids run the blocks, working as lookouts, innocent ambassadors to basements and back alleys. Tompkins Square Park is its own nation of tents, milk crates, bonfires, tattooed people, and dogs that stutter and function in debilitated rhythms. A man jauntily threads through a crowd on First Avenue,

T-shirt on his head like a sheik, singing — raised among so many people, at home and on the streets, that he doesn't see them as obstacles but rather as water or air, a medium to move through, that moves through him too. Holding hands, Elise and Jamey kicked through candy wrappers and avoided dog shit. Then they found this place.

On the first floor, the landlord Mr. Gorowski lives with his wife, who only speaks Polish, so he speaks Polish to her when he's moved to translate something, and Elise can't help wondering why he translates the sentences he does and then doesn't translate anything else. The elderly couple has houseplants and fake flowers in the living room, an indoor garden of metaphysical proportions.

The second-floor apartment is old but scrubbed and repainted, a bathtub in the kitchen, two windows looking into an apocalyptic courtyard, and two windows looking onto Seventh Street. The one thing left by the previous tenant is a dozen airplane whiskey bottles shoved into the toilet tank. A found sculpture of obsession.

The new tenants lie on the mattress, sheets pooling on the floor.

Elise runs her hands through his hair.

"Remember how you acted in the very beginning?"

He grunts, animalistically pleased by her massage.

"You didn't know anything," she says, pulling his hair now to hurt him.

"Nothing," he agrees, and turns over on her. He nips her now with his teeth, his breath between her legs.

They do it the old-fashioned way, missionary, but the unfamiliar smells here, the disturbed dust, the hollow drawers, the way air travels from this window around this room, the shush of leaves in the trees, strangers outside shrieking names they don't know — all of this pinpricks their skin, making this seem like the first time.

They fall asleep, and the afternoon nap feels illicit, against the order of the day. They really don't know what they're doing. Jamey stands at the window, watches evening take over the streets. A stray dog sniffs down the sidewalk, no collar, no owner. Someone waits for something in a tinted-window Chevy, the radio so loud the whole car shudders with the bass. Jamey flattens his hand on the glass, meeting the future.

These days he eats lunch alone, perched on a Fifth Avenue bench, watching kids in uniforms on the next bench. The light moves fast through grand elms above.

One kid has a nosebleed, and boys and girls are nursing him, skipping in circles, taunting him. It's amazing how fast a society forms around an emergency.

Jamey finishes his sandwich with a bittersweet smile. He's not in school this September, and he misses it, but not Yale. Not even high school.

He misses third grade. He misses kickball. He misses long division.

He misses Jack London.

She gets to know the neighborhood with the curiosity of an army wife who understands they could get transferred tomorrow. Behind the dry cleaner, a bicycle with no wheels, no chain, and no handlebars is still padlocked to the window bars — a useless torso. Empty whipped-cream canisters have collected under the Kiev's dumpster.

She discovers the pungency and shadow of this corner, or the green dank tingle of air in the alley, the way kids get acquainted with woods or attics or fields, knowing the molecules and milliseconds of a place. She looks at the red velvet boxes in the jewelry shop window, and the white cat with rheumy eyes, stoned on sunshine, that guards the chains and crosses and medallions.

Oil stains dot the gray tar, like cheetah spots.

She goes to the Third Avenue Cheese Shop. It's like walking into a chapel that smells of sex. Or a morgue where you feel comfortable. The staff shows a devotedness like miners or nurses. They know their work, having made a commitment that's private and stoic. They're beautiful and rank; they're people with a holy, boozy, creamy, rotting idea of love.

Buck looks at squirrels with a stare that says: *I could, but I won't waste my time.* He's unguarded while playing catch, and bounds around like a fat woman doing ballet. But when the game is finished, he pulls himself together and walks carefully through the streets, sniffing the wind. He looks at her as she unlocks their new building, and his eyes say: *Yeah, this is the right place, but just for now.* That's what she was thinking too.

Elise navigates by faith, because she believes in love, has always known it in her bones. When she saw Jamey for the first time, she recognized him, in a way.

Jamey has always wanted to believe he believes in something good, but deep down, he fears he believes in nothing. Without fanfare. He's not an extravagant and charismatic nihilist. He sees himself as someone who slips through the crowd at Grand Central, or stands in line at Duane Reade, or crosses the street at Mercer and Prince, a sculpted white face whose eyes and mouth are static at moments, inhuman. He might seem to belong, but is trespassing on land that belongs to better people. Love, he thinks, is accidental, fleeting — he can't possibly deserve it.

Very often, when Elise and Jamey talk in the apartment, drinking coffee, she sits with knees spread, feet tilted on the dirty outer edges of her sneakers, seeming bored and sullen. He'll falter, sensing animosity. It's just that she can't look at him — he's too much. He's a prince of this apartment, his eyes black and doubtful, uncertain of the maple burning in the window even while he's enchanted by the red leaves.

She's ahead of him, and while she does think he'll catch up someday, it's lonely waiting for it.

"Is something wrong?" he'll ask, shy and concerned.

She'll look like: *Duh,* and laugh. "*No.* Why?"

She can't force him to know things.

There's a deli on Tenth Street she likes.

The Pakistani cabdrivers, with their burnt-yellow or salmon button-down shirts and creased brown hands, get her drinking tea and eating English muffins toasted with cheap strawberry jam.

Lester owns the deli, and his retarded son Brian does most of the cooking while Lester gossips and handles money. Brian is obsessed with baseball cards, and customers bring them to him. Brian acts like a woman who just got a sapphire bracelet from her lover, squealing and clapping his hands to his chest. Everyone makes lopsided smiles when this happens.

"You got it, Bri," they say, pleased and embarrassed by his effusive thanks.

The bells jangle above the door; it's mainly men who come and go. A dollar bill is thumbtacked to the wall, and so saturated with the fumes of grease and coffee and sweat, it must weigh five times its normal weight, and it hangs there like leather.

Old East Village natives come in.

"Gimme a bacon egg 'n' cheese and a coffee light wit cream," they say.

Elise can sit here all day, with no sports section in front of her, no notebook to scribble in. She barely listens to the soap operas playing on the TV above the refrigerated sodas, a strange choice of channel but

Elise thinks the men are comforted by women being vaguely present, in their chiffon robes, hair body-waved, not demanding anything, gliding into gardens with fountains and through hospital rooms full of lilies.

She brought Jamey here once, and he couldn't see why she thinks the place is so great.

"See yez 'round," says one guy, folding the paper under his arm.

"Till tomorra," says Lester, and he grabs the metal spatula and fixes something, chastising Brian, but he promptly hands it back, kissing Brian on the cheek.

Elise already knew he would kiss his son like that, right then. Her heart is set to the same time.

Jamey's come to love his sidewalk-bench lunch on Fifth and Seventy-Second, and when he feels in his blazer pocket for a napkin, he finds a valet ticket from a yacht club in Massachusetts, and the nub of a lime Life Savers roll, and a key to something. Like clues to a crime that he still has to solve.

He looks at life around him — a nanny walking children, who are animatedly talking over each other about lions and candy apples, the light filtering through trees and buildings and clouds, the yawning pretzel guy on the corner, and a gray-haired man in a tweed jacket walking a Pomeranian. Jamey receives it all like ocean spray on his face, smoke from a bonfire, pollen on your soul after a day in the garden. He's roosting in the heart of the city, among human lives, getting stink and oil and spit on his hands. This daily baptism of the city — he loves it. He collects it. Maybe he *is* gaining on Elise.

Their phone rings and Jamey answers.

"Jamey! It's Binks, darling. How on Earth ah you?" she purrs.

"Great, I'm great, how are you?"

"Bats and I would love to have you and your lady friend for dinner, Jamey. How would next Thuhzz-day evening work, darling?"

"I think it would be fine," he can't help saying. "Sure."

"I could just tell at the christening that things are amiss. I left the church that day, and this is what was going through my mind: *Make things right for my Jamey.*"

"That's — thank you, Binkie. Thank you."

Binkie — what are *you up to*? She's diaphanous, but in a flinty way, like a seashell. Metallic layers. She's the sound of a martini pitcher stirred with a sterling spoon. The smell of Après L'Ondée and thin cigarettes. She was handed more personality than other mortals, and chemically fertilized in a glasshouse — now her bionic strength allows her to teleport platters of watercress sandwiches from the kitchen to the library, where she's beating her friend at backgammon. Her own dogs fear her. Her staff never needs disciplining because they live in terror — her authority hums on a subsonic level to all the creatures in the land.

Jamey's ventured before into her Newport bedroom — the vanity set reminded him of a war throne.

She believes her grandson will do what she says.

Goddamn, she can gossip and growl and coo, and he suddenly understands that her star power — the part of her that really sells tickets — is the abyss between the two Binkies. It's exciting to experience such a discrepancy, and he knows he's performed in the same split manner in the past, and it's a demonstration of control to keep the selves separate. Her public persona and private person are so distant from each other. He can't help but wonder if they ever meet, and if it's once a day, or once a year, and what it's like.

"Jamey?" Binkie says suspiciously. "You sound fah-r away."

"I'm right here," he assures her.

Ah, pale yellow roses and Rolaids and gin. Breakfast trays painted with horses and riders. Binkie, the one and only. He can hear her rings clacking on the plastic phone, and he chuckles, envisioning with amusement the bejeweled suntanned manicured grip his grandmother thinks she has on his balls. And she does.

Jamey and Elise are welcomed into the home of Binkie and Bats Hyde, at Fifth Avenue near Sixty-Fourth Street, by a black woman with an eye patch.

Two Westies race down the staircase, and a squid of candles hangs from an iced cake of a ceiling. The silk curtains shine, still and demure like a dress worn by a matron to a ball, pressed against the windows' sides, and on the dappled, rainy street beyond, headlights and brake lights surge and stop mutely.

It reminds Elise of *Gone with the Wind,* and she can smell housework done by many hands — polish and cream and soap, the bad breath of a vacuum. This place is a domestic stadium.

Jamey and Elise are quickly separated, like

kids at a police station, hauled into rooms for questioning.

But they're not questioned.

Elise is shown the orchidarium.

"The what?" Elise asks, as she stumbles into this damp atrium.

Pointing to a hot-purple bloom with a hairy gullet, Binkie says: "This is a Venus Slipper. Found in Finland, of course."

"Right," Elise agrees.

"This is a Blood-red Odontoglossum. Ecuador."

Walking through the greenhouse, Elise feels like this woman is drugging her. Binkie puts orchids and more orchids into Elise's face, then looks into Elise's eyes to see if she's succumbing.

At the tour's end, Binkie hands Elise her own orchid, writes a gilt-edged note.

"Instructions. These are temperamental creatures, darling. Ring me if you run into difficulty."

Meanwhile, in the wood-paneled salon, Bats is making a presentation of a 1925 Patek Philippe watch, a relic from Great-Grandfather Aaron Balthazar Hyde.

"*Wear* it for godsakes, James."

Bats believes it's gauche to buy luxury possessions. They should be won in a bet, or inherited and worn daily — even if they belong in a safe-deposit box. Or acquired and neglected. He loves that the fishing camp upstate is rarely used, the *LIFE* magazines moldy in its tartan-couch living room. He owns a corn-yellow Beechcraft, which sits in a barn at a friend's Florida estate, and he thinks of the plane the way a man thinks of a woman he fell in love with on a trip and lusts for *because* he won't see her again.

"Watches weren't made for sitting in drawers," he says testily, as if Jamey had said they were made for sitting in drawers.

At dinner, Elise thinks everyone — staff and grandparents — have the faces of nurses: expressions that combine lonely eyes and very big smiles. They watch as if a dazed and bloody girl is stepping from a car wreck to live a last couple lucid moments. It's a stoic high point in their manners to interact with her straight-faced, refraining from shock or disgust.

"And what ah your interests, Elise?"

"Um, I don't know. Basketball?"

What did Binkie mean by saying they wanted something good for us, when she and Jamey talked on the phone? Do they see he loves me? Can they tell we're good for each other?

She keeps smiling, because she forgets to smile when she's nervous, and then people think she's a cunt. Elise picks at the truffled scallops and spinach soufflé. Jamey shrugs at her; they're both just waiting.

The maid who greeted them now bends stiffly to Elise, offering almond cake.

Elise picks up the flat shovel of a knife, slides a slice onto her plate.

"What happened to your eye?" she asks, gesturing at the patch.

A tsunami of silence crashes over the table.

The maid straightens her back, and says, in monotone: "An operation."

And moves to the next guest.

But a black hole in the night has been rent, and finger bowls and cigarette packs and pearls risk being swallowed into the void.

They retire to the den, and dogs wing the fireplace like beastly angels.

Everyone is served sherry on a silver tray, and Elise takes one sip of the sour cough syrup and tries not to spit it out.

Mr. Graham Smythe arrives, like a spontaneous friend, even though he's the family lawyer.

"Ah! Graham, you know my grandson James Hyde," says Bats.

"Of course," says Graham, beaming.

Hands are shaken.

"And this is his friend Elise Perez."

"Elise, pleasure," he says, offering his big white hand.

"I'll leave you all to it!" Bats says, and does just that.

Elise and Jamey look at each other as Graham takes papers from his briefcase. Jamey is not the first Hyde to be handled — although the indiscretions usually take place on private and massive playgrounds and are easier to navigate.

Marital infidelity, drug treatment in the guise of a month-long African safari, or curing someone's homosexuality condition, Binkie and Bats conquer all.

"Where shall we begin?" he asks them.

"I guess I don't know," Jamey says in a very careful and even tone.

"Ah!" he says. "I take it Bats hasn't explained what he wants us to discuss."

Jamey looks at Graham as if daring him to continue. "He hasn't, no."

Graham smiles, wrinkling the corners of his yellowing eyes. "This, I think, could be a solution for the whole family."

A maid arrives with Graham's drink diapered in a napkin. Graham twinkles his eyes at her too, and, after sipping from the crystal glass, earnestly explains. "It's a little agreement that spells things out clear as day."

"It's a prenup," Jamey says darkly.

"It's much like a prenuptial agreement, yes, and this one" — he clears his throat — "covers cohabitating, as well as being with child."

Elise looks to Jamey; she's embarrassed by whatever is happening. "A pre-what?" she asks.

Jamey smiles for a minute, sickened, then shakes his head. "I'm not even going to stoop to argue," he says in a bitter voice. "Game over."

He takes her hand and gets up.

In the main foyer, Jamey yells: "We're leaving!"

Binkie flutters in from wherever she was waiting. "James, stay," she says soothingly.

Elise surprises herself by not being able to meet the woman's eyes.

Jamey politely says: "Can you please tell me where our coats are."

Bats glides into the foyer. "Let's have another drink."

Jamey opens rooms and closets. "We're going out in the cold without our coats unless you tell me where to find them."

A maid looks on — anxious, paralyzed — until Binkie nods at her and she fetches their coats.

■ ■ ■ ■

Outside, Elise realizes she has the fucking orchid in her hand. She doesn't want it — but it's a living, breathing, blameless thing. It shouldn't be left on the street.

They get in a cab.

"*God,* I'm sorry, Elise," he says.

"I know."

"They're not going to stop, apparently. The whole family — is rabid," Jamey says.

"No, I get it now," Elise agrees.

Jamey thinks she means she finally sees through his family's bullshit. But that's not it. She sees through his.

"You can say I told you so," he says.

"Nah," she says, looking out the window.

The flower nods over potholes and bumps.

"What's that you got there?" asks the cabbie with curious eyes.

"An orchid," says Jamey.

The cabbie looks like they're trying to pull one over. "That ain't real!"

"It is too," Elise says sullenly, and looks away.

"Wait a minute, why you mad? What'd you do to her, buddy?"

"Long story," says Jamey.

"You should say you're sorry," he warns

Jamey via the rearview. "Even if it ain't your fault. Trust me, I been married twenty-one years."

"I *am* sorry," Jamey says.

"He *is* sorry," Elise corroborates to the cabbie. "That's not the point."

She holds it together until he leaves for work the next morning. Alone, she makes coffee like an automaton. Why didn't she tell them to screw themselves! Because that would confirm everything they think. They're not about to be defeated in a parking-lot cock fight — *They've rigged it so they can hang shit over your head while looking innocent, and you end up looking like the lunatic, the aggressor, the problem.*

She sucks on her cigarette at the kitchen window, dirty sunshine streaming onto her bare feet as she contemplates the bottom line.

Why can't he stand up to his goddamn family for real?

She packs a bag. Her body is light like she can float out of this trouble. She takes the two hundred dollars she stashed in a menthols pack the way her mom always hoarded a twenty in a tampon box, or a ten in the crib.

Holding Buck's face, she rubs her forehead on his.

"You know what's up," she murmurs.

He freezes as she opens the door to leave.

When she closes the door, she stands a minute on the landing because she feels Buck waiting on the other side, can sense the heat of him two feet away from her. He never panics, knowing good behavior is his best chance, but she can hear a low, quiet whine. She can't bear to listen.

She heads to the St. James Hotel, bag slung over shoulder, chewing gum, aviator glasses reflecting New York City, hands shaking. She shacked up at this motel once with a guy who'd just run from home and still had money from pawning his stepdad's power tools.

The candy-pink neon sign is comfortably familiar.

This is where she'll start.

In the room, she sits against the headboard, playing with a nicked switchblade she's had since she turned sixteen.

Why does it have to be so hard? Elise remembers sitting with her mom's friends while they watched game shows and smoked, snow coming down. To them, men are enemies. The more you want a man, the harder you lie and fight.

These women, from teenhood on, had the

guys' babies, mailed pictures and letters to prisons, battled girls in his ladder of lovers.

"Don't let them get comfortable. Make sure they see you touchin' another man's shoulder, you know? Shit, even if you get a smack. Keeps the blood up."

"I wear them little shorts and vacuum when he's watching TV with his crew, and I bend down, girl. He doesn't like that, me showing it off, but it fires him up. Later that night, he comes to me, you know what I'm saying?"

Elise looks onto the warzone of the West Side, onto tarpaper roofs and bodies splayed on the sidewalk and rusting cellar doors and a curbside mountain-scape of garbage bags.

If they were here, the women from her hood — the girls, cousins, aunts — they'd circle her, gesturing like their fingernails are wet, leading with the chin, showing support. It's a riptide — she could drown in their affection and good-intentioned fury. This is when it hurts to be gone, but she can't, she *cannot* go back to them.

When he gets home, there are Elise's keys, with the cobalt rabbit foot, on the kitchen counter.

No note.

He envisions an animal blithely gnawing

off its limb to escape a trap.

How dare she? How could she . . .

Come evening, she buys a hot dog and a Coke on the corner, and sits on the Alice-in-Wonderland-blue bed. A roach watches from the corner of the room, antennae waving.

She's come here to imagine life without him. He's everything now. He is her life.

Picture him gone. She's not being sincere in imagining separation. It's like running her finger through the candle flame — it should hurt but doesn't.

Come on. Feel it.

There, that's it!

Everything diminished to ordinary proportions — a spiritual reality that can kill a person fucking dead. The world shrinks, loses inner light, becomes a gray and hard site. *I just don't want to go there.*

The TV is stricken with lines but she watches it anyway, her big feet in athletic socks crossed on the bed.

Gorbachev says Chernobyl shows the sinister force of nuclear energy. United States calls it premature to draw conclusions about Syrian complicity in recent terrorism. Haitians are destroying voodoo temples and killing priests and priestesses.

A pornography panel has called for a reversal in the nation's law enforcement and prosecution of distributors. A whale who charmed people as she swam off the Connecticut coast for fourteen months has been found shot to death.

Elise stubs out her cigarette, turns sideways on the bed, and spends the night with eyes open. Around seven a.m., when light starts fingering the curtains, she falls into dreamless sleep.

Jamey walks the East Village with Buck, past the open jaws of bars, past cats licking a tuna can, past the guy with a ghetto-blaster on a stoop. He looks into hallways, yearning for a fight — his bearing makes everyone uncomfortable, as if Baryshnikov is loitering in the streets.

"Can I help you, boy?" spits one guy in a bell hat.

"Looking for my girlfriend," Jamey says.

Buck growls at another man who shuffles too close.

At a Third Avenue deli, Jamey buys a cheese sandwich and a root beer. He eats the sandwich, pops the soda, and drinks the whole thing. He burps, staring into pool halls and church foyers and burger joints.

Jamey sizzles through the environment like acid.

He's brain-dead at work, hair curling over one eye, pale as an opium addict.

"Did someone party like a rock star?" Clark asks coyly.

Jamey languishes in the apartment, with no idea how to reach her mother. No friends' numbers — he's not sure there are friends. Robbie's in Miami or some other fantastical paradise.

She's an orphan and he liked that until now. She was dependent on him and without a jury of family and friends.

This fall day is flat. No forgiveness to the afternoon, just straight particles of air. Buck watches Jamey from where he can also see the door if his lady returns. There's a measure of blame in the dog's eyes.

Jamey imagines the fuzz on her braids, the way she hides her smile when he comes home from work, her standing in a man's wife-beater (that barely covers her pussy) in the morning light and watering the plants, her pigeon-foot strut down the sidewalk as she tells a long story with hands splayed.

He's been sitting here for an hour, fully clothed in the empty bathtub, smoking menthols from a pack she left behind, and ashing in the drain, bare heels on the rim.

His hair is greasy and his dimple acts up when he grinds his teeth.

He thinks this whole thing looks like a prank.

It always struck him as suspicious — how she showed up, the girl next door, and kept after him until he fell in love, this choosing between her and his family — it's too biblical, too tragic, too concise a conundrum for a life as amoral as his.

He's never had to be moral. He falls into one of those crevices: a certain kid in a certain society in a certain generation where no decisions remain because his ancestors have finished every single thing within reach.

While tapping ash into the drain, he feels a revelation like adrenaline: *If everything is already done, maybe I'm here to undo things.*

He pictures himself on a pyramid, lugging off its top stone, and sending it to the ground, where it bounces silently. He takes a last drag and crushes the butt on the worn porcelain between his thighs.

She smokes out the window. The night drips and pops with prostitutes, drug dealers and addicts, runaways, drifters. Her fourth-floor room is too high to hear anything but the shrillest hooker-to-hooker "Girl!" and car horns held for psychotic lengths of time.

She does jumping jacks to get her blood flowing.

She smokes on the bed, her consciousness a kingdom where many things take place but nothing wins or loses. Growing up in a hood whose one playground had one working swing, whose candy stores sold more heroin than candy, whose public library was a carcass of a building, she knows how to amuse herself.

After a while, she ventures out, spends seventy-five cents on a Wonder Bread loaf, feeds pigeons from a church stoop. Their feet are red like gum that's been chewed.

"I'm gonna pay for another night," she says to the front desk. "Four-oh-Four."

The clerk takes her money without saying anything.

A man whose flattop is bleached yellow leans against the lobby wall and sizes her up. Elise imperceptibly shakes her head no. He looks away.

The room is very lonely, but she doesn't feel lonely. She feels the presence of her childhood, but doesn't reminisce on things like they were completed incidents. The past is layers of cake with cream in between, and she can bite through it on one fork; it's a deck of playing cards being shuffled and shuffled and shuffled; it's what she sees when she spins and spins, light streaking her mind with white and ghost-pink and nuclear-blue. It's poodles coughing, rough kisses from her mother, blood in the bathroom sink, policemen knocking in the night, flowers from the supermarket, funerals in damp churches, melted popsicles — all of it is still happening, it's alive and recurring. Her memory works like a beat.

"Buck. Where is she?" Jamey asks, half expecting an answer.

He's lying on the bed, looking at a Polaroid from a Jones Beach afternoon. She's wearing a string bikini and black sneakers, holding up her hands as if to stop the hours, laughing, aviators reflecting him.

Jamey limps to work. Clark sends him home before lunch.

"Whatever you have, child, I do not want it, thank you very much," Clark says from a safe distance, and shoos Jamey out of the office.

Clark can taste heartbreak like a rotten egg.

In his building's hall, Jamey hears the phone, sprints upstairs.

He's jamming the key into the lock when the phone stops. He storms into the apartment, and Buck hides in the bedroom.

Jamey sinks onto the couch.

The phone rings again. "Elise?"

"Yeah."

"Jesus fucking lord," he says.

They've grown up years in a matter of days — they know it when they hear each other.

"I had to *think,*" she explains.

"Why did you leave to think when you could have stayed and talked?"

Silence for a moment. "So let's talk."

"Where are you?" he says impatiently.

"St. James Hotel."

His taxi gets stuck in traffic around Forty-Second Street, among sandwich-board evangelists, under beaded-light LIVE SHOW signs, so he pays the guy and jumps out.

He enters the lobby in a way that makes the clerk sit up.

"Four-oh-Four," Jamey tells him without stopping.

He flies up the staircase like a cat.

"That was fast," she says as she opens the door.

She's sullen and unreadable. Shoulders and boys' hips cocked in opposition.

He walks by without touching her.

"Say whatever you need to say," he says.

"Fucking calm down first!"

"I'm pissed. You left without leaving a note." He's sitting with legs crossed, as if meeting with businessmen in a parlor somewhere. His face is calm, the broad mask trained to be flat, while she can see the red in his eyes.

"Jamey," she soothes.

"Just tell me."

Elise looks at the ceiling.

"Speak," he says loudly.

"Why do they have such a hold on you?"

Expressionless. "My family?"

"If you can call them that."

"They've given me everything, Elise," he says like he's breaking horrific news as gently as possible.

Elise shrugs. "So give it back."

It takes him a while but he finally grins, considering this. Then he laughs, that golden, filthy laugh. It fractures his skepticism — yolk runs from the cracked shell.

"What?" she says.

"That's such a good idea."

Her eyes — outlined in black — open. "Really?"

"Come here." He buries his head in her waist.

They rock, and laugh.

"Elise, Elise . . ." He sighs.

"Jamey, Jamey," she says, to be funny.

"We're fucked," he says, muffled.

She kisses his head.

"That was way too simple," she says, and they laugh more.

"Goodbye, fortune," he says, and lets it go like a balloon zigzagging up to the sun.

October 1986

Sunshine sifts through white oaks and mulberries on Seventh Street, and someone in the building sings scales. Two guys in leather trench coats sit on the stoop across the way, sharing a pint of Gallo in a bag. Upstairs, Elise folds his laundry while he cooks her eggs for lunch.

"I could literally divorce my family — I've heard of people doing that," he tells her, closing up an omelet.

Albert Peterson, a fellow Buckley mate, got himself emancipated at fifteen, and his SoHo loft was promptly overrun with street kids and parasites. Albert separated from his parents but not from his trust fund, and the ants found the sugar cube.

"I think Albert went at it backwards," Jamey says. "No need for divorce if you just get rid of the capital."

He and Elise scour the Yellow Pages as they eat.

They come upon Rodion Slavin Flits, Esq., at 199 Neptune Avenue in Brighton Beach. *Serving Brooklyn since 1978. A Personal & Empathetic Friend. Specializing in Wills, Family Law & Probate.* Mainly they like his name.

"What's 'empathetic'?" Elise squints.

"He cares about us."

That weekend they get a cold front. One evening, they're walking Buck on Third Avenue and see a sweatshirt on a fence, white with *Jordache* in gold letters, the stallion in mid-gallop. Elise holds it up to her shoulders.

"I don't want to know where that thing's been," Jamey says, watching her in the lamplight.

"You have this whole plan to be broke, and you can't handle a sweatshirt on a fence?" she tells him.

At Goodwill, she buys him a red wool sweater (which she washes in the kitchen sink and dries on the radiator), and Isotoner gloves. She finds a wok on the curb. She takes scissors to the coupon section of the paper.

She thinks about Lorena, a diabetic Puerto Rican lady who wore her white hair in a bandanna — her Turnbull apartment spun and glittered with junk. Lorena gardened in the summer on her "patio," a tiny enclave where she grew herbs and vegetables, watering them from her wheelchair. During August, she'd let Elise pick cherry tomatoes off the plant. Elise can still remember the heat of the fruit as she bit into it. The little seeds were orange tinged with green, the liquid a viscous blob.

"Su-*per*-ior to store-bought," Lorena said in an imposing voice. "You best believe that."

Tuesday morning is one torrential rain, the street gutters carrying beer cans and dead leaves into drains. Right before they leave the apartment, it stops.

The sky is now deafeningly silent.

On the subway, he reads the newspaper while she sits forward, elbows on knees, and he rubs her back with one hand. It's a long way to where they're going. The train finally rattles up from the tunnels and into the cityscape. Elise watches graveyards and junk lots and scorched buildings fly by.

"What stop is it again?" Jamey says.

"Ocean Parkway. It's next."

They get off to a cheap block. In the barbershop window, neon shears glow. Every house has a different look: new brick or red siding or butterscotch-yellow cement. But this world is tidy. The gates all lock and open, the mailboxes aren't crooked, the beach chairs in each fenced-in sidewalk front yard are in good shape.

"Here it is," Elise says, biting her thumb.

A damp American flag hangs from the peaked porch roof. The sign by the metal screen door says: BY APPOINTMENT ONLY.

Jamey rings the bell.

A woman opens the door, offers her hand. "I'm Marianne, Rodie's wife, we talked on the phone, how you doing."

Her shirt is zebra-print, and a blond pile of ringlets is bobby-pinned on her head. She has lavender eyes and marionette lines around her smile.

Jamey almost trips, the carpet is so thick.

"You two want coffee? Something stronger? Get the rain out of your bones?"

"Mmmh, coffee," Elise says.

Turquoise-and-gold-wallpaper hallway, past a dining table stacked with mail, to a tiny office, where Rodion, white-haired, in a velvet jacket, plays a wobbly Haydn record on a turntable. The cave is tangy with European cologne.

"Good afternoon." He shakes hands, his Brooklyn accent etched with Russian.

When they sit, he lights a brown cigarette.

"Well," he says. "What does this regard?"

Jamey and Elise look at each other.

"My inheritance —"

"You're competing with stepsiblings," Rodion suggests.

"No."

"You're worried about the tax."

"Completely the opposite."

"There is no opposite," Rodion says, amused. "You're not excited by taxes."

"I don't want the inheritance." Jamey looks apologetically at Rodion, because he knows this is a silly thing he's brought to the man's doorstep.

Rodie grins, shakes his head at the strangely decent boy sitting in his office, while Marianne delivers dark coffee in bone-china cups. She points to a sugar bowl and creamer, and mouths: *sugar* and *cream,* then winks and leaves.

"If whatever *incited* this decision happened in the past week, we're not going to discuss anything today," Rodion says.

"It started the day I was born."

"What did?"

"They try to own him," Elise jumps in belligerently. "They use his trusts against him and shit like that."

"Ah," says Rodion, and then he offers cigarettes, and Elise takes one. He holds a gold lighter to it while he evaluates the couple.

"It's called a renunciation," Rodion says. "Why don't you give me a sense of where we stand."

Jamey tells Rodie his net worth. Then he watches Rodie consider that number with operatic drama.

"Who are you, for chrissakes?" asks Rodie quietly.

"James Balthazar Hyde, of Hyde, Moore & Kent. The problem child."

"James Balthazar Hyde," Rodie says, sipping black coffee from the delicate cup.

"Yes sir."

"I fear you're being idealistic, or vindictive — neither of which are criminal actions — but I want us to consider your best interests here."

"I have."

Rodie shuffles papers, and nods his grand head. "What's harmful in thinking about it some more, James?"

"I'm wasting time."

"Why not take these millions and do good?"

"When something is poisoned at the root, it won't flower," Jamey says.

Rodion smooths his lapels, keeps nodding. Then he sighs: "I don't feel right about this.

But we can do it if you say so."

While Jamey and Rodion start the carbon-copy forms, talking in that low-voice litigious way, Elise smokes and watches. Whenever Jamey glances up at Rodie, he almost looks like he could kiss the lawyer — his mouth is so pure.

As Rodion adds up numbers, Elise thinks: It *is* too bad it has to be all or nothing. She realizes her hands are sweaty, and her mind is racing with lost possibilities. She didn't know she'd harbored a secret dream of buying her mother a house, but she knows it now, as the dream gets extinguished.

"How do you feel about everything, Elise?" Rodion asks, tapping a Waterman pen in his palm.

She shrugs, tosses her braids back. "Got to do what you got to do."

Rodion stands up to stretch, and asks them to have lunch with the family.

"I *insist,*" he says.

They wander into the kitchen, where Marianne is cooking beef stroganoff, the window valance making a shadow of lace on her face.

A girl, around five or six, is rolling tiny balls out of Play-Doh at the table. When she looks up, Jamey knows by the hanging mouth and shark teeth, plump cheeks, round eyes, that she has Down syndrome.

"This is Bethany," Rodion says with tenderness.

"Hi sweetheart," Elise says.

Elise asks to help make Play-Doh balls, and Bethany grins wetly: "Yeah!"

"Look at that, she's good with children," Marianne says. "How long you two been together, long time?"

"Only eight months," Jamey says. "It feels like longer."

But Elise is looking at the lustrous open request of Bethany's eyes, the chubby dimpled hands that rub a tired face, the tiny bum plunked on the chair, feet kicking air as she works the assembly line of dirty yellow clay.

Now Elise can't block out a row of phantom kids' eyes from another home, all beaming from one bed, reflecting a Bambi night-light plugged into the wall.

Those kids wonder where Elise went, why she's not there to kiss them good night, to tell them morning will get here soon. Elise used to stamp fear from their hearts. She told them *You're safe* even though it wasn't true. They knew the fear could come back, they would recognize it like a sleeping face knows the legs and wings of a roach crossing your cheek even before you wake up.

Or worse, the fear would return as your brother's friend, who invites you into your own mama's room, because she's at work, to show you something, and you get a cookie after, and he'll kill you if you say a word.

Yeah, sorry I couldn't stick around, kids! Elise thinks. *It's been fun. Good luck with everything. Oh, the world will treat at least half of you like half a person at best, not worth any investment cause you're already damaged and undereducated and emotionally weird, even though yeah, they can see something kind of great in you, but isn't it just a losing battle, throwing good money after bad? Your environment is so fucked that your behavior gets more and more impossible, till society claims they can hardly use you for anything but its lowest tasks — an orderly at an old folks' home, garbage-truck guy — and you'll barely support yourself.*

BUT you could try this little piece of candy you put in a pipe, and you'll be beamed into white light and heavenly love, which will in five minutes turn into a greater problem than you ever knew, so you'll then have a new problem to solve, and you'll solve it by doing things you never dreamed of doing. Good luck with that!

Not sure in the meantime who's gonna dress your little bodies, make a ghost costume or Magic-Marker a Batman mask onto your face for Halloween, guide your hand to spell your name 'cause you keep making the s *backwards, change your pajamas if you wet the bed, tell you you're special on your birthday, hold you after you had a nightmare and you can't stop crying, put you on the bus your first day of school, teach you to catch snowflakes in your hand on the last day of winter. . . .*

The kids in Bridgeport know her now as another person who just vanished — like their dad went upstate, and their sister hit the streets. *So sorry! Hope you manage. I'm sure you'll understand that I felt like there was no other way for me to leave than to leave completely, absolutely, to never fucking see your mischievous and hopeful eyes one more fucking time.*

It's getting dark early as they stand in line. *Coney Island Cyclone, here we come.* They move through a labyrinth of fences, the late sun collecting like gasoline rainbows in garbage-can water and gutter puddles and bottle caps.

"How you feel?" Elise asks.

Jamey shrugs, tries to smile. "Liberated?"

They're first, they're next. A carny wipes

down a seat for them. Elise holds Jamey's hand, presses it, for her comfort or his assurance.

They sit in the cab. They get belted in, the clunk of the metal bar closing and locking, and then the silence, the emptiness of time and thought as the roller coaster is sent into movement.

And then the glide and click, jewelry rattled and bones jangled. The face drawn open then closed. The stomach distended then crushed shut, exultation and nausea. Seeing and smelling the top of the sky, on a lonesome New York ride, not in each other's arms but instead in the arms of the day.

Amazing that such a rickety old machine can take them so high.

Clark's in a mood today. His morning bloody mary hasn't helped his hangover. Now he's just cockeyed. He's bawling out anyone who gets in his way, cursing Gillian up and down for lukewarm coffee, and telling Mitford he's dressed like a Mexican pool boy and should go home and change.

Jamey tries to be invisible, the way he's always done when the adults around him rant and rave. He's the little boy pressing himself into the backseat of a swerving car.

Jamey stares at his own hand, clutching a

mug. It's not a child's hand.

"I think I'll go home too," Jamey suddenly tells Clark.

"Excuse me?" Clark says, mid–pain au chocolat, licking a flake of croissant from his oily finger.

"I'm done at Sotheby's for good, actually. But thank you for having me here this whole time."

"You're . . . quitting?" Clark asks.

"I just quit. Yes."

Clark stares at Jamey swaggering down the hall, jacket slung over shoulder while his other hand undoes the top buttons of his shirt.

"Don't come back then!" Clark feels venomous, and they both understand something greater happened than Jamey resigning from an auction house. Jamey has somehow spit in Clark's eye. Clark wants nothing to do with him, sniffing treason like a bloodhound. He's heard rumors anyway. Before Jamey's even sealed into the elevator, Clark is whispering with anyone who will gather to his desk.

Elise gets butterflies when Jamey tells her he left his job.

"Really?" she asks. " 'Bout time, I guess."

Swinging, he let go of one branch before

grasping another.

She also explored that in-between place, after leaving Bridgeport and before arriving at Robbie's. Hitchhiking with sweatshirt hood up, she looked like a boy, then she pulled it back to say thank you once in the seat. Her eyes slid back and forth, *blink-blink,* as she devoured polluted Queen Anne's lace along highways, Indian town names on green signs in Pennsylvania and New Jersey, truck-stop counters with lemon meringue under Saran Wrap in a pie case. She panhandled in Syracuse, alone on the median, while cars passed in either direction. When you don't have to be anywhere, you can figure out where to go.

Now Jamey and Elise look at classifieds, draw hearts around listings. They hang in free fall from one life to the next. Jamey's got a few grand left in his account so they just doodle and talk.

Cocktail Waitress. Pharmacy Technician. Milk-truck Man. Limo Driver. Front Desk. Aquatics Coordinator at YMCA in Bensonhurst. Macy's Merchandiser. Coffee-shop Counter Girl in Dyker Beach. Experienced Fish Cutter in Midwood.

They hear a poetry reading by a tall man whose pale red hair falls over his face as he bends above his pages at the microphone.

Later she play-pushes Jamey on the sidewalk: "I'll die for your sins if you live for mine."

"What?" he says, pulling the knit cap over her eyes.

"It was in the poem!" she says, moving the hat up. "Didn't you listen?"

They go watch *After Hours* by Scorsese, then see *Breathless* by Goddard. They eat cabbage soup at Odessa, watch the girls with massive teased hair, cat eyes, and sleeveless shirts as they laugh raucous and high with leather-vested boys, all picking fries off the plate in the center, dragging it through ketchup and slapping it on a tongue.

Their days and nights are spent in cafés and bars, movie theaters, parks, and they talk about the things people near them are talking about: AIDS, women's rights, the welfare system. The topics jump from one group at a table, smoking and drinking beer, to another, like fleas from one dog to the next dog.

It's a chilly day, not raining but all the yellow and orange leaves are vaguely wet.

Alex receives the first clues of Jamey's renunciation as Rodion closes accounts and files motions.

"Jamey," his father growls on the phone.

"Alex," Jamey says in a low voice, trying to be calming, but he ends up imitating his dad's voice.

"What is the *problem* with you?" His dad sounds like Phillip Drummond.

Jamey bites his lip. He thought he'd feel guilty when this moment arrived, but he feels great. He felt guilty *before,* knowing he'd never fulfill the contract of being a Hyde but getting paid anyway. "I just don't want money that doesn't belong to me —"

"It's family money."

Jamey pauses. "Robber-baron money —"

"Oh, you kids *love* to throw that term around. Do you know what the Hyde Foundation gives every year?"

"For tax deductions, you mean?"

"I *make* jobs in this city — *I* create work for people who would be *homeless.*"

Jamey shakes his head in amazement. "*You* do?"

"*Yes,* I do," Alex says, his voice hoarse. "We provide a better life for so many folks —"

While Alex is blustering on, Jamey disconnects the wire from the wall, permanently, walking outside to leave the avocado-green telephone on the curb. He lets hatred mushroom-cloud in his head, after years and years of cold war with his pops.

He stands and looks at the phone on the clammy cement. He gently kicks it over, the receiver clattering out of the handle, the coiled line stretching. He skips up the steps, whistling like a farm boy.

One day, Elise enters the building and suddenly the landlord's door opens. It's Mrs. Gorowski in a lace-collared dress, eyes wide under her Dee Dee Ramone bowl cut. Meat is cooking, and this joins the smell of ginger, ancient secrets, amber, and old leather in their apartment.

The landlady fervently waves her in, then pulls Elise onto the couch to watch a PBS special with her. The show *is* beautiful, hallucinatory. Elise stares at orange and turquoise saris, palaces so massive and ornate they seem imaginary, dark men with white mustaches walking barefoot through mist and woods, children with gleaming exquisite ways of staring at the camera, paint on their forehead.

"Mother India," the narrator intones. "The *cradle* of civili-*za*-tion. The only place where history has *not* been forgotten."

When Jamey asks later about her afternoon, Elise says it was random, and awesome.

Elise and Jamey walk up Second Avenue. It's brisk, the wind reddening everyone's cheeks and causing people to look down while they walk, and hold hands, or wrap arms around shoulders. Jamey likes the rude and undiscerning weather today.

Approaching the market on the corner, whose shelves are crooked and whose floor is covered in roach traps and rat shit, Jamey asks her to wait while he goes in for milk and cereal, he'll make it fast.

An automated horse is stock-still on its metal stand, and Elise checks her fur-coat pockets for coins. She pops in a quarter, and sits while it moves in a suggestive way. Her legs are too long, her shins almost touch the ground.

The pale horse gleams against the dark sidewalk.

Jamey comes out with no paper bags. Just a crazy look.

"What's up?" Elise asks, worried.

The horse has stopped.

Jamey moves toward her.

He gets down on one knee, takes a gumball-machine ring out of his pocket. Its chip of glass shines.

"Elise," he says. "Will you marry me?"

She can hardly look at him, overwhelmed with emotion like a kid who has to hide her face in her mother's skirt. But there's nowhere to go.

And this drab avenue, with its somewhat hostile breeze ruffling litter and sending plastic bags into the sky, this ordinary afternoon, is suddenly alive with candy hearts.

"Will you?" he says.

The dark traffic of possible answers moves in his eyes.

"Yes," her voice cracks. "Yes. . . ."

She jumps onto him, almost knocking him over, and they stand up, she's clinching her legs around his waist, and they stagger, laughing, and she howls at the sky, not giving a fuck who's watching them. Elise thinks she's going to have a heart attack, she can barely breathe. Eventually she falls off, and they kiss again, and again. She holds out her giant hand like a starfish and they both stare at her ring.

NOVEMBER 1986

November is laden with parties and feasts and business in New York City. The cold streets make everyone feel alive, the cold plush and rich now, as opposed to March when the cold is cold and makes the city feel hard up.

Every day, Elise passes the cherry-red neon sign reading PSYCHIC next to a gold hand painted on the glass. She finally peeks in.

"Don't be shy," beckons the woman sitting at a silk-draped table. "I'm Zelda." The woman holds out fishnet-gloved hands. She's manly, with a bulbous nose and blond wig, but her eyes are tired in such an antique and drastic way, she must have the magic.

"Elise," she says, swiping off her knit hat and stuffing it in her pocket. "I got a question about . . . about timing."

"Sit down, honey."

Zelda and Elise hold hands and shut their eyes.

Sandalwood incense burns in thunderclouds of sickly sweet smoke, and a child complains beyond the beaded curtain, and a soft female voice answers in another language.

Zelda's black-lined eyes press closed. "You're straightforward. You don't lie. You tell it like it is."

Silence as she reads the hand-holding.

"You love. You're a lover. Unafraid."

A cat purrs against Elise's leg.

Zelda's brow crumples. "You need to do it soon, whatever it is. I feel urgency in your stars."

Zelda shakes Elise's hands so she opens her eyes too.

"Something's coming. Do the deed."

Elise hands Zelda a twenty as the fortuneteller lights a clove cigarette and snaps a can of Tab open. "I like your jacket," she says as Elise zips up her white fur to leave.

Elise tries on white dresses at Gimbels. The store connects to the Herald Square subway station, so she used to shoplift there. Everyone did — it was so easy to get away. Back then, she watched women browsing, and wanted to walk out one day with her own brown Gimbels bag.

A saleswoman approaches, head tilted like it's a medical condition.

"You know that there's a summertime dress, right?" the woman says in a Southern accent, with smiley antagonism.

"Oh. No, I didn't."

"That's why it's on sale, honey," she says through nicotine-striated teeth. "What are you looking for?"

"A wedding dress," Elise says. "But not for a wedding."

"I'm not following, sugar."

"We're going to the courthouse," Elise says.

"Uh-huh."

Elise then looks at the lady, pulling her braids insecurely.

"Baby! You're not gonna cry, are you?"

"I just want to look like a bride."

"Well, praise the lord! Let *me* find you something, honey," the woman snaps her gum. "And I'm Cheryl-Lou, got that? What's your date?"

"November nineteenth."

"So soon! We're gonna try wool suits, honey. Let's do Audrey-Hepburn-daytime-wedding, mmkay? Real class. Grace Kelly at a royal luncheon."

She hangs garments around the changing

room, whose carpet teems with silverfish, as if serving a queen.

Elise finally likes a suit with pearl buttons. The shoulders stand up, and the pencil skirt tapers.

"That. Is. Divine," says Cheryl-Lou, manically destroying her gum with her tongue and teeth.

"Yeah?"

"Hold on," the woman says, putting up one finger. "Shoes."

She brings back Fendi pumps. "Try these."

"How much are they though?" Elise asks.

"They're eighty percent off, girl! That's because of these here marks," she says, pointing to damage. "Who's the lucky man?"

"His name is Jamey."

"What's he *like,*" she singsongs.

"He's — I can't explain him."

"You don't have to. I can tell by the way you say his name."

Cheryl-Lou arranges Elise's hair, and they both look into the mirror.

"Beautiful," the saleswoman says quietly.

Elise looks at the reflection, worried. "Really?"

Cheryl-Lou is mad. "*Yes,* really. Are you scared or something?"

Elise holds the woman's eyes in the looking glass and shrugs.

Cheryl-Lou shakes her head vehemently. "Life's too short, sweetie, to think twice."

"I know this is what I want."

"Then what's the trouble, little lady?"

That's a good question, Elise thinks.

Standing in line to pay, she thinks about being sixteen and trying to make up for leaving her mom high and dry, doing penance one baby's bath at a time, cleaning up beer bottles and ashtrays every Sunday morning, handing over a hundred dollars a week from her Payless job, fifty from the Burger King night shift, a kiss on the cheek, coming through on a promise made, patience.

Every time she walked the block back then, sweating in the July sun, or using an umbrella in the soaking rain, picking up greasy food in white bags, the grit of the sidewalk sticking to her wet legs — she would always walk slowly on the way home, and she would know that not everyone was walking with intention the same way she was.

Outside Gimbels, Elise stops to watch a crew breakdance in the drab midtown nowhere land. The star is skinny, shirtless, sweating in the cold. He smiles as he pops and locks, spins on the folded cardboard, his boys moving on the sidelines, calling out, *uh-huh*-ing when he backflips. She wolf-whistles, drops a dollar in the hat, watching, suddenly grinning.

Jamey puts a quarter into the corner pay phone, and dials the lobby number he knows by heart. He watches girls draw in chalk on the sidewalk while it rings.

Teddy the doorman sounds wary when he hears Jamey's voice. "What is it, little fella?"

"Teddy — I want to ask you a big favor."

"Uh-oh," he says, and means it.

"Can you be a witness at my marriage? At the courthouse this Saturday?"

Jamey cradles the phone to his ear.

Teddy quietly laughs. "Yes, son. I can and will. My oh my. Wait till I tell Claudia."

"Will she please come? Lunch is on us — we'll drink Champagne," Jamey says, warmed and moved, his voice thickened. But then he laughs. "You think it's strange I'm asking."

"I do indeed. And I'm not even gonna inquire about why you having a courthouse wedding, son." Teddy laughs again. "I'm just gonna show up."

"You'll be happy for me."

"Very good," he says eventually, with

tenderness, or concern.

Before daybreak, Jamey lies in that half-sleep state when the heart just goes feral, attacks the brain, shits in it, scratches the backs of his eyeballs, howling and frothing. Then he wakes, and can't recall a single dream, and there might not have been any dreams.

He's going to ruin her if he marries her.

You're confused and irrational, he tells himself sternly, *just get up and go forth.*

He takes a shower, makes coffee, forcing one thing after another.

In the shadowy bed, Elise looks up, bleary-eyed, to accept the mug. "Yo, I didn't sleep *at all,*" she claims angrily, like a child, even though she did.

He cups her chin for a kiss. "Good morning."

She pulls away to light a cigarette. "What's good about it?" she jokes.

Her heart is like a bird caught in a house — she can't even catch the poor thing to calm it down and set it free.

They walk hand in hand down the street, a gangly girl in white with cornrows and a red mouth, and him in a suit, hair slicked like an Irish gangster.

The day's so cold it burns throats, and the air irradiates bodies, cell by cell. The leaves are done, so the city is light and pigeons, and windows reflecting sun.

They wait in line at the courthouse. Gretchen and Jacek arrive, and hand Elise a bouquet of violets. Teddy and Claudia huff up the stairs in elegant coats, with a gold-wrapped present.

Teddy takes Elise's hand. "Very nice to meet you," Teddy says.

The line of couples winds down the street, waiting to pass through the secretary's X-ray vision — this old gal in Lucite spectacles makes private bets on who will last, and has been doing so for years.

In the City Clerk's Office, the judge — a man with broad Nigerian cheekbones and an aura of goodwill — reads vows.

"James Balthazar Hyde, do you take Elise Dawn Perez to be your wife?"

"I do."

"Elise Dawn Perez, do you take James Balthazar Hyde to be your husband?"

"I do."

Gretchen uses their Polaroid to take a loud picture of the couple kissing.

At Chanterelle, they clap when the waiter pops the Champagne. Everyone glows from butterscotch shadows reflected by the walls and sun leaking in the ruched curtains.

Jacek toasts with an e.e. cummings poem, and the words bounce like rice around the bride and groom.

Teddy pushes his chair back, crosses his arms. "I thought I would mention today something from your childhood, Jamey. Like how you'd ride your tricycle in circles in the lobby. Or how you always left your encyclopedia on my desk. Or your obsession that year with butterflies."

Jamey smiles at the crumb-strewn tabletop, embarrassed, and Elise curls his black hair around his ear, looking at him.

"Good lord, butterflies this, butterflies that," Teddy complains.

"I know," Jamey admits.

"But I'd rather talk about today then yesterday," Teddy says. "I don't know if I ever saw you happy like this before."

Jamey thanks him, then turns to Elise, chin down, eyes tilted up to hers. "Yeah — this is one of those things people say" — he bites his lip — "but I didn't know I could — love someone like I love you."

Then she sobs, awkwardly raising her flute, its rim stained with red gloss, and Gretchen and Claudia coo and soothe, feed her tissues.

"Why you crying, baby?" asks Claudia.

"I don't know!" she manages to blubber.

She hiccups through lunch, and they all laugh at each tiny *yeep.*

"Champagne helps," Jacek says, pouring.

"It makes it worse!" Claudia chides, laughing.

Walking alone now through the pale-gold afternoon, Jamey takes Elise's hand and she takes it back.

"What is it?" Jamey asks.

Her Fendi heels drag the cement, shoulders low, the way a teenage boy walks.

"We're *married,*" he says.

They pass a pet store, where sickly kittens wrestle in sawdust. An apothecary, with glass jars of herbs and roots, the labels written in script.

"Till death do us part," he says.

They pass a school, its halls dark and empty.

"It just happened so *fast.* And now it's over," she complains, her wires short-circuiting, blinking, and burning up.

"It's only beginning!"

"And nobody in our family saw it," she pouts.

"But we agreed we'd just have friends?"

They march a few more blocks, the winter sun caulking the seams and gaps with black light, until she halts — she lost her flowers!

"We'll find them," Jamey says.

"We're *not* going to find them!" she bawls.

Passersby glare at Jamey consoling her.

The red church door across the street catches his eye. Maybe a little ritual will help, he thinks, panicking.

They walk into the silent space — a bank of candles burns against one wall. Elise cranes her neck to look at the ceiling — robed figures, luminescent lilies, shepherds leaning on a cane.

"Okay, wait here," he whispers, and seats her in the pew.

Jamey finds a priest reading in an alcove. Embroidered tassels hang over his chest, and his chin is red.

"Father," Jamey says quietly. "I hope I'm not interrupting."

"Not at all, son," the man says, lowering eyeglasses, making it clear that Jamey is interrupting.

"My wife is sitting in the pews. We just got married, and she has some questions."

"Ah. How long have you been married?"

Jamey looks at his watch. "Two and a half hours, Father."

The priest opens his eyes like an owl.

They find Elise, kicking one leg, biting her nail. The priest expects drama.

"I understand you two are newlyweds," the priest says.

"Can you, like, make it official?" Elise asks.

The priest looks like they're swindling him. "Official? I don't know of anything fitting your request, young lady, besides an actual ceremony —"

"Could you — just bless us?" Jamey suggests.

"Well, I —" the priest protests.

"Please?" Jamey pulls out his dimple.

"I suppose I could devise something —"

"If you would. As a man of God. As a spiritual leader," Jamey says desperately and condescendingly.

"Well, then. A blessing for your marriage."

The man hums incantations, lights a candle, holds their hands. Elise's blood pressure slowly — slowly — comes down a little.

They walk into the cold night.

"You feel better?" Jamey asks hopefully, and she nods, smiles for him.

They hold hands.

As Jamey talks, she pretends to agree, but she can't hear him. She sees their vague reflections moving from some dirty apartment lobby doors to the amber mirrors and metal shutters of storefronts, and she knows she loves him almost too much to bear.

At home, they take off coats and move around, flaunting a new identity in this familiar context.

"Would you like a drink, Mrs. Hyde?"

They open wine, look out the window, lock the door, stand up and sit down, animating an hour or two.

They meant to have dinner out, but suddenly they lie down. It's like nothing they ever felt. It comes from someplace deeper than existed yesterday or the day before. They lie on their sides, looking at each other, Jamey puts his thumb on her mouth, and she flicks her tongue. Her eyes are pained.

They wake up starving at three a.m. and cook eggs, naked, and toast each other with orange juice.

"I'm nothing without you," he says plainly, holding up his glass of Tropicana.

"And I'm nothing without you," she answers, and they clink.

As filthy as any night was, a New York City morning is always clean. The eyes get washed.

Flowers in white deli buckets are replenished. The population bathes, in marble mausoleums of Upper East Side showers, or in Greenwich Village tubs, or in the sink of a Chinatown one-bedroom crammed with fifteen people. Some bar opens and the first song on the jukebox is Johnny Thunders, while bums pick up cigarette butts to see what's left to smoke.

The smell of espresso and hot croissants. The weather vane squeaks in the sun. Pigeons are reborn out of the mouths of blue windows.

Elise and Jamey look through the classifieds, circling jobs with a felt-tip pen, and drawing rays of sunshine around their favorites.

He asks her to choose where they go for their honeymoon. The only place she knows is Mount Airy Lodge, from its commercials of doe-eyed born-to-party couples in bikinis or parkas.

Elise and Jamey spend time in the heart-shaped bed, and in their very own pool — a cup of chlorinated water, casting spooky blue shadows. They screw the living daylights out of the room, hooked on the sweet pornography of the place. Elise bought a white garter belt and seamed stockings for the weekend. But the most interesting thing happens outside.

As they eat gluey pancakes in the dining

room, Elise stares out the window at the horses in gray snow, and Jamey asks if she wants to ride.

"I never did it before," she says.

"Even better."

Billy's hair is shaved on the sides, long down the back, and he's missing teeth, but he doesn't seem jaded. Elise wonders if he's done so many drugs he's gone back to a child's mind-set, or if he just never developed, and grifted his way through train hopping and circuses and stables with wonder and innocence untouched.

"Most horses feel fear, you understand?" Billy says. "But that don't mean you should be afraid."

"You'll be good," Jamey tells Elise.

Elise puts one sneaker in a stirrup and, with Billy's help, throws her other leg over.

"Holy shit!" she says, breathless.

"There you go, easy now," Billy says, his lower lip fat with tobacco.

The horse side-prances, then stays.

Its bristly flank is more than human. It exceeds life! The hairy and prickly hot flesh outdoing anything of this world she's known so far. Giant muscles and heavy bones moving under her, between her, and with her. Elise bends to lay her beating heart against the horse's back. *So, this exists — this can happen.*

"You're a natural," Jamey shouts as Billy leads them around the corral.

She's never seen an eyeball bigger than her own. The globe is an obsidian jewel in the galactic head. It's a girl — a mare, to use the language — and her hooves move in a pattern like bluegrass or jazz, nothing even-tempered, nothing expected.

"What do you think?" Jamey calls.

She just shakes her head. "Oh my God!" she eventually answers.

Jamey's seen many girls on horses, mostly riders with complex styles and skills, and total authority. But with Elise, black sneakers in the stirrups, her face mottled with incredulity, Billy leading them slowly back to him, he sees how power can be shared to make a different kind of elegance — one more immediate, and less negotiated.

DECEMBER 1986

They're about to be flat broke.

Sparkling winter afternoon. Elise jokes with construction workers down in Battery Park City, walking Buck, lured to this mammoth half-built structure. She asks to try the jackhammer, and they say no — but the boss is looking for runners inside.

"They like girls for that job," says one guy, giving her the up and down.

Elise takes metal steps into the trailer office, where Tommy Bricks is smoking Lucky Strikes and paging through a *Bon Appétit* in his sweater turtleneck.

"Could we help you?"

"I'm looking for a job?"

Tommy looks at Salvatore, whose knees are spread because his belly hangs low, and Salvatore supposedly looks back, although smoky gold-rimmed glasses hide his eyes.

"What kine?" says Tommy.

"Runner?"

Tommy puts a hand on his glossed hair. "You got to spend the days walking around this site, showing perspective residents they future home. Last girl, she threw a hissy fit and she left."

"She thought it was *too cold,*" Salvatore says, mimicking a girl whining. "She said she didn't feel safe."

"I'm not afraid of the cold."

"You look tougher than her," Tommy says after a moment.

Salvatore reaches out his cupped hand. "Wanna Tootsie Roll?"

"Sure."

Tommy shows her around, shouting for the cage elevator that runs outside the skeletal building. All thirty floors are at a different stage of completion, the top still nothing but an idea — open to the wind, to the sky.

"The Realtors send clients down here. You get seven an hour to show them what the Realtor wants them to see. Dress nice and talk nice, but don't wear shoes where you get a nail though the sole."

He gives her rolled lavender plans to take home. Battery Park is like a space station being erected. Looking across the river, New Jersey's pale jumble of factories and office buildings is just a gentle and easy sorrow, written in urban language, and far enough away to be sweet, to be precious.

The Statue of Liberty is being restored too. Her scaffolding looks like the halos doctors put on car-accident survivors.

Gulls occupy the sky like flies.

Jamey asks cabbies, guys behind the pizza counter, even Mr. Gorowski, about jobs.

No one trusts a rich boy looking for work, and they feel ridiculed by his questions.

"Nothing, huh?" Jamey says, gently disappointed, to the landlord.

Mr. Gorowski looks at his tenant a little longer, rubbing knobbed knuckles in his palm. "I do know a night job. My cousin Karl just left it is why."

And that's how Jamey ends up at the Iris Residences, with its pearl-gray awning and glass doors. In a few days, he's hailing cabs in a charcoal suit and cap.

The lobby is a box of mirrors, an infinity room, where reflections make more reflections.

There's a million teens on crutches, a million women with green beads, delivery guys with pimples and scooter helmets, men tilted forward like executives in cartoon strips.

And Jamey — in white gloves — shrinks

from image to image.

The dreaminess of the night shift is constant, and objects float — keys and coffee cups and Chinese containers and tissues. Time seems free to do what it wants.

In the morning, on his way home, Jamey looks at the buckets on the street, asks the guy how much for the snapdragons — (a guy whose hands are casually scarred, the hands of an immigrant, standing in the cold for ten hours with a snotty nose and thin jacket). The man grins, speaks no English.

Elise smells the flowers before she puts them in water. "They're real nice," she says.

Sex is beautiful when they're tired. When he works nights and she works days, and he gets home from the shift and she has yet to leave, they lie together for one hour. The hour is like an island in a river. He's exhausted, and she just woke up. His body buzzes with work, and she sleepily rubs his back until she feels a new weight to his body, a solemnity.

He goes under the sheets — to her little heart, feels it harden, his chin wet in the otherworldly humidity of her reddish hair, her hands roaming his skull with no consciousness, they could be someone else's hands — and she grinds against his tongue, everything dear and alive about her pinpointed in a pearl — that he's licking, licking — she groans — he slows down — *Oh come on,* she says, stern, *come on* — he licks — he licks —

Sunburst ravensblood snowstorm rosepetals kittenfur shootingstars!

It's a drug of stuff, glugging through her veins, gilding her smile now, the best smile, eyes closed — but his eyes are open — looking at this girl he knocked out, angel in a coma, she's pale with pleasure. . . .

Then she kisses him, and he puts his hand behind her head, gently sets his weight on her. They're quieter than usual in this orphan hour, slower. Sometimes he falls right to sleep after, and snores as she pads around, getting dressed and drinking coffee in the new light.

It's so cold and windy, people stride backward. A cop on a horse looks like he'll be sucked into the evil frozen sun. Everyone should just stay inside, where the radiator clanks and shudders like a beast that wants to care and protect the only clumsy way it knows how.

Walking Buck, Elise grips Jamey's arm so she doesn't slide on the ice.

"We should go to my mother's house one day," she says casually.

"Really?"

"Maybe . . . for Christmas?" she says, as if she hasn't been thinking about it.

"Let's go. You know that I —"

"What?"

"I've always wanted to meet them. You just seemed . . ."

"Seemed what?"

"Reluctant."

Elise lights a smoke, looks at him, waiting for him to go on.

"I felt," Jamey says, "like you didn't want to be judged."

"Is that right?" she asks, blowing smoke out her nostrils.

For Jamey, Christmas is parties, driving from Greenwich or to Southampton, stress, fighting, caviar and Veuve Clicquot, black velvet, giant fir trees and eggnog, Labradors with red ribbons around their necks, tangerines in stockings, cigars, candles, Yule logs, carols. He could spend an hour looking at the ornaments, gently holding a blue-silver dove that is weightless. If he closes his eyes, it's like he's holding nothing. *What are you doing thuh-r, son?* asks Mr. Armistead in his cashmere turtleneck. Jamey is the one who creeps into the kitchen, asks the catering director where she gets her plum pudding. He happily spends an hour sitting in the library with the spinster aunts from Philadelphia, in monastic silence, avoiding the Mullworths' daughter, who adjusts her silk plaid dress and flips her hair by the fire, stealing looks at him.

Elise and Jamey watch Buck drop hot turds in the dark afternoon.

This Christmas was looking pretty solitary, but now they have a plan.

"I don't want to go empty-handed," he says. "I do have about five hundred dollars left of the old money."

Elise squints against a newspaper blowing down the street. "I was hoping we could, like, impress them," she says bluntly.

"Sure," Jamey says, trying not to seem surprised. "Something special for your mom?"

She shrugs. "Yeah."

"I'm not necessarily suggesting it, but should we get something for your . . . dad?"

Cabs nose through walkers at the corner.

"Angel's not my dad."

"Your stepdad, sorry."

They pass foyers with names scribbled on buzzers, an advent calendar of brass mailboxes. Stir-fried rice on the sidewalk that looks thrown up, undigested.

"He's not my stepdad. He's my mother's boyfriend."

"What about the kids?"

"That would be cool, get stuff for the kids."

Buck loops his urine on a hydrant, and Jamey thinks it's odd how she's always been weird with him about presents, but suddenly she's all about it.

"It's a deal," he says.

Elise puts her arm around his waist and leans her cheek on his chest while they walk, awkward and lovely.

On his way to work, he eats dinner at a Greek joint, his thighs spread on the stool and shoulders hunched over the newspaper that he reads at the counter while people bustle in and out. Eventually the "mother" of the place grabs his arm whenever he arrives, her eyes practically closed because she's grinning madly, and leads him to his hallowed seat by the steam and clank of the open kitchen. She always sends the blondest, curviest girl to take his order like a madame pleasing a beloved client.

In the mirror box of the lobby, he learns the residents by name, and knows who needs what. He hands out a lot of shirts to young professionals. These flags of ambition, starched and strung on wires, shimmer in plastic. He likes holding the door. He likes hailing taxis. He likes helping old ladies over the brass threshold into the building. Not because he's a good person, made for service. It's the same pleasure a kid gets from playing with someone else's toy when he has that exact toy at home.

Bessie Jameson, 12C, always gets flowers or a package hand-delivered from Bonwit Teller or chocolates, which she orders for herself. The front desk knows because Felix signs receipts and sees her name.

Rumor is she had a nice divorce. Bessie spends the days with a mud mask and Richard Simmons, and when she sashays from the elevator, all businesslike, she makes a noise as she pretends to wonder what's inside the package. Her body pressed up and out, her face newly shiny. Jamey knows her coming down to the lobby is a sexual act, even if she'd never admit or understand that.

Once she wore a blouse with no bra. When she was gone, Jamey jacked off fast in the staff bathroom. He would never want her, never make love to her. He washes his hands without looking in the mirror. She's not real to him; she isn't real to herself. When he does imagine her naked body, he sees it as fiberglass.

■ ■ ■ ■

Elise always shows a prospective client the model units first, the fake residences that look like someone lives in them. Lorenzo the interior designer targeted the Wall Street sensibility, using Ralph Lauren wallpaper and tobacco-brown leather couches, and there's even toothbrushes by the sink and books on the shelves. Then she takes them to the actual floor to see the site of the apartment they want, usually an empty space with no walls, the Hudson winking below, helicopters sensuously twirling at eye level, a shiver in the knees.

The clients are often Europeans, sent for a year to Deutsche Bank or Credit Suisse. Or traders, whose wives and children live in Greenwich or Oyster Bay, looking for a pied-à-terre.

Elise does Vanna White — *Here's your brand-new dishwasher!* She has to shout over the circle-saw's shrill cry, and the nail gun's shot and echo.

Up top, as they stand among rat pellets and lost bolts and Styrofoam cups, she points out Miss Liberty, the girl next door.

Night shift.

Jamey raises his arm, and a hundred arms are raised.

He smiles, with thousands of teeth.

Jamey thinks of Narcissus bending to the pool. He thinks of how a swan on a calm lake is one with its reflection, and then, lifting off, the bird divides from its self, and both parts become smaller and smaller. Division is more interesting than duplication, and an ax is a fascinating tool. It makes a fallen tree into wood that will keep your family warm. It does more than separate a whole into pieces; it changes the spirit of the thing, its use.

He thinks about Elise checking her compact, and how he looks over her shoulder to catch her outlined eye in the mirror. Her eye, separated from the rest of her, floating. Normally he doesn't let his mind split into pieces, because it frightens him, but he's in a container here. He has so much time to think on the night shift.

Jamey and Elise board Metro-North on Christmas Eve morning, and the Gorowskis look after Buck.

Grand Central is busy but not with businesspeople. Fur coats, a woman carrying a potted amaryllis, children running wild who are normally behaved. A homeless man sucks on a candy cane, the stick glistening out of his scabbed mouth.

Elise and Jamey carry Toys "R" Us and Bloomingdale's bags, their hands turning red.

The scratched train windows refract light through the cabin. The seat headrests are oiled from men's pomade over the years. A coffee cup rolls in a twirl, clockwise then counterclockwise. Even though the car smells like soot and urine, there's a sense of holiday and goodwill, and Elise and Jamey lean against each other and drink coffee and eat cinnamon doughnuts out of paper bags, and are very happy.

The conductor looks lost in time, like he'd been punching tickets since 1931. His sandy hair combed back, his face handsome in a blustery, committed way. Keys jangle off his belt, a schedule pad and leather pocket of tickets hanging from it too. All his equipment sways with the train. A gold cross on a chain is barely visible under his pale-blue uniform shirt.

"Where you kids headed?" he says, clipping their tickets.

"Gonna see my family in Bridgeport," Elise says.

"Yeah? Sounds nice. Happy Christmas to yous."

"Have a merry Christmas too," Jamey says.

"I'm gonna," he says, whistling as he moves down the dirty aisle. "Soon's I get done with this shift."

And Jamey feels included, assumed into the ethics of finishing the shift, commiserating with other working stiffs without disrespecting the job. Last year, the conductor wouldn't have said much to him if Jamey had been on this train, and he wouldn't have been on this train.

When they get off, their cabdriver is a fat lady whose dyed-black hair has an inch of white at the root. Her radio is tuned to Christmas oldies, and she rolls through every stop sign. The town seems empty — as in deserted forever — and Jamey's nervous. They pass a boarded-up theater, a hair salon with a bullet-cracked window.

They pull up to barracks set unceremoniously in rows, with zero landscaping. A sign says WELCOME TO THE SALLY S. TURNBULL HOUSES. The brick units are flat, and a white iron barrier enclosing every lawn says prison yard more than picket fence. Dead grass is clumped with snow. A pink kid-sized car is bleached by weather and wheel-less.

He's meeting his wife's family — his heart rate explodes and his testicles are drawn up into his groin. Now, too late, he sees it was obscenely rude not to request her hand in marriage from the family. He never even wondered what they said when she told them.

"Elise!" shrieks someone from a window.

They lug shopping bags from the trunk to Building 5. On the ground are malt-liquor empties, and a face peeps out the door.

"Yo, Elise is here!" says the face.

Elise looks at Jamey. "Here we go."

Jamey has met hundreds of people, been left to entertain famous strangers, been relied on to charm parents' friends or schoolmates' siblings or Alex's business partners. He can smile like a cat, make them nervous, be intimate and faraway, warm and cold — he can whip out the survivor skills of charisma. But he'd rather be honest for once.

The yard smells of piss. There are audio echoes of television, EPMD, children shrieking. The smell of food cooking all day.

As they enter the hallway, kids jump around Elise, talking about Santa and stockings and toys, pulling at the bags. Jamey's heart is skipping. He can tell Elise is scared, because she won't look at him. A paper wreath is scotch-taped to the door of the apartment.

"Get out of my *way*!" she grumbles at the kids sweetly.

Walking into the fluorescent-lit room, Jamey braces for scrutiny, and he grazes the faces, but mainly he's ignored.

"Oh my fucking *God*!" Denise throws her spoon into the pot and wipes her hands on her apron and tackles Elise with a hug.

Mother and daughter hold each other, rock back and forth, and everyone is silent, murmuring.

Jamey's speechless, shocked by this love, that Elise has been away from it.

Denise is a ghetto Mae West, with huge half-lidded eyes, globes of breasts, and a strut. She flings the dishrag over her shoulder and evaluates Jamey, her pupils smoking.

She grins, wet and mean. "Well, if our girl loves you, we got to love you too. We don't have no choice."

Jamey tries to smile.

Angel is a mountain, with a mullet, curly on top, hair so thin his scalp is visible. "How you doin', man," he says to Jamey, and his hand is a cinder block.

"This is Dawn, Jesus, and Little Marie," Elise says, and the children stare with mouths open.

"Who *are* you?" Dawn asks.

"My name is Jamey."

"What are you doing here?"

Denise swats at her head with the dish towel. "Shut the fuck up, baby. We don't talk that way."

The dog is like a cotton ball pulled out of a drain. Teeth and gums so nasty her breath transcends a closed door. (She torments Angel, waking him by standing over his face and breathing into his nose. Jamey will hear all about it later. Angel opens his eyes every morning to this gremlin. When he moved back in recently, she shat in his disco loafer, a twirled army-green turd, curlicued with malevolence.)

A blue tinsel tree is wired with lights the colors of Jujyfruits candies. The same Elvis songs from the taxi play on this radio: "Blue Christmas," "Merry Christmas Baby," and "Silent Night."

A silent night it's not! Jamey sits with the men, where Angel rules. Someone hands him a snifter of Hennessey and an El Presidente. The men smoke cherry cigars, the windows cracked. The kids chase one another, shrieking. The kids he met seem to have spawned more kids.

Everything is out in the open. The second someone gets angry, there's a fight. Then it's resolved. Denise and the other women catch children who come and lie against their laps for a minute, languidly scratch the kid's head with their long nails, then let them go.

Elise is overwhelmed by how different everything seems, and how it's the same as when she left. Even while she's in here, talking and arguing and laughing, she's also coming down the hall, nine years old, in a clothing-drive parka with a grocery bag on her hip. It's stacked with bread, milk, and diapers. She's putting her key in the door but she forgot the beer! She goes back into the cold because she'll get a beating if she doesn't.

On the fridge, Jamey sees a photo of Elise in a basketball uniform.

"Look at you," he says.

"I played on the boys' team. For one year."

"That team, what a fucking tragedy," Denise says. "Them boys, the second they got good, they was arrested, hooked on drugs, or they family was falling to pieces and they hadda take over. Like, two kids would show up at those practices." She laughs hoarsely.

Jamey looks at Elise looking at the picture. She doesn't seem bitter — just curious about the girl on one knee, greasy hair parted in the middle.

The ladies drink Amaretto sours for the holiday.

"Cheers, all-a you!"

Aunt Shay busts in from her house on the next block. Cracks jokes about Jamey — but won't look at him. It's an aggressive shyness. A shy aggressiveness.

"I keep expecting you to like start *waltzin'* or some shit," she says, gesturing loosely at Jamey and looking around at everyone else, a comedian.

"Oh, she flirtin' with your man," Tara says to Elise.

"No, I ain't!" Aunt Shay protests with sass and a hand spread over her heart. "*I* like em tough. You know what I like."

"You can't talk like that, sister!" says Terrence, and there's a whole argument about Jamey that doesn't actually involve Jamey.

Shay's high on cocaine, her own private eggnog, or blizzard.

There's Barbies, remote-control cars, baby dolls that speak in robot voices. The dog doesn't stop yapping — it's like she's keeping time, and no one stops her.

They eat Christmas nachos (with red and green peppers), cheeseburgers Angel cooks on the grill in the freezing cold, then cherry pie with Reddi-wip.

Manic honking from the street, and Angel's eyes light up.

"Aw, that must be Goldie — he got a new ride for his mama!"

The men make an exodus onto the front stoop.

And there it is: a Champagne-pink 1980 Cadillac Seville with the bustleback and a Rolls Royce–like grill, fake belt strap on the trunk lid. Stadium seating in coral-red leather.

Jamey is jammed into the back, where he's pretty much sitting in Raul's lap.

"Shit, brother. This is bananas, man!" says someone.

"V8, man," says Goldie. "Hey, who's the rich boy?"

"Some kid Elise brung in from the city."

Jamey's high on cognac, so he gives a polite wave. "Hey there. Jamey Hyde."

Goldie glares in the rearview with wasted, happy eyes. "How you know Elise?"

"Well," Jamey says. "I'm married to her."

Angel looks at Goldie and looks back at Jamey.

"Stop the fucking car!"

Goldie screeches on the brakes and the big pink ship sails to a stop in a cloud of smoke.

"What do you mean, you're married?" Angel asks.

When Jamey sees everyone's expressions, he understands.

The Cadillac is headed to the house.

Angel smiles as he busts in the door. "Dah-neese," he says.

She doesn't hear, jabbering with the girls.

"Dah-*neese,*" he says again.

The room is quiet.

"Your girl got married."

Denise swivels giant eyes at Jamey.

No one says anything.

Jamey clears his throat. "I feel extremely fortunate about it."

You can hear a pin drop. Elise looks at the floor.

"I feel as though perhaps I should in fact start waltzing, ha-ha," he tries.

Denise drags Elise by the wrist into the bedroom and slams the door.

Mother and daughter sit in the dark, ignoring the drunk cousin snoring against the headrest.

"Talk to me. Did you change your name?" Denise asks.

"Yeah."

"Did you go on a honeymoon?"

"Nah, just a short one."

"What the hell does that mean? You do a honeymoon or not, not no short one or long one. Did you even have a wedding?"

"*Ma,* we got married at the courthouse."

"But you're not pregnant?" she says quietly.

"No."

Elise is glad it's dark so she can't see her mother cry, intoxicated and crushed her baby didn't want her at the wedding.

"What'd you wear?" Denise asks gruffly.

"Not a real dress, Ma," as if that would make this better.

Denise sniffles and they sit there.

"I can tell you love him," her mother says.

Elise looks toward her in the gloom.

Denise continues: "I think you love him too much."

Her mom seems like the frightened kid, face round, eyes glistening, shoulders hunched. Elise takes her hand instead of answering.

"Do you?" Denise presses.

"It's not possible to love him too much, Ma."

"Oh, honey. You're gonna learn the hard way, like you always done."

Elise pulls her hand away. "We're happy. We have a life together, he's got my back, in a way you wouldn't even understand."

"Yeah? I don't understand? Fuck off."

"You know what I mean."

"You don't know shit, little girl," Denise says.

Sirens. Lots of them. Someone's tree must have caught fire. No matter how many public-service announcements they run on TV, there's always fires on Christmas Eve.

"I feel like I lost you for good this time," Denise says.

Elise wraps arms around her mother, her own face wet. "Ma, please don't say that."

They hug in silence. When they pull apart, Elise fishes the Tiffany pin out of her pocket and puts it into her mother's hand. "Here. This is a little extra. Jamey wants you to have it. I mean, he doesn't know about this, but still. Take it to Easy Pawn."

Denise snuffles at the object shining in the dark.

When they come out, holding hands, they walk into a dance party — toddlers and grannies, Aunt Shay, Angel, even Jamey, everybody getting down and doing their thing to Marvin Gaye and Stevie Wonder and the Pointer Sisters. Jesus swivels his six-year-old hips like a sex machine to make everyone laugh.

And right before dawn, when teal leaks into the ragged horizon, Elise and Jamey pull out the couch in the living room, its mattress so thin they feel every spring and hinge. The kids bed down in the corner with Snoopy pillows stained from Marie's nosebleeds.

In the morning, everyone's hungover. Angel comes out of the bedroom, stepping over drunk people on the floor, his eyes wild and red. He drinks Kool-Aid from a pitcher and slams the fridge door. A kid begs him for pancakes, and Angel shakes his head at the child, who then asks again, and Angel grabs his jaw and pushes it so hard the kid falls.

"Get the *fuck.* Outta. My. Face."

Jamey rubs Elise's shoulder.

Angel back in the bedroom, Elise sits up, hair tangled, and pats a spot between her and Jamey. But the little boy retreats to his makeshift bed with the others, proud and sleek like a kicked cat.

She wants to leave before seeing everyone, tucks Pop-Tarts into her handbag on their way out.

She can hear the chaos of the past right outside: the ice cream truck's melody, kids with stolen bikes shouting to come play, girls fighting over a candy necklace.

As they stand on the threshold of the cinder-block hall, knotting scarves and surveying wreckage, Elise seems worried.

"What is it?" Jamey asks.

She shrugs unhappily.

The cab honks again downstairs.

"What?" Jamey asks.

She's annoyed. "Nothing. It's hard to leave."

"Why are we in a rush to go?"

"Because."

They slide into the cab, and ride through blanched, wounded streets to the train. This neighborhood is burned and deserted, the sidewalk weeds siphoning poison groundwater into their leaves.

He waits for her to kiss his fingers, or do one of a hundred other things that let him know everything is okay. He rubs her neck muscles with no response. She sits up straight, and looks out the grimy window, her face deeply irradiated with sun, except where it is very dark in shadow.

For a few days, she's quiet. He asks if she wants to talk. He's really glad they went out there, he tells her.

"Yeah," she says, absentmindedly.

She knows she did the right thing by leaving home, but, *fuck,* it feels so wrong.

They go to Little Italy one night for comfort food and red wine. Their table is in the corner of the big-windowed restaurant, looking onto Grand and Mott. The snow coming down vanishes once someone steps on it. The footsteps of the few walkers are exact.

They get a bottle of Chianti, and their hustler-waiter winks at Jamey and points to Elise, pantomiming that she's too beautiful, he's too lucky. He makes a hundred flourishes in turning the corkscrew, and they're so enchanted someone could easily pick their pockets, but the performance is just the cherry on top of dinner. He flips the corkscrew closed and tosses it in the air and catches it behind his back, slips it into his apron.

Over clams linguini, Elise gets misty.

Jamey steamed the window and wrote their initials.

"I love you more than life," she says.

"You're drunk," he chides her, but he likes it when she says things like that.

Before work, he decides to drop off Teddy's gift — a Canon 35mm camera for Teddy and Claudia's birdwatching trips upstate.

Martin mans the door, and Jamey greets him on the icy sidewalk, squints to see if Teddy is at the desk.

"No sir," Martin says without looking at him.

"Shoot," Jamey says. "Think I could leave this here for him?"

"Teddy doesn't work here anymore, sir."

Jamey gets queasy. "What?"

"He — well, sir. They let him go."

When Jamey walks into the apartment the next morning, the camera, bow on top, is under his arm. "They fired Teddy. For coming to our wedding. I know it."

Elise sits heavily at the kitchen table. "Are you serious?"

The trees make bony shadows on the cabinets.

"Yup."

Jamey takes off his coat, suddenly too hot. He stands behind a chair, holding its back with knuckles facing out, shoulders high. They look at each other.

"I didn't want to go to Bridgeport," Elise confesses. "I just felt guilty. Now word'll spread I married a rich boy."

"I'm not a rich boy anymore."

"You'll always be rich deep down."

"Fuck you!" he says sort of playfully.

"Trust me, there's family of mine could show up."

"Oh come on," Jamey says halfheartedly.

"What are we going to do?" Elise asks.

Jamey rolls his sleeves, takes out a skillet. "Let's fry some eggs." He can't look at her.

■ ■ ■ ■

New Year's Eve. They feel too heavy-hearted for partying, but Jamey at the last minute buys paper hats that say HAPPY NEW YEAR! and rainbow-foil blowouts.

"We can't not celebrate," he chides.

So they plan to go to Times Square, watch the red apple drop, kiss strangers, stay warm by crowding against bodies. They hit the streets, which feel like anarchy, people meeting one another's eyes, daring to connect, intoxicated, jacked-up.

"You got any resolutions?" he asks.

Elise's hands are deep in the white fur, top hat at an angle, as they turn onto Sixth Avenue. Someone throws a Champagne glass from a window to break on a car.

Thumping music from a kid strutting by with a boom box.

"Maybe I'll quit smoking," Elise says.

They're paused, shivering, while she lights a smoke, when Jamey's eyes wander down Twenty-Second Street to a dark clump of motion, distress.

"Hey!" he shouts, and moves in that direction.

The clot of people freezes, and Jamey starts running, and three silhouettes vanish in the opposite direction.

Elise chases Jamey, and they arrive at a boy, sequins torn from his shorts, feathers from wings, blood trickling from his mouth.

"Oh my God," she panics, kneeling.

His blue eyes pop open, one false eyelash askew. "That's what I get," he says wryly, "for being an angel."

"Who were they?" Jamey asks.

"Strangers. Fuckers."

This kid is now anointed with violence, his glitter stuck to those boys' hands. This was the finishing touch to his costume.

They take a cab to a Ninth Avenue address Frankie gives the driver, holding a tissue to his mouth.

"Where you going?" Elise asks as they drive.

"You guys should come!" he says suddenly, clapping. "*I'll* take you to the best party in town."

They hold him as he hobbles to a door (wedged open with a copy of *Grimm's Fairy Tales*), and into a freight elevator. "We're going all the way up, if you know what I mean," he says.

The elevator door opens, and they're about to climb an iron ladder when Frankie asks how he looks.

"Divine," Elise says.

He grins, showing a lost tooth.

And they ascend, into the night.

Into a forest of recycled Christmas trees on the roof, woods inhabited by unwashed beasts of art and vaudeville — grown-up delinquents — who glued and spit and stitched (with dental floss and shoelaces) a world. The seams are invisible at night.

"Welcome, welcome!" says a guy roller-skating through the crowd, tossing iridescent dust.

His nose is giant and chin minimal, and he skates into the arms of his Hawaiian girlfriend, twice his size with gold rings in her lip. But like the other misfits here, their faces are not hidden or corrected. Instead the features glitter and shine, transmuted into authentic humanhood and transcendent character.

Jamey and Elise make their way through the woods, past a bar carved out of ice, past a DJ whose turntable blasts remixed Bananarama, and Frankie introduces them to someone in a pink wig, robed in seashells.

"I'm Neptunia of the Netherworld," she says, brandishing a trident.

"Hey!" Frankie points to the stars.

The moon is new.

Many hours later, Elise and Jamey go home, after dancing and fire-juggling and ice queens, and they never see Frankie again. He was reunited with his tribe. Everything that was odd and ungainly about him became beautiful in the right crowd.

Maybe Elise and Jamey are their own tribe, and they belong to no one else, to nothing larger than themselves. *Can we live like that?* Elise thinks about this question as she wearily unlaces her black sneakers, soles coated in gold.

January 1987

One of the first mornings of the year they hear sirens down the block, and the sirens don't end. Later on, Elise walks by news crews camped in front of a building.

"These ladies were torturing a little girl," an onlooker says, hugging his shoulders.

She and Jamey watch the TV, eating lasagna at their coffee table, but soon they can't eat, and dinner congeals.

The reporter braces against the wind in her scarlet coat, the camera light glaring at her.

"Leticia Broadman is being accused today of killing her only daughter, six-year-old Shawna Broadman, with an exorcism gone awry. A neighbor here at 152 Second Avenue heard screaming, but when the police arrived, the damage had been done. Leticia Broadman allegedly made her daughter drink Drano, according to sources inside the police station, because *God* told her to.

This is Cindy Drecker, Eyewitness News."

Shawna's school photograph comes on the screen. She's beaming, hair braid ending with a red plastic ball on the elastic. The blue "sky" is mottled behind her.

Elise's seen that kid at the corner, carrying a giant laundry bag.

Neighbors and tourists make a shrine of candles, bouquets, and posters against the building. Strangers weep, and a coalition keeps an overnight vigil for the first few nights. Jamey stands in front of it one dawn, after work. Granted, he's tired, but for a moment he sees the flower petals move like worms. He abruptly leaves, walks home as quickly as he can without running.

Then the news releases footage of the mother in shackles and an orange suit, face streaming with tears. *I did it because I loved her,* she screams.

He comes home, she wakes up. They make love in the shower, her hands splayed on tile. He finds a white Bible on their stoop. Elise gets her period. Jamey gets stuck on a subway car with British tourists — older ladies and gents all with identical bobs, mad gleaming eyes and snaggle-teeth, completely decomposed faces — who sound like recently hatched birds. She comes home, he wakes up. She dreams of unfinished rooms, hallways leading to the sky. He watches rats forage in the subway track. She's walking down the avenue, glances up to see a poinsettia on a sill.

The snow looks like thin felt when he peeks out the window. Jamey walks Buck on his leash down the stairs and feels the searing white radiant cold from the other side of the front door. He braces himself before turning the knob like before shooting vodka or diving into a chilly lake, with an extra heart thump and an earache on the way. He walks around the block grinning because his face is reacting to the sun-spangled panorama out here, and Buck prances through the blinding wonderland of his master's world.

The city is emptied of its holidays, and Jamey feels the echo from his first Christmas away from his family. This is what he wanted. Now he wants to *enjoy* ordinary time with Elise as they go to work, come home, eat and drink and make love and sleep, instead of overthinking it or being anxious. But a merry-go-round still operates in his head. It starts up on its own, whenever it wants, music jangling, the animals (frozen in expression but mobile in their prescribed circle) beginning again. . . .

■ ■ ■ ■

It's not like he ever thought about doing this; it just happens one day when Jamey and Elise coincidentally end up in the same subway car.

Pink graffiti reads PROPHIT, next to a spray-painted Doberman with satanic eyes and a diamond collar.

The way he saunters up, body swinging with the train, she has a feeling.

"Haven't I seen you in the neighborhood?" he asks quietly.

"Maybe," she says, twirling her hair.

"Let's have a drink. At your place."

She sinks her hands in the white fur. "But I don't know you."

An old woman gives Jamey a look of disgust.

He tails Elise off the train.

Why is she scared? She measures her walk like when she's terrified for real.

"You're following me," she says without turning.

At the building, she smiles, thinking they can't sustain this.

He smiles back, but not like Jamey, and follows her in, his breath steaming, unbuttoning his camel-hair coat as they mount the steps.

On the landing, he gets under her skirt, tears the pantyhose, not kissing her.

She's stiff.

"Open the door," he says gruffly.

Her hand shakily unlocks it, they walk in, door open, anyone can see —

Jamey pushes her to the couch, bends her over . . .

And Buck lunges, fights him to the floor, roaring, snapping his teeth!

After a silence, Elise starts laughing. Buck's lips still twitch over his black gums at Jamey. She soothes the dog and gently pulls his collar.

"You're a bad man," she says to Jamey.

"Buck," he says, beseeching, only half in humor. "I was playing!"

They watch *The A-Team* and *Miami Vice,* stuffing their minds with helicopter crash landings and gold crucifixes. Jamey tells himself they were just experimenting. *Right?* He feels as if the guy he was, just a few hours ago, is still in the apartment, hiding in a closet with a baseball bat, ready to attack Jamey next time.

But Elise has drifted into television world without looking back, a liter of Sunkist between her legs, mouth slightly open, as she tracks the detectives on screen who stalk a man through a marina, pastel loafers glowing in the moonlight.

"He's gonna fall in the water," she says to no one.

In bed, Elise sends smoke rings into the lamp's light.

"We're on a gangplank these days," she tells Jamey. "Way up, above everything."

"Looking over the city," he says. "I know."

She imagines exotically infinitesimal buildings. Itty-bitty cars, people are fleas. Roofs glitter silver or black.

She puts her forehead to his and holds his face, closes her eyes.

"I want you to see what's in my mind," she says earnestly.

They press their skulls together, eyes closed, breath synched, the oil of her skin seeping into his skin. There's the vague groan of a vault opening, a flood of green like a tornado sky, and then damp silt that moves in still water. Little dolls and cats and monsters in the shadows, the puppets of memory, almost emerge. Wet cement pouring into the cavern, and they drag themselves out before it dries, pulling skulls apart.

They look at each other.

"You're a weirdo," she tells him.

"*You* are!" he says, laughing. "That was your fucking idea!"

Terry and Simone, a couple who live a couple buildings down, knock on the door one evening. They're '70s hippies, cosmic, and high on heroin — and this week they're selling vitamins door to door. Jamey and Elise always see them with their kids, Chloe and Star, psychedelic ragamuffins with knotted hair, on the neighborhood swing set.

"Hey, man, feel like getting healthy?" says Simone.

"Hell no," Elise says. "But come in for coffee if you want."

The couple put down their B12 samples and take off their boho coats. Jamey's at work, so Elise pours Folgers into the machine and wonders what to talk about.

She doesn't have to come up with anything, because Terry and Simone raspily relay every detail of their own lives for the next couple hours. Elise finally says she has to get up early, she needs to go to bed.

"Well, fuck, no problem! God, we got to get back to those sleeping babes, anyways," Terry says. "Hey, let's have dinner sometime!"

They leave her a Vitamin E sample and

some dehydrated garlic. If she wants to earn extra cash, they confide, she should talk to them about selling supplements. They won a waterbed last month for top sales in the hood!

Whenever Elise and Jamey walk past the Variety Playhouse, they look away from the guys hunting there like wolves, smoking, pulling a flask now and then. But why?

This time it's her idea — she's restless — she feels like pushing him — she whispers it in his ear one night.

And here they are — everyone standing at attention when Jamey in his camel-hair coat wanders like a general onto the territory.

In the clammy recesses of the deteriorating theater, men cruise with dexterity that comes from practice and desire. There's one kid with high-waisted slacks and corn-silk hair — but he's too girly.

A man with roan sideburns and a cut-off Garfield T-shirt looks better. His jeans are skintight, his sneakers ultraviolet-white. The connection is triggered, although his eyes turn skeptical when Elise follows — *I'll just watch,* she whispers nervously — and he keeps walking, self-conscious, resentful, and showing off.

They end up in worn velvet seats, Jamey

in the middle. The guy deftly unbuttons his jeans and takes out his cock — skinny and snake-like. The hair is trimmed. Jamey takes out his own, uncertain. The guy strokes himself, and looks at Jamey's face then at Jamey's cock then at his own cock, and then makes the rounds again, with an expression that's fierce but emotionless.

He gruffly directs Jamey to stand, facing him, his bare ass on the seat back. And now the stranger takes Jamey's cock into his mouth.

Jamey loses it and gets it back. His legs are trembling, his thighs go rigid, but he won't touch the man's head, keeps his fists on his own waist. He does raise himself by tilting his hips — he can't help it — his hips are getting higher — higher — higher!

Later in bed, Elise asks questions.

"It was the same but different," he answers, still in awe.

"Would you do it again?"

"Most of what I felt came from you watching."

"I loved watching," she says, eyes bright with jealousy.

She talks about the dark auditorium, how other men were near but invisible, the heat and the illicit big space — and Jamey just observes her face. She licks her lips, holding braids like a rope. She's amped up and tumbling over observations.

"You used me," he says jokingly at one point.

She doesn't deny it like he expects her to — she just laughs, shrugs. "I'm bored. It's wintertime. We need things to do."

Washington Square Park. Hash smoke twirling, ice in the fountain, a girl with broken fingernails strums her ukulele. Elise thinks she sees Jodi — someone she knew in Bridgeport — pushing a stroller with another girl, and she pulls Buck to a halt to watch.

Jodi looks at the beeper clipped to her tight black jeans. The girls part with a hand slap, one of them says something funny because they laugh, turn their high heads and strut in opposite directions with smiles.

Yeah, it's Jodi. Fur-trimmed hood, like a German shepherd.

Elise squints. It might be cool to say *Hi,* to say *Holy shit whatchu doing here,* talk gossip, meet the baby. She watches her walk under the arch, stopping once to fuss with the kid. Gone.

Let her go.

Brainwaves from the old world, marcelled

squiggles of energy, infrared forces try to hijack Elise's own ways. It's like that — it's science. When she's with the tribe, it's hard not to live like the tribe, think like them, love like them, die like them.

When she was at the juvenile center, girls were all on the rag at the same time, their bodies synched up with no intention or permission.

Back in Bridgeport, life repeated itself every day. The women would lean elbows on the kitchen counter and bitch. Pile into someone's car, babies on laps, laughing and smoking. Take over a section at the playground or Dairy Queen.

A girl is in or she's out — she can't loiter on the threshold with the door open.

Denise drags girls in synthetic lace dresses and plastic Mary Janes to church, shouting hello to people, her giant face shining with love. An addicted, compulsive, close-minded, gambling, pre-diabetic, angelic, giant-busted survivor, resurrected from minimum wage, from last night's battle in the bedroom, from self-loathing. But when Elise tried to drag Denise away from that world, her mother made it clear that if Elise was going to jump ship, she better jump alone. And so she did.

And here she is.

■ ■ ■ ■

Jamey and Elise haven't driven the BMW for weeks, and today it makes a strange rattle.

He pops the hood in brittle sunshine.

"What the . . . ?"

They don't even know what they're looking at.

An old man limps by, carrying a newspaper, and peers over their shoulders.

"Aw, shoot. Know what that is?" the stranger asks, smiling lopsided.

"What?" Elise says, fixated on the tiny bones.

"Rats is eating they dinner up in your engine. Ha-ha, that happen to my sister Maureen."

"Chicken bones?"

"Yup. Must be from the KFC 'round the corner, you know. They gets all their bones from the dumpster, then use this hidey-spot for they dinner."

Jamey and Elise collect skeletal parts from their machine. Grinning with absurdity.

A week later, Jamey sees blue glitter on the sidewalk before looking up to the crushed window. Inside: tinfoil burned with grime, seats pushed back.

The car is his big, black ceramic pram. Why does he keep it? He wonders that while waiting in the oil-reeking garage for it to get fixed.

It's a queasy little afternoon, and they're hungry — but there's nothing in the house. Jamey doesn't want to go outside, but Elise lures him into the brisk day with the idea of Broome Street Bar hamburger pitas. The place is quiet, a calico cat stealing from corner to corner looking for scraps. Jamey and Elise are greasy-fingered and laughing when a shadow falls across the table.

"Jamey! What the hell, man!"

It's Matt.

"Hey," Matt says to his entourage, "this is my buddy, Jamey Hyde."

The two guys — shirts untucked under yellow cashmere sweaters, sockless ankles in duckboots, eyes bloodshot — shake hands with Jamey. They barely nod at Elise.

"Dag."

"Shep."

Jamey is speechless.

"Dude, you're the most gossiped-about human being I know," Matt says. "Everyone says you two are holed up shooting dope together."

"Who's everyone?" Jamey asks. *And where*

did Matt learn language like "holed up" and "shooting dope"?

"Bennett told me you're painting now? You got a gallery or some shit?"

Jamey manages to clear his throat. "Gallery?"

"Are you coming back this semester? You're like living the anarchist dream." Matt hungrily memorizes Jamey's threadbare camel-hair coat and demeanor. He flicks his gaze at Elise, then away.

"What are you doing in New York?" Jamey asks.

"I've been spending most of my weekends here, these days. Hanging. Shep's folks live on Crosby Street," Matt brags.

Shep is dipping Skoal and Dag has coke powder on both nostrils.

"Crosby Street, that's great," Jamey says.

"I'm sure we've met, man," Shep says grandly. "I know who you are."

Dag pipes up. "We're headed to the Palladium. I'm promoting tonight with my buddies."

"Maybe we'll see you there." Jamey stands up. "Matt, good catching up."

Jamey drops a couple twenties on the table and leads Elise out.

As they walk in ruptured moods, hands in pockets, Jamey looks at Elise.

"Don't you think it's odd?" he says, holding his coat closed at the collar.

"What?"

"Him showing up like that."

"Weird coincidence."

Jamey squints into the distance. "*Is* it coincidence?"

Elise snorts. "What else could it be?"

"I didn't want to leave the house for a reason," he says testily.

"Now you stopped making sense," she says, and they walk in silence, both annoyed.

Jamey wants to hide out all the time, but Elise is at work today, and they've run out of toilet paper and coffee, so he's forced to go to the deli. It's ugly out here, as he thought it would be, and he walks into dank wind.

Dim faces look down from the roof: kids smoking. Snow hangs, unspent.

Jamey thinks he's hallucinating: it looks like a guy moving a grandfather clock (which he can hardly hold upright) down the cracked sidewalk on a skateboard.

The guy is wearing wraparound sunglasses and a denim jacket.

"Yo, help a brother out," he says.

Jamey gestures to see if the guy means him.

"Yeah, you, I got to get this pain-in-the-ass clock into this truck but the truck ain't here yet. Let's move it into the Holiday!"

"What are you doing with this thing?" Jamey asks.

"My grandma needs it fixed," he says with a straight face.

Jamey stares at him, deciding.

"I'm Tony. I live here." The guy scratches the blemishes on his white chin, then grins. "I'll buy you a drink, man."

Jamey shrugs, amused, and uses his back to push open the door as they guide the tilted clock into the dive bar. Smoke and old wool. A tiny dog sleeps in a knitted red bed on the cigarette machine.

"We're just resting it here for a second," Tony tells everybody as he positions the clock by the door.

The bartender: square face, dead eyes, and a gold hoop in one ear. He gives Tony a look Jamey can't decipher.

"My grandma," Tony says conspiratorially to Jamey, twirling whiskey in the finger-printy glass, "is a woman of God. She prays every minute she's awake. She prays for you and she don't even know you yet. You should come meet her sometime. She'll make you cocoa. She got three cats and two of them is blind. They were born blind," he says matter-of-factly.

The clock strikes a quarter hour.

A lady with a lipstick ring shakes her head. "Why the fuck am I in here if I wanted to sit next to church bells ringin'?"

"This ain't no church, Gwen," Tony says.

Tony follows the horse race on TV. He looks like a grasshopper: huge eyeballs, spindly limbs, and a predatory mouth. He probably gets laid but has to spend all his money to get her drunk and high, even though he could spend the same on a hooker, but won't.

"We should hang out sometime," he says to Jamey. "You seem like you from somewhere else."

Tony springs off his stool to see if the truck arrived, then asks Jamey for a quarter.

The clock watches over them all.

"Hey Jamey, order us another round?" Tony yells from the pay phone in the corner.

When Tony sits back down, he scratches his arms. He sees Jamey see that, but it doesn't stop him.

"My grandfather died three years ago," Tony offers. "He took care a his old lady, he was good to her, he worked for thirty-nine years in this factory over in Red Hook." Tony considers life and fate for a moment, then continues. "She's the shit, my grandma. She barely got any friends left, and the ones still alive, they down in Florida. But she loves New York, man. She got her butcher, her cheese shop, her tailor, all on one block. Same block she grew up on."

"She sounds amazing."

Just then, a man in a work jumper, dusty and mad, arrives. Jamey wonders if this is the guy with the truck.

But the bartender backs up and smiles, crosses his arms to observe.

Tony sees the man and his jaw drops.

The man pops Tony in the mouth, and Tony cradles his face and looks with pure hurt at his attacker.

"Wally, what? Why'd you do that?" Tony asks, his lip bleeding.

"Where do you even think you can sell a fucking clock, Tony? This is the third time you done this. Are you retarded?"

Tony looks blamefully at the bartender. "Did you call?"

The bartender shrugs.

Wally hustles Tony off the stool. "Your grandmother deserves better than a turd like you. Get up, and help me get this back into the apartment."

"The clock drives me crazy! I'm not selling it just to sell it."

"Everybody knows why you would sell it,

Tony. Not a big secret, you faggot."

The two men sourly collaborate on moving the giant object over the threshold and into the dark light of an East Village evening.

Jamey has another whiskey. Gwen makes him sit next to her and she studies him.

"Who are you, anyway?" she asks.

"Nobody special," he says, giving her a sideways smile.

She cackles hoarsely, and her lips work over the too-perfect dentures. "Oh, join the club, my love," and she gestures for the bartender to pour Jamey another.

When she reaches into her coat pocket for beef jerky, and breaks herself off a piece, she offers one to Jamey, who accepts, and then she feeds the last bit to the dog. He suddenly doesn't think he should eat it, and watches to see if the animal gags. When he can, he delicately drops his jerky on the floor. Gwen talks while he sits politely, wondering what she wants.

She narrows her eyes at him after a while. "You got the look of a bona fide paranoid."

He finally makes an excuse and escapes.

The Gorowskis come over for dinner. As a gift, Mrs. Gorowski brings a paperweight with a sea anemone in it, and Elise presses it to her heart. Elise makes beef stew and potatoes from a magazine recipe.

"So is your son visiting anytime soon?" Jamey asks.

"No," Mr. Gorowski says.

"Are you going anywhere, taking any trips?" Jamey asks.

"No, just making it through the winter, sitting tight," says Mr. Gorowski.

And Mrs. Gorowski looks on with beautiful eyes but her husband doesn't translate. It's an awkward hour because she'd be the one to get the talk going. So they eat in genteel quiet.

They have Entenmann's banana cake for dessert. Debussy trills and plings among static on the transistor radio, and Elise fake yawns until their landlord and his wife finally leave.

"I feel sorry for her," Jamey says when they're gone. "He controls her, don't you think?"

Elise shakes her head. "She *likes* not having to talk. That's what I figured out tonight."

"I don't know about that."

Elise looks at Jamey. "You're, like, suspicious of everyone lately."

Jamey blinks innocently. "Not suspicious of you," he says, and clears the plates.

The next afternoon, Chloe and Star play

hopscotch on the sidewalk, and Terry knocks and invites Jamey to see their baby raccoon.

"Sure," Jamey says reluctantly, after racking his brain fruitlessly for an out.

Jamey stands awkwardly in this home of incense and watercolor sets and narcotics and pyramid schemes and LEGO, a place that will one day implode but is happy for now.

"We named him Mad Max!" Chloe says.

Jamey watches Simone adjust the nest of towels in the kids' room. The raccoon is still a tiny, clumsy, grunty creature that will only become more nimble and true, the way animals do. Jamey looks at Chloe and Star, born revolutionaries. But they might become hypocrites like their parents, the way human beings can do.

They both have the day off. Elise boils hot chocolate, and the man on the jazz station talks in a monotone about a Miles Davis track for longer than the song lasted.

"I don't ever want to go outside again." Jamey sighs.

Jamey pulls up her sweater, dabs a half-melted marshmallow on her tit, licks it off. She giggles.

They play sex games with honey, maraschino cherries, whipped cream.

The bed is sticky and stained. He's lying on his stomach, his hair unruly, long enough to curl down his neck.

"You got an ass like a black girl," she tells him.

She smokes, contemplates him like a painter evaluating a model.

His body always seems stilled, inactive, but it's gambling and tricking and delighting the world.

Why is he hard to look away from? He doesn't invite it — fantasy is just built into the meaning of his body the way a swimming pool is made for water and a cemetery for graves.

"Turn over," she commands for fun, looping her cigarette in the air.

He's like the statue at the Met, supple and melting with sensuality, and closed. But she knows her way into the marble. She thinks his gentleness comes from being sure he'll hurt someone. An eternal restraint.

Hail pelts the windows.

"It's too *cold* to go out," he groans.

"I know."

"I mean ever again."

And they lie in bed and smoke. He picks up a hardback *The Call of the Wild,* which Elise found at the Salvation Army.

"Why don't you read it to me?" Elise says.

He holds the book open and scans for a good passage. *"Deep in the forest a call was sounding, and as often as he heard this call, mysteriously thrilling and luring, he felt compelled to turn his back upon the fire and the beaten earth around it, and to plunge into the forest, and on and on, he knew not where or why; nor did he wonder where or why, the call sounding imperiously, deep in the forest."*

They lie in a penumbra of light coming in the door. Buck sleeps, whimpering as he hunts.

"How were you so sure about us?" he asks.

"I just knew," she says, without drama.

"Okay, Confucius."

She doesn't laugh. "Seriously, you think you should know the reason for everything."

He's quiet. "I keep thinking about the blackout," he says.

"You didn't do *nothing* till then. I had to wait."

"I was so scared of you."

"You still scared, baby." She yawns, and curls up to sleep.

He watches her, propped on an elbow. *Scared?*

"You can't just say that and then go to sleep," he argues.

"I can do whatever I want," she says,

pissed off, eyes firmly closed to make a point.

"Oh yeah?" he says, and stands on the bed, backed into the corner like he's in a wrestling ring, gearing up.

She lies back and flashes him, pulling up her Public Enemy T-shirt and throwing it down. "Scaredy-cat," she taunts, laughs.

She switches moods in a heartbeat not because she's out of control — she just doesn't care what it looks like to switch. She watches other people stay in moods just to seem committed to something.

He tickles her, and she pants, hunched over, between laughing hysterically: "No, no, Jamey, no . . ." And then she squeals as he attacks again.

February 1987

Elise walks with head tucked to the morning wind, past the shoe-repair shop (front window stuffed with orphaned loafers and lavender pumps), past a man sleeping in a brittle churchyard, past a vase (luminous like a woman, but empty) in a dark window.

"How ya doin'," says Rob at the construction area entrance, and Elise salutes him.

Guys move around, tools clanging from belts, faces smug against the chill under hard hats. The coffee truck is on site, Stan telling Irish jokes and blonde jokes and Jewish jokes, making change from his money apron.

"Morning, sunshine!" they call to her. "Kinda cold, don't ya think?"

"Mornin', fellas!" she calls back. "Yeah, fuck *this*. What can you do about it, right?"

"Yeah, right!"

Trash is collected in the bottom of the

chain-link fence like spinach in teeth.

One night at work, Jamey finds Teddy's home number in the phone book.

"You heard," Teddy says when he answers.

"I want to make it up to you," Jamey states, dimple working, earnest and embarrassed.

"Aw, no — don't pull that shit on me."

"Can I meet you somewhere?"

Teddy hesitates, and Jamey can tell he doesn't want to see him.

But he relents. "Why don't you come over for dinner tomorrow? Claudia's visiting her mammy in a home up in Philly, so I'm by my lonesome."

Jamey drives the BMW to Brooklyn, the Manhattan Bridge swaying under the tires. At a stoplight, a woman knocks on his window for money. Her sweatshirt is filthy, her lower face burn-scarred, and she looks at the tinted window (unable to see him) with an abnormal fearlessness.

He drives through industrial Flatbush, then through the Greek Revival row houses in Fort Greene, and past abandoned buildings dissolving like temples of soot.

Jamey parks and walks, passing a stoop with lions, bird shit on one statue's eye. Chestnut trees tower.

Buzzed in, Jamey is the specter of some white boy from yesteryear, lurking around black clubs, obsessed with jazz. Goofily happy to get in the door. Jamey takes the gloomy stairs, feeling stupid.

The apartment was meant to be full of kids, but things didn't turn out. It's Spartan, sort of Christian minimalist, and smoky from Teddy cooking pork chops.

Jamey opens the bottle of red he brought and pours glasses.

"Thanks, James."

"Least I could do," Jamey says.

Teddy makes a face at that. Teddy's face is not a kind face, but it's not unkind. Kindness just isn't relevant because his jaw, his forehead, his cheekbones are *right.* He's walking evidence of proper actions taken over many years.

"It *is* because of the wedding, right?" Jamey says, his voice undramatic but serious.

Teddy shrugs. "Most likely."

"I just — you worked there forever. You have a relationship with these people —"

"What people?"

Jamey leans against the counter and stares at Teddy. "The building."

"I most certainly do not," Teddy persists, taking the pan off the fire. "Not in a way that will disrupt my life, now the connection is broken."

"How could you be there so long, and . . ."

Teddy takes off his oven mitt and grimly considers Jamey. "Things are good between me and *my lord.* How you think I made it this far? If my dignity was hung up on those people, no offense to you, Jamey — I would have no self-respect, no peace."

Jamey smiles. It's like finding out a friend has been having an affair for years. *That's* why he was distracted. It's obvious now!

They eat, and the meat is tender, briny, pink in the center. The phone rings and Teddy looks at his watch.

"Claudia's calling at nine, Jamey, I gotta take it, man."

Jamey watches Teddy talk to her, mainly *uh-huh*-ing, and then laughing, picking his teeth with the edge of a matchbook all the while.

Teddy says Claudia sent her best.

They play chess, and swirl Courvoisier in glasses.

"Can I ask you something?" Jamey says.

"Well, I could tell you had something else on your mind."

"You and Claudia — really love each other."

"Yesssss . . ."

"I feel . . . lucky these days," Jamey admits, smiling, chagrined. "Sometimes, I just wonder if, I don't know, if I'll screw it up."

"You worry about what you got?" Teddy looks at Jamey with pleasant scorn and disbelief, which amounts to: *Ah — white people.* "That's your problem right there. Think about it."

They get on the subject of Valentine's Day presents, and Jamey tells Teddy how much he loved Christmas presents from him and Claudia as a kid. (The gifts were wrapped in cheap drugstore paper. It was usually candy, or a remote-control car that broke on its second day, or cologne. They were real, unlike the Steiff animals and Barbour jackets a personal shopper picked out "from Father.")

"Well, your dad tipped the bejesus out of me."

"Right, of course." Jamey looks down, the dimple flickering.

Teddy sees the reaction and pauses. "I did always have affection for you, James. None of those other children were curious. You were different."

When Jamey gets ready to leave, he feels jittery, knowing this could look like noblesse oblige — but that's not how he means it.

He's going to put faith in his intention and screw the appearance of things.

So he takes the BMW keys and a pink slip out of his coat pocket. "Almost forgot," he jokes.

"What the heck is this?"

"Your new car."

Unflappable Teddy: flapped.

Sometimes the mirrored lobby makes Jamey claustrophobic, and he folds this fear into paper airplanes, performing origami on the hours themselves.

He writes Elise love letters on scraps and receipts. He sketches the dahlias in the vase, his hand, the midcentury modern ashtray standing by the elevator, his key ring. Nights go by, time itself converted into cartoons he draws for her, haikus he writes of rambling thoughts, hearts in black ink.

After her last appointment, Elise smells smoke from the first floor. She knows the odor, like plastic burning but more toxic. She peeks into the room — two drywall workers are smoking rock.

Seeing their faces — in blank rapture, big eyes looking but not registering — doesn't scare her as much as what will happen after they've smoked it all.

She runs across signs everywhere. Teeth ground down, burned fingers. On the street — wire hangers, scouring pads, wet cigarette filters. . . .

This poor city.

Early morning, waiting for the bus, she stared at a lace sock covering a swollen, poisoned foot, sticking out of a cardboard hut.

Yesterday kids with pinned eyes jacked an old man on her train, with a Rambo Survival Knife, while passengers watched.

A dead woman was found in the McDonald's entryway on Tenth Street; the police tape was going up when Elise walked by. The cops were talking about the Knicks game.

Crossing through Wall Street after close of market, no light straggles into those canyons, and the old buildings are grimy caves. Elise passes a three-piece suit in the hollow of a gothic stairwell, a hooker sucking his cock while he sucks a burning pipe, his shoe buckles shining.

She's lonely. There's a chasm between Jamey's days and her nights.

Elise wakes early to be crushed and smashed against him, sealed in heat under the comforter in the dark stink of the bedroom, the accumulated gas and breath of humans in a small room, for one hour. Light touches the edges of the blinds, a thief finding its way, and she nestles her jaw between his ear and shoulder, and he makes a dream-heavy noise acknowledging her and everything. Usually, in this gray light, they hear a gunshot or fire engine or domestic fight.

Good morning, East Village.

The other night, Teddy told Jamey his only advice was to give women what they *actually* want.

"It's a logical recommendation, but rarely followed," Teddy said wetly, far from drunk but loosened up.

So on Valentine's Day morning, Jamey hands Elise an envelope — with tickets to the Prince concert at Madison Square Garden that night.

"No. You. Dint," she says.

Hallelujah!

Elise was raised on the Supremes, Smokey Robinson, the Isley Brothers — Denise played records, night and day. Prince is the son of Motown, born early and underweight, an over-incubated child raised in a bedroom with a white grand piano.

Anemic genius.

He summons Haitian spirits, Pentecostal

virgins, drowned witches. If James Brown and Baudelaire had a hermaphroditic bastard, babysat by Mister Rogers, who grew up to wear lilac matador pants — it would be Prince.

"Happy?" Jamey asks.

"You don't understand," she says.

Elise gets ready like she never got ready before.

Madison Square Garden is ready too. The city (and Jersey and Long Island) launches an army of pilgrims to meet their lord, him with the rolled curls and beauty mark and white dance shoes.

Everyone surges to the stage, pushing. Dark hearts, kids ready to sing their brains out.

Girls with shirts smaller than bras, pouts, and violent stars in their eyes; guys with combs in pocket and little street spats and minty gum. All eyes are tilted up, waiting for the moon to rise into the black sky.

Like a unicorn on a rampage, he emerges. He slumps into every cherry-red note and electric piano chord and lightning streak of guitar.

"I'm in heaven!" she yells at Jamey.

She dances like a demon took hold.

She signs with her fingers: *You . . . I would die for you. . . .*

Dancing dancing — no one's in charge. Everybody just smiling. Tits and ass thump, big hands in the air, fancy feet — everybody do their thing — yeah — moving and grooving.

In the river of LIFE . . .

Dancing is when the devil holds your tail and keeps yanking down like a chain. A woman onstage with glowing suspenders plays the key-tar. Elise can dance for hours, sweat rolling down her rib cage, soaking her shirt, and she smiles like a heathen.

Sparklers and chimes tear through the stadium, flash-bulbing as every heart goes: *pop-pop-pop!*

Life . . . can be so nice. . . .

And then, the crying game, the tearjerker, tears that run down your neck into the bathwater.

This one's for you, Jamey.

Elise sings: *Sometimes it snows . . . in April.*

Lighters come up, a giant field of tiny fire flowers.

She's blind and happy as they make their way with other dazed boys and girls out the doors, and they're part of the mob of vulnerable freaks. On the subway, kids — whose silk shirts are drying — light one more joint. *That was a dope show.* Slowly, their snakeskins grow back, and everyone is strangers again.

When they get home, Elise and Jamey have sex, spending sweaty hours in bed.

He comes, and comes again, inside her.

Those swimmers hunt the egg.

Elise and Jamey fall asleep, and the work is done without them.

Collision — the spermatozoa dig through the outer layer, headfirst, flagella waving behind them, carrying a library of identities.

Elise's dad, picking almonds in Adjuntas, is joined with Tory's mother listening to Eisenhower on the wood cabinet radio. Binkie as a teenage girl crosses a ballroom floor, dropping one pink glove like a petal. Denise swims in the cold lake, blind underwater, safe for an afternoon. Denise's dad watches farm fields unfold beneath a bomber plane. Trembling, Tory studies her first headshots, paid for with babysitting money. Elise's grandfather, tall and slender in a dark room, watches Elise's father delivered from a dying woman's thighs. Alex bleeds from the ear on a New England football field in the dying sun. Denise's Dutch-Irish mother wakes up in the tank again, and the lady officer knows her name, hands her an apple for breakfast. Tory's dad is a teenager driving through Pennsylvania woods, elated, beer bottle between thighs, deer strapped to roof. Bats is ten, smokes his first cigar in a hotel room in Havana with his lilywhite uncle.

This is the hour of blood-binding.

Elise wakes up later to piss, sitting on the cold toilet seat — she had an extravagant dream. She's *tired* from dreaming. She wishes she could remember it.

March 1987

If she does feel funny, dizzy or off-kilter, ravenous for pickles or cream puffs, she doesn't notice. Because Elise heads to work one day, ratty fur belted tight around her, and gets a surprise.

It's an arctic morning, and she envies the woman on the train with a floor-length down coat that moves like a bell. She can't feel if her nose is running, because her face is too cold as she stands in line at the coffee cart. Her numb fingers can barely count out the right change, and she and the coffee guy joke about that.

The site is still open at the top, no roof, no walls up there, and she squints at it as she approaches. Rays of sun pierce the structure, gild the steel girders.

She makes her way around chalky dumpsters, but when she walks into the office, she gets silence instead of the usual fist bumps.

Tommy Bricks holds up the *National Enquirer,* March 3, 1987.

The headlines: *Tatum O'Neal's Trouble; Princess Stephanie's Rock Album; How to Live Forever; Losing Weight in the Winter; Dynasty's Bloody Plot Twist;* and:

Hyde Heir Marries Ghetto Girl, Slumming in Style!

With a photograph of Jamey in sunglasses, arm around Elise in her white fur, emerging from the Dugout after a liverwurst sandwich and root beer, both of them — very obviously — in love.

Dawn breaks into the lobby with shards of yellow light, and Jamey stews in disbelief — Elise brought the paper to him this afternoon. Then at four a.m. a man supposedly delivering Indian food snaps a shot of Jamey at the front desk and runs, leaving curry on the lobby floor.

Now Bessie sidles out of the elevator in a mohair dress, and slaps down Page Six of the *Post.* "Well, good morning."

> Finance royalty James Balthazar Hyde, whose mother, Tory Boyd Mankoff, and father, Alexander Hyde, battled in one of the bloodiest divorces NYC ever saw, has taken up with Section-8 Princess Elise

Perez, whose criminal record is as long as Jamey's tuxedo coattails, and she's apparently gotten him to shower her with Tiffany diamonds and Moët et Chandon even as they slum it up down in the East Village. Word has it they're cooking more than caviar in the spoon.

"You're a secretive boy."

Jamey pulls his doorman cuffs. "It's a long story."

Claire from management arrives in a houndstooth coat, her face ruddy with discomfort. "James, can we talk in the office?"

They stand among file cabinets and umbrellas.

"We can't have people taking pictures of the doorman," she says.

"Well, that won't last."

"I wish you told me, coming in."

"Told you what?"

"Who you are."

"I did."

"You know what I mean," she says, flustered.

He looks at her. "Yeah. I do."

He walks out, numbly high-fiving Gregory, who smiles ruefully at Jamey, and he disappears into the pastel city.

■ ■ ■ ■

Elise is eating lunch at White Castle when she gets flash-bulbed.

"What the fuck?" she says, spilling her Diet Coke.

The camera catches her face for the world to relish.

She goes back to work in soda-wet jeans. The construction guys aren't mad — their women (like Godiva and Mercedes, stars at Billy's Topless) get in trouble all the time. These men *enjoy* policing the site for stringers, and protect her like Bullmastiffs.

"How's our ghetto princess today?" they call out affectionately.

"This was bound to happen," Jamey says as he mopes around the apartment, smoking too much. "I could feel it coming."

Elise sits on the couch and stares at him. "Really?"

"It's never-ending."

"What's never-ending?" she asks, annoyed.

He lights another of her Newports, winces when he inhales.

She watches him look out the window — at Puerto Rican ladies walking Chihuahuas, at skateboarders, at old Cadillacs double-parked with flashers blinking.

"What I really don't get is why you didn't tell Claire to fuck off," she says.

"I don't want to work there anyway," he says.

"But you need the job," she tells him sourly.

He won't answer, just looks at the street.

Over the weekend, she and Jamey cook mac and cheese and eat Cheerios from the cupboard. They don't even order delivery because Jamey doesn't want to open their door.

"What are you scared of?" she asks.

"Why do you keep saying that?"

"Saying what?" she says, playing with her sweatshirt zipper.

"That I'm scared."

"You're scared of everything."

She goes to eat alone at the pizzeria, watching *Star Search* on their TV, and pushing red pepper flakes around the tabletop with her fingertip. Nobody looks twice at her.

One evening, she puts hands on hips. Jamey's unshaven, reading in bed before the sun has even set, and the apartment stinks — he hasn't been out once.

"Let's go to Wo Hop," she says. "I'm

gonna be fucking crazy if we stay here one more night."

He looks at her, his dimple coarse with stubble.

"Duck lo mein . . ." she says in an enticing voice. "Dummplingssss . . ."

He finally brushes his teeth, throws on a trench coat and borrows her mirror aviators, and they hit the street. In the crushed, steamy, loud restaurant, they're so invisible, he feels stupid.

"And besides, *I* got dissed," she says, licking plum sauce off her thumb. "You're the rich boy, I'm the grifter."

His cheeks redden. "It's not like I feel sorry for myself," he says.

"But?" she asks with impatience.

"It's — that —" he falters.

"Fucking *what*?"

"I keep putting you in — these situations," he announces. "I just feel guilty."

Her face softens, and she finishes the last emerald shreds of bok choy in silence.

After dinner, they wander by the East River.

There's an old man with a pole, a newspaper spread on the ground so he can filet his fish before packing it in recycled plastic containers. Pearl drops of light glisten fuzzily on the bridge.

"It's good to be out," Jamey admits.

An ancient Chinese lady with a man's blunt haircut walks by — a shirt with tiny flowers under her jacket, ivory cane glowing in one hand, and her other arm looped through her daughter's elbow.

"Yeah," Elise says, and loops her own arm through his. "It's a pretty night. . . ."

Saturday feels like spring — it's in the low fifties but the sun is sincere.

"Maybe we could go to the park?" Elise says in a carefully noncombative way.

Jamey nods. "Let's do it."

They take the subway, in hats and sunglasses, and get out at Eighty-First Street. They walk by Belvedere Castle scrawled with hieroglyphics, look at the scummy lake.

Central Park delicately offers its first crocus, a couple daffodils, forsythia opening their yellow buds, a few dangling snowdrops.

Jamey and Elise sit on grass, which dampens their asses. They eat hot dogs glopped with mustard and relish. The day is chilly enough to warrant sun on their faces, and sunny enough to need the breeze. A push and pull, petals falling occasionally, birds working in the sky. It's the thrift of March, measured-out abundance. She needs to tell him she hasn't gotten her period, but she keeps putting it off, and before she knows it, they're walking home in twilit streets.

Someone knocks, and Jamey looks through the peephole, and hesitates before unlocking the door.

"Tory!" Jamey says, when he can finally speak.

"My poor child," she says, hugging him. "Dragged through the mud. I've *been* there — I know how it feels." And she keeps hugging him.

Annie hovers in the grim staircase. Outside, a white limousine trembles.

Elise raises her palm in an Indian *How* so they don't touch her.

Tory claps her hands together. "I have a surprise. We're going to France. Get you out of the limelight, away from these assholes."

"I don't understand," Jamey says, after a moment.

"*We* are going to France. All of us! Today!"

Elise and Jamey look at each other. "I have to work," Elise says unsurely.

"I'm sure you can get off for a few days!" Annie says benevolently — Annie who never had a job. "The plane is on the tarmac, and the house is ready, and the trip is *all* planned!"

Jamey frowns at Elise. "You don't even have a passport."

"Oh, yeah. I don't."

"We can't go," Jamey says brightly. "It's a great idea, but some notice would have been helpful."

"But it's a surprise!" Tory says somewhat disingenuously.

"Thanks but no thanks," he says.

"It's your birthday," Tory insists.

Elise touches his arm: "You know what, babe? Go. What's a few days?"

"A few days is a few days," he says to her with meaning.

"Honestly? I could use some time. Clean house, get my head straight. Go," she says, fingering the bandanna holding her braids back.

He looks at her, confounded. "What's the story, Elise?"

"There is no story," she says as sweetly as possible, kissing him quickly. "I'll miss you like crazy and want you to come back. Please go."

Tory might barf. "Okay, then, it's settled!"

On the plane, the ladies snuggle in red blankets monogrammed for Annie's mother.

Jamey sips club soda while Pilot Dick Keye gives the safety speech, politely flirting while also presenting an unexcitable, militaristic competence. He links his fingers and uses his fused hands to gesture. He is God, father, and servant, all in one buff, trim, diplomatic fellow.

They eat steak au poivre with golden forks. Then the ladies pop pills, turn chairs into beds, and mask their eyes.

Jamey opens his shade because he can't sleep, and sees a vast and spawning field of so much nothing — or so much something.

Delicate night. But is it night? It's just a darkness. Night loses meaning when separated from time, and the whole thing seems random.

The cabin feels like a chamber of ethylene, and Jamey suddenly pictures himself striking a match. *Don't,* he tells himself gently, *even think about it.*

They get picked up at the airport by a Frenchman with criminal eyes but very silly buckteeth. He drives with what seems like bitter, silent pride — but could just be distraction — through dark hills in a Peugeot.

"I'm *so* happy we're here together," Annie says.

To Jamey, this sounds like Chinese. Is he "happy"? Are they "together"? Why or why not? Who are "we"? Is this beautiful or violent, that he's in the French countryside, on a starless ride, with no control?

The car radio is tuned to the news, and the news sounds more serious here. He tries to imagine what they're passing: lavender? Goats?

When they arrive at the house, the staff take bags and run baths. Jamey's brought to his room. A portly woman turns down his duvet. She does a desperate ballet, saying "wah-ture" when indicating the bedside bottle, then speaking French when showing him the bidet and the steam cleaner.

"It's hot," he says, flicking his fingers as if burned to show her he knows what she means, and she grins and holds his hand, squeezes it.

Jamey feels ill from flying. His stomach is bloated with gas. When she leaves, he drinks Perrier and burps quietly. Something moves and he flinches, then recognizes himself in a mirror, broad shoulders in a tattered black cable-knit sweater, circles under his eyes, his white chinos stained with red wine. It took an opulent room for him to see what he looks like these days.

■ ■ ■ ■

Elise pisses on the wand. She doesn't understand how this could be — she's taking the Pill! *One* day she forgot then doubled up the next morning — but that can't really matter. . . .

Buck watches as she waits. He licks her knee once because he can tell she's anxious.

When she sees the result, she puts her hand over her mouth, crumples to the floor, silent, not even rubbing Buck's face.

At breakfast time, the trio wakes crankily.

"How you doing?" Tory asks Jamey.

"Fine, thanks. And you?"

"You don't look so good," she tells him.

"Well, I guess I don't feel great."

"Try to feel better. We didn't bring you here to feel bad."

"Right," he says, privately amused.

He remembers his first jet lag. The phrase was so odd, and the sensation was sinister. It was profoundly different from being tired. Someone was dragging him down through the bathtub, through the hotel-room floor, and the hotel rooms below him, through the London sidewalk, through the hotel's basement, into hell. He was six. His father instructed the nanny to keep him awake all day, no matter what, or the trip would be ruined. "It's *crucial,*" Alex said. The nanny nodded, and so ensued her ridiculous day of dragging the boy through Harrods, putting candy in his mouth, buying him a tartan scarf and tying it around his neck while he stared drunkenly at her, walking him through parks, patting his face in a way that wasn't friendly.

Jamey butters his croissant. "You must have known Elise didn't have a passport."

Wide-eyed. "I thought that might be the first thing you'd do for her upon getting *married,*" Tory retorts. "Loved finding out in the paper that my son is married, by the way."

"She did think Elise would have a passport!" says Annie. "Your mother really believed Elise was coming and would be with us today."

It's hard not to love Annie — she accepts everything, except cruelty to animals and nuclear war. She soothes, chiming and making music of conversations. Her face is like a plate or a clock — no mystery but very useful. She can lie without knowing it.

"Annie, come on," Jamey says gently.

Elise goes to the Passport Office on Hudson

Street. She arrives early, and stands in line for three hours.

Finally a weary man with a ponytail hands her the booklet. "Check to make sure it's your correct identity."

She looks angry in the square photo, chin up and eyes narrowed, the white fur shoulders tapering into the unseen, the gold *E* glimmering on her sternum. She likes it.

At home she looks at the blank pages, turning them, one after another.

Coming back to the villa after strolling unbloomed gardens, Tory and Jamey have the Big Conversation.

"Baby," Tory begins. "I just don't want you to make the mistakes I made."

"Which of your mistakes do you mean?"

"You should get what's yours. You're a *Hyde.*"

"But you hate them. Why would you want me to take their money?"

"*Because* I hate them! What, do you think it's dirty?" she asks facetiously. "Money is what you *do* with it. It has no inherent character, James."

Sitting on a chair upholstered with black damask, Jamey traces patterns in the silk with one finger, and he doesn't hide his boredom.

"When *I* demanded my share, they called me a gold-digging whore. They claimed they wanted custody for *your* sake. And then did *nothing* to raise you."

"I did somehow get raised, though," he points out.

"They just didn't want to lose the game."

"I wish it *was* a game."

"They've *mastered* the art of looking like the good guys," Tory continues, not listening to him. "They know how to cover their tracks, boy." She lights another cigarette.

"But I don't care anymore."

"Come on. You can't flick off emotions like a light switch." Tory tells him about the detective the Hydes hired during the divorce. "He got pictures of me in *private* bathrooms in *private* houses. They're *shameless.*"

"I'm aware of that," he says softly.

"And you will *never* get away from them," she warns, seething.

"Tory —"

Suddenly she starts to cry, eyeliner running like watery paint. "Leave me alone, Jamey. Go."

Jamey looks around, and remembers again that he's in France.

That she commandeered him here.

And now she wants to be alone.

■ ■ ■ ■

Denise calls to Elise's window. The late afternoon is murky, and her mother's pale face looks up from the street. Elise takes the stairs, barefoot, opens the door and rocks her, won't let go.

"Shit, girl, wow, good to see you too." Denise cackles, snapping gum.

Elise sees her mom did her makeup, eyebrows drawn, rouge on the monster cheeks.

"*Thank you* for coming," Elise says.

Upstairs, Elise offers tea.

"What's with the tea?" Denise asks contemptuously and lovingly.

"It's from *England,*" Elise jokes.

They sit at the table, under the frilly, opaque light full of dead flies.

"When's the due date?" Denise asks.

"November something?"

Denise takes her daughter's manlike hands, looks into her eyes. "I love you. I am so fucking happy for you. This baby is blessed. Hear me? This baby is loved."

From his window, Jamey overhears them on the dusky patio by the heated pool.

"Let's be real, sugar," Annie says. "It's

better than shooting horse and fucking men and getting gay cancer."

Annie holds a gold tube of mascara and pulls a bunny face as she applies it in the mirror of a compact. Opium perfume amplifies the electric blue of her St. John dress.

"He's not *just* kissing his inheritance goodbye — he's choosing this *worthless* girl. . . ." Tory is frantic.

"But — didn't you think there was something between them?" Annie speculates.

"He just picked her to piss everyone off."

Annie's family villa is like a colony on the moon. The exoskeleton of the house is Provençal, and the inside is Texan. There's horse magazines, sheets from Neiman Marcus, and a certain hay and oil and Mercedes-leather smell to the air. A vague sense that people might come down the stairs at any moment dressed in tuxes and gowns for museum balls in Dallas.

Instead, British expats named Evelyn and Rhys, in equestrian outfits not meant for actual riding, arrive for dinner. Jamey says hello and eats in silence. He wants to be cruel when they ask about his mom's sweet birthday surprise for him, but he'll look spoiled, so he blandly smiles and bites his tongue.

By dessert — a Meyer lemon cake —

Tory's had it. "Feel free to retreat to your room," she says icily to her son.

"No thanks!" he says, being friendly now. "I'm happy right here."

In the morning, she's got a masque on her face, and drinks fresh grapefruit juice.

"That was some attitude," she says. "Ruined my night."

Jamey looks at his mother. "I could hardly give a fuck," he says cheerfully.

Tory gasps. "You can't talk to me that way! I *love* you."

Elise serves chicken with tall glasses of Diet Coke.

"It's weird you live here," Denise says with her mouth full, looking around the kitchen.

"Why?"

Denise laughs. "I don't know," she says earnestly. "It's my little girl's house. In New York City."

"And here you are, eating chicken at my table."

"Still don't understand why he's not here, taking care of you right now."

"I told him to go. I needed time to think." Elise's face is pale and makeup-less. A pimple by her nose.

As she chews, Denise takes a sidelong look at her daughter. "You all grown, now, aren't you," she points out. "You're changed."

Elise blushes.

"I'm serious!" Denise insists.

"I have *no* idea what I'm doing, Ma."

"Look, I know I told you what to do before. But don't go by nobody else's ideas but your own." She cackles, and sparks her Bic under a cigarette. She exhales. "Shit, I didn't listen to *my* mother."

Elise plays with rice. "Never?"

"Oh, you know that story, El. Her head wasn't right. But I got to say — when she wasn't howlin' in the gutter? She treated every single day like *the* day. Every hour is *the* hour. You don't have nothing else. You pick the meat off the bone gets handed to you. She — she had problems . . ." Denise rubs her bottom lip with the back of her thumb. "But her soul, when it was lit up, man, it was *ablaze.*"

Unearthly mauve twilight. A broad-backed masseur arrives for Annie, who giddily leads him to her room.

Jamey sits outside, smokes an unfiltered cigarette he bummed off the cook.

In her room, Tory looks out long glass doors onto a wet land, a place of rabbits and cottages, roses, of new growth and old families, stars, the pool shining deeply, and sees none of it, nor her son, who is a dark form among the sculpted hedges.

She closes the doors, pulls her robe, and looks once more at her reflection. She paces, takes a magazine into the bed, and puts it down and stares at nothing.

Why did it take him until this trip, this evening, to realize his mother was bankrupted in the divorce in more ways than one? That Annie takes care of her? He knew she was bitter, but didn't understand she lives on hate, that it's her sugar and meat and oxygen, and she'll never recover. She's destroyed.

Beautiful morning. When Jamey wakes, he decides to leave.

He walks along the sunny road and steps into the high grass each time he hears a car growling and screeching through the turns and hills. Others walk this route: a man with a baguette under one arm, teenage boys (shirts tucked into high-waisted jeans) who talk very obviously about Jamey but without menace. An old lady converses with herself, face animated under a straw hat.

He looks into a cottage whose door is open, and terrible French rock sizzles from a radio. A baby cries in the darkness of those rooms, and food is cooking.

He's in love with the sky, which is tart and robust and ever-changing, the clouds pulling, swelling, bursting. Everything is in motion, the lilac branches trembling with wrens, flowers spitting pollen. Chipmunks and field mice leap in the air, and butterflies swirl around his head, the farm cat winking as he goes by, like the countryside is a Hanna-Barbera scene. It's a diabolically merry afternoon.

His feet are bleeding and he doesn't notice.

He waves at a housewife hanging laundry in her yard.

It's four in the afternoon, and he's done swimming in a pond, and is drying in the faint sun and feeling alarmingly cold and lost, when the chauffeur, driving slowly around the village, finally finds him. The driver can't speak English, so he motions Jamey into the car without hiding his antipathy.

Jamey doesn't speak to Annie or Tory when he gets to the house. Instead he takes a bubble bath like an old diva, and falls asleep early, naked, exhausted. He can't remember his dream when he wakes, but he knows he was terrified. He smells of gardenia from some face cream he found last night and smeared on his bloody feet.

■ ■ ■ ■

Denise sleeps in bed with Elise, like old times. She snores louder now, the bed sagging under her mountainous body. After the light is out, she still makes raunchy jokes and tender observations, playing with Elise's hair.

"You're gonna be the best mother, hon."

"*You* were."

Denise laughs raucously. "Yeah right! I did good at times, and I *definitely* fucked up."

"It was Angel who screwed us up."

Denise is quiet. Then she says: "Yeah, babe, but I asked him in the door, you know?"

"You slept for what, six months after he got sent upstate. You were like Sleeping Beauty."

Elise can see the gleam of her mom's eyes as she stares at the ceiling. "Yeah well. It had to go like that," Denise says quietly.

And suddenly Elise knows her mother turned Angel in, to regain order, so the family could survive.

How didn't she figure that out till tonight?

Jamey packs his stuff, staring at his clothes

in the suitcase as if they belonged to someone else. Morning makes the room glitter and shine, everything is golden. After a while, he realizes someone is watching him.

He turns to see Tory in the door, her face ashen. He sighs. What now? He just wants to be on the plane, this continent shrinking beneath them.

"Yes?" he says antagonistically.

She shrugs weakly. "I just want to know . . ."

He waits. "Want to know what?"

"How you justify what you're doing to her." And she turns, vanishes into the dark hallway.

When Elise wakes up, her mother is gone. There's a box tied with curling ribbons, and a Hallmark card: *Congratulations!* It's the christening gown Elise wore as a baby.

He carries off the plane a *Le Figaro* with a flower pressed in its pages for every day he was gone. He also brings a baker's package of lemon tarts. In the airport bathroom's mirror, he combs his oily hair with his fingers. He looks more like a man coming back from a year of shooting drugs with bohemians in Marrakesh than a movie star's son who vacationed in the patrician French countryside.

He'd made a formal bow as a goodbye to Annie and Tory. "And thank you, Annie, for what I know were good intentions."

From the taxi window, he stares at the city, so forced, menacing, and crowded after the hills of Provence. When he opens the apartment door, he hides his mood, tells himself it's jet lag. He looks sick.

Elise hugs him and won't let go. "I'm so glad you're home," she says.

"I still can't believe you sent me away."

"I didn't!" she says in a playful voice, because she did.

He gives her a look. Then: "God, I missed you." He's thinking about telling her all the fucked-up things his mother said.

"I have your birthday present," she says, climbing into the bed, nervous. She's wearing a wife beater, and her gold necklaces fall to the side.

Jamey gets under the covers, looking skinny in his boxers. "Oh yeah? What."

They lie facing each other, and prop cheeks on hands.

"Guess," she tells him.

He looks from one of her gray eyes to the other. "I'm not good at guessing."

"It's right in front of you."

Jamey looks around the room, then falls

back dramatically to look at the ceiling. "Ummmm . . . where?"

"Use your imagination."

"Hmmmm, I —"

Elise pulls his hand to her belly.

He looks from her tummy to her face. He can't speak.

"Yeah," she laughs at his reaction.

He presses his mouth to her belly, kissing her, kissing her. There's no bump yet, but he can see what everyone says, that a woman becomes radiant. He holds her braided head against his chest. This is *wild.*

She's doing holy work.

And she throws up French toast the next morning, the chartreuse bile floating on the toilet water as he kneels beside her, holding her hair.

"This part sucks," she says as she wipes her mouth with a shaky hand, sort of embarrassed.

He comes back from the store, wide-eyed from the things the pharmacist told him, a paper bag of the recommended aspirin and hemorrhoid cream and Pepto-Bismol in his arms. He's going to be a daddy.

Jamey and Elise are giddy, plums hanging on a branch, fat with sun.

The day seems innocent enough. They

drip out of bed, shower together, lazy, whistling, shaving. They feel like taking an epic walk.

The East Village is bright — dark — bright with fast clouds.

They head north, see addicts being lured out of boxes and bushes by the big silver drug of hunger. Cats in bodega windows. Block by block by block. Petals like confetti in the seams of cars. They pass parking-lot guards locked into bulletproof stalls. Gold-leaf numbers on glass doors to buildings. The sun turns the fire escape into a sideways shadow.

"Sandwiches?" Jamey asks, swinging her hand.

"Take them to the park?" she answers.

"Sure."

They walk, the dragon's roar of a subway under their feet.

Barbers, tailors, delis.

Central Park has a minty flush of new life. The horses drag carriages in endless ovals.

They eat on a bench, wipe mayonnaise off a knuckle, squinting at the lake.

"Check it out," Elise says.

Swans rise from the water, about to fight, wings raised and necks curved.

"They can be violent," he says.

A couple with a baby lie on a blanket,

speckled in light, sequins on their black skin. Elise and Jamey sneak looks at them.

Back in the day, Jamey wouldn't lie like that on this ground — it's the kitchen floor, the toilet, the filthy sheets of New York. Wine and urine saturate the dirt — but now he barely cares.

They watch people eating strawberries out of a Ziploc bag or reading the *Post* or buying drugs or pushing twins in strollers or talking to themselves.

Elise will always think back to the atlas of this day — the peacefulness and fighting swans and the light-spangled baby — and Matt.

"Holy shit," Matt says. "Again!"

He has a girl by his side — she's tiny and hot, coughs like she has emphysema.

"We keep running into you," Jamey says.

"Destiny." Matt holds a hand up at Elise. "Hey."

"Hey."

"You guys, this is Valentina," Matt says proudly.

"Hallo!" she says in a thick Italian accent, now that she's unleashed upon them, and she gives hugs and cheek kisses. "I'm so, so happy to meet each of you, okay!"

Her perfume is amber — spicy pollen off a forbidden flower — and it lands on them, coats them. She's wearing couture clothes too big for her bones, but the way they fall, in conjunction with the chains on her sallow neck, and the sandals slipping off her feet like she's meant to be barefoot, give her star power. Her hair is tangled down to her ass.

"What-a should we do!" she says.

Matt takes in Jamey's self-cut hair, second-hand clothes, and fuller mouth, fascinated.

"Yeah, we should all do something," Matt says.

"We got to get home," Elise says.

Jamey looks at her. "We do?"

Elise bites her lip. *"Yeah."*

Valentina claps her hands. "Dinner at my place, next week? You cannot say no." She drapes her arm over Matt, squeezes him, steadily unsteady.

Elise and Jamey look at each other.

But Jamey accepts the invite. "Where are you?"

Valentina squeals with pleasure, tells them her Trump Tower address. "Fabulous," she pronounces.

Jamey and Elise watch them walk away, among hot-dog-cart fumes and kites and pigeons, into a tunnel where someone surely was raped in the last two weeks if not two hours.

"Why on Earth did you say yes?" she asks, in shock.

"Didn't you say we should get out more?" he kids. He feels invincible.

April 1987

Jamey and Elise have lunch at Paolucci's: asparagus and burrata and prosciutto.

"Vivien? Jacqueline," Jamey says. "Or Sandrine."

"Why do you think it's a girl?"

"Just a feeling."

They eat dark-chocolate mousse for dessert, watching Italians saunter outside in weak sun, running errands, greeting one another with generations of familiarity. Two heavyset brothers, or cousins, jaws big with experience, one with gold chains and one without, walk in absolute synchronicity.

"Northern California," Jamey says. "We could even have a farm."

"We should move near Disneyland?" she asks. "We could bring our kid there all the time."

"Disneyland is not that great," he breaks it to her.

"Um, neither is farming," she says.

They don't sound like themselves. They're acting like they're not scared shitless, pretending to be lighthearted.

"But seriously. It's a *little* fucked up to bring a kid into this world, right?" Jamey says, hanging on to good humor, but the line falls flat. Elise doesn't answer, because she doesn't like what she hears in his voice.

They watch two guys unloading a big truck — one has a braid, might be Dominican. The other seems angry, as if freshly sprung from Rikers, but then he giggles, cute as a panda bear.

Dinner at Valentina's. Elise and Jamey dress in silence as if for a funeral, but there's something heady about the evening. Jamey barely slept the last few nights, ideas rushing through his mind about where to live, how to make money, unstoppable thoughts that have him seeing stars.

A radio on the street blares KRS-One. Sautéed onions rise from downstairs.

"Trump fucking Towers," Jamey says.

"It's just stupid we're going."

"I can't wait to tell them," he says.

She stops putting on eyeliner and gapes. "Tell them what?"

"That we're having a kid!"

"I'm seriously not going unless you swear

to God you won't tell them."

"Why not?" he asks, his eyes wicked in the broad cheekbones.

"Jamey," she says, getting really upset. "You just never know —"

"Hey, hey," he soothes her, hugging her. "I'm teasing. I won't."

"Don't tease about that shit," she says stubbornly, letting him hold her.

"You realize he's tried to find his own Elise," he says into her neck. "That's what Valentina is."

Elise smirks, reluctantly flattered. "Whatever."

She wears a tight white dress, and he kisses her belly, makes her smile. "You're exquisite," he says.

"Shut *up.*"

They take a cab, the city flashing by in its grit and radiance.

Pulling up to the monolithic address, the taxi is opened by a doorman.

"Thank you, sir," Jamey says.

The young couple — the doorman will remember them when police question him.

Yeah, Officer, he'll say. *I opened the door to their cab. They were laughing, but they sorta seemed like they didn't wannu go in there. Into the building. She was, how can I say, rough around the edges. She thanked me —*

she was just a little street. Outta her league. But not for hire or nothing. Just not on his level, you know? He looked all prep-school and high-dollar. Maybe a little run down, but the real deal. I remember thinking that, even.

He tips his cap. Arms linked, the couple enters the smoked glass doors.

No, Officer, I didn't see 'em after that. My shift last night ended at ten o'clock, so I was out of there. I guess they were just getting started.

The gold sign outside makes Jamey and Elise feel they're entering a chocolate box. Inside, the apocalyptic waterfall roars.

Valentina is on 57, right under the Trump family. They take the penthouse elevator, and a Taiwanese tenant gets out on 46, into a minimal space with a poppy-red couch.

"Here you are," says the elevator man when they surge to a stop and the doors open.

Valentina is barefoot in a long gray Versace dress, cigarette in her mouth as she hugs them, squealing like a pig. "You found-a me! We can start to party. I've been waiting all day."

Matt grins. "Welcome to the penthouse, kids."

They walk around this aerie of glass and clouds, dreams and money. Darkwood chairs with arms gnarled into swirls and flowers. Threads of gold that shine in the Persian rugs. Oil paintings hang — a still life with a radish and a fish, a portrait of a noblewoman with a grungy face and satin gown.

"We've been doing I Ching all day," Matt (the jet-set outlaw) says to Jamey, showing off. "Smoking weed and reading the future."

Elise forces a smile. "Cool place."

"It's radical, right?" Matt says, and it's the first time he really speaks to her since New Haven.

In the corner, a Pac-Man makes noise.

"I ordered dinner, okay? Arcadia bring to me. You have to be hungry and eat like crazy!" Valentina twists out her cigarette in a crystal ashtray.

"Jamey, come here," Matt says, beckoning into a hall. "I got to show you something."

Jamey lets go of Elise's hand, looks back as he walks away.

He's strange tonight, she thinks.

Matt shows him a Picasso in the guest bedroom. "Can you believe this shit? Know what her dad paid for this?"

Valentina drags Elise into the kitchen for a drink, but Elise wants soda.

The phone *bring-brings.* Porters haul in a silver cart.

Valentina claps. She's seventeen, indulged and entitled to the point of being mentally ill, with Krug Clos du Mesnil bottles filling the refrigerator, and — in her bedroom — acid tabs between the pages of a Marilyn Monroe biography. (Her childhood was a gold kernel. It was a germ of love. Her family built a wall around her but she scrambled over it, lost her virginity at twelve to her best friend's uncle in a Mexico City nightclub. Her father was the king of sex and romance in Milan. She has jewels in safe-deposit boxes in countries she's never visited. She thinks of her toys and silk gowns, the little Ferrari waiting for her in Ibiza, as her "children"; she'll raise them when she's ready to be maternal.)

"Let's eat!" Matt says.

Elise sits down with dread.

Champagne is poured for everyone but Elise. They make small talk — about Whitney Houston, MoMA, old friends of Matt and Jamey's, Yale gossip, Valentina's name, rack of lamb — which they're eating. Elise pushes around her food.

"You like it?" Valentina asks with a face of demented concern.

"Yeah," Elise says without looking up. "Just not that hungry."

After dessert — melted îles flottantes —

Valentina dramatically pushes plates away to put a mirror on the table where a lazy Susan usually goes. She taps cocaine out of a sterling-silver vial.

"Now it's time for the really fun," she says, hitching up her gown and kneeling on her chair to cut lines.

Elise looks at Jamey, then flicks her hooded eyes at the bitch, shakes her head slowly.

Matt watches.

"None for you?" he asks.

"Oh!" Valentina looks up from her work with childish hospitality. "I want you to enjoy."

"None for me either," Jamey says.

Valentina laughs with strange intonations. "Wellllllllllll, Jamey, you're taking acid."

"I'm sorry?" Jamey says.

"In your Champagne! I put a surprise!"

Jamey looks at his empty flute.

Matt laughs now too. "You did it? I thought you were joking," he says to Valentina, then looks at Jamey. "Might as well go with it, right? I *totally* tripped last weekend out in Montauk, and my mind was officially blown."

"I like what he say!" Valentina says, cutting lines. "Go with it!"

Jamey doesn't want to trip — *or does he?*

— but he feels the lights go down and the curtain rising.

"I guess you're right," Jamey says.

Elise maintains a neutral face, knowing bad energy leads to bad times. "Yeah."

Valentina makes an exalted *ohmygod* face and claps. "Yes! Jamey, you're my hero!"

"What's to fear but fear itself?" Jamey asks, like an actor in a western.

The first hour is spent giggling at the table, the three of them shy as if flirting with the drug, courting it. Elise watches with forced benevolence.

Then Jamey notices that everything — furniture, faces — are coated in Plexiglas. Everything gleams, protected.

"You feel it." Matt grins.

"You feel it first," Valentina says to Jamey, "I given you Elise's tab, *bonus*!"

Jamey nods, laughing. "Great!" he says.

He hears offshoots of noise, like a purring, after words.

Latin translations appear above Elise's head when she talks.

"What?" she asks, smiling back, keeping her commitment.

"Latin," he says. A long silken trail of glitter follows words out of his mouth.

Valentina and Matt sneak away, made innocent by their high, and curiously investigate objects in the bathroom, turning over a toothbrush and tittering, hunched down.

Elise is left with Jamey, who is extremely occupied.

"My God on Earth," he says, burdened by awareness.

There's a movie happening on the black windows. The images shuffle so fast and he realizes they're memories, and moments from the future. His brain is transmitting these pictures to be felt more than seen. There's a leg with black stitches, then wild roses in Rhode Island, and a white Jaguar. But he just feels the air displaced by them, or he almost tastes them — they're not visible.

He watches lights change in the chandelier, the glass tubes like ice pops in cherry and lime and orange flavors. He tries to stand on the dining table to make the chandelier move, but Elise holds his hand and says something to him.

Her face morphs into an albino doe's head. She blinks the big eyes.

She lets him feel her face and shoulders like a blind man trying to understand what she is. He looks at her with trepidation.

"Everything is good, Jamey," she says, like telling him the time. "I love you."

He takes his hands off her quickly, as if she just barked.

Four hours later.

"I'm freezing." He looks at Elise like a child in the snow.

She rubs his arms briskly. "We'll warm you up."

"I'm so cold," he says pathetically.

Elise sighs. "Do you want a blanket?"

He drawls like a dandy: "I want your fur coat. Can I have it?"

"It might not fit."

He looks like he might cry.

"I'll get it, I'll get it," she says.

When he puts it on, they hear a seam break like ice cracking beneath their feet. He looks ridiculous.

"I'm warmer already."

At the window, he slow dances like a charmed snake. He watches himself in the glass.

This lasts a long time.

Then he looks at her with dead certainty. "I need to go outside."

Elise squirms. She got bored and lax while he danced, thinking maybe there would be an end to this. But his face is even more altered. He's puffy, his face muscles operating in a foreign way, clenching and relaxing.

His eyes syrupy with light.

"Well," she says, reasoning with a toddler, "maybe in like a little bit, we'll go out."

"I need to go now."

"Jamey, I don't think this is the best idea you ever had."

Matt and Valentina are making sculptures with salt and butter, still giggling, and Elise suspects they're coming down from their one tab each, and can't let go. She doesn't want their help but is sick of babysitting, and she blames them.

"Hey," she says. "Jamey wants to go outside. Can you help explain *why* we shouldn't do that?"

Valentina purses her mouth. "Why not we go outside?"

"Hey, James," Matt says. "Maybe we'll go for a walk in a little bit? Want to come over here and give us a hand?"

Jamey stands at the window, looking left out. "I want. To leave," he manages to say, his mouth dry.

Elise looks at Matt, suddenly an ally.

"Why don't we go out in like five minutes?" Elise asks, planning to manipulate Jamey's sense of time.

Jamey looks down, then bolts for the door.

Matt and Elise get him before he opens it.

They instinctively know not to be too

physical, but just pulling his hand from the doorknob makes Jamey jump like they hurt him.

"Maybe we can have a little quiet time, Jamey, and just calm down," Matt tries.

"Let's sit on the floor together!" Elise proposes, like it would be fun.

"No," Jamey finally whispers.

Valentina traipses over. She puts her bony, diamond-braceleted arms around everyone. "We go out! It's no problem. Come on. We have fun."

She slips into her coat, her own face smeared by the trip, still beautiful.

Elise's stomach flips.

"Jamey, we do what *you* want," Valentina says, and presses for the elevator, jangling her keys.

"Do you want to wear that coat out?" Elise asks him carefully.

Jamey nods, his hair standing up like a gutter punk.

Matt puts on Jamey's camel-hair coat, and Valentina hands Elise a yellow Moncler jacket.

And they get into the elevator and the elevator man presses the button for the ground floor and they all look at their feet.

In summary, on April 6, 1987, at approximately 0313 hours, officers were dispatched, along with EMS, to the Trump Towers building lobby at 725 Fifth Avenue, after being notified by Central Dispatch of an incident in progress.

Upon arrival, Officer in Charge noticed the offender, James Balthazar Hyde, walking in agitated circles and cursing. Officers Drake and Tomlinson announced office and proceeded to inquire whether Hyde was able to talk with them. Hyde stated, "I will not need you."

Then Hyde pointed to his friend Matthew Danning, going up the escalator, and he began to hyperventilate. Hyde's extreme distress seemed to be triggered by/fixed on Danning.

At that time, Hyde began to run up the "down" escalator, shouting unintelligible words. His wife, later identified as Elise Hyde, and Danning and Valentina Corsicona (family is Tenant at Trump Tower), shouted to stop, that police officers needed to speak to him. Hyde responded: "You don't matter!" Officers gave multiple verbal commands for Hyde to get off the escalator. Hyde took the escalator to ground level, but instead of allowing Officers to cuff him, he proceeded to skip around the lobby, frightening residents trying to exit.

"That's it!" he was heard to say.

Officers showed weapons, at which point Elise Hyde became hysterical and begged the offender to stop running. He refused all verbal commands, and proceeded to give chase around the lobby, eventually speeding up as Officers closed in, tripping and skidding, breaking the glass wall of a boutique.

Officers at that time used necessary force; the Trump Security Guard was required to help, as offender was extremely aggressive. Officer Drake was injured on the left side of his face, and Hyde was injured in multiple places, including the forehead, mouth, teeth, left rib cage, and left leg. Central Dispatch had already sent EMS to the location, and the EMS attendants Jackson and Gertz spoke with Danning, who explained Hyde was under the influence of LSD. Officers agreed Hyde should be taken to the hospital, and at approximately 0422 hours, Hyde was given temporary sedative by injection, strapped into a gurney, and transported by ambulance to Lenox Hill ER. End of Report.

Jamey is wheeled into triage while Elise answers questions from someone with a clipboard.

Elise cannot believe this is happening.

When she hesitates with details, the EMS guy shakes his head. "They got to know, for his safety. This is not no bad thing, okay?"

"He took one hit" — she holds up a fingernail — "no, *two* hits, of LSD, of acid. He's never taken it before, he doesn't do drugs at all. This bitch made him do it."

"Is he on other substances tonight?"

"No. Champagne."

"How much?"

"Like, four glasses?"

"Marijuana, cocaine, heroin, PCP, pills?"

"Nothing."

"Any prescribed medication?"

"No."

"Has he had an episode like this before?"

"No!" Elise says, offended for him. "He didn't even want to do it!"

"He was forced?"

"He was tricked."

"By a stranger?"

"We were at a dinner party, with his friend."

"You can press charges if you want, but it's gonna be a he-said she-said."

"Just make him better," Elise says desperately.

Elise sits by Jamey's stretcher, where he's

hooked to an IV, the orbs of his eyes moving but not seeing, hair drenched in sweat. A nurse touches Jamey's wrist, counting, and says the doctor will be here soon.

"Hang tight," she says.

Elise smells lemonish bleach and urine. Blood travels the threads of Jamey's arm bandage.

Suddenly another team busts in, talking to each other, and injecting him again.

No one notices Elise. "What's going on?" she asks.

"You are?" asks a woman in pink scrubs whose black hair is oiled into twists on her head.

"Jamey's wife."

"Oh, okay. We're taking Jamey to Gracie Square Hospital, toots. You wanna ride with us?"

"Why's he going to a different hospital?"

They all look at each other. "His family want him there."

"How do they know he's here?"

The woman shakes her head. The hair doesn't move. It's like hard plastic.

As they ride in a van tricked out like a luxury ambulance, Elise realizes Matt called Jamey's parents.

Jamey's maneuvered into the new hospital under a royal-blue awning.

"I'm Jamey Hyde's wife," Elise says to the front desk.

The lady looks meaningfully at her. "We're all set, dear."

"Okay," Elise says slowly. "Where should I go?"

"You can wait here, if you like," the woman gestures at a couch. "They'll call if they need you."

Dr. Brandywine comes out to tell Elise that Jamey will be asleep for the next eight hours. He's got both hands in his white coat pockets, as if to show he's not combative.

"I'll stay anyway," she says, her feet reddened in the high heels, mascara blurred.

"Well, that's not necessary," he says, looking her up and down.

"I want to."

"The Hyde family asked me to make *sure* you don't talk about what's happening to anyone."

"Why would I talk?"

"It's for Jamey, the privacy," he continues, as if he had to finish the paragraph before being done with his task. "He doesn't need attention for an accident like this."

"Do I look like I'm arguing?" she says, head starting to cobra-snake.

"Easy now. I'm just stating the obvious.

We're here if you need anything."

"I need to know when he wakes up."

"We'll be sure to let you know as soon as he wakes up."

She sits primly in the waiting room, bare thighs in the short white dress sticking to the pleather couch. Even though the family knows he's here, no one shows up. A soda machine vaguely surges with light, and she reads pamphlets written in periwinkle.

Gracie Square provides an individualized treatment plan based on a complete evaluation. They give medical, neurological and psychological consultations, perform detoxification, assess and treat psychiatric symptoms, offer education programs, hold daily group therapy, along with nightly twelve-step meetings where patients share experiences while focusing on abstinence and recovery. They've got a twenty-four-hour, seven-day-a-week internist and psychiatrist, progressive discharge planning, and weekend support groups for family.

She falls asleep on the couch, drooling.

Morning. Private room on the third floor. Scrubbed and glistening. He's propped in bed.

Light comes through the window in clear

blue waves, and terror is clamping its teeth on his brain.

There will be no rationale, no logic, no emotions — just terror.

Like trying to get comfortable in a scalding bath.

A doctor. Jamey can't open his mouth to answer. He can't hear the questions, that's part of the problem. He can't use his hands because he has to clutch the mattress on each side.

He can only make it from second to second, sustaining a minor consciousness — he'd rather be unconscious but can't do the work of getting there.

Terror has taken his system and all he can do is feel it.

It is his one activity.

A nurse checks his temperature and pulse, he's injected with a sedative, his eyes close.

Elise buys a vending-machine doughnut and weak coffee. She eats in the waiting room, and it comes roaring through her intestines and she barely makes it to the bathroom.

She calls in to work, and Mrs. Gorowski walks Buck.

Elise's story is that Jamey collapsed in the subway — it might have been a mild heart attack, they don't know yet. Everyone is oohing and ahhing, asking to help.

Elise just wants him home. She leafs through a battered *Time* magazine.

The longer this goes on, the less likely it ends well.

Her panic is animalistic — *Get him away from here. Get it done. Run.*

Dr. Brandywine comes out to say Jamey is sedated again all day.

"You'll be doing yourself and Jamey a favor by getting him books, taking a nap, eating something. I've seen couples go through this many, many times, Elise. Come back when you're ready."

She looks at his white beard and lumpy face. Breath so bad, something's fundamentally wrong with him.

"Shouldn't he be okay by now?" she asks.

"Well, many patients would be done with the crisis. But there are cases where the patient doesn't emerge for forty-eight hours, say."

"I want it on record he can't be moved anywhere."

"We would never do that."

"He was moved from Lenox Hill without them asking me."

"Be glad he was moved from Lenox Hill."

"I never had a say is my point."

The doctor smiles tightly. "I'll make an

addendum to his file."

"And can I please, please see him?"

"You can't go into the room."

"Can I *please* just look in the door?"

A nurse takes her to the third floor. The nurse opens the door and Elise looks at Jamey, supported on pillows, sleeping, his face melted and insulted by the sedative, his body strewn in the bed.

A bruise like a dark flower fills his eye socket.

"What's he on?" Elise asks.

"Three milligrams of etizolam, it's a tranquilizer, for severe anxiety."

"What's gonna happen?" Elise says, sounding younger than she is.

"You know, when patients come in here experiencing a psychedelic crisis, they usually get out in one to three days. Usually the acute anxiety subsides, and we talk them through the experience, decide if they'll have lingering psychotic feelings or not. And eventually they're discharged. That make sense, honey?"

Elise nods. Looks one more time. There is nothing repulsive about this vision, but Elise walks away breathless, as if she'd just seen his stomach cut open and his guts hanging out and he was leering at her.

At home she lets Buck into bed, and

sleeps with him, his heat passing into her bones.

When she wakes up, she peels off the white dress, showers, scrubs herself of Valentina's apartment, of the Trump Tower lobby, of the ambulance, of the hospital waiting room. She has to use Vaseline to take off her eye makeup, which has stained her skin.

Eating buttered toast, her eyes tear up, certain that she made all this happen. She chased his ass in New Haven, she loved him first.

Dr. Brandywine asks her to his office, where a plaster model of a human brain is labeled in a rainbow of words.

"I'd love to be blunt, here, Alissa."

"Elise."

"His family says you all *have* been using drugs."

"We do *not,* except this one time when he took acid."

"You've never used drugs *at all?"*

"That's not what I mean."

"But you *have not used drugs,* is your wording."

"We never used drugs together."

"Look, Lisa —"

"Elise. Elise Hyde."

"The truth is, I don't care really about *your* drug use. What I need to know is what drugs Jamey's using."

"Jamey don't even really drink. He never does drugs."

"Except when he does LSD."

"Once. That girl made him."

"Heroin? Cocaine?"

Elise stands. "Do you have a hearing problem?"

Dr. Brandywine pushes a button on his phone without taking his eyes off her.

An assistant enters the room.

"I'm leaving!" Elise says. To Brandywine: "You suck."

She makes it to the turquoise couches before sobbing.

A nurse sits next to Elise, says: "You're okay, love, you're gonna be fine."

Jolie's hips are almost busted like an overripe tomato. She's maidenly, an artist of tenderness.

Elise cries on her shoulder, wetting her scrubs.

"I hate that doctor —"

"I understand," Jolie soothes her. She unwraps a mint for Elise and unwraps one for herself. "I'm gonna put a word in."

Elise hiccups, and nods.

■ ■ ■ ■

A bouquet of a hundred white roses gets delivered by a Jamaican man with a hand-cart.

The note from Tory Boyd Mankoff: *I so wish I could be there. Thinking of you!*

Elise tells the nurses they can redistribute the flowers; he wouldn't want them in the room.

Finally, Alex shows up. No one has been allowed to sit with Jamey yet, but Alex and Brandywine have a closed-door conversation. The doctor makes an allowance for this suffering father, who is gracious, as Hydes are known to be.

Once they're alone, Alex pulls a chair to Jamey's bed, livid he has to sit in this melodramatic configuration of furniture and bodies. He rubs the bridge of his nose, displacing his glasses.

"James. Why are you doing this?"

Alex stares at his son.

Jamey smiles for the first time.

"This isn't funny. Everything is pretty damn stressful as it *is* right now. Cecily is buried in work for the Sloan-Kettering Ball, you *know* she's on the board this year. You *know* what that means. I've got my hands full with Daley-Cray in London. I'm not even supposed to be in New York, for godssake. And I *know* you don't want people talking, but the longer you're in here, the worse it looks."

Alex paces in topsiders.

Jamey's eyes follow his father in his spearmint-green Polo shirt.

"You've put me in this *position.* I don't want to lie to our friends, but I can't tell them what's going on. Not a one is going to understand how a kid with everything just up and throws it away. Jamey — you were given the world. Your grandparents are too horrified to visit, and I wasn't even going to tell you that, but I had to. They're disgusted."

Alex stands squarely in front of his son, looks at his watch, then: "What do you have to say?"

Jamey stares at his dad.

"I'm going to count to ten, Jamey."

Jamey shakily puts his legs over the side of the bed for the first time.

He holds the IV pole, and slides off the mattress — slowly — till he's standing.

Alex, hands on hips, nods with triumph. "There you go, son," he says.

Jamey squats, eyes closed, and Alex starts

to wonder.

Jamey grunts, and a huge coil of shit hangs from his buttocks, and it peacefully finds the faux-granite vinyl floor.

Cecily and Elise sit in the waiting room without talking, staring at a watercolor of a robin in a blooming apple tree on the wall.

The kids read books on the carpet.

Then Samantha sweetly asks Elise: "How come your hair's like that?"

"Sam," Cecily says, face reddening.

The girl asks Elise: "Are you black?" in an angel voice.

Elise laughs. "I *am* black."

Cecily gathers her daughter onto her lap, says "Well, then," to Elise, meaning: *No you're not, and stop talking like a fool.*

Alex storms through the doors.

He glares at Elise, and gathers his family, and leaves.

Elise goes to work, somehow putting on lipstick and finding her way to the site, picking up a bagel on the way but she doesn't remember where.

"It was a little stroke," she says, without meeting their eyes.

"That happened to my brudda," Salvatore says.

"It'll happen to *you* if you don't stop with them cheeseburgers and sundaes," Tommy says to Salvatore. "Elise, where's he at?"

"Um, Lenox."

"Oh yeah? I spent a lot of time there with my ma. Which wing?"

"Let's see, not sure what the name is."

"Well, we're all rootin' for him to get out soon. He's gotta take care of the mother of his babe."

She knows they know he's not at Lenox when Tommy slips her an envelope of cash the next day, from the boys. They smell a rat — they think it's drugs too. They just want her safe.

She works, she walks Buck, she takes deep breaths like Jolie said, and she can visit Jamey now — even though he's either asleep or propped up with eyes open, but never awake.

He won't speak. Day after day.

She puts his hand on her tummy. "Feel that?"

One evening, he blinks when she takes his hand to her belly.

She tells Jolie, who writes it on the chart. "That's great."

"Soon? It's been two weeks. He'll pull out of it?"

Jolie chews gum and shrugs. "I hope so, love. You should just try to trust what's happening. He apparently needed to be like — removed from reality right now. He'll come back when he can. That's sometimes how psychotic breaks function."

Brandywine strokes his own beard; he smells of red wine and garlic from lunch.

"He won't talk still, I see," the doctor admits, "but let's get his vitals."

He takes the stethoscope from around his neck and listens to Jamey's heart:

Remember little child of God what this is. It's a drag show. It's fake. It's a snow globe. Golden cigarettes and little kittens. Someone keeps setting fire to blanket like sparkler. It's a TV show, the blocks of primary color signify God the father. You're in this kaleidoscope. It's a play your mom made in third grade. Esoteric and out-there, man. For children. Those kids of God were killed. Black dresses. A tiger in a dormitory. A rich girl who ate arsenic. This is a terrarium. This is joyful.

Brandywine shines a light into Jamey's eyes:

It's powder. A fine dust from heaven. You could lie outside and slowly get buried. It's gold flake blanched into meaningless drift. It's a black sky somehow made darker by white fluff. Everyone knows how to make an angel. You get up without wrecking the print you made and everyone does a shadow.

He presses the gauge against his Velcroed arm:

Blackberry like the eye of a fly. Cut the liver out of the clock, wrap in wax paper and write a number in grease pencil. Do what they say and survive. Cut flowers for the table. Tell no one what day it is. Sleepwalk instead of dream. Run don't walk. Go to town on Thursday — buy gingham and salt. Forget the dead. Keep singing if you forget the words. Love the ferns.

Dr. Brandywine avoids eye contact with Elise. "We're going to keep him under observation," he mumbles. "Patience."

In the smoking room, which she's gotten to know well, Elise has just lit another menthol, exhaling out the cracked but chained window.

"He said your name!" Jolie exclaims.

Elise clutches pack and lighter. "He did?"

She runs through the hall, sneakers squeaking, and pushes into the room where Jamey looks out the window.

She falls onto him, and he almost laughs.

"Hi," he says, in a new voice, his bruised eye lavender now.

"Oh my fucking Jesus Christ."

He runs a hand over her hair, breathes her in, kisses her cheek.

Something moves at the base of her spine — a worm of truth. "Are you okay?" she says quietly.

He tries to smile. "I have questions," he says.

She smiles uncertainly. "Ask," she prompts.

He bites his lip. "How long have I been dead?"

There's silence.

"Like, how long you haven't been communicating with anybody?" she asks.

He tries to understand her. "No, dead."

She laughs. "You're fucking with me!"

He grins, polite, unsure. "Is this purgatory?"

"This is a treatment center," she says, firmly, still smiling. "In Midtown Manhattan."

"Actual Manhattan?"

She glares. "I don't think this is fucking funny. If you don't —"

Jolie walks in with Dr. Eva Lessing, a very tall woman with a jet-black bob.

"This is Dr. Lessing. She'll be taking over, okay?" says Jolie.

"Great," Elise stumbles, in shock.

"How you feeling, Jamey?" Dr. Lessing asks.

He turns away.

Dr. Lessing asks Elise if he spoke.

"He did, actually," she says. "He wanted to know where he is, stuff like that."

The two women look at Elise.

"Anything else?" says Lessing.

Elise shrugs and tries to smile and forces her dry mouth to say: "I wish."

May 1987

Sunshine bores into the apartment, and dust hangs in chutes of light.

It's been five days since talking to Jamey about his death, and she hasn't been to the hospital once. She's abandoned him.

Elise called in sick to work this morning, planning to get it together, and she just lies in bed with Buck. Never in her life has she been paralyzed like this. Every time she gets up to brush her teeth, or put on shoes so she can go back, she starts crying so hard she can only stumble into bed.

"I hate you, Jamey!" she calls out, like a kid.

But in the darkness of the bedroom, Buck's garnet eyes gleam.

"I know," she finally admits to him, whose tail thumps once.

Elise drags on sweatpants, a jean jacket, the Yankees hat. Gold earrings.

"I'm going," she tells the dog.

At Gracie Square, Elise finds Dr. Lessing's office. Calligraphied degrees on the wall, lilacs in a Japanese vase. The window is dirty.

It's confession time.

"He hasn't said a word since you left," Lessing muses.

"Really?"

"Really."

They watch each other across the desk.

Elise says: "I should . . . tell you something."

The doctor tilts her head. "Shoot."

"He asked me . . ." — Elise fiddles with her earring — "how long he's been dead."

"What was your answer?"

"I explained he wasn't dead."

"Of course. And then?"

"The way he looked at me, he *knows* he's dead. Like, I can't tell him otherwise."

"Gotcha." Lessing suddenly smiles widely. "People think all kinds of things, don't they?"

Elise is taken aback by this breeziness. "Yeah?"

"Look. I've seen stranger stuff. We'll get him sorted."

One little flower-bell falls from the lilac head, unprovoked.

■ ■ ■ ■

This is a sickness that doesn't start or end in the bowels, in measles, in a high temperature or a tin pan of vomit. It's all light and darkness, creeping through his cells, staining the molecules of his soul one by one. It's the photosynthesis of ideas and memories, impressions, dreams. The body actually likes to host sickness, courting this rash or feeding that tumor, letting those chemicals glitter and shimmer through the blood. There's a way to resolve chaos and that's to finish what was started, and every organism knows this emergency plan without being told.

He's thankful the curtains remain closed in this room. He doesn't have to see humanity. Little kids always peering into the window, runny noses pressed to glass, eyes flickering over him. Keep them away.

He tries to figure out what his "body" is made of now. It seems to be bleached or processed or desiccated wood — like toy airplane wings — *balsam,* he thinks — is that correct? He gently mauls his "flesh" and decides this is right — it's turned into something airy, light, but not too fragile. So interesting!

Morning light burns through the shade, and Jamey gets meds with red punch. A nurse stands by while he showers.

When Elise and Lessing arrive, Jamey's back in bed, hair side-parted by someone else.

"I don't bite, promise," Dr. Lessing says, sitting in the chair.

Jamey shoots daggers at Elise for bringing in this stranger.

"How old are you, Jamey?" Lessing says, scanning a sheet.

Jamey hesitates. "Do you mean — how old was I when I died?"

Elise smirks because he sounds stupid, fiddles with her earring.

"Sure," Lessing says.

"Twenty-one."

Dr. Lessing ponders his demeanor. "You seem . . . calm for someone who's dead."

"I've never felt this calm."

Elise drums her nails on the meal tray.

"Jamey, any brain injury in the last year or two?" Lessing asks. "Concussions? Any little car accidents?"

He shakes his head. "No."

"Are you on meds?"

"Just the ones you make me take," he says.

"Have you been depressed this past year?"

Now he rubs the long scab on his chest, thoughtful. "I've always been depressed, maybe."

"Have you been *suicidal* in the past?"

"Not literally."

"Do you have thoughts of suicide now?"

Jamey smiles with condescending amusement. "That would be superfluous."

"Is there mental illness in your family?"

"Just profound unhappiness on both sides."

"Substance abuse history?"

"None."

Lessing leans back, hands clasping one knee. "Do you want to tell me what happened that night?"

"I watched my soul go up the escalator to the next world," he says.

Elise says: "That was *Matt,* in your coat."

Lessing assures him: "It's okay if you were confused, if you thought that was you."

Jamey evaluates her for a moment. "I know you're testing me, and I don't appreciate it."

Elise stands up, infuriated. "Wow. You're being *crazy,*" she says, her voice shaking. "You better quit this right now because you're *pissing* me off —"

Lessing escorts her out, soothing her as

they walk down the corridor, where wheelchairs have left black stripes on the walls.

Elise and Lessing eat albino lettuce and sludgy carrots in the cafeteria.

"People who have psychedelic breakdowns do occasionally think they're dead. But the delusion is persistent *while* under the influence, and then they come back to reality."

"Yeah, he needs to come on back."

"A French doctor, Jules Cotard, called it *délires des négations.* A delirium of negation."

Elise eats her Jell-O.

"Something is breaking the circuitry. Either in the amygdala, the part of the brain that recognizes human beings as human, or the fusiform face area, the *visual* system that recognizes faces." Lessing tosses a vanilla wafer into her mouth. "He's self-negating."

"Self-negating."

"We'll keep trying different meds. I'm going to double the Haldol."

"Is that . . . does that have side effects?"

Dr. Lessing looks at her raisin pudding as she says: "Oh no, not really."

Elise curls up on his bed, lying across Jamey's shins. "You're Cotarded."

"What?"

"You're alive, you do realize."

He seems exhausted by her argument. "Don't you think *I* would know if I'm alive?"

Elise pops her gum, staring. "That's what I *would* think."

"You think I'm lying?" he asks, trying to muster up anger.

Elise makes thin bubbles with her gum, then snaps them.

"They said you didn't sleep last night," Elise says.

"I don't need to sleep anymore."

"Can you do *me* a favor and fucking go to sleep tonight?"

A blade of sadness steers him away, like a centerboard on a sailboat that lost its rudder, and he can't get any more words out.

You go through life thinking there's a secret to life.

And the secret to life is there is no secret to life.

There is just the palest blue light seeping through the curtain, there is Elise's long hand, there is just this kiss, this cathedral of a moment when she presses her mouth to his, her eyes brimming with crystals.

The hospital gift shop is small, banked with cards, travel-sized toiletries and romance books with embossed covers. Thousands of people have stood here, selves unsheathed, picking up key chains and deodorant and putting them down and picking them up.

Why, Elise thinks, *is this happening?*

Thousands of people have wondered that too.

He hasn't been eating, so Elise buys him a box of chocolates.

But when she poises a bonbon at his mouth, he shakes his head.

"Please just eat one," she says.

"You eat one."

"Is that how this is going to be? Fine. I'll eat chocolates for you," she says sadly.

The May sky is so bright that people look past the skyscrapers and actually notice. Everywhere, at bus stops and crosswalks, heads tilt back, eyes shielded.

Elise connives a service-dog pass and brings Buck upstairs.

Buck sniffs, starry-eyed, at everyone.

But he whimpers when he sees Jamey, and he crouches low, his bushy tail between his haunches.

"Hey there," Jamey says softly to the dog, like a scientist watching a laboratory mouse.

Elise wonders, despite all her protests, if Jamey could actually be dead.

■ ■ ■ ■

A celebrity is carried into a private wing like a queen in a palanquin. Her bodyguard's gold chains rustle as he works a walkie-talkie.

In Jamey's group meeting, they go around the circle, and everyone has to say: *Today I feel . . .* and pick an adjective from the blackboard.

"I feel . . . amazed," he says when it's his turn.

"Do you want to tell us more about that?" says the therapist.

Jamey shakes his head. "No."

He likes the sterility of his room, after so much grubbiness in life. There had been beetles in his head, bugs crawling on glistening pink matter. He'd been infested with acquaintances and small talk and manners.

He loves his white gown! His body is lost, scattered in this place, eyes exploding with galaxies of revelations. Then his head lies deep in the pillow, face turned to the ceiling, his mouth curved the way coroners know, even though his chest rises and falls.

A white stuffed rabbit, with a red ribbon

and black glass eyes, is delivered with this note:

Dear Jamey Hyde,
I feel like a stupid girl. My father and me, we talked about this whole thing that happened, and I decide that I miss you.

I can't understand what you are thinking now. Jamey, you're alive! How can it be possible for you to not know this?

That was a made-up dream about you on the escalator. We need to go back and remove this dream, this fantasy. It was Matt wearing your coat!

You're not dead.

Love, Valentina

P.S. You were the only one who had trouble with what we did, but still, I'm sorry.

Jamey spends time on the dayroom's orange sofa, watching patients solve jigsaw puzzles.

One person on this floor never wakes.

Someone else walks the halls day and night, never sleeps.

A nurse tells Jamey he has a visitor.

"Hey there, brother!" Matt says in a jovial way he'd been practicing in the mirror.

"Hi," Jamey says eventually.

"How ya doin'?"

Jamey doesn't answer.

Sent by the Hydes, Matt was almost psyched to tell his buddies about his trip to the insane asylum, but already he wants to leave — the odor, the monotonous cursing down the hall, and — Jamey. "The doc said we should take a look at old photos, man, stir up some memories."

When he gets no reaction, Matt opens an envelope of deckle-edged photos.

Two boys in sport coats with baskets of pastel eggs. The year they both had braces, eating lobster and corn at a clambake on the beach. Madras shorts and glowing red eyes. A blurry shot in their first tuxedos at the Gold & Silver Ball. Jamey as a baby, wrapped in white, in a cradle.

"I know these guys," Jamey says.

"Right," Matt says, collecting the pictures but avoiding Jamey's eyes. He can't tell if Jamey's kidding.

Matt launches into some disorganized news, pulling his windbreaker, playing with the brim of his Drexel Burnham hat. He looks at his watch. "Shoot, you know what, I gotta run. I'll be back soon though."

Matt looks at Jamey sipping juice through a straw, lashes blinking, his cheeks hollow and lips chalky at the edges.

"Do you . . . want to hang on to these?" Matt asks, holding out the envelope.

"No thanks," Jamey gently declines.

The four-point cuffing system. Hourly blood-pressure tests. Ten-minute phone calls. Thorazine. Decks of cards. These are the rules of this holding station.

One day, he tells nurses his organs are rotting, he can't eat, it's time to let the flesh starve itself clean for the hereafter. Dr. Lessing orders a nasogastric tube through his nose.

He does have clarity sometimes, and realizes that everything is a test to pass out of purgatory. But he can't tell, no matter what anyone says, if this hospital or that person or the city itself is real or a semblance. He stops asking, frustrated.

He does for a moment doubt it all — that Elise exists, that he actually met and fell in love with her, that he left school, and cut off his family. He seriously wonders if he died a year and a half ago, and this has been a long dream.

Then he thinks — *Jamey, you're being fucking crazy. You just died a month ago.*

■ ■ ■ ■

In the art therapy room, Jamey sits next to a barefoot woman.

"I'm Kim-Ly," she says, her red-lipstick mouth amused.

"Jamey."

The woman laughs. "My real name is Lan. I trick you."

This Vietnamese girl cut quarter-inch bangs with the same scissors she then dragged down her wrists. The bandages on her wrists are fresh.

"You have lots of flowers in your room," Jamey says, able to talk to her in a way he can't with others. "I've walked by."

"Yah! My motherfuck husband send every day."

"Oh."

"Yah, I meditate in cafeteria this morning. They say to me I meditate in wrong room. No such thing, wrong room."

Kim-Ly/Lan gawks at the paintings on the walls. Stick figures spew blood out of heads. Dinosaurs eat cars. A demon with pretty blue eyes. A house fire.

"This shit crazy," she muses.

With markers they draw a yellow elephant, palm trees full of coconuts about to fall, boom boxes pouring out music notes, a cake, an orchid, a lion.

They fill notebooks with block-letter poems. Lan and Jamey see their selves, as the afternoon dims, in the window. They cut shapes out of colored paper. The scraps fall onto the floor. These hours are snips and shreds of indigo and lime-green. No one knows they're here. They're lost. He feels an almost sexual pull to her, they're orphans, both isolated in nowhere land.

It's a confection of a sickness, a pink sugar nest of problems, an airy whipped cream of illness. The caramel is burned, gives off a nasty ash. Sickness is sweet in bed, in life, the goopy cherry flavor of medicines and ideas if one is willing to be sick. They bring you balloons and flowers, and news from outside, the crime rate, the president's plan for the underclass, record highs at a Sotheby's auction, the military budget, and you — you just lie there in folds of white taffy sheets, your mind a sea of honey.

Elise brings him *The Call of the Wild, The Catcher in the Rye,* and the *New York Times Magazine.* He doesn't touch them.

"Here, remember this?" she prompts, handing him the Polaroid of a white flower between her legs.

He stares at it.

"And this one?" she says, watching his reactions suspiciously.

The tiger fish at the sushi place.

He looks at it solemnly.

"Answer me," she says in a low voice.

His eyes take her in, looking at her from a long distance.

"Jamey, I'm right here," she says.

She pulls his hand to her face, then to her breast, then between her legs. He looks at his hand, and back to her face. She starts crying, eyeliner running like turquoise ink down her cheeks. "I really hate you," she sobs.

That night, around four a.m., he has a seizure or fit — no one is very clear about what happened.

She finds out about it the next morning when she brings him a doughnut covered in pink icing and sees restraint marks on his wrists. His medication has been increased again, and they added Phenobarbital to the mix, and he stares at her, squinting, as if looking through smoke.

He lies there, just one of the patients in this bleached labyrinth: no different from the woman talking to Steve McQueen on an invisible telephone, or the shaved-head girl who carries around her empty suitcase, or the man who keeps exposing a rosy, flaccid penis.

"Do you feel like harming yourself today?" they ask at room check.

He shakes his head. They give him more Seroquel anyway.

He bends over the butterfly coloring book but doesn't color.

He listens to the echo chamber of midnight.

The furniture is heavy so it can't be thrown, and he wouldn't throw it anyway.

He occasionally talks to Rodrigo, a slim male nurse — built like a dancer — with a tongue ring, who is captivated by Jamey and seems to believe anything Jamey says about purgatory.

Tania, another RN, with a Filipino accent, just sighs checking his IV, feeding him red pills in a pleated paper cup. *Sigh. Sigh.* He sometimes mimics her but not cruelly.

The days break down into building blocks.

Dumbbells.

Candy Land.

Treadmill.

Snack time.

One evening, Elise brusquely hands him his

apple juice. “Do you understand I’m knocked up?” she asks. “That we — you and me — are having a kid?”

He looks away.

“I don’t know how much longer I can do this,” she says.

He doesn’t answer.

Later, Elise walks slowly home, unaware of hawthorns blooming in the night, her footsteps preoccupied on the greasy sidewalk. When she unlocks the building door, at the bottom of the stairs is a lumpy manila package with a New York Police Department label.

Addressed to James Balthazar Hyde.

In the kitchen, she cuts it open.

It’s her jacket, the fur and metallic-almond lining stained with blood.

June 1987

Jamey opens the curtain. The city is ablaze, constructions go on and on. Stars are dulled by the flaming city. Planes cross the sky, passengers gazing onto sleepless chaos, the FDR clotted with red dots and white dots, pools shimmering darkly on roofs, smoke chuffing from pipes.

What a planet.

Contraptions and structures, inhabited and driven by animals.

Dr. Lessing comes into the room, studying her clipboard, and doesn't look Elise in the eye.

"Change in the program," Dr. Lessing says. "Looks like Jamey's family wants ECT."

"I'm his family," Elise says.

"They've started some paperwork."

"What's ECT?"

"Electroconvulsive therapy."

Elise actually grabs Lessing's arm. "No way."

"Elise." Lessing looks at Elise's hand until it's removed.

A patient hangs himself, and dawn's pink fire finds the body.

Cary Naughton was a short, zitty army brat with impossible skateboarding stories. In group, Jamey wondered how Cary could be so diabolically insecure, twirling his bleach-blond rat tail, jiggling his knee. The kid's eyes rested on every person, trying to get attention, by love or hate. And then he figured out the best way to do that.

Elise sits with Jamey while staff tends to the tragedy. He has a window of semi-lucidity because the nurse forgot his round of meds this morning.

On his tray: clam chowder and translucent balls of melon.

"I'll do anything I can for you," he says to her.

"Really?" she asks.

He nods.

On the subway home, she touches her belly. She's constantly scared this stress is bad for the baby, but then being scared adds to the stress, so she tries to calm down.

The next day, Elise corners Jolie in the

cafeteria. "Can I ask a favor?"

Jolie sips a pebbled-plastic cup of grape juice. "You can ask."

"Three blocks away is this ice-cream shop —"

Jolie's eyes darken. "He's not on the list to leave premises."

Elise rolls her eyes. "But maybe he'll, like, come to, without ECT."

"I can't."

"I would love you forever," Elise says, rubbing her belly.

Jolie blows her bangs up like: *Are you really gonna push it?* Then she looks away for a long moment. "Goddammit. It has to be quick. Tomorrow, during my lunch shift."

That night, Elise asks the Gorowskis to take Buck for a few days.

"Thank you so much," Elise says evenly.

She drops him off with food and a leash. Mrs. Gorowski loves Buck like a grandmother loves a gangster grandson, and she pets him awkwardly, giggling.

Buck knows. He can't stop moving, pacing and whimpering.

Elise holds his face. Her fingers tremble.

"You such a good boy," she says in a baby voice that isn't steady.

He looks with big amber eyes, inquiring,

frightened.

Oh, how he wagged his tail like a maniac every time she walked in the door — he'd jump vertically, then squiggle around at her knees, in love, forever grateful he'd been taken in when he was ugly and sharp-ribbed and he had no home, and he and Elise walked those New Haven streets, both lost but finding their way, block by block, together. *Bucky Buck, the big boy, my Buck,* she called him, and he came to her every time, head down and eyes up, used to being beaten but knowing she would never. Shadowing her around rooms, watching to see what she'll do on any given day, trotting up and hanging his head so she can click on the leash to walk. How can this be goodbye? How can she leave him? He looks to his leash, as if asking: *Don't you want to snap it on right now, take me with you, do anything but leave me here? Please?*

She walks out of the apartment without him, bites the heel of her hand until she gets upstairs and then bawls into a pillow. She hits the mattress, over and over, her face red, until she's exhausted, hiccupping from crying.

The next morning, she shows up at the hospital, face bloated.

"What's wrong?" Jamey asks with half-lidded eyes.

"It's a surprise," Elise tells him nonsensically.

Jolie shows up. "Ready?"

They tiptoe down the emergency stairs without talking.

The sun floods Jamey's brain the second he walks out the door, almost getting through to him. He holds out his hands like it's rain.

They walk down bright and bustling blocks to the ice-cream shop with the yellow awning on Seventy-First Street. Jamey orders mint, and Elise gets strawberry, even though she can't imagine eating.

"Jolie, come on, get something," she says in forced cheerfulness.

The nurse orders vanilla with rainbow sprinkles.

Elise devours hers, hands tremulous, and throws out her napkin. Jamey has pale green cream on his lip and is taking his time.

"You done?" she asks Jamey meaningfully.

"I guess," he says unsurely.

Elise takes his hand and stands up.

Jolie looks at them, stops licking sprinkles off her hand, stricken. "You're not going to do this."

"I'm sorry, Jolie."

Elise puts her switchblade on the table. Jamey watches.

"Is this a joke?" Jolie asks, looking at the knife.

"You can say we made you," Elise says apologetically. "I dropped the knife and ran."

Elise marches Jamey down the street to the Korean nail salon where she paid twenty bucks to store their backpacks. The owner twirls a pink telephone cord around her finger, and nods *You're welcome* without breaking her conversation in another language.

"We got to hurry," Elise says, forcing him to run.

Tokens into the turnstile, they take the C train to the A train to Port Authority, heads tucked.

At Port Authority, hands reach up from the floor like monsters out of a swamp. A woman approaches, in slippers and bathrobe, with no teeth, holding out a claw. A man hollers at everyone, shit staining his sweatpants. A suburban kid with a Hello Kitty backpack moves through the crowd, doomed. Elise and Jamey scan the departures board, numbers and letters flipping, while hustlers scrutinize newcomers.

"Where do you want to go?" Elise says.

"I want to go where you want to go," he says dully.

"Choose!" Elise says, panicking.

He stares up. "Wyoming?"

It leaves in five minutes. They buy tickets and rush to the gate on the lower level, where twenty buses all lean and cough, ready to be boarded, and they climb up the steps to theirs, find seats together, and collapse.

They pull out of the netherworld, and the bus careens into the Lincoln Tunnel, burping and hissing.

Jamey looks at Elise's reflection in the window, as she watches the vanishing city.

"Shit, they were gonna electrocute you," she says without turning to him.

En route to Baltimore first. They pull into a gas station.

"What do you need?" he asks her, already sharper than when they left, although his eyes are still half-lidded.

"Mountain Dew?"

As the bus rolls out, he massages her back as she leans forward and sips her soda.

"You're knotted up," he says.

Now she cries, the stress caressed out, tears dropping off her cheeks.

She sleeps with her head on his shoulder. Late afternoon, she wakes, bleary.

Her eyes consume everything they pass — amazed and skeptical.

"What!" she'll say suddenly, pointing out something ordinary like cows gathered under one big tree. "Is that *cows*?"

They stop and start through the ruins of Detroit.

"My ass hurts," she says.

She sleeps for much of the night, snoring, head on his shoulder.

And he barely sleeps. He doesn't want to miss anything.

This morning, he studies a carnival that isn't running, a field of spinach. Vultures spiraling.

Everything he sees is significant. There's little time left, and everything matters.

A biker in the next lane doesn't glance up to the bus window — blond, a craggy face, denim vest, her arms browned in the sun. Jamey looks at the humid sun blinking off the motorcycle, at the scrappy woods beyond, at the dead possum whose mouth opens to ruby entrails, a sign for Honey Creek, the telephone wires rushing by while the sky is stationary. Someone is holding his jaw — *Don't look away, Jamey.* He squints his tired eyes open. He's committed.

And he suddenly understands that he's waiting to see a signal to leave.

Not today, or tomorrow. But soon.

Grand Rapids.

The passenger is tall and maybe a hundred pounds, hair soaked in oil and combed — his face narrowed like a ferret by the speed he's been doing for so long. His body reformed by addiction, curved into endless need, refusal, humiliation, and perseverance.

He perches on their armrest with a brown unlit cigarette hanging from his mouth. *Hey kids! Daddy's collecting money for the next rest stop, where I'll grab us all snacks to share. No? Well, need some gum? I got Doublemint at a dollar a stick? Shoe shine, fifty cents?*

When they stop talking to him, his mega-smile drops and he stares with hunger, moving to the next row, puts on his mega-smile. It's a terrifying performance — perfect, stellar.

It's a population of misfits, changing at each stop as they discharge riders and take on new ones. An ex-con with a ginger-blond mustache whose last meal was behind bars. A woman with a beehive hairdo carrying a parcel of dried meat. A pretty child in a watermelon-print sundress who keeps asking questions but whose mother never answers, paging through a magazine with empty eyes. And the obese man, taking up the last row by the bathroom, with three chins and deep creases in his flesh, aromatic in an ancient way, stinking ethereal, more beautiful than hell.

They doze on each other's shoulder, conscious of hands moving under the seats, reaching for a wallet in a backpack. They stamp at the ghostly fingers the way you scare roaches.

Sunrise behind them, and they're passing another town in Iowa. This place, a blink of fellowship, people and buildings and animals — folks meandering around this fine morning, sunlight caught in their hair like dewdrops, all believing that where they are is where life begins and ends, even if they know better. The gravity of any location pulls citizens to its heart, organizing people by abstractly spiritual geography.

The speed of the bus isn't grand but it has the effect of slowing down any activity it passes, so a farmwoman lifts a crate into her truck sluggishly, and the man trudges the field at a funereal pace, even the dust kicked up by his boots billowing in languorous, illuminated clouds.

■ ■ ■ ■

They drive into the falling sun.

At a diner in Nebraska, they break and grab a quick breakfast: sliced ham and scrambled eggs. She tries to get Jamey to eat, but he plays with his food like a girl who thinks she's overweight. She pushes a forkful of fried apricot pie to his mouth, and he almost retches.

Back on the bus.

They drive past white crosses.

Past an Indian reservation.

Past floodlights at night shining on giant tractors, working through late hours.

They drive along barren highway and then a town begins: a gas station first, then raggedy houses, a grocer, then a liquor store, a stationery, a diner, a gun store, culminating in a church at the midpoint, then deescalating with a ladies-wear store, a barber, raggedy houses, the other gas station . . .

Wyoming!

They make it to the Wagon Wheel Motel, its name written in neon script above the office. The Wagon Wheel offers a daily newspaper delivered to their door, a hot breakfast every morning. A bar with wagon wheels for lamps, and a motor court with picnic tables.

They register as Buck and Esther London, names they came up with on the bus while looking out filthy windows onto clean land. They take number 186 from this single-story horseshoe of rooms.

Home sweet home.

The room has faux-wood walls, and an Aztec-patterned comforter, 1950s bedside tables. Ashtray with the Wagon Wheel logo. They brush their teeth and fall onto the bed, and wonder if they are in fact different people than when they left New York three days ago.

Jamey looks around the room from his horizontal position and can taste the smoke of thousands of cigarettes. He can feel a lady in a nylon peignoir cutting corns off her feet, right there. A man watching game shows in pinstriped boxers as he flosses. Salesmen must have looked in this mirror. Rodeo contenders would have prayed. The old lady held the shower walls as water pummeled her frail body, then set out in an apple-green Pontiac Catalina for a last Thanksgiving at her son's house.

"What are we doing?" Jamey asks.

"I don't know."

"I thought maybe you had a plan."

"My plan was to get away."

They lie in silence.

They meet the old cowboy who lurks around the motel. His name is Don, and he runs his hand through white hair under his hat then replaces the hat. He wears dark glasses too. He has a peg leg, and gets violently drunk every night, and does motel chores all day. He shoots a couple rotgut whiskeys, runs to the loo, vomits, comes back for more, patting his mouth with a gingham hankie.

"Lost my leg in 'Nam," he tells them one morning in the parking lot, and runs a hand through his white hair.

Later they overhear him at the bar telling a Canadian couple it was a mountain lion tore off his foot.

The air! The air is so different. She breathes it, and the novelty doesn't fade. This world brushes her arms, touches her face, like something getting to know her. She can't help but smile at the clouds ringing the knees of snowcapped mountains, or at the constellations at night. She hadn't known that stars do twinkle, that squirrels eat mushrooms, that birds fill a dusk with song. This place is a surprise, pulled out of the big American road map like a Cracker Jack prize.

Thickets of grass and wildflowers bend with the wind.

Jamey looks at ravens weighing down the branches of a tree so heavily it seems they're in the wrong tree, since everything here is calibrated.

The breeze moves different trees differently — aspen leaves wink and tilt like sequins — the cottonwood flutters. The young aspens don't have white bark yet. The rose hips look like red marbles.

He can't imagine the moment he and Elise will say goodbye to each other.

He didn't know he could have this volume of feeling, this intensity — sadness lights every cell like adrenaline. Stabs of it run through his loins, bolts of grief up his arms.

Just watching her now, spreading peanut butter on bread at the motel-room table, the way she looks at what she's doing, licks the blade, her shoulders rising as she cuts the sandwich in two — who dreamed he could love someone this much?

"You could do fine without me," he tells her.

"Shut up," she says without looking away from the TV.

She hates seeing him like this: skinny,

ghostly, his tooth cracked.

He still has the basic face he brought to every occasion — the mask that can outlast anyone's prying except hers. She could tell, from the day they met, that he hadn't given up. His act was to pretend to care, but to pretend so badly it looked like he didn't care, protecting the dear and tender truth that he did care. He wanted to love somebody.

Don mentions they need a dishwasher at Dragon City, a random Chinese joint down the highway; their regular guy shot his sister in the hand last night and is in jail.

"Maybe I'll go down there?" Jamey says.

"Make an extra dollar, why not, I say," Don says.

"Why do you need to work today?" Elise asks.

"Got to make as much money as possible."

"Why?"

"To *live* on."

She knows he means for her to live on with the baby *once he's gone.*

He's the only white boy in the house. All the cooks are Chinese guys with thick elbows and a way of bantering and laughing as they sizzle food and sink steamers into pots like all kitchen crews everywhere and just like this one kitchen, here. Universal and also a subset. Jamey can't understand but smiles along, and no one cares. They assume he's a junkie, a strung-out loser with twine to hold up his pants, a broken tooth.

With their muscular jowls or jaundiced eyes, balding heads or prison tattoos, they seem far away from anyone Jamey knows. The heat in the kitchen makes everyone pink, as if there's some excitement, but when they break between lunch and dinner to eat, he sees normalcy in everyone's eyes. It doesn't matter that they're Chinamen in Wyoming. Nothing can ever stay strange for long.

He smells fetid at the end of every shift. It's odd because all the food smells good, but combined it's too many ingredients, accelerating some kind of decomposition. He comes home rotten.

He arrives at the motel with little confetti strips from egg-drop soup in his hair, and grease on his hands so deep and indelible it's healing. He showers but Dragon City stays like golden plugs in his nostrils.

When he walks home, hands in pockets, he can't help looking back at his life.

Odd moments surface — sailing a Beetle Cat alone, eating a tomato-mayonnaise sandwich, the wind's power moving the hull . . . sleeping in Martine's king bed, the loft filled with never-ending light . . . clamming as a kid in a cold bay, feet working in the mud, hair blown into a salty twirl . . . a red rose blooming in a stranger's yard, in the September streets of New Haven . . .

They walk the hallway of the motel to get breakfast. Sometimes a door opens, and the moment is spiked with cheap shave cream and halitosis.

These foreign smells make her think — again — how impossible it will be to wake up in a bed without him. What's the point of anything? Why did we make it this far, she thinks, through hours in our own lives before we met, even after we met, when we were sure we were worthless, but we somehow got to the other side of those times, holding it together, ashamed to be hopeful but being hopeful, when we had no protection and no direction but we kept going anyway, and then we got rewarded, and now it's being ripped out of my hands? I didn't give up and I didn't complain, she thinks, furious. Why can't I have what I want, what I earned, what I deserve?

He plans to learn to hunt. He talks to Don

about it at the Wagon Wheel bar, the sound of pool balls clicking behind them.

"It ain't the season," Don says.

"Yeah, but I could brush up my target shooting and be ready."

"Well, what you need, a shotgun?"

"Yeah, a twelve-gauge?" Jamey asks casually.

"How much you want to spend on this here shotgun? I can get you something that works but it's not very pretty, fer about one-fifty."

"Perfect."

Everyone thinks he's on drugs, which is ironic since now he's lucid, but he's wasting away. His jaw bone, brow bones, hollow eyes — and a mouth that's still plush. He ties his pants with string.

They cook on a hot plate. She hates cleaning his dish afterward, which is full since he just pushes food around. She scrapes it into the garbage. She does it in slow motion, trying to keep her face together. She takes the plate to the sink.

A stubborn, poisonous feeling is creeping into her, and she recognizes it.

She loved block parties as a kid, the hot dogs, the cake, playing tag through all the adults, who cursed and laughed and smoked reefer — everyone happy, all night they'd dance, grandparents, kids, the bad boys, the dirty girls, everyone was invited, no one stayed away. And then that feeling, as the crowd shrank, they were folding up the long metal tables — *See yez — G'night, now —* stumbling and giggling, fighting, sealing Tupperware, stubbing out smokes, finishing bottles, someone throwing up behind a car. She'd feel rage, a disappointment so vicious she couldn't be consoled, touched, even approached. *I hate you!* she said to anyone nearby. *C'mon, shug,* her mother would say, firmly gripping her little arm. *Party's over.*

They spend the day with Don as he checks fences on the Rhoner ranch, riding the truck through fields, tagging wires that need mending.

Don has the twelve-gauge and takes them shooting near Clover Lake, taking aim at a dead tree.

Jamey knows how to load shells from hunting with his uncles. It's been a while since he fired a gun, and he winces at the kickback.

"You're a damn good shot!" Don says, surprised. "Want to give it a little try, Elise?"

She shakes her head.

Lying in bed later, Jamey can feel it all

coming to an end. They both can.

The gun is the new sun in the room. It's a star. They revolve around it.

He's in pain; he throws up anything he eats.

She hands him a Saltine, and he pushes it away, gently.

"Let's go to the hospital," she says.

"No, Elise," he says. "Not going anywhere like that."

That morning, at dawn, he stands at the doorway to the room. A doe is in the brush, but she's not scared away by him, which is unusual. She looks up then back to a movement in the grass. It's a damp fawn, just born, with brittle tiny sticks for legs, barely walking. And mama won't leave its side. This is what he's been waiting to see, and he's breathless.

The motel room itself is a puzzle. It reminds Jamey of *himitsu-bako,* these Japanese puzzle boxes they had at Sotheby's. Exquisite parquetry, a mosaic of black walnut, yellow mulberry wood, and blue cucumber tree. Only one unique series of moves could open a box, those moves built into the box itself. His favorite box had 66 moves, but it was more complex and difficult than the box with 115 moves. He liked that fact.

He makes his proposal, laying out the options.

"The bottom line is that I have to, you know, leave," he says with difficulty.

"Jamey," she pleads with him.

"I can go alone."

"What the fuck are you saying?"

"But" — he seems uncomfortable — "from where I stand, I do know there's — somewhere to go."

They look at each other for a while.

"I'm not staying here without you," she says.

He stands at the window, and looks at the sky for a while.

"You been planning this!" she accuses him finally.

"Did you really think I wanted to go hunting?" he asks gently.

She comes to look out the window too. "Why is this happening?"

They get ready to do it without talking, Jamey seating himself in the middle of the room. Elise kneeling at his feet, muzzle to his chest.

It's her mom she sees in her mind right now. Her mom's colossal face, the metallic eye shadow, a worried grin, a cheap cigarette lit between her teeth. And then she sees the baby in her belly, a shadow of promise, a rosebud mouth and virgin eyes.

Yet believing in the next world is an act of love.

Her mother, then her baby. Then the act of love. Mother, baby, act of love.

This wheel turns in her mind.

"Don't you love me, Elise?" says Jamey.

And then suddenly her eyes close and a huge red ledge tilts in her, an avalanche of logic, crumbling, disappearing. There are no words but ribbons come untied, knots loosening by themselves. Form is unlocked, and the fall is a bird's dive from high in the air, and the finger is on the safety and it clicks the catch forward and the gun is a form too and soon the walls and structure of flesh and history can dissolve, sugar in hot water, a new thing glistening and abruptly liquid, the sugar bubbling as it goes — she's been coming this way her whole life, now she's letting go, on to the next place, to destiny, pale finger and violet rhinestone nail on the cold metal trigger —

He sees it coming, a blue rush in her gray eyes before she closes them, the soul of Elise welled up in her long bony hands, and she's gonna do it, and he actually smiles, grins like a fool, and there goes the safety catch, and there's her finger on the trigger —

He pushes the muzzle at the last millisecond and the shot hits the wall, a focused spray of powder, one almost-deadly *thunk* in the fake wood — the deafening shot — kickback to her shoulder — she's now staring at him — unfocused like she just woke up — gun tilted crazily at the ceiling — and he takes the weapon, opens it to pop the smoky shell from the top barrel onto the orange carpet. He pulls the live shell too.

He pissed himself. And it's this, as he laughs at it, his laughter — she knows he's alive. Warm urine, soaking denim. His mouth, she kisses him, and they hold each other as someone frantically knocks, and the door is opened by the manager, who finds the gun open on the floor, and a girl cradled like a child in the guy's lap, the two of them laughing like lunatics. . . .

They rush to the Wagon Wheel diner. The table is too small for their order, so they scrape eggs onto the cheeseburger plate, baked potato onto the pork chop. They hardly talk, devouring hash browns and lemon meringue cake. Jamey laughs, says

Holy fuck, with his mouth full, every once in a while.

Out in the parking lot, he holds his hands up and shouts: "I'm alive!"

Then he vomits up half of what he ate. But still — he feels *good.*

They turn in early — right after sundown. She's so tender and painful in bed, like a princess isolated in a tower for years. They're relentless under their geometric-striped coverlet, in sheets that smell of cheap soap, and he does everything he knows how to do.

At sunup, he slips to the hotel door, barefoot, to watch. It's a subdued dawn, wavelets of dark cloud over petal-pink sky.

All day, they talk and talk. She pushes one idea, and he listens to her bizarre and beautiful reasons.

The next morning, Don drives Jamey to Laramie, where he pawns the Patek Philippe watch, stowed in Elise's underwear for the Greyhound ride, and he buys tickets at a travel agency. They have two connections, a long trip for a girl who's never flown. He buys Don a milkshake at a drive-thru and a bottle of rye on the way back, and the cowboy mixes them and drinks, and sighs as they head into dusk, animal eyes shining like pearls from the landscape.

■ ■ ■ ■

They go to the airport in Don's truck too, the old cowboy driving slow since a pregnant lady's on board. They sit three across on the cracked leather seat, backpacks in the truck bed.

The windows are down and the breeze is sharp. The sky is so massive and so blue, it can't be fully understood. Elise looks up at the mountains, their white caps shrinking day by day as sun melts the snow into rivers and springs, feeding thimbleberries and musk thistle and columbines.

She is wild with happiness.

The airline agent is surprised they only have carry-on bags, but they get checked in and wait at the tiny airport for their plane. When they board, Jamey gives her the window seat so she can watch the land get smaller as they rise. It's such a clear day, the mountain range looms in crystalline detail.

They fly to Chicago, then go through customs at Munich, board another jet. Jamey tells the stewardesses that Elise is pregnant, and the ladies with lipstick and blond bobs wait on her, bring her extra pillows, fresh OJ, a cold compress for her hot face.

They land in New Delhi, stand in the customs line for an eternity, where Jamey asks the American in front of them (a white-haired, gin-blossomed retired professor) for directions, and the man offers to share a taxi into the city.

The cab is shining and bulbous, British racing green with a yellow top, and the driver wears a turban.

"What are you all doing here?" the American asks.

"Just wanted to come somewhere we'd never been," Jamey answers, enthralled by the long hotel lawns and polluted sky, stacks of lush jungle bushes and white houses, highways that look like highways he knows but are crammed with smaller, tippy cars in unusual colors: custard, burgundy, powder-blue.

Their taxi jerks through a neighborhood, and they finally get out, Jamey slinging both backpacks over his shoulders.

"Hotels in either direction," the man says, pointing at the wide dirt lane. "Come up for tea first if you like."

"That's really kind," Jamey says, "but I think we'll move on, thank you."

The couple walks slowly through crowds,

past buildings molded from dirty putty, the store signs painted in rainbow colors, their Indian letters like drooping flowers soon to stand and bloom, extravagantly dotted and twisted, the roots and shoots of an alphabet.

People shout, rickshaws are driven by men in striped shirts and loose short pants, sweat flicking off their faces. The language buzzes like flies or birds. Fumes and gases are unknown. Food bakes and crackles at corroded carts, and Jamey and Elise don't know how anything tastes yet.

The people here think this street is ordinary!

They keep going, dazzled, high on life.

And children watch Elise, this dark-braided woman who walks with strong shoulders, chin up. They stare at her. They seek out her gray eyes, which are soft in the hard turquoise lines.

Except one girl. Her eyes are milky and phosphorescent, and she tags along with older kids.

Elise remembers that she has strawberries, wrapped in an Air India napkin, in the backpack's pocket. She brings them out. She takes hold of the blind kid's tiny hot hand, and puts the bundle into her palm, closes her fingers for her. The girl changes the tilt of her head, as if to hear the strawberries, but she doesn't unfold the package yet.

Seeing herself do this, Elise realizes she always knew she would give the fruit away, at this exact moment, to that girl, with this exact feeling in her heart.

ACKNOWLEDGMENTS

My love and thanks to:

My phenomenal agent, Sally Wofford-Girand; my exquisitely wise and kind and visionary editor, Alexis Washam; Lindsay Sagnette and Molly Stern for their faith and support; Jillian Buckley, Rachel Rokicki, Lisa Erickson, Claire Posner, and *everyone* at Hogarth for bringing this book into the world; Mr. Swink, Brush Creek Foundation for the Arts, Writers Omi at Ledig House, the Ucross Foundation, the Edward F. Albee Foundation, Steve Stern, Sweet Zoe and Lady Olive, Kathryn Davis, Captain Bob Morris, Nicholas Delbanco, Charles Baxter, Eileen Pollack, Patricia Jones, Marjory Reid, Barry and Lorrie Goldensohn, Rachel Hanss, John Andrews, Shaun Dolan, the work/playmates and Swedish Fish at 4710 E5, Jim Lewis, Alyson Richman, Bruce Mason, Barbara Purcell, the beloved citizens of AHAB, Austin Film Festival,

Melissa Tullos for the books, Bradley Bechtol for the walks, Justine Gilcrease for black-and-white lilies, everyone at Truth Be Told and the women at Lockhart Correctional, Fleurs du Mal Syndicat, Neil Little for *everything,* Anabel; my extraordinary parents, Deborah and Jack Libaire; Julien, Jake and Erin, and Gus and Edie for inspiration.

ABOUT THE AUTHOR

Jardine Libaire is a graduate of Skidmore College and the University of Michigan MFA program, where she was a winner of the Hopwood Award. *White Fur* is her second novel for adults. She lives in Austin, Texas.

The employees of Thorndike Press hope you have enjoyed this Large Print book. All our Thorndike, Wheeler, and Kennebec Large Print titles are designed for easy reading, and all our books are made to last. Other Thorndike Press Large Print books are available at your library, through selected bookstores, or directly from us.

For information about titles, please call:
(800) 223-1244

or visit our website at:
gale.com/thorndike

To share your comments, please write:
Publisher
Thorndike Press
10 Water St., Suite 310
Waterville, ME 04901